Tree of Life

The Corescu Chronicles Book Three

ellen c. maze

TREE OF LIFE
The Corescu Chronicles Book Three
By Ellen C. Maze
©2020 by Ellen C. Maze Sallas
All rights reserved.

ISBN-13: 978-1734047431
Also in eBook

Cover photo © Fernando Cortes – Spain, 123rf.com
Cover Design: Elizabeth E. Little, Hyliian Design
Little Roni Publishers
Clanton, AL
www.littleronipublishers.com

The following is a work of fiction. Names, characters, places, and incidents are fictitious or used fictitiously. Any resemblance to real persons, living or dead, to factual events or to businesses is coincidental and unintentional.

Let's stay in touch!
Enter your email address to join my newsletter. You'll receive exclusive deals and special offers, and be the first to know about new releases. *You can unsubscribe at any time.*
I included a free book!
https://dl.bookfunnel.com/z0c7dpe1am
OR www.ellencmaze.com

PUBLISHED IN THE UNITED STATES OF AMERICA

IT HAD BEEN TWENTY-SIX DAYS and the pain only escalated.

Sure, he was hungry; his gut pulsed and cramped in miserable waves—but he had not succumbed. He was still pure and clean as of his last transgression.

Maybe God was helping him.

Maybe God was *healing* him.

Maybe he had found the answer.

Meditating on the Scriptures had so far prevented him from lusting for blood bad enough that he succumbed to the temptation. So far, he wasn't a slave to the sin. So far, his Biblical quiet time fed his gut as well as his spirit.

But…

Twenty-six days! Please, God, let this trial end soon. Please...

Tony prayed and his stomach gurgled. It was not unbearable.

Yet.

1

And there is no creature hidden from His sight,
but all things are naked and open to the eyes of Him
to whom we must give account.
Hebrews 4:13

A Month Ago in Egypt

A DOZEN LOST, HUNGRY, AND ORPHANED BOYS SCATTERED
at the sight of their oldest member clutched tight to the vampire's chest.
Rakha did not wait for them to disappear before plunging vicious fangs
into the child's throat, the pleasure payoff flowing into his mouth at
volume. The escapees' cries of alarm would reach no one; Rakha had
chosen this tomb well. If younglings squatted there as he slept, they
now understood the purpose of the stalwart no-entry barrier.

Trespassers will be eaten, he thought and drank on.

No doubt the orphans had been surprised by his appearance, but
finding them in his hideaway had been unexpected.

Immediate food—how fortuitous…

Perhaps the Unseen led the boys there knowing Rakha would
require sustenance upon awakening. It had been a long slumber, four
hundred years, although he'd learn the exact date once he exited his
sanctuary.

It is good to be alive! he said inside and withdrew his teeth from the
dead boy's flesh.

Minutes ago, he had been awakened by the screeching of invisible
spirits. From the unseen realm, he had awaited this moment, when the
stars aligned to allow him access to the host; a young man who gave
himself to the Dark, to be possessed and owned by the next spirit in
line. Returning entities followed a strict timetable of astrological
windows; if it missed, it went back in line. In two thousand years, Rakha
had never blown an assignment.

His belly full and his face smiling, Rakha considered his tomb.
Located outside the Nile village of El Nar, Rakha found that this desert
soil received him best, perhaps because the land claimed him having
been first born only three kilometers away. This underground hollow
was the best place to rematerialize ….

1

Ahhhhh!

A bolt of pleasure shot through Rakha's system then and he closed his eyes to the elation it brought.

This host is magnificent!

The body had been well preserved, its cohesion and vitality maintained by spirits specifically assigned to that task. It was male, Egyptian, and young, maybe twenty-five in mortal years. Having no mirror, Rakha used his hands to examine its face, its neck, a nearly hairless and muscled chest, a tight abdomen that gave way to shapely thighs—a runner's legs. Oh, this one was pretty. He'd chosen it sight-unseen because of the circumstances of 1640, when while in Hungary, lucky villagers destroyed his former host by yanking him into the sunlight. And he had been enjoying the priest so very much.

My priest...

Rakha allowed the memories, enjoying the sensation of recollection. In the spirit realm, there was no tactility; spirits had no nerve endings to experience or eyes to see into the fleshed dimension. Every sensation given the Unseen came through the use of a consenting human or lower creature, looking through their eyes, hearing with their ears, and feeling with their touch. Rakha had been jumping host bodies since his master turned his original corpus into a vampire two thousand years ago. He'd been barely twenty when he allowed the creature to swap blood with him. After this, Rakha became like his master, and over the course of millennia, he learned to wield the Dark Power as well as any of his kind.

My kind...

Rakha had few offspring, recognizing from the start how difficult it was to cohabitate with a direct competitor. But after four centuries, Rakha grew bored and longed for a companion. As of his forced hibernation in 1640, of his direct descendants, only the priest still lived.

"He returned to the Carpenter," Rakha whispered in the dark and grinned at the sound of his voice. This host had a sweet, little-boy quality to his accent. It would appeal to men and women both, and Rakha repeated the phrase in a few other languages for his own entertainment.

But he had not arisen to find the priest. Corescu had already been defeated, deceived, and turned into a bloodthirsty miscreant like his master. During his slumber, Rakha had been granted access to the priest's subconscious and he had tormented him often. When the priest-vampire fed his blood to his underlings, Paul and Reuben, Rakha spoke to them too, using their fears and selfishness against them to his own end. So, no, he would not seek Corescu.

And Paul Black…

From the spirit dimension, Rakha manipulated the priest's servant, guiding him until they could eventually meet in the flesh upon Rakha's scheduled reawakening. But Paul was dead, leaving Rakha rudderless and seeking a new mission. Was there any vampire out there worth his attention?

"We know of a vampire you cannot subdue…"

Rakha raised his brow. This was the guiding voice that resided always in the spirit dimension. Rakha called them "the Unseen," for they were plural and invisible, guiding him as well as all those – mortal and vampire – with the ability to hear the Dark. With respect, Rakha awaited more.

"In fact, we waste our time even mentioning him. You cannot defeat him. There is no chance…"

Rakha took offense. *"I can and I will. Who is it? Direct me there at once. I have never missed."*

Rakha sensed a huddling of minds before they replied, *"Seek out Anthony Agricola, recently brought to the Thirst. Our bondees say he resides in Alabama of the United States…"*

Rakha offered a thoughtful nod. The spirits referred to their human mediums—witches, psychics, black magicians—as "bondees," their information most helpful since they had feelers in both worlds.

"It will be fun watching you flounder as you see what we are saying is true…" the Unseen prodded, but Rakha was not provoked.

Anthony Agricola, an unassuming name.

Rakha would do it; he required aggressive diversion to regain his full strength. He exited the tomb, its heavy access already worked free by the desperate orphans seeking haven from the weather and local slave traders. The moon sat high revealing he had a few hours to discover the year and the general state of the mortal world. He'd awoken in the middle of a war once and that had been a dangerous time.

Rakha filled his lungs with the fresh night air and headed for the horizon. His memory would show him the way, and in another hour, he'd reach Cairo. There he would find shelter and discover how much—if any—his new host could tolerate the sunlight. Usually, he could manage the sun at dawn and dusk and he hoped such would be the case again. After this, he'd travel to America. It would take him a few weeks to locate Agricola, narrow down a specific American town. Rakha had not visited the United States in the flesh, but his advanced intelligence would make sure he assimilated with haste. Once he found a suitable dwelling and settled in, he'd show the Unseen he could destroy whomever he wished.

Anthony Agricola... Sounds like an easy mark.

Rakha smiled and jogged on.

2

Let him who glories glory in this,
That he understands and knows Me,
That I am the LORD…
Jeremiah 9:24

IS GOD CONCERNED THAT I'VE BECOME A VAMPIRE?
He cares for the lowliest sparrow, right?

Pondering his unfathomable situation, Anthony Agricola jogged down the covered gangway into the belly of the waiting 747, leaving Hamburg, Germany, for Atlanta, Georgia, USA. Three hours ago, Doctor Mark Corescu volunteered his blood so Tony would not be overcome by bloodlust on the long flight home. An hour before that, he and the doctor along with his friend Hope Brannen had gone to battle against the devil in Mark's assistant, Paul Black. When the dust settled, Paul was dead, and Tony was still a vampire who needed to get home.

But why me? Shouldn't God have protected me from this curse? I sacrificed myself, threw my neck into Paul's teeth so John's wife could escape!

Tony's brow furrowed with the memory. A scant week ago he'd done this, offered himself to a vampire hoping he'd release another innocent victim. Paul had accepted and drank him dry. When Tony awoke, the same monster was plunging an enormous hunting knife into his chest. He had watched paralyzed as Paul then poured his cursed blood directly into Tony's open wound.

This is how they reproduce, Tony thought with great misery. He had learned more than he ever wanted to know about real-life vampires over the course of the past year.

Paul tried to make me his slave…

Tony found his seat and fastened the safety belt. Watching the flight attendant tend passengers, he thought about that *other* night. When months before Paul turned him into a vampire, he forced Tony to drink his blood. This made his body heal like a vampire while remaining human. During that time, when Paul was hungry, Tony sought to protect the innocent by volunteering his blood. But he never bowed the knee which enraged Paul beyond measure.

Well, Paul's gone, I'm still here, and I have to go on…

Mark and Hope took a separate flight to points unknown, the vampire doctor promising to contact Tony when everything died down. Weary concerning what lay ahead, he worked to focus on God's promises and not the curse in his flesh.

Tony's job had been laid out earlier this morning at Corescu's German hideaway: Paul Black's final words as he passed from the flesh indicated Tony must find Reverend Sarah Tracey. Why? Had Paul infected her with his blood? Had he turned her into a vampire, too? The unknowns put a fire in Tony's spirit to proceed without haste. Yet this mission's perceived difficulty paled in comparison to the larger issues, such as, what happens when his abominable hunger returns? On top of that, how does he continue the Lord's work?

Preachers cannot be vampires. Vampires cannot be preachers.

Tony closed his eyes. The answers hadn't come and he expected nothing new from on high. Last summer, he discovered the world of vampires when his friend Hope fell for Dr. Mark Corescu, a four-hundred-year old vigilante killing sinners for God. In a cascade of snowballing events, Tony was first bitten by the doctor, turned "immortal" by Paul Black, and finally, transformed into a vampire on Paul's whim.

I need to reclaim my life…

Could he? At the moment, he didn't see how. He'd need a fresh infusion of faith to simply survive the thirteen-hour flight home.

Tony's cell vibrated, a reminder he hadn't shut it off. Glancing at the screen, he read the opening lines of John's message.

"Have a safe flight, see you Wednesday."

Tony's lips tightened and he switched the phone to plane mode. Big John Jenkins had been under Paul's teeth a few months and suffered quite a bit before the megalomaniac vampire passed. The big man promised to maintain the house and grounds while Tony and Paul traveled to Germany. John's text revealed he would continue to come by, which would be a huge help. Tony did not know how long he would live in Paul's house, but he couldn't maintain it alone. Plus, he didn't want to. He liked John, he enjoyed his companionship, and more than anything—John wasn't tainted by ingesting Paul's blood, which meant John still heard from God. Tony wanted assistance in that department more than anything. With confirmation that Big John would stay on, Tony would have the peace of mind to locate Reverend Tracey. Once he discovered her situation, the next order of business would be to have the hugely anointed woman of God pray for him to be delivered of the curse.

"Yes, please God," Tony mumbled, where again, he heard nothing in return. When the attendant began emergency procedures in German and English, a gentle voice on his left roused him to attention.

"Pardon me, but would it trouble you greatly if we were to switch seats? I will be airsick on the aisle…"

Tony turned his head to greet his seatmate, a matronly woman in her sixties, stout and crisply-dressed in a tailored business suit. She spoke with a brisk British accent, had bright blue eyes, and a sparkling smile. Tony stood to make way.

"Not a problem," he said and stepped into the aisle for the woman to maneuver past. When settled, he offered his hand. "Tony Agricola."

She shook his fingers and beamed a new smile. "Lucinda Louise Langley."

After a polite nod, Tony leaned back to avoid small talk. As the plane rumbled away from the gate, she also kept to herself and he smiled behind closed eyes; unexpected blessings were the best kind.

As the plane reached altitude, Tony rolled his eyes open and looked about the cabin. The rumble of the jet engines did not drown out the thumping of dozens of hearts. But thankfully, the air-controlled cabin smelled more of honeysuckle deodorizer than the blood of his fellow travelers. His exhaustion enabled him to drown out the whispered and uninvited thoughts of other men and women captured inside the jet, and for the moment, his stomach remained satiated. Corescu had been right; the old vampire's blood had indeed carried Tony farther than any other he'd consumed.

Uneasy at the memory of drinking blood, Tony lowered his eyes to his lap where his hands rested atop his thighs. His clothing had been purchased in the airport since the ones they fought Paul in had been ruined. Because of this, he wore a German flag T-shirt and loose jogging pants. Wearing short sleeves on a plane before he met the vampires would have meant he'd be freezing the entire flight. But since he'd been made over into Paul (and Mark's, he thought with a frown) image, cold and hot did not register the same way in his flesh.

Tony huffed at his loss of sensation, stretching out his arm and, without thinking, traced with one finger the scar inside his elbow. Only two shiny white circles remained of the terrifying ordeal he had survived upon his first meeting with Dr. Corescu. They would be friendly now, connected by blood and curse, but that night, Tony had feared for his life. The memories resurfaced and Tony replayed the evening in his mind. The events of the past month had certainly given Tony a new perspective. He understood the vampire's need, the creature's lust for blood that out-purposed his desire to do the right thing.

I know that feeling, Tony said to himself recalling the first time the bloodlust hit. He had been three thousand feet up, accompanied by Paul Black, the vampire that pushed the curse on him mere days earlier. Shame arrived then, consuming him as he stared at the scar unseeing. Only a few hours ago, he had taken Mark's blood without fuss or argument. Drawing from Corescu's strong forearm, the crisp, hot fluid filling his mouth...

Tony's breathing grew short as the memory brought a new arousal, his viper-like fangs elongating unbidden behind closed lips.

Oh, God! Tony grunted with surprise and focused on nothing. *Blank. White. Blank. White. Blank...* By sheer will, the red images faded and Tony's unnaturally pointed teeth returned to his gums.

"Will you look at that..."

Startled from his thoughts, Tony turned to his neighbor and attempted to sound normal. "Pardon me?"

"That. On your arm." Lucinda Langley pushed aside her silk shirtsleeve. "How did you get that scar? Don't you think it's oddly similar to mine?" She stretched out her right arm and held it in view.

Tony sat up. *If she only knew,* he thought as he focused. It took him a full five seconds, but the healed punctures on the inside of her elbow were not similar—they were *identical* to his. Tony's gut tightened as he maintained a poker face. His seatmate spoke again when he had no words.

"Heavens me! There's no way we received them the same way. No way in the world." Lucinda finished with a laugh and allowed her sleeve to fall to her wrist. Then she pressed the recliner button on her seat and eased back. With morbid curiosity, Tony waited for her to elaborate, but she closed her eyes and turned away.

Tony inhaled, counted to five, and exhaled in a like manner. It couldn't be. It was ridiculous. And he didn't need to dig; the woman said it—they could not possibly have gotten the wound the same way. Tony pulled his eyes off his neighbor's resting visage thinking a little rest would be nice.

Will I sleep like Paul said, only twelve hours a month?

He'd only carried the vampire curse a short time. Dealing with the super-sensory elements of his transformation were the most disturbing. Besides those he resisted as he entered the fuselage, he had incredible strength. Earlier, when washing his hands in the airport toilet, he'd inadvertently broken the faucet. He thought he had turned it with normal human effort, but when his fingers touched the metal, the item spun off and skittered across the tiled floor. The other occupants sent him irritated glances but nothing else. Thank goodness they saw nothing odd in the gentleman wrestling spigots. With a half-amused grin, he closed his eyes and rest his head to the seat.

"Roll up your sleeve, Lucy."

Tony sat up in a jerk. The voice had been raspy, male, and not one he recognized. He had heard it in his ears, yet knew it had been *transmitted*. Tony's gaze went to Lucinda fast asleep on his right.

"Why?"

"Roll up your sleeve and I'll make you another one to match."

With an urgent inhale, Tony covered his face with his palms. In his mind's eye, he saw a teenager from another era dressed in a frilly knee-length smock. Across from her stood a tall, dark man with a sharp nose and protruding brow. He held out his hand, waiting for the teen to do as requested. Tony groaned as the girl giggled and put out tiny fingers.

"I told my mum about you, Mr. Haman. She almost sent me to hospital," the girl said and giggled again. The dark man smiled, too, but his teeth were much too sharp.

Tony groaned again and clenched his jaw.

The movie did not end.

"Oh, yessss," the tall man said and pulled the girl's proffered wrist to his mouth. When he pressed his fangs into her flesh, Tony rose to his feet. The tiny restroom was twelve strides away and by the gasps of the people he passed, he reached it faster than he should have.

"No, no, no, no," Tony told his reflection as he doused his face with water. Lucinda's memories had grown hazy now, so much like his own did when he pushed them down. It was going to be a horrible existence if strangers' bad thoughts could so easily worm their way into his own. Tony ran his finger against his gums, rubbing the itching sensation that grew much like the erections of his old life.

Tony scoffed. *That* part of his life had died. From the day he awoke with Paul's curse in his blood, he had no sensations in his pants. Add to that, since he didn't eat, he had no use for waste, which meant no bathroom breaks.

Can't eat, can't sleep, can't have sex.

What else did God expect him to sacrifice before he fell off the vampire-monster deep end?

"I'm hanging in there, but you better deliver me soon," Tony mumbled to God under his breath. Once back in the aisle, he avoided the faces of the passengers he'd spooked before and slumped into his seat. Lucinda was awake and she gave him a humorless smile.

"Maybe we *did* get our scars the same way," she whispered, leaning in. Tony forced a blank look.

"Just a little airsick. I apologize."

Lucinda faced front and said in a soft, breathy voice, "I saw him three times."

Tony pretended he hadn't heard.

"Three bites is what it takes, right?" she chuckled and her delicate hand went to the lacy collar of her blouse. "He put me in hospital the third time."

Lucinda lowered the lace and Tony's gaze fell on a mass of scar tissue that had healed two inches long and at least a quarter-inch wide. Whatever bit her had not gone easy.

"I was a foolish child." Lucinda released the cloth and sat up with a shrug. "How about you, Mr. Agricola?"

Tony swallowed and looked straight ahead. "I have no idea what you're talking about," Tony replied his voice raspy. "It's an old injury. I don't even remember how I got it."

Lucinda lowered her seat tray and rubbed the smooth surface with her palms. She turned to Tony and winked. Tony offered a curt smile and pressed the button to relax his seat back.

"I'm going to catch some sleep, Ms. Langley. I enjoyed chatting with you."

"And I you," Lucinda said and clicked off the light above her head. In a teasing but clear whisper she uttered a few parting words. "I may be older now, but I see my mystery man in your eyes."

Tony rolled his head to the side and met her eye. "Ma'am?"

"I'm a very light sleeper," she whispered with a knowing smile. "If you try to bite me, I'll know it…"

Tony held her gaze, his face lax. Had she pegged him as a vampire? Was it going to be obvious to those with previous exposure? When she showed no sign of budging her expression, Tony looked away and allowed a smile.

Closing his eyes, he whispered as eerily as he could, "Yes, ma'am." Then only slightly less creepily, he added, "I promise to keep my teeth to myself."

He felt Lucinda's eyes on him a few more moments before she settled into her seat and leaned into the small window. Tony pondered her mystery vampire and wondered who he might be.

Mr. Haman...

Did Corescu make any vampires besides Paul? If he did, he did not admit to it. All of these things and more circled his mind until the plane landed in Atlanta eleven hours later.

As he departed the jet and entered the busy terminal, gut-wise, he still felt sublime.

Thank God for Mark's blood, he mused. And then shook his head. *What an odd thing to thank God for.*

But then, he had become a very odd creature indeed.

3

But the LORD your God
Turned the curse into a blessing for you,
Because the LORD your God loves you.
Deuteronomy 23:5b

26 Days Later

MARK CORESCU PACED THE FLOOR OF HIS CAVERNOUS living room, his heels causing staccato clicks on the marble tile. It was good to be home, although he hadn't occupied this particular dwelling in decades. He held property across Europe and the 14-room stone edifice he liked best sat atop a wooded cliff surrounded by a hundred acres of untamed forest. In the day (and on her whim), a short car ride would get Hope into town where Marburg provided basic food and products particular to her American tastes.

Hope...

With a wistful sigh, Mark listened for her on the other side of the castle-like abode. She would not awaken for hours; Mark's tenant enjoyed her rest.

Tenant? That is hardly accurate...

He enjoyed referring to the young woman he shared space with as his *muse*. But for now she resided with him, gave him companionship and entertainment as he catered to her every impulse. Eventually, Mark would need to quantify their communion.

And what would that be? I am not a man, I cannot be any woman's husband.

Mark turned his eyes to the heavens, afraid to speak the real reason he kept her near. Maybe he would admit it to himself one day, but Paul came to mind and Mark resumed pacing. Life with Paul Black, the uber-subservient and affable blacksmith he'd acquired in 1910 had been perfect, enjoyable, and peaceful.

"No!" Mark whispered with clenched fists. When his hands relaxed, he exhaled and forced a smile. He refused to long for the past when he played god and judged the living. Every night for four hundred years, a new Judging victim met his or her end under his teeth. Their sin had called to him and he went, giving them a chance to repent before he filled his need.

Oh, how I loved their blood!

Mark waited. Nothing.

This is progress!

No bloodlust rose in his middle, which meant God was helping him move on, forget the demons that empowered Markus Corescu, Markus Crump, Mark Faircease, Doctor Mark Corescu—any number of aliases he had used over the centuries—that man was dead.

I am a new creature and I will not long for the days of old when I murdered killers in God's name.

He learned with Tony's help that God had never called him to do this, that he had been hearing the voice of the devil. So Mark spent eleven months in stasis until Tony and Paul came to his resting place and changed everything.

So now I live here, with a beautiful twenty-five-year old self-absorbed female who has no idea what she wants in life or even from her aged host.

Well, that wasn't entirely true, for Hope knew what she wanted from him. She may be unable to say it aloud, but she longed for a "Hollywood vampire" experience. She wanted to be held in his arms and feel her blood rush out of her body into his—in her mind, it would be the most romantic thing in the world. Mark read this in her private fantasies, but if he did that, he'd be committing an act he had vowed to put behind him forever.

If I take her blood, I become the vampire I am working to expunge.

Mark resumed pacing and this time, ignored the sound his shoes made on the cold floor. It was nearly three in the morning and the room was as black as the sky outside. He did not need light to see by and he rarely lit the fire.

Am I a vampire?

Anthony Agricola believed God would deliver them from the demonic stronghold that gripped them. Tony also believed God brought Paul to Himself at the end, saving his soul.

Mark forced Paul's memory away once more, the pain too great. He had never loved a person as he loved the young man he proselytized more than a hundred years past and the loss remained raw. In addition, if he pondered Paul too long, he may have to face his improper desire to work the same deal with Hope.

Eh, neither Anthony nor Hope are the reason I'm up at this hour. There's something else…

Mark dropped into a chair beside the cold fireplace.

I am anxious because of the nightmare…

He slept once every twenty-eight days and rarely dreamed. But tonight his mind had returned a disturbing night terror he'd experienced during his rest a month ago. Tonight, it awakened him early, causing him to miss most of his refreshment period. He had been *alarmed,* and this made him angry. Mark concentrated on the details and as it filtered back, he reclined to watch it replay.

It had started innocently enough, Hope riding at the stable, loping around the ring, laughing with delight at the power and agility of her mount. Then another rider appeared, this one a silhouette, with no features or dimensionality. The other rider approached Hope and without provocation, began to absorb her into its shadow. Her blood-curdling screams spurred Mark to leap the arena fence to her rescue. But she was gone. The shadow remained, larger, and more menacing than before. Its featureless horse stomped its hooves in the pool of blood Hope left behind.

When Mark confronted the creature, it responded, *"You disappoint me, reducing yourself as house-boy to a female and bond slave to an invisible Deity. I am returning and I will right this for you. I am very close now. So very close…"*

Sitting upright in his stiff Queen Anne armchair, Mark wiped blood-tinged sweat from his brow. He knew that voice. He knew that featureless rider, knew him all too well. That creature was long dead, burned to death by villagers four hundred years ago. If his spirit lived on, could he return to the flesh? Not knowing precisely how the spirit realm functioned, Mark hoped the demon stayed where he was, in a separate dimension, a disembodied voice and that's all.

He turned his mind to Anthony, the time difference putting his cohort's clock at late afternoon. In a split-second, Mark's stomach folded over with starvation, experiencing the pain via his telepathic link with Paul's reluctant offspring.

"Tony, Tony, stop," he sent and got no reply. The young vampire heard him, but another peek revealed he was deep in prayer, working desperately to erase his bloodlust with Scripture. Mark wished him the best and returned to his own troubles.

☙❧

"Father! Help me! Come on!" Tony growled, his middle twisting with hunger. His pain continued to escalate no matter how piteously he petitioned the heavens. Sitting in the room he claimed as his study,

Tony clutched his stomach, a grimace morphing his face into a mask of pain. He'd been at the desk working on arranging his assets when the newest discomfort brought tears to his eyes.

In the three and a half weeks since he'd been back, the doctor had handled the paperwork that deeded Paul's house to Tony. This had been extremely generous since Tony had no money of his own. Before he met Paul, he worked for his dad's church and delivered pizzas to create his $32K/year income. Now he owned an executive home on eleven acres in Montgomery, Alabama. Corescu had also transferred Paul Black's financial holdings to Tony's name, so no matter what happened in the days and weeks to come, money would not be a problem. *Forever.* One accounting sheet alone described a cash value of $1.2M. Tony didn't open the others. If God allowed a curse to eat at Tony's faith, at least he'd have a comfortable place to endure it.

"Not funny!" he gasped aloud in the empty room and with purpose, turned his mind to the police detectives. They'd located Paul's house the day before the escape to Europe. Tony contacted them when he returned as being on the lam would not work for what he had in mind as he worked out his troubles. He had called Detective Jonah Miller, the cop assigned to Paul's case. The department said Miller retired and turned the call over to his replacement, who took Tony's statement over the phone. He was released and as a result, the case of Paul Black/Saul White had been closed.

At that moment, Tony's hunger fired acidic flames into his esophagus. "God! Help me!" he yelped and returned to his mantra. *I can do this. I can do this. I will NOT drink blood!*

It had been twenty-six days since he had consumed blood and he was hungry; his gut pulsed and cramped in miserable waves. But he had not succumbed; he was still pure and clean as of his last transgression when he took blood from Corescu's arm in Germany. Maybe God was helping him. Maybe God was *healing* him. Maybe he had found the answer. Meditating on the Scriptures had so far prevented him from becoming a slave to the sin. So far, his biblical quiet-time adequately fed his body as well as his spirit. But right now... tonight... Tony's pain expanded, causing his head to pound in time with his heartbeat.

Please, God, let this trial end soon! Tony prayed and opened a blank document on his PC.

This is the prayer of a God-fearing monster—

He paused, lifted his fingers from the keyboard, and closed his eyes. When he reopened them, his vision blurred with tears tinged red.

The curse. The curse caused this. Tears of blood.

In the past, keeping a journal had given him pleasure, but since returning home, he deleted every post. Today, he would save an entry to study his evolution, note his successes, learn from his failures, express his predicament in diary form.

The vampire's curse, still a part of him, ate away at his soul, moment by moment. Tony resumed typing, hoping soon, he'd be posting about his deliverance.

> *May God have mercy on my soul.*
> God will turn the devil's curse into a blessing. The lust for blood is a demonic oppression. It's an addiction, no more, no less. A manifestation of man's sinful nature, inherent in all flesh, as common as a cold. A craving for cigarettes can be ignored. Withdrawal symptoms from cessation of drug abuse can be toughed out. People do it all the time.
> And yes, they fail sometimes.
>
> Oh, God, my body yearns for blood!
>
> I will wait to be delivered. God will set me free. Until then, I'll pray. I won't allow bloodlust to ruin the life God gave me, even if its God who allowed this to happen.
>
> Why? Please, God, why?
>
> And there's Mark. Doctor Corescu drinks the blood of animals and he's comfortable with that compromise. I hear a different voice in my heart. I just can't do it. What the hell? How is that fair?
>
> I know vampires are the stuff of legends. The devil took a myth and made it real enough to change me and a few others into blood-thirsty immortals.
>
> <u>I'm not buying it. I don't believe in vampires.</u>
>
> I'm still a child of God. I didn't do this! It's not my fault! This is God's doing!

Tony—focus!

My mission hasn't changed: deliver the Gospel.
This curse is only the devil's distraction.

Or is it a test?

Wiping another pink tear from his cheek, Tony closed the document without saving.

4

"Those who war against you shall be as nothing,
As a nonexistent thing.
For I, the LORD your God, will hold your right hand,
Saying to you, 'Fear not, I will help you.'"
Isaiah 41:12,13

ELIZABETH CLOSED HER LAPTOP AND STOOD FROM THE barstool, stretching her arms to the ceiling. The low-wattage bar pendant illuminated her area leaving the remainder of the house in quiet darkness. Her new neighborhood was peaceful and she adored her tidy rental with its arched doorways, ceramic tile floors, and uber-modern kitchen. Divorce left her scrambling to start over, but she was twenty-five, still young enough to do anything she put her mind to.

When she and Aaron split, the home equity they halved did not go far. It got her to Alabama, allowed her to put down first and last on a refurbished one-bed-one-bath cottage in Old Cloverdale, and left four thousand dollars in the bank which would supplement her alimony until new income rolled in. Thankfully, the studios in Los Angeles that sold her sculpture made two sales this week and those checks would be nearly as much as her bank kitty.

God is awesome, Elizabeth thought and crossed to her small sofa. It was ironic that the closer she got to God, the more things in her life upended. Elizabeth allowed a smile and looked to her hands resting in her lap.

"Pastor Aaron Hawken," she said and sighed.

Raised a nominal, feel-good Christian, Elizabeth used church as a social club through high school. The summer before college, she fell in love with a visiting preacher fifteen years her senior. Because he was a successful televangelist, her parents did not dissuade her interest. Over June, July, and August, he took her to movies and to dinner, all the while sweeping her off her feet. By the time Elizabeth began her freshman year of college, they were engaged. Aaron traveled the west coast preaching and reconnecting on weekends, and when Elizabeth finished her degree a full year early, they were wed. Four years later, the month of her 24th birthday, they were *un-wed*.

Elizabeth's phone rang just then and she startled.

"Lizzie? Did you get my package?"

It was her mother. Elizabeth switched on the side table lamp and the cozy living room came alive with soft light.

"Not yet. What is it?" Elizabeth's mother had been vehemently opposed to her moving across the country, but that had more to do with the fact that her only daughter might reconnect with her estranged father than the three-thousand-mile cushion Elizabeth now enjoyed.

"Oh, just a little thingy I picked up at the beach. Sean and I spent the week in Tijuana and they had so many great shops! Watch the mail. I sent it last week."

Elizabeth promised she would and made an excuse to get off the phone. The house returned to its earlier delicious silence and she opened her phone's Bible app. The verse of the day made her grin.

"Thus says the Lord, the King of Israel, And his Redeemer, the Lord of hosts: 'I am the First and I am the Last; Besides Me there is no God.'"[i]

Aaron had preached on that verse the first time she saw him. Now whenever she came across it, the fond memories paraded past her consciousness. The trick was to move on to something else before the bad times filtered in and ruined her mood. A Jewish believer in Jesus, Aaron preached with power and filled every sanctuary that hosted his ministry. His celebrity came with devotees, many of those being starry-eyed young women. Two years into their marriage, as Elizabeth grew closer to God in her private time, studying and growing in her faith, Aaron allowed himself to be led astray. Twelve months later, their divorce was final. His income and the laws of California allowed her a monthly alimony payment of $1200, one of their two vehicles, and half the home equity.

Thank God we didn't have children.

She wanted children, but the old-fashioned way—with a mommy and a daddy who loved each other forever. Her own mother divorced her dad because he loved his job more than he loved them.

At least that's what Mom always told me.

But Sean, her mother's second husband, told Elizabeth privately that her dad was an okay guy. That he worked hard at a tough job, and in private, Sean attempted to give ten-year-old Elizabeth a rosier picture of her biological father than her mother allowed.

Now I'm here, one state over.

With her setting up house in central Alabama and him in Whitford City, Georgia, Elizabeth was spatially closer to her father than she had been since her parents' divorce. Over the years since her mother moved her across the country, her father never once visited. He sent greeting cards, and as she reached high school, he sent emails. But never did they meet up. Still, it would happen soon. Inside, she understood that God wanted her to reconnect with her earthly father. Maybe it was time. Right now.

Elizabeth thumbed her phone contacts and found one for "Jonah Miller (Dad)." He had given it to her a few years back and she had never used it. Of course, he'd never called her either, so they were even. Elizabeth wanted to make contact. She touched the speech bubble icon beside his number and the text box gaily opened, making it so easy to send a little, "*Hi, Dad, I moved to Alabama. Let's have lunch.*" Elizabeth whispered a prayer requesting courage and then spoke those very words into the speech-to-text. The words appeared, she added an exclamation point, and hit send.

There it was. The Dad had been texted.

His move.

Elizabeth set the phone to silent, and strolled to the front door. She wanted a little fresh air, a little *world,* feeling cooped up and isolated. She enjoyed her solitude, but… a glance at her watch revealed it was not quite 6pm.

I'll find a bookstore.

Her search engine app informed that the closest, Collegiate Bookstore, was less than a mile away, its ad bragging, "All your reading needs for school and pleasure!" With a smile, Elizabeth headed to her old Camaro and pondered seeing her father face-to-face. How would it go? She grinned wider.

Everything I've done since turning my life over to God for real has been an adventure.

Elizabeth was game.

❧

"Sweet Jesus! look at this!" Former homicide detective Jonah Miller stepped to Jennifer's side to show her the screen. "Didn't you say just this morning that we needed to get in touch with Elizabeth and invite her to the wedding? Look!" Jonah waited for his bride-to-be to read the words before looking at it again himself. "Damn," he whispered, and then, "I'm sorry—*dang.*"

"Why you want to watch your tongue around me, I'll never know. My mouth is far worse than yours ever was," Jenn said and put the last dish in the dishwasher. "So the child makes the first move. Promising."

Jonah texted a few words and stopped. "Geez. Maybe I should just call." He looked to Jenn for her opinion.

"No, trust me. She's nervous, too. A short text is all she needs."

Jonah typed a few more words and Jenn stepped over to supervise.

"No, look," she said and plucked the phone from his hand. "Say this," she mumbled, typing with both thumbs. *"Hey, babydoll! I was just thinking about you, for real! Must be psychic! Can I meet you for lunch tomorrow? You name the place!"* Jenn returned his cell and crossed her arms.

Jonah read and re-read her message, wrinkling his brow. "That's pretty girly, isn't it?" he retorted and Jenn shrugged.

"Then say what I said in your own words."

"Okay... *Elizabeth, I am so happy to hear from you. I would love to have lunch. You name the place.'"* He showed his partner the screen.

"Put an exclamation point after *you* and it's approved," she said and walked behind him to wrap her arms around his middle. "Let's see what she says next."

Jonah sent the message and watched for a reply.

"Does she know you retired?" Jenn asked, still hugging his back.

"Probably not. I last sent her a note at Christmas, and I'm not in contact with her mother since she graduated college."

Jenn chuckled and squeezed him. "She doesn't know her sexy cop-dad now grows mushrooms in cow-manure for a living?"

"Sexy, I like that part. But no, and we're creating a legacy. She'll inherit every acre of this cow-manure, thank you."

"Nicely said, rabbi," Jenn teased, referring to his tendency to quote the Bible and because he resembled a Jewish relation on his mother's side. "But she's taking too long to reply and I gotta get my relaxin' on," Jenn said and released him after popping his rear end. "Come sit beside me, but don't forget my M&Ms."

Jonah promised he wouldn't and he watched Jenn saunter away, swaying for his pleasure. They had been partners on the Force five years and how he ever convinced her he was worth keeping, he'd never know. He loved the woman with his entire heart and he thanked God every day that she said yes when he asked her to be his partner for life.

Jonah looked back to his phone screen. Nothing. He had so much to tell his only daughter, so much to apologize for. Her decision to send him a text opened up a whole new future, for now, Jonah would have an opportunity to ask Elizabeth to be part of his life.

Jonah pocketed the phone, but only after cranking the volume to the top in case she responded. He grabbed two colas and the bowl of candy and joined Jenn on the couch. Part of his mind, though, listened for the ding.

∂∞∂

Rakha scowled as the pious young woman mewled to the cashier about Jesus. On and on and on she rambled until Rakha fantasized dashing her head against the counter. But he stopped his processes, not needing the trouble he brought by indulging his imagination. He'd been in-country two weeks and so far only killed one mortal in anger. As he assimilated to his new host, he found it possessed incredible rage, was easily offended and struck out before considering the consequences. Tonight when he arose with the sunset, he had found it calmer, easier to tame, so he headed out. First stop – his target's business, a college bookstore of all things. Rakha counted heartbeats and waited in line.

"I grew up in California, but I belong here. Alabama is wonderful. The trees. The people. *The food!* I'm a southerner, deep down. God knew that. He always knows," the female customer said. Rakha stood three feet away and inhaled her scent, her shampoo, her soap, the day's perspiration. All these things he stored without effort and as she babbled on, he studied the back of her head, her soft sienna-brown hair dropping to her waist in thick ringlets.

In a perfect world, I'd have this one tonight. Bring her to my home, not slay her in an alley. She'd need to be nude, I'd want to feel that skin, it's so tight, tanned and glowing. How old is she? She can't be more than twenty-three, twenty-four… I'd take her blood from her neck but go shallow, yes, she needs to last. Rakha's head tilted as he sought her profile, and yes, she was classically attractive. The women still rambled so he returned to his delicious fantasy. *I'd run my hands into that beautiful mane and grip it tight enough to pull some loose. Oh, yes. And when she finally expired, I'd shear it off and keep it in my box.* Rakha smiled to himself. It was time to start a box. He'd done it in previous incarnations, collect something of interest from his victims to remember them by. Church Girl would leave him her hair.

"I better let someone else check out, but thank you!" Church Girl said then with the pudgy cashier nodding like a mindless bobblehead.

Rakha made a small "ahem" and the women continued to swap joyful stories.

Rakha held his temper. He needed Agricola's information.

Now, now, calm yourself, Rakha…

He cleared his throat, hands becoming claws at his sides. The cashier finally met his eye and offered a curt nod. Rakha relaxed his shoulders as Church Girl, laden with three sacks of books, leaned away as if to leave. Then, she had one last thought. In a flash, both women were back at it, one miracle after another dribbling from their wet mouths.

Mouths I could fill with soil.

A tiny smile reached the corner of his mouth and he backed away, pivoting to the right, avoiding their notice and that of the other patrons. Facing the nearest bookshelf, Rakha waited for his arousal to fade. Familiarizing himself with his hosts strengths and weaknesses was part of the awakening. When he fantasized of shedding blood, this one's fangs slid free of his gums and protruded enough to be seen by casual observers.

The sheep needn't witness that.

Rakha wanted to be invisible, not attract attention. He had come to Montgomery, Alabama, with a succinct mission and he would not waver.

A teenaged female entered the aisle and reached for a book inches from his right elbow. He did not give way, but allowed her into his personal space, enjoying the heat she emitted. His own flesh was interminably cold, and only when he feasted on the mortals did he experience such warmth. The woman tilted her head at the apex of her rude reach, gathered an impression of his face, and backed with a flirtatious smile. She hadn't met his eye. She saw merely a handsome shopper, perhaps a student. She hadn't seen Rakha; he lived in the host's eyes and hid well.

The cashier said goodbye to her mouthy customer and Rakha checked his teeth. As Church Girl shuffled away, Rakha watched her exit the bookstore into the dark lot. She climbed into an aging red sportscar and rearranged her wavy hair. Remembering her conversation with the cashier infuriated him anew and he imagined his hands around the girl's shapely throat, squeezing until she took her words back. He could see himself pressing his thumbs together over her larynx, insisting that she deny every word about the Carpenter from Nazareth. But...

What if the woman could be seduced and led away from her ridiculous faith? Wasn't that the best vengeance of all?

Rakha licked his lips. In the past, he had enjoyed destroying life in its prime. But he also enjoyed the *game*, the pursuit, the effort of bringing the righteous to the mud.

Rakha turned from the window and refocused his energy on his current target. He stepped to the counter and smiled at the manager.

"Yes, sir," she said. "Did you find everything you needed?"

"Madam, I am interested in getting in touch with Mr. Anthony Agricola. I understand this is his store. Please give me his number and address." Rakha did not know if the woman was simpleminded enough to volunteer the information so he removed his sunglasses to catch her eye. The woman paused and Rakha waited while she cleared her throat. Satisfied that her mind had been adequately scrambled, he replaced his sunglasses and waited.

"Tony lives in Fox Hollow off Vaughn Road." In a faraway voice, the manager gave Rakha what he asked for. "His phone number is unlisted, but I'll jot it down for you."

"And that young woman with the long brown hair. Put her information on the reverse."

Rachel, according to her nametag, fished for the credit-card receipt, used it to look up the girl's name in her computer, and then copied it onto Rakha's memo.

"Thank you. You have been very helpful. Good evening." Rakha tucked the folded piece of paper into his pants pocket. Smiling at his victory, he waltzed out the door.

So easy.

5

Set me as a seal upon your heart, as a seal upon your arm;
For love is as strong as death, jealousy as cruel as the grave;
Its flames are flames of fire, a most vehement flame.
Song of Solomon 8:6

SARAH TRACEY SAT CROSS-LEGGED ON THE LIVING ROOM floor having not yet joined the others in the yard. The hostess, a friend of a friend, promised her a good time among humanity to get her mind off her recent bereavement. Now, three weeks after Ira's death, finally God had sent her a release from her grief period. When the invitation to congregate with strangers arose, she accepted. Now that the word had spread of her celebrity, five young women gathered to talk about the Bible. Each introduced herself and when the circle completed, she offered the group a genuine smile. Besides this room, the house sat empty, the other guests outdoors, soaking up the warm late-afternoon breeze, their laughter wafting through the open windows.

Across the room, leaning against the doorframe, a man watched on with polite interest. He was in his thirties with shoulder-length dark brown hair pulled into a ponytail at his nape. He wore wire-framed glasses and a neatly-trimmed goatee. His clothing drew no attention, plain khakis and a light blue dress shirt, open at the top with no tie. He looked comfortable in his skin and Sarah realized too late that she had been staring. She returned her gaze to her impromptu audience and after a minute of chatting with the girls, found herself drawn to the stranger once more.

His magnetic gaze hinted at a deep-seated confidence and at that moment, his mouth pulled into a tiny grin. Or was it a smirk? Sarah wondered at his spirit. Was he a believer? The Lord had gifted her with incredible discernment, which served her ministry well over twenty years, but this guy... In her spiritual eyes, an incredible energy enveloped him, which without further investigation, could go either way. Sarah trained her eyes to her circle and concentrated on the young people's questions rather than the sultry brown eyes across the room.

"Reverend Tracey, aren't you that evangelist who caused all that commotion last year at the civic center?" Soon-Ye, a quiet Asian twenty-something asked. After which, the others chimed their interest.

"That was God, not me!" laughed Sarah. The previous summer, she and Ira had enjoyed a particularly anointed evening at the Montgomery Civic Center. Several local broadcasters had been there to catch the revival on tape, not that anyone believed what they saw.

"My mom said that you were casting out demons. That's really cool," Soon-Ye said and blushed, avoiding the other girls' eyes.

"My husband Ira headed up an amazing ministry," Sarah said with a sad smile. Then she sent the girl a wink. "We'll miss him a lot."

"Yeah, I heard he passed. I'm sorry." All occupants of the room fell silent for a few moments before the girl spoke again. "Are you leaving the ministry, Reverend Tracey?"

Sarah didn't have an answer so she said what she could. "We'll see. I'm waiting on the Lord. I'm here to do His will, not mine."

A soft amen sounded from the direction of the man in the doorway. Sarah didn't look over, but she wanted to.

The group of women became quiet, the only noise being the instrumental humming of a CD player in the corner and laughter from outside. Sarah sipped her punch and uncrossed her long legs. A movement to her right had her turn and the man from the hallway approached and stood nearby.

Sarah gave him a nod and he returned the gesture with a wink. She looked away and blushed, heat flooding her cheeks.

"I have a question," the one named Cammie said. "Is it okay for a Christian to watch horror movies? My sisters both said it was evil, but I like being scared. What's wrong with that?"

Sarah's eyebrows lifted and she smiled. "I get that question a lot. The short answer is if a movie or book causes you to sin then you should avoid it. If it merely entertains you, than it is simply that— entertainment."

"Do you think that watching *Twilight* will make you want to have sex with a vampire?" Amy, the blonde in the retro green pantsuit asked. "My pastor said we shouldn't watch sexy vampire movies because they make us have bad thoughts."

Sarah's smile tightened, movie monsters not her forte. She parted her lips to answer, but the man hovering above them cleared his throat.

"If I may, I can answer that," he said, his voice rolling about the room with substance.

Sarah looked to his face and gave him a nod. He smiled and her head rushed. She averted her eyes, inside admonishing herself for flirting. *Come on, Sarah! You're a forty-year-old widow. Leave that poor man alone.* And Ira, only gone twenty-one days. Sarah cleared her mind, smiling at her own silliness.

The stranger peaked his fingers below his chin and met each girls' eyes in turn as he began. "There are plenty of kids—boys and girls—caught up in our supernatural-seeking culture. They fantasize to be with or even *become* witches, warlocks, vampires, werewolves... They want to have sex with angels and demons and demigods—"

Some of the girls tittered and he sent them a fatherly wink.

"It's not necessarily the movies and books making them that way, but such media provides fodder for these unclean desires. If you can control your fantasies—control your *thought-life*—this type of entertainment will simply pass the time. It doesn't have to control you or make you sin. Master your thought-life with intention." The man tapped his temple and met each girl's eye one last time.

"Amen to that," Sarah said, looking at the girls and not the man speaking. He stepped to her side and held out his hand to her seat on the carpeted floor.

"Reverend Tracey, I'm Tony Agricola."

Sarah rose to her feet before taking his hand. She was taller, but at 5' 10" she towered over plenty of men. She shook his hand, noting the cool, dry firmness of his grip.

"We met some time ago at a worship conference, although I don't expect you to remember me."

"I'm happy to meet you now," she said nodding.

The young women also got to their feet and made their goodbyes. Sarah waved to the last one and turned to see her new friend close by, watching her every move. She wondered if she should be unnerved, but she wasn't.

"I'm sorry about your husband. He was a powerful preacher."

Sarah nodded and smiled, enjoying the man's soft gaze. Why was she acting so strangely? Her school-girl heart palpitations made her blush and the man smiled as if he noticed. Sarah turned for the door, thankful he couldn't read her mind.

"I didn't mean to run you off," the man said, humor in his voice. Sarah had entered the hallway and he trailed her to the front door.

She laughed. "You didn't. It's time I headed out. Thank you for your wise words in there," she said amused that he recognized she was trying to escape. The man shrugged, his hands in his pockets, a humble look that pulled her heart.

He gave her a new grin. "My pleasure. Can I speak to you before you go? I am tickled to have you to myself. It's hard to make friends with a woman who normally has ten thousand people competing for her attention."

Sarah laughed. He referred to the mega churches she and Ira frequented during their ministry. Still, should she stay? Sarah thought to decline, but was surprised to hear herself invite him to her house for coffee.

"Really? It wouldn't be too much trouble?" he asked, true interest in his gaze.

Sarah laughed again and shook her head at God for putting words in her mouth. "Don't be silly. I live just around the corner."

"Thank you, Reverend," he replied with a debonair bow.

"Please, Mr. Agricola, call me Sarah."

"Sarah, yes, and you call me Tony, eh?" he said and gestured for the open door.

Sarah led the way into the front yard, absently wondering if her place was tidy enough for guests. She was a decent housekeeper, but since Ira passed, she did not give much thought to vacuuming and sweeping.

When they reached her Volvo, she pointed to the stop sign. "Just follow me. We'll go left at that stop, then it's only three streets down on the right. Sound good?"

The man nodded, waved, and piled into a green pick-up.

Why aren't I afraid to bring a total stranger to my house?

Sarah put her car in gear and chuckled at the notion; a month ago, she'd allowed a dangerous miscreant named Saul White into her home and nearly been murdered shortly after. God had protected her and had His hand on the entire affair.

"Lord, Lord, what do You have in mind this time?" she asked in a whisper and finished with an internal joke for God: *Let's hope this one doesn't want to kill me, too.*

ß

"If God were your Father, you would love Me,
For I came from God and now am here…
You belong to your father, the devil,
And you want to carry out your father's desires."
John 8:42,44

WITH THE ADDRESS THE BOOKSTORE MANAGER PROVIDED, Rakha tracked the man in question as he traveled from his own home to a boisterous outdoor party.

But this cannot be the man. He is a fop, an innocent, a mere boy…

Reclining in the driver's seat behind deeply tinted windows, Rakha watched as the young *vampyr* settled into his truck a block away. After all of the miles he had covered, had he found his prize? Rakha did not doubt the Unseen, although he grew irritated at their scheming. The spirits indeed revealed that the "unbeatable equal" he sought owned a bookstore in Montgomery, but it had been up to Rakha to sniff out the details.

No matter; he had found the place by intuition. Picturing the store in his mind, the zealous young woman he had observed there resurfaced in his memory.

If I could get my hands on her, I would make the Unseen so proud…

Tonight as he waited for Agricola to emerge from the party, he researched Church Girl online and found her cyber footprint extensive. As if afraid of nothing, her life lay exposed to the world, and although he didn't find her current address, he found her previous one. Then he found her cell number. Before long, he located a personal email account and made a note to himself to play with her later. Oh, how he loved the technology of this era.

Send her some fan mail. An art collector who heard of her work all the way from Manhattan!

A deception would be easy to concoct, a spell to get close, get her alone, and then to strike her deep in the heart. To see her eyes when she learned no God could save her from his grasp.

Rakha frowned banishing the delicious fantasies; his current mission needed his focus. The Unseen assured him this young vampire living as Anthony Agricola would be the one to give him the most sport of all.

"But look at him!" Rakha said to the Unseen. *"He's picking up women at parties. How can you have made a mistake such as this?"*

No reply, and this did not surprise him. The Unseen had their ways, even after centuries of hearing their ethereal voices, Rakha could only guess at their motivations.

Rakha started his Jaguar and fell in behind the green truck, keeping a good distance to avoid notice. Not that he need worry, for the man's attention did not turn from the woman he tailed.

Still, the Unseen are very sure…

Every time Rakha awoke from hibernation, the Helpers would come. Never seen, but ever present. Helping, guiding, and tutoring him to procure his needs, desires, and fantasies. Such is what this Agricola was to be—a *desire*. A plaything.

Since his newest resurrection, he peeked in on his other children—a moronic devil called Haman and a silly vampire playing magician named Androni. Neither of these interested him. No, he sought a worthwhile opponent. Was there any man or vampyr, mortal or immortal alive in this century that could offer him a proper challenge? His helpers said, yes, right here, Anthony Agricola, a brand-new addition to the immortal family. Rakha scoffed as he stared at Agricola's truck.

They want me to believe that this man is my equal? My worthy adversary? Just because he is a descendant of my priest, I do not believe that this man is the most powerful vampyr on the planet.

"He can destroy youuuuu…" a quiet voice giggled deep in his mind.

"Rubbish," Rakha thought, watching Agricola follow the tall woman into her house. He could be a toothbrush salesman, a pharmacist, or even a small-town preacher.

Unless, perhaps he masquerades in this innocent form, keeping his opponents open to attack. That would make sense.

Rakha narrowed his eyes.

I will follow him, watch him. Then, when the time is right, I will approach.

Rakha shut off the black Jag several houses down from Agricola's truck and determined to wait; there was no need to lose patience now.

2

Then the Lord God said, "Behold, the man has
Become like one of us in knowing good and evil.
Now lest he reach out his hand and take also
 Of the Tree of Life and eat, and live forever..."
Genesis 3:22

SARAH TWISTED AT THE WAIST TO WELCOME TONY ACROSS
the threshold of her home. Unlike the party house down the road, her
street sported rows and rows of new-construction townhouses with
sunshiny paint choices and immaculate landscaping. But it wasn't the
plants that held his attention; Sarah Tracey was beautiful. She
mesmerized him. She wore her frosted blonde hair just long enough to
flip with the movement of her head. And he loved her big hazel eyes
and clear rosy complexion. She was unusually tall for a woman and
impossibly slender, as if every bone in her body was longer than
necessary. In another life, Tony would have found her very attractive,
but there could be no romance in his current state.

Tony sighed and closed the front door behind him. Alone in Sarah
Tracey's house, he wondered anew how she had been affected—or
infected—by Paul Black. Had she been tainted? Is that why she stood out
as she did in his eyes? Or was it God in her that made her so special?
Tony hoped this evening he would find out, answering the questions
that plagued him since Paul mentioned her name in his dying breath.

"If you find a mess, ignore it," Sarah said and Tony smiled.

"Your home is very lovely."

She smiled and gestured for the living room sofa. "Have a seat and
I'll start some coffee."

"None for me, thanks. I'll be happy to wait for you, though." His
host nodded and entered the kitchen. Tony soaked up the peaceful
energy. From the other room, Sarah offered him a few more beverages
and he politely declined. When she returned, she sat in a petite mauve
chair across from Tony's perch on the sofa.

"So, how do you know Janice Garner?"

Tony raised his brow. "Who?"

Sarah laughed. "The hostess at the party."

31

"Oh, heh," Tony chuckled. "I crashed it. I was looking for you." He grabbed her eyes then with purpose. "It's important that I speak to you about something that happened to you a few weeks ago."

"My goodness," Sarah said with mock worry and crossed her knees. "That jibes with what I'm getting in my spirit and the mystery has me curious. I'm not normally this familiar with perfect strangers."

"I'm sure," Tony said and looked at his hands, buying time. He loathed broaching the subject, but her wording gave him an opening statement. "Since you put it that way," he began, "a few weeks ago you had a run-in with a man named Saul White." Paul went by Saul those last months and when Tony researched the news-clippings, he discovered the papers referred to him with that alias. His new friend paled and she put her hand to her sternum.

"Was he a friend of yours?"

"No, not a friend," Tony said to assuage her growing fear. "I was his *keeper.*" Her brow furrowed, and Tony forged ahead. "My job was to prevent him from getting into trouble. Sort of his divine parole officer."

"I'm not following. You're a parole officer? So they caught him?"

Tony shook his head. In the news article, the police chalked the attacker up as Wanted and Tony knew from speaking to the detectives on Paul's case that the manhunt had ended until new evidence presented. As for Sarah... why did Paul say he needed to find her? Tony chose his next words with care.

"Wait. Start over. I read about the attack. Can you tell me about your encounter? In detail?"

"Tony," she started, but didn't say more.

Unsure of why she hesitated, Tony tried another tact. "I need to know the extent of your relationship."

"We didn't have a relationship, thank God!"

Tony gave her a smile that garnered an immediate effect. Her heart rate slowed and she stopped wringing her hands. "Did you meet him before the night he attacked you? Tell me about that," Tony said, unashamed for hypnotizing her a bit.

"Yes. I met him earlier, one night after church," she said, her eyes locked in his own. "He was insane, he *oozed* evil."

"I know. What happened?" Tony pressed.

"I needed jumper cables, he was outside. Oh, Tony, his eyes..." she said and trembled. "The Lord gave me a word for him, but he scared me so badly, I shouted it at him and ran away."

"What was the word?" Tony asked, remaining calm and happy that she did as well.

Sarah replied with reverence, "I told him, '*You can't get away from God. The Lord is watching over you and protecting you. He is not going to let you die without knowing Him. You will travel to a distant land looking for one master, but finding another. Listen to your little shepherd and do what he says.*'"

Tony's eyes widened and Sarah noticed his reaction.

"You're his little shepherd?" Tony gave her a slow nod. "What does it mean?"

"It means," Tony began and met her eye once more, "he should have done as you told him." Had Paul heeded that advice, he might still be alive. Maybe even been delivered from vampirism. *Maybe we all would have been—Mark and myself, too.* Tony fell quiet and studied the floor. Paul made his choices and a new path had been set for Tony because of those. With a resurgence of purpose, Tony steeled his nerve and clasped his hands in his lap.

"So, was Mr. White saved?" she asked in the awkward silence.

Tony offered a gentle nod. Paul had seen Jesus, received Him, and died. The experience remained a fresh wound and Tony didn't realize how fresh until that moment. Paul had been awful, but Tony was attached to him—odd as it sounded. The vampire's death *hurt*.

"Halleluiah!" Sarah said with a glee that brightened his heart. "Mr. White was as lost as a man could be. Where is he now?"

"He passed away," Tony said and she exhaled, working through her emotions. Tony needed more. "Sarah, this is important. When he attacked you, tell me how it went down."

Sarah shuddered. "He tried to kill me when I left the mall one night," she said whispering. "You might think I'm crazy, but when I looked into his eyes, I saw a creature as evil as the devil and old as time."

Tony nodded, glad that she headed down a supernatural path. "Do you think he wasn't human?"

Sarah uncrossed her legs and leaned forward as she moved into what appeared to be ministering mode. "You have a huge burden on you about this man. Ask your question. I'm a big girl."

Tony smiled. He would blurt it out if he could. *Did Paul ever bite you, suck your blood, make you drink his blood, give you a transfusion of his blood…* all of the wrong phrases came to mind. He tried his best. "When you had your encounter, did he hurt you physically?"

"Besides trying to kill me?"

"Yes, tell me what happened. Don't leave anything out."

"He was waiting for me near my car," Sarah answered without hesitation. "He tried to drag me away but I fought back, and with the help of angels, he was thrown off twice."

"Angels?" Tony had seen an angel at the height of dealing with Paul's growing insanity.

"Yes, had to be. I barely shoved and that monster was thrown several feet. And when I hit his face, a powerful force broke his nose. It wasn't me. My hand was fine. Not a scratch."

"Broke his nose? Did any of his blood get on you?"

Sarah sat up, alarmed at the idea of contagion. "Did he have a disease?"

"Please, in detail, what happened when his nose was broken."

"My head had hit the pavement and I called on Jesus. I swung my fist as hard as I could. I heard the crack of bone. I might have been holding a brick, but it's not clear if that was real or something God did."

Tony nodded for more, having no problem believing either.

"You look so worried. Please tell me he wasn't sick with AIDS."

Tony shook his head no. "Now think hard, could you have swallowed his blood? Even a drop? It's very important."

"It was all over my face, Tony. Maybe." Sarah paused. "Wait... I licked my lips and I remember being disgusted when I tasted blood."

"Oh, God," Tony exhaled, stood and turned away. If Sarah ingested even the tiniest bit of Paul's blood, she would be changed. *But why, Lord? Why persecute Sarah? Why stick her with this uncleanness?*

Sarah's heartrate had increased in Tony's new ears. He would need to explain it the nicest way possible; sweet little evangelists don't believe in vampires. He never had before he met one in the flesh.

"But I'm fine. The doctor released me without restrictions. What aren't you saying?"

"If you ingested his blood, even a drop, we have a lot to talk about."

"What's the big deal? What in the world did this man have inside of him that is so dangerous?"

Tony bowed his head to collect his thoughts. Would she freak out or be calm?

"Spill it, Tony. I'm tired of dancing. I can take it, I promise."

Tony took a deep breath and leveled his gaze. "Okay, people who ingest his blood become immortal."

"What?" Sarah scoffed. "Explain."

"Look, I was tossed into this storm last summer and it still amazes me. We have to determine if it's happened to you. Maybe you didn't ingest enough. Maybe you're still normal…"

"God placed a limit on the number of man's years." Sarah spoke as if Tony was kidding.

"It's God, not me." Tony maintained eye contact. "Answer me this, have you hurt yourself since then? A cut? Abrasion?"

"No," Sarah shook her head. "And I'm perfectly healthy. That's good, right?"

"Normally, yes, but in this case, it could mean that you were infected." Sarah's expression remained pensive and Tony tried on a smile. "It's not so bad. It just takes a little getting used to."

Sarah's eyes lit up and she leaned in. "You, too…?"

Tony offered a slow nod. He had resolved to not tell her his other peculiarities, hoping God would save her the horror of learning her new friend was a monster.

"I'm sorry, I don't believe it." Sarah turned away. *"Lord, you could have warned me this nice man is crazy."*

Sarah's thoughts trickled into his ears and he'd almost forgotten it could happen. He tried again.

"How can I make you understand? None of this was my idea… I'm not happy to be the bearer of this news."

Sarah gave him a kind smile. "I sense that you're sincere. Really, I do." She thought a moment. "Can you prove it?"

"Sure. It's easy to prove. Ghastly, but easy." Tony stood and disappeared into the kitchen. "Come in here," he called. "It'll be easier to clean tile than carpet…"

Sarah entered the kitchen praying under her breath. He held up his hand to get her to stop where she was. Her eyes widened when she saw the knife he held and he gave her a smile.

"Don't be afraid. It is painless. Watch."

Holding out his hand, palm up, he put the sharp blade to the pale underside of his forearm. When he was certain that she was paying attention, he brought the steel across sure and fast slicing deep. It pinched, but as expected, delivered no pain. Sarah cried out at the sudden movement and hushed just as quickly, covering her mouth. They both focused on the line of blood that welled up before dripping to the floor.

"Tony, why…" Before she could finish her sentence, the sliced flesh began to knit itself together before her eyes.

"Watch," Tony whispered. It would take fifteen seconds for the deep gash to heal and neither of them breathed as the skin magically came together. Thankfully, Tony resisted the urge to lick the wound clean as the healing completed. "Can you grab me a paper towel?"

"Here." Sarah snatched one off the roll and handed it over without stepping close. After he set the knife onto the counter, she watched him wipe the wound clean.

"Gone, healed." Tony held his arm out for inspection as he knelt to swipe up the blood from the floor. "This is what I meant by immortal. This is the most obvious evidence of someone who ingested Paul's blood."

"I have to sit down," Sarah whispered and turned for the living room, collapsing on the soft couch instead of the chair. Her prayers zoomed past his mind. *My Father, my Father, is this for real? Can this be so? Have You allowed access to Your Tree of Life? Have I tasted of the fruit of this tree? How can we know?*

"You don't have to spill your blood, Sarah," Tony said from the doorway, hoping she wouldn't become aware that he could hear some of her thoughts. "You only need to know what has happened. It doesn't have to be a bad thing." Sarah didn't reply and Tony crossed to place his hand to her shoulder.

"I told you I was strong…" Sarah chuckled, shaking her head. "I want to know if I'm changed. I want to know right now."

"I understand." Tony waited for Sarah to build the courage to do what he did. Deep inside, his hunger tapped on his consciousness. Unintentionally, he thought of John Jenkins. John donated blood to Paul Black many times and Tony hated recalling that fact. What if John should offer such a service to Tony? Could he resist?

God help us all, he prayed in the silent moment.

"You do it," Sarah said then, soft and sure. She got to her feet. "I don't think I can stab myself. I'd be too afraid. But I could stand it if you did it and I looked away." With a shy grin she added, "Like when I get a shot at the doctor's office."

Tony swallowed and said he would. "And it doesn't have to be dramatic. A tiny incision is all it takes. If you're not infected, no big deal."

Sarah nodded and reentered the kitchen. A bit stunned at her courage, Tony trailed her in. Was she really going to let him, a practical stranger, put a knife to her flesh?

"Use this. The one you used hasn't been sharpened in decades." Almost jovial, she handed Tony a paring knife out of the knife block. She held out her arm and turned her face.

"Okay. Here goes," Tony joked and took her wrist in his free hand. "I'll cut right where I cut my own arm. There are no major arteries there and it should heal nicely if you turn out to be... you know... normal." Tony took a deep breath. "This is weird, isn't it?"

"Definitely," Sarah muttered, her eyes closed. *Ira would have a heart attack if he knew I was letting a stranger stab me in the arm...*

Tony sucked his teeth at her silent transmission. Aloud, he sighed and touched her skin with the knife-tip. "Try not to flinch."

Without waiting for a response, Tony drew the blade across her arm, just light enough to nick the top layer. He watched mesmerized, as Sarah's blood pumped to the surface and gradually welled into a drop. It was a beautiful thing and for a moment he forgot where he was. Only the audible grumble in his stomach brought him around and he looked to see if Sarah had witnessed his strange behavior. Thankfully, she hadn't, her face still turned away.

"Are you going to do it? I'm about to lose my nerve."

In a faraway voice, Tony responded, "It's done. Have a look." They both looked to her arm and watched the thin scratch disappear. "It's a girl," he whispered with muted humor.

Sarah yanked her wrist free and held the healed wound to her face. "This can't be! It's impossible! Give me that!" She yanked the short knife from Tony's hand and plunged it into her other arm to the hilt.

"Sarah!" Tony yanked the knife from her arm. A string of blood splatter accompanied the excision and he dropped the blade. The deep wound dredged dark, oxygenated blood that dropped to the tile in an obscene waterfall. Sarah stared incredulous as the new wound also healed before her eyes.

His head swimming with the aroma, Tony made a grab for the remaining paper towels to catch the excess. Once again, he fought the impulse to bring the blood-soaked towels to his mouth. He knelt to swipe at the crimson mess but converted to sitting cross-legged as the room spun.

Twenty-seven days...

Tony's mantra came to mind as he wadded the soiled paper into a loose ball.

"This can't be. Father, what does this mean?" Sarah mumbled, still watching her arm, ignoring all else.

At her feet his eyes half-closed, Tony brought his hand to his mouth and touched his tongue to the towels. Daring a second go, he then ran his bloody fingers to his lips. The minuscule amount he ingested magnified as his stomach swelled to welcome the nourishment. It had been less than a teaspoon, yet it erased his hunger.

A tiny voice that could only have come from the devil taunted, *"See? What's the harm? A tiny drop is all it takes. What are you afraid of? Why torture yourself? No one has to die…"*

But that was a lie. The few times Tony had imbibed in the awful stuff, it had been nearly impossible to stop. His flesh took over as soon as he gave in to the lust. This demonic voice would have him *start* because it knew he would not be able to *stop*. Rather than allow the realization to haunt him any further, Tony turned his attention to Sarah. He met her eyes as she leaned against the counter. She held her arm out for Tony to see the healed wound.

"You are white as a sheet," she said low. "Are you okay?"

"Yeah, sorry. I get wigged out at the sight of so much blood." *And that's the truth.*

"You, too, eh?"

Tony nodded and fell silent, waiting for his head to stop spinning.

"What do we do now?" Sarah slid down the cabinet to the tiled floor to sit across.

After a long moment, he sighed for her to hear. "Nothing. Everything. Pray. I have no idea why God allows what He allows. Let's see what happens next."

Sarah sighed the same way. "It looks like Saul White was some sort of walking, talking Tree of Life."

"That's one way to look at it," Tony allowed, thinking the man had been more the *Tree of Death* in the time he knew him. But Sarah did not need to know the ugly details. Tony prayed he'd never have to tell this beautiful woman he was not so far removed from the monster she knew as Saul White.

"Heavenly Father," Sarah said, eyes closed and head tipped to the ceiling, "your servants await Your command."

"Amen," Tony agreed and sucked his palate. *Maybe this is as bad as it will get.* Which he didn't believe for a minute.

8

In the day of prosperity be joyful,
But in the day of adversity consider:
Surely God has appointed the one as well as the other,
So that man can find out nothing that will come after him.
Ecclesiastes 7:14

BIG JOHN JENKINS TROMPED ACROSS THE DARK YARD,
his six-foot-six frame casting a long shadow. He was a giant by man's
standards, made even more so because of his incredible bulk. A former
body builder, not an inch of John's body lacked bulging muscle. He had
been over-sized since the third grade, so when his friends began
referring to him as "Big John," he took it as a compliment. Now
everywhere he went, folks exclaimed at his size.

Pulling his handkerchief from the back pocket of his Levi's, John
wiped the sweat from his brow and then rubbed his entire head. He
kept it shaved to conceal a bald spot, and his face clean-shaven to
complete the look. His chocolate brown skin was without blemish and
his wife often chided that it was even smoother than hers. Of course,
she exaggerated; no one's skin was as soft as that of his Opal. John
allowed her beautiful face to surface and blew her a kiss. He checked
the time on his phone. Tony would be back soon.

John spent the day clearing one of Tony's pastures. He finally wore
himself out removing felled trees that had blocked the stream feeding
the one-acre pond. After two hours of futility, one huge trunk finally
rolled away from the water. Then the tractor pitched forward, lost
balance, and tipped onto its side. John had slipped out in time to watch
from safety as the machinery sank twelve inches into the wet bank.

Where's Superman when you need him? John thought with a smile. Tony
could pull the machine out with his bare hands. Ever since his friend
had been transformed, they constantly tested the limits of his new
abilities. So far they had not found any definitive boundaries when it
came to brute strength.

Entering the backdoor of Tony's house, John shrugged off his
boots and trudged in. He crossed through the mudroom and into the
kitchen reflecting on Tony's other peculiarities.

And there is still that one very big drawback…

His smile faded as he pulled out a stiff wooden chair at the table. After dropping his bulk to the cushion, he lifted his eyes to the vaulted ceiling and thought about praying for Tony. Every few hours, he would get the urge to pray for the guy and he wondered if it was his idea or God's. John closed his eyes, lifting Tony Agricola to the Throne of God.

"Heavenly Father, help him remain holy. He needs all the help he can get…"

Out of words, John glanced at his watch and stepped to the front windows. No sign of Tony's truck. How did his evening go? Did he find the reverend? Did she talk to him about Paul? And the main thing, had Reverend Sarah Tracey been tainted by his blood?

Big John peered down the winding driveway toward the electronic gate. It was eleven o'clock and after a few more seconds watching for his truck, John headed to the den. The television flickered on and he fell onto the sofa, determined to stay awake until Tony returned.

Poor Tony, I mean, geesh…

John shook his head, still sorry for everything that had happened to them both over the past eight months. He was increasingly thankful he had Opal at home. Tony had only John.

John continued to think on all these things until he dozed off.

ॐॐ

The clock chimed midnight as Tony reached the house, parking beside John's red Cadillac. Although he'd rather be alone, the big guy deserved an update and Tony no longer had the privilege of having his own way. John had been an invaluable asset as he worked out his new (hopefully temporary) existence, and had priceless insight on everything Tony brought to the table. He entered around the side and heard John's heart-sounds in the area of the den. He started that way, thinking of how quickly he'd grown accustomed to using his superman ears.

"So, how did it go?" John asked in his deep baritone when Tony stepped into the room. "You didn't call. I was worried." John sidled up rubbing sleep from his eyes.

"Well, mystery solved," Tony replied. "Paul infected her."

"She's not—" John said and stopped.

"No! No way," Tony jumped in realizing his error. "She ingested his blood when he attacked her. So she's like he was—like I was—before, you know."

"Oh… God help us. What did you tell her?" John asked and followed as Tony left the den for the study.

In the doorway, Tony turned and met his eye. "I didn't tell her any of the *mosquito* stuff." He looked over his glasses at his use of his friend's euphemism from the Paul days. John offered a tight smile and waited for more. "She has great discernment so it won't be long until she sees the rest. I just couldn't go into it tonight.

John commiserated and Tony walked to his desk. A gnawing cursor in the back of his mind told him the guy needed to leave. He met John's eye as he leaned on his desktop. "Head on home. I can fill you in tomorrow. Go be with Opal."

"Forget it. Opal's out of town visiting her mom. I'm staying here. Spill." John dropped his weight into a sturdy winged-backed chair. Tony went behind his desk to shuffle papers and John watched him. "You look different," he said with a chin tip.

"What?" Tony looked at his shirtfront and then his hands.

"Yeah…" John crossed his arms at his chest. "You're moving different, sorta rolling, smooth-like." John huffed. "That vampire blood is making you over. You're much more… lupine? Is that a word?"

"Lupine?" Tony furrowed his brow. "Like a wolf?"

"Or a cat," John replied. "I tell you what, if you keep changing into this creature, the folks we meet are going to be unnaturally attracted to you. It would make resisting all the bad stuff more difficult."

"That's all I need," Tony said. Exasperated at the thought, he sat in his office chair. "That reminds me, I need a favor. I asked Sarah to come by here tomorrow, to talk, to see what God wants us to do now." John parted his lips, unable to guess the favor. "I want you to tell her everything. Tell her about you and Paul, about me and Paul, about how I came to be like this…"

John nodded. "No problem. I'll tell her. Why?"

Tony shook his head. "I can't do it. I saw her face when I told her about the contamination. You tell her the vampire part and I'll come in when you've done it. I sure appreciate it, buddy. I'm strong, but not that strong."

John chuckled. "No worries. So is that all you can tell me about Reverend Tracey?"

"She's beautiful," Tony said with a grin. "I've seen her before, from the audience last year at a worship conference. But she was someone's wife then and I was an innocent little seminary student seeking a movement of God." Tony shook his head with a wry chortle. "I wish I could rewind the last eleven months."

"I'm right there with you," Big John agreed. "I figure you'd like some alone time, but tell me the short version. How did she get contaminated?"

"Sure. When Paul attacked her, she broke his nose. Some of his blood got on her face," Tony said in a rush and closed his eyes. A fresh wave of nausea rolled over him and left in its wake a creeping stomach cramp. To John, he said, "I reckon you better go on up to bed."

John caught his eye and pointed to Tony's middle. "How's *that* going?"

Tony stood and leaned his palms on the desktop. "So far so good. Twenty-seven days and counting."

"How do you feel?" John asked. Then Tony heard in his friend's mind, *"God, don't let him get hungry…"*

"I feel fine, but go on upstairs." Tony met John's eyes and his stomach grumbled again. John's smile faltered. "We'll see what happens tomorrow."

"That bad, eh?" John asked, his eyes full of sympathy.

"It's uncomfortable, but I'm beating it." Without intention, Tony captured John's gaze and the big man began rolling up his sleeve.

"Well… I'm going to bed…" Unblinking, John spoke in a dreamy voice. He took two steps toward Tony before both men simultaneously snapped to attention.

"John! Get back!" Tony barked hating that again, his flesh attempted to have its way without his official consent.

"DAMN!" John yelped, jumped back, and then jerked down his sleeve. "Damn!" he said again softer and apologized.

"It's not you. Just GO!" Tony's voice had grown raspy and he moved behind his desk chair. John backed into the hall, blinked a few times, and turned away cursing under his breath.

"I'll be in my room," he called. "And you stay *the hell* away from my door."

Miserable and embarrassed, Tony nodded. The close call had his hunger and the accompanying nausea coming in great waves. He was never sure how severe the pain might be and he didn't want John to see him suffer. He also didn't want John to offer himself as a substitute as it became increasingly difficult to resist.

Tony listened to John climb the stairs, both of them having glimpsed the monster he worked so desperately to hide. Holding his gut against the cramps, Tony resumed his seat at the desk and reached for his Bible. In the Book of John, he read aloud, his voice too guttural to be human.

"Whoever drinks of this water will thirst again, but whoever drinks of the water that I shall give them will never thirst…"

After a few long moments of reading, the pain receded from Tony's middle. Tony leaned back and sent a mental memo to his friend. *"It's working, but don't come out until morning. Just in case."*

"I'm way ahead of you," John replied. *"Locked and loaded."*

Not offended at John's threat, Tony closed his eyes and replied in his mind. *"Pray for me."*

"I always do, man. I always do…"

Tony switched off his desk lamp and smirked at the glow his cursed eyesight caused.

"Whatever…whatever. So long as I'm not drinking blood."

Tony relaxed into his chair, head nestled into folded arms.

If I don't drink blood, then I'm not a monster. I'm just a super strange and supernatural guy.

Smiling, Tony prayed for sleep.

9

"The LORD will be awesome to them,
For He will reduce to nothing the gods of this earth."
Zephaniah 2:11

"EATING THE WORD OF GOD?" GRUMBLING TO HIMSELF, Rakha returned to his car and slid into the leather seat, barely making sense of what he witnessed. Agricola was insane.

In an absent manner, Rakha held out his left hand studying the shiny new skin. Earlier that day in a gross error of judgment, he had left his thick curtains open as he dozed on the floor. He sighed. It seemed the older his soul, the further from the sun he awoke.

Now, what is it about Agricola that has the Unseen so agitated?

Rakha returned to the task at hand. He had followed Agricola home and planned on introducing himself. *That* was before he heard the inane conversation inside. Before he realized the toothbrush salesman *was* some sort of preacher, and he was defying his bloodlust with power drawn from his religion.

I am wasting my time. I will never trust those buggers again.

"You cannot beat him..."

"What?" Rakha whispered in the close confines of his sleek new car. His insults had riled the Unseen and they hissed in his mind.

"You wanted a challenge. We give you Anthony Agricola. You cannot defeat him. But if you do... your reward will be greater than you can even imagine..."

Rakha scoffed, watching the outline of the house in the distance. "A preacher. You think I can't snap his head off?" He waited for a reply, but only heard more of the same challenge. The ancient spirits saw Agricola as a true threat, which meant they knew something they hadn't revealed. Rakha apologized to the Helpers and focused a new question.

"What do you know about this man, this vampyr?"

He discerned a quick huddle as the Unseen decided what to share, and finally, one voice answered for them all. *"Just know that he has bested two of your kind without lifting a finger... that is all we will say."*

Rakha squinted his eyes toward Agricola's dark house.

"I will keep on him," he promised. *"I will wait for my time and then I will show you how a real vampyr operates. I will have my fill of his blood before the summer is out."*

Rakha backed his car a few yards and then exited the man's neighborhood. He would bide his time. If this man, this *preacher,* was so powerful, he had better get to know him, uncover his weaknesses. Rakha headed toward downtown.

All I need is a few well-laid plans…

Rakha schemed along the way, turning finally onto Union, seeking the forgotten places. The streets where thugs and prostitutes dawdled their lives away, unprotected and alone. He soon spotted his prey walking along the crumpled sidewalk. It was a young man, black and presumably homeless, and as vulnerable as they come.

He slowed his Jag and rolled alongside, waiting to be acknowledged. He could see the boy's profile. With an aristocratic nose and haughty brow, the youth might have passed as an actor if he had taken better care of his health. But his hope had been long ago snuffed out by a heavy drug habit and Rakha discerned it had almost finished its deadly work.

The kid heard the smooth engine slow and follow, but he stiffened his jaw and refused to look. Rakha rolled down the passenger side window and cleared his throat. The boy stopped walking and stood still, considering whether or not he should address the driver of the fancy car or take off running. Rakha cleared his throat again and the boy turned to meet his eye.

"What do you want? I ain't no queer. Buzz off." He stood square and placed his hands on thin hips. His face curled into a fierce scowl and he waited for the driver to be cowed and pull away.

"One hundred dollars says you are anything I say you are." Rakha never abandoned the boy's dark gaze. The kid could not have been a day over sixteen, but he had already seen the worst side of life and there was no light left in him. Rakha brandished a crisp one hundred dollar bill.

"I said I ain't your boy. What do you want?" The youth stepped to the car door and leaned in, bracing both palms through the open window. He eyed the bill and licked his lips.

"Get in," Rakha whispered with a glance up and down the dark street. He did not intend to leave the boy alive and he didn't want stories in the morning of police looking to question someone driving a dark blue or black Jaguar XJ6. "Get in and the money is yours."

Still eyeing the bill, the boy yanked the door open and fell into the passenger seat. Once inside, he raised the tinted window. The kid looked to his right, left, and then behind before flicking his fingers toward the windshield.

"Get off this road and go up there. Turn on Washington." He clutched the tops of his thighs and did not look at his driver.

Rakha did as he suggested. No one had driven by and the only other person in sight was passed out on the stoop of a dilapidated apartment building. He chuckled at the boy's fevered thoughts; he was quite familiar with selling his body for drugs, and although he didn't enjoy it, the lust for cocaine would not go ignored.

Rakha turned on Washington and checked his passenger's profile.

The boy pointed to an alley. "One hundred dollars," the boy said and turned to face the driver. He did not maintain eye contact but watched the money in the stranger's hand.

Rakha parked and reached for the boy's wrist. The kid flinched, but then relaxed, looking at Rakha with a mix of fear and self-loathing.

"Relax," he cooed, reeling the boy close by his arm. "Sit still and be quiet." His victim did as commanded, his young mind easy to hypnotize due to his desperation. He watched with round eyes as Rakha brought his wrist to his mouth. He did not move and he did not cry out, even as the vampire forced sharp teeth through his skin. When the blood flowed into Rakha's mouth, the fire in the boy's eyes dimmed, his furrowed brow softening as his life drained out.

"One hundred dollars..." the boy whispered, slumping forward until his right temple rested on the dashboard, leaving a swath of sweat in its wake.

Rakha watched him die. He wanted to witness the very end, when the kid stood at the precipice of death and peeked over the edge. It was wonderful to behold. Almost as pleasurable as the feasting itself.

And I will see Agricola's life fizzle out as well. Oh, yes. He will be to me as this lost child: helpless, hapless, and hopeless.

Rakha stared into the boy's sunken eyes until his heart stopped its labored pulse. He thought once more of the bothersome Agricola. He imagined that the young man in his car was actually his *vampyr* prey. It would come to pass. But for now, he would feed on the forgotten people of the city. He reached across the boy and opened the door.

Planning and scheming, he thought as he pushed the youth from the car with his foot. *It is all part of the hunt.* And it was all part of the fun.

10

"I will love You, O LORD, my strength.
The LORD is my rock and my fortress and my deliverer."
Psalm 18:1

SARAH'S CLOCK READ 7AM AND SHE'D BEEN AWAKE SINCE 5, unable to go back to sleep once her new acquaintance and his huge news returned to her consciousness. Was it too early to try his number? Sarah reached for her cell on the bedside table and did not think on it again. She had a ton of questions and he had told her before he left that she could call any time, day or night.

Morning, it is.

She pressed the number and waited.

"Hello?"

A very deep African-American voice issued the greeting and for a moment, Sarah wondered if she had the wrong number. The man must have sensed the pause and he clarified with a follow up.

"Agricola residence."

"Oh! Good morning," Sarah stammered and wondered about the man answering the phone. Did Tony live in a commune of folks infected by Saul White's blood? She smiled at her inner questions. "This is Sarah Tracey. Is Pastor Tony in?"

"Well! Hey, Reverend Tracey! This is Big John Jenkins. Tony told me you'd be calling. How are you?"

"Thank you, Big John, I think I'm fine but..." Bordering on being rude, Sarah did her best to sweeten her tone. "Can I come over? He and I need to talk."

"I'm sure he'd want you to come over. Let me try to get him to the phone. Hang on..."

Sarah said okay and strode to her mirror to fluff her bed-hair. After a few seconds of silence, she started to her kitchen to put on the coffee.

"Hey, Reverend Tracey, it's all quiet on his side of the house," the man said. "Do you have the address? By the time you get here, he'll be presentable."

"Yes, I have it, thank you! I'll be there in an hour." Elated, Sarah made her goodbyes. After a quick sip of go-juice, she sprinted to the shower, afraid to learn more, but more afraid to remain ignorant of whatever God wanted her to know regarding Tony Agricola and the deceased Saul White. Sarah sang to the Lord until time to leave and did not worry about any of it for twenty whole minutes.

At 8AM on the nose, Sarah waited at Pastor Tony's electronic security gate. It inched open and she wound her way to the house. He lived on a street populated by executive homes, two- and three-storied estates situated on multi-acre lots. Sarah pulled into one of four parking spaces between a shiny red Cadillac and Tony's familiar green truck. On the front porch, she pressed an ornate bell. The door opened without delay and she smiled into the face of the largest man she had ever seen.

"Reverend Tracey! So nice to meet you. I'm Big John Jenkins. We spoke on the phone." The man backed to allow her to enter, but put out a huge hand.

"Nice to meet you, too, Big John," Sarah said, trying not to gawk. He wore a workout tank with loose joggers and it seemed every viewable muscle had been developed to the max. When she gave him her hand, his grip was gentle. "I hope Tony's up. I have a zillion questions."

"Come on in," he said and she crossed the threshold. "I heard him stirring. Make yourself at home and I'll get you some coffee. How do you take it?"

"Black is fine," she said and dropped her small handbag on a chair by the study door.

Big John made sure she found a comfortable seat and left her for the coffee. Sarah looked around and took a deep breath. A hefty desk took up a quarter of the room, and on it sat a banker's lamp, a few ink pens, a pencil sharpener, and an empty leather-lined outbox. If Tony had any mess, it wasn't on his desktop. The back wall on either side was filled with built-in shelves, although very few books lived there. In fact, the décor was sparse all-round, and Sarah wondered if he had just moved in. Before she pondered it further, John re-entered with two steaming mugs.

"Thank you," Sarah said receiving the coffee. They both sipped saying nothing until Sarah broke the silence. "So, are you like me? Did you catch this bug from Saul White?" she asked, a finger to her sternum.

The man's eyes widened and he released a nervous chuckle. "No, ma'am. Thank God." Then he met her eye. "No offense."

"None taken," Sarah said and inclined her head. "You're mighty calm about it. I'm freaking out, and I'm supposed to be trusting God in all things." She gave a tight laugh; depending on God did not erase all human worry.

"Yeah, I apologize," Big John said with a softened tone. "I'm used to it, that's all."

"Mr. Jenkins," she began and he asked her to call him by his first name. "Sure, John, how do you think God fits into this?" Sarah watched Big John's face; he had something to say, but held back. "What are you thinking?"

"I have a few ideas, but I'm not an expert on the Bible."

"Please, share," Sarah said. The memory of her skin healing before her eyes gave her the sense that there was to be no need for politeness. "God reveals Himself in pieces so no one man can boast. What do *you* think God is doing?"

John didn't look comfortable and replied looking into his mug. "It's like I told Tony, why can't God do a new thing?"

"Behold, I will do a new thing," Sarah said under her breath, awaiting confirmation or rejection from God.

"Exactly. 'Now it shall spring forth.' Isaiah 43:19."

"Go on," Sarah added and Big John grew more animated as he continued.

"No matter how much we study, there's always something new to learn." Big John sipped his coffee and leaned forward. "There're still things for us to comprehend. This is probably one of those things."

"Huh, maybe there's something to that."

Big John sipped and when he leaned forward to swipe the top of his shoe, Sarah spied a horrendous scar on his upper back. Another moment and she noticed one, two, and maybe three more partially eclipsed by the straps of his tank.

"John, how did you get those scars?"

"Oh, these?" John clapped his own upper back. "This, ma'am, is what I need to tell you about. Tony said you could take some tough talk. You ready to learn a little more about Paul?"

"You mean Saul?"

Big John shook his head. "Saul was an alias. His real name was Paul Black. I mean to tell you the whole thing, so get ready."

Sarah rest her coffee cup on a nearby coaster. "Oh, boy."

"Oh boy, is right," Big John laughed and set his cup down, too. He leaned over his knees and softened his deep voice. "Tony asked me to tell you a few things that he's a little, well... too squeamish to tell you himself. Once I'm done, he'll join us. You ready?"

"So this is worse than what he told me last night?"

"It's all pretty awful, but here goes." John took a slow breath. "I met Paul and Tony last summer when they moved into this house."

John gestured to the room and Sarah watched him with wide eyes, trying to imagine what he was about to reveal.

"I own a moving company with my wife. The day I moved them in, Paul took a perverse liking to me and challenged me to an arm wrestling match."

"You're kidding."

"No, and he knew he would win. Here's why." John leaned forward another inch and lowered his voice. "Paul wasn't human. He knew he could beat me because he was a vampire." John paused only a moment before moving on. "And he beat me easily. Right here, in this house, up those stairs, second room on the right."

"He beat you at arm wrestling?" Sarah whispered, not willing to comment on any of the rest.

"Easily," John replied. "Then he offered me five hundred dollars cash if I'd let him drink my blood. Now, don't judge me. I needed the money. I had a baby on the way and no savings. I took the money, and on several occasions, I let him drink my blood."

"John," Sarah said, speaking as if he were a confused child.

John twisted a few inches yanking his tank top over his head and revealed every jagged scar on his upper back. "My choice, he didn't force me."

"John..." Sarah said again, her mind reeling.

"If you think I'm lying or crazy, I'd prefer you just leave," John said, his tone gentle. "You've seen the evidence and I'm telling you events precisely as they occurred. I have nothing to gain, except Tony asked me to tell you. I consider him my closest friend, and I would appreciate it if you would open your mind to these revelations."

Shamed and convicted, Sarah nodded as the blood drained from her face. The man was telling the truth; Saul White—*Paul Black*—had been a vampire. *A vampire.*

"I'm sorry. You're right. What happened. Tony said he is dead."

John nodded. "Paul went nuts on us. I won't pretend to understand his psychology, but he went bananas. He tried to kill me, he tried to kill Tony, and when he threatened the life of my wife and baby, things really got crazy."

"Oh, Lord," Sarah whispered.

"They're okay, but only because Tony saved them. Which brings us to the last bit I need to share with you."

Tony saved them? Sarah's heart swelled with emotion as she imagined the courage in the man she had begun to think about nonstop. She waited for John to continue, which he did after sipping his coffee.

"A *real* vampire isn't like those in the movies. I mean, turning into a bat, running from crosses, afraid of holy water, and all that crap, I didn't see any of it in Paul. *But...* Paul had super strength, the devil's conniving, teeth that slid out like a viper, and a lust for blood he could barely control. At the height of his insanity, he attacked Tony and turned him into a vampire, too." John continued in a rush. "That is what Tony couldn't bear to tell you himself. He is a vampire now and he is hoping you and I together can convince God to deliver him from that curse."

"Oh, God, please," Sarah said, shaking her head. "John," she said and got to her feet. "Please stop. That sweet man?" She gestured for the staircase. "That adorable sweet man isn't evil. I would sense if he was possessed. I can *see* demons, John, and I didn't see them on Tony."

John didn't stand when she did. "It really don' matter how much you deny it. Tony has it—he has the strength, the teeth, the bloodlust. Think about last night. When you first saw him…" John sought her eye but she stubbornly looked away. "Did he seem unusually attractive? Did he mesmerize you? Be honest. You took him to your house after a single hour of chatting. You let him stab you with a knife. Hello? Think about it."

Sarah rubbed her eyes and then forced a tight nod. "I'm sorry, you're right. I'm ashamed that I resisted the truth. I just wanted you to be wrong. I wanted Tony to be... well, *not* possessed by a demon."

"To be fair, he's not possessed," John said, but Sarah was already agreeing.

"I misspoke. Poor Tony is *o*-pressed. He's oppressed by satan, and I'm most certainly going to do all I can to make sure he's delivered!"

"Praise God, amen to that," John said and stood to walk to the door. "He's going to join us now and he heard our entire conversation."

Sarah subconsciously fluffed her hair and straightened her blouse. John caught her primping, but thankfully, only smiled a tiny bit.

11

The Spirit of the Lord shall rest upon him,
The Spirit of wisdom and understanding,
The Spirit of counsel and might,
The Spirit of knowledge and of the fear of the Lord.
Isaiah 11:2

"MELLOW MUSHROOM AT 2PM, GOT IT. SEE YOU THERE."

Elizabeth read her father's text and hit sleep mode, but the phone immediately chimed again as he added more.

"I'm driving a blue Jeep Wrangler with a Georgia Bulldogs license plate. Should stand out, in case, you know. See you soon!"

In case she didn't recognize him, that's what he didn't want to say, and Elizabeth was fine with that. Whatever they could do to ease the awkwardness, the better.

Elizabeth's laptop buzzed the familiar tone of new email on her personal account. Hoping it was an art dealer, she sat on a stool at the bar and watched the computer power up. If she made three hundred dollars more this month, she could hire a landscaper to get the tiny lawn under control. She didn't mind yardwork, but she left Los Angeles with no tools, not even a pair of hand pruners. So until she replenished her collection, she would hire it out.

Fifteen emails were deleted before she found a legitimate non-spam message. The sender was FrogAndLizards@yahoo.com, which made her think of gardens and ponds. The subject line read, "Buying your sculpture". The letter was formally styled with proper punctuation and grammar. Could be interesting.

"Dear Ms. Hawken,

Yakol Kinner gave me your email last week after I visited his gallery in Claremont. He said you had moved to Montgomery, and I have a hotel chain in Alabama. My newest venture is in East Montgomery. I want to commission you to make thirty sculptures like the one you made for Yakol, one for each hotel lobby.

I look forward to hearing from you,

Rakha Tep"

Elizabeth read the email again and marveled. Yakol had been her art teacher at Claremont McKenna College and he'd purchased three of her works before she left. Which one did this businessman like? Elizabeth opened the photo albums in her phone and selected "Sculpture." Soon, she located Yakol's purchases and all three had been built with brightly colored polymer clay. The Turkish-born art professor had chosen a fifteen-inch white biddy hen wearing blue jeans, a fifteen-inch-long pink dachshund wearing red spiked high heels, and a nine-inch-tall grasshopper with long blond hair playing a saxophone. All silly contemporary pop art that Elizabeth never had any problem selling in her Los Angeles home or college town, but during her short time in Montgomery, she had no takers. Smiling, and thanking God for His providence, Elizabeth typed a professional reply.

"Dear Mr. Tep,

Thank you for writing. I would be honored to share my sculpture with you and your hotel patrons. Call me Monday when you have time, and we can set up a meeting in Montgomery. My phone number is 555-563-3352, voice or text.

Thanks again,

Elizabeth Hawken"

Elizabeth checked her spelling and sent the message. That job would pay enough for six months, not to mention give her plenty to do over the course of a year. After a short victory dance, Elizabeth jogged to the tiny bathroom to shower and prepare for her date with Dad.

❧❦

Tony entered the den and both inhabitants met him halfway. John shook his hand and stepped back for Sarah who gave him a hug, despite having just learned he was a monster. Taking this as a good sign, Tony chuckled.

"So, you still like me a little?" he said with humor and thankfully, Sarah matched his expression.

"Of course, and I don't blame you for wanting John to break the news. I'm so sorry. I'm sorry you have this trial upon you and I'm sorry for last night— I mean," Sarah walked to her chair and sat. "I mean, if I'd known you had this—" She gestured to his head area. "This demonic oppression on you, I wouldn't have stabbed myself and bled all over the place. You were very cool. *Very.*"

Tony huffed and sat in the chair closest as John took the one across. "It didn't bother me," he lied, then continued to disguise his deceit. "I was only concerned with finding out if you were okay. You have nothing to apologize for."

"Okay, Tony, Sarah, what do we do now?" John asked, leaning

forward. Sarah jumped in with a question before Tony could reply.

"Excuse me, but John didn't tell me how Paul died. You said Jesus saved him from hell, but he's dead. What happened to him?"

Tony swallowed and bought a moment to consider. The telling of Paul's demise included the doctor, and that meant everything associated with Mark would be added to the mix. Tony glanced at the wall clock and Sarah gave him a stern look.

"Are you taking medicine?" she asked moving her upper body between Tony and the clock. "Go ahead. I'm listening."

Tony lifted his hands in surrender. "I'm going to tell you a little about Paul's life leading up to when I met him, and that way, you can better understand his death, okay?"

Sarah nodded and John leaned back to get comfortable. He hadn't heard much of the story either.

"Last summer, I got a call from a friend of mind named Hope Brannen. She was dating a doctor who had some twisted ideas about God. She asked me if I'd talk to him about it." Tony then added, "I was in seminary then. My father was a pastor and I wanted to be one, too."

"Gotcha," Sarah said and then fell silent.

"I agreed to talk to him and eventually, I ended up at the doctor's house in Whitford City, Georgia."

"I've been there a few times to preach," Sarah offered.

"Yes, that is where I first saw you and Ira. Anyway, when I get to the house, Paul and the doctor are waiting for me in the garage. Hope was in the house, oblivious to what was about to happen next." Tony had worn a comfortable black T-shirt so he brandished the crook of his arm. "The doctor decided to keep me in line by showing me he was a vampire. Here's where he took my blood."

"Oh, God," Sarah gasped.

"Yes. I was terrified. And Paul held me down while he did it. Paul wasn't a vampire then. He was like you—he had ingested Mark's— that's the doctor, Mark Corescu—ingested his blood and had already lived a hundred years at that point. Anyway, Paul held me still, and when it was over, Mark left us alone. This is when I learned Paul fancied me a little too much."

"How do you mean? Like he fancied John?" Sarah asked.

Tony nodded. "John and I think he was attracted to *God* in us. At any rate, he obsessed over me and as the night wore on, I spoke with and prayed with Mark while Paul disappeared somewhere—I don't know where."

"You prayed?" Sarah asked.

"Mark wanted to be delivered, so I prayed. Anyway, long story short, something happened to Paul and Mark went to help him. While they were gone, Mark transformed Paul into a vampire."

"Geez," John said and shook his head.

"Soon after, Mark went to Europe, sad and mad he hadn't been delivered, and I stayed with Paul to keep him from attacking innocent people. I thought God wanted me to watch him and introduce him to the Truth."

"The word from God!" Sarah whispered. "He gave me that word for Paul that he should listen to you, his 'little shepherd,' until God saved him."

Tony nodded. "So now we're up to when he died. Mark told me that he was miserable not drinking blood and he wanted me to come and bury him. When Paul and I got to Germany, Paul shoved me down a cliff and got to Mark first. It took me hours to climb out, and by the time I did, they had killed an entire family of forest dwellers."

"The doctor changed his mind again," Sarah said as a statement. "He changed his mind often."

"You discerning that or guessing?" Tony asked and John grunted agreement.

Sarah licked her lips, appeared to be considering the question, and then nodded. "I'm discerning it. I can almost *see* him, too, in the spirit. I sense him even now," she said and closed her eyes. "It's not clear, but is he still living? You didn't bury him, did you."

Tony looked around the room. *"Doctor Corescu?"* he sent to the area of his subconscious he usually found him. In moments, he understood why Sarah felt his presence: Mark was eavesdropping on them and had been the entire time. Tony cleared his throat and jumped back into the story, no desire to attempt to discern what the vampire was up to.

"Yes, Doctor Corescu is still living, and he is capable of hearing this conversation. That's why you sense him," Tony asserted and John made a small noise.

"Incredible," he whispered with a single head shake.

Sarah said nothing, but looked into the corners of the room before settling back in her seat.

"This is what happened next. As I reached the doctor's house, Hope showed up, too. Mark greeted us politely enough, but Paul was crazy with jealousy. I think because Mark had chosen Hope over him. Paul tried to kill Hope and I stopped him. Then he tried to kill me, and

God stopped him. After that. he went into a trance and I heard him say, 'I saw Jesus,' and then he said, 'find Sarah Tracey,' and he died."

"Just…geez," John whispered.

"*Find Sarah Tracey.* I'm so glad you found me. I'm just… speechless," Sarah said, her voice soft.

When no one spoke several moments, John added, "What happens now?"

Tony met his eye. "We have to figure out how to get rid of this vampire oppression."

"Tony, I don't know…" Sarah began and then stopped.

"What? What is it?" Tony asked, afraid she was backing out.

"I see a timeline, I—"

"You see *my* timeline?" Tony asked leaning forward.

"It can be hard to explain, but let me try. I see there will be more time passing for you in this form." She gestured for his hand and he held it out. "I don't know anything about delivering you from vampirism, but I see that you have more jobs to do for the Lord in this form. I see some highs and lows, bright spots and dark. Do you understand?"

Sarah had taken his hand and Tony looked at her long fingers and soft pink nail polish. She still wore her wedding band and he rubbed it with the pad of his thumb. He couldn't comprehend how Sarah knew these things, but it was ironic she had superpowers even before she ever met a vampire. Sarah clucked her tongue and Tony met her eye.

"Have you considered that *vampires* don't exist?"

Tony readied to interrupt, but she continued.

"Hear me out. Sure, they exist to us, to man. But look at this from God's viewpoint. Have you considered the spiritual implications?"

"But I'm here, living it. Right now," Tony said, not following.

"Let me pray on it further, but there is something to mankind believing in something unreal and causing it to manifest." Sarah rubbed her eyes and fell silent. Tony could almost see what she was trying to describe, but not quite.

"All that aside, what do we do now?" John piped in, his deep voice echoing in the quiet room. "Does God say anything to you about that?"

"Yes. We're going to feed the sheep," Sarah said, but did not elaborate.

Tony released her hand and rose to his feet. With his back to his friends, he said, "There's no way I can preach in this condition."

"I agree," Sarah said very quietly.

Tony was curious at her tone. He turned. "You know quite a bit about this *next thing* God has for us, don't you?"

Sarah stood and crossed to his side. "Yes. I see Big John and myself on the stage and you in the wings. You're the stagehand, Tony. You have to wait on us."

Sarah whispered the last part and looked mortified at her words, but Tony nodded.

"No way," John objected and joined them. "Tony is a million times more experienced preaching than I am. I've done it maybe five times in my life and I'm usually awful. God wouldn't put me on the spot like that. No way," John said again and went to the open doorway. "I'm getting more coffee," he said and left the room.

"It's a humility thing. I get it," Tony said and Sarah took his hand. She stood a few inches taller and he looked up to see her eyes.

"You'll get a call from a big church this week, wanting *you* to speak, but when we arrive, you'll introduce *us*. It's the way God is going to introduce our ministry." Tony nodded and Sarah placed her warm palm on his cheek. "And I'm going home now. I'll come back Wednesday and see what God will have us do next."

Tony sighed and without planning to, moved a few centimeters to kiss her palm on his face. She remained there a few moments until John returned, caught their moment, and again retreated.

By the time she had explained herself to John and was gone, Tony's stomach rumbled to life. Thankfully, John took the sound as a hint and headed home. Tony collapsed in his desk chair and stared at his open Bible, ashamed that he was growing sick of the Scripture that kept him fed.

12

Let your light shine before others,
that they may see your good deeds
and glorify your Father in heaven.
Matthew 5:16

RAKHA LAY ON THE COLD TILED FLOOR BEHIND THICKLY
curtained windows and stared unseeing at the ceiling. The church girl
indicated via return text that she would call him around one and set up
an appointment. It was now 1:15 and his mind raced with options. The
Unseen had no apparent opinion or position on what he did with the
pious upstart, which gave him free rein. Earlier, he enticed them with
the idea of turning her faith to mud, but they showed no interest. They
reacted only when he toiled in his main mission to defeat Agricola.
Rakha would enjoy the diversion and at that moment, the cell rang.

"Rakha Tep," he said rolling his voice into a smooth tenor.

"Hi, Mr. Tep, this is Elizabeth Hawken, the artist. Thank you for
that email. Which sculpture of Yakol's were you interested in?"

The woman spoke in a rush and Rakha sat up in the dark room.
He ran his fingers through his host's smooth brown hair. "If you
replicated the dachshund, fifty-percent larger, my customers would love
it. Do you have any pieces I can see today?"

"No, sir, I had them shipped to my studio space in town and
they're not unpacked. But let me give you the address and we will meet
there this week. I'll unpack a few boxes now that I have an impetus."
She laughed as she spoke, and Rakha forced a grin.

"That would suit me fine," he replied and calculated sundown. "I
am free tomorrow after six. Can we meet around seven?" The woman
took a few seconds to respond and then she agreed. Tuesday, 7pm, at
her studio. Rakha jotted down the address and said good bye.

Pretending to be a mortal art lover, businessman, hotel chain
owner, single young man—Rakha laughed. The young woman should
find his new host dashing enough; Rakha rubbed his smooth cheeks.

The church girl is single, Rakha is single...

He laughed again. "I shall need a suit," he told the air. Church Girl
would see a devilishly handsome Arab man who will emerge as her

greatest new fan. He would woo her, ruin her faith, and then drain her dry over a period of weeks, maybe months if he was careful. Rakha's teeth ached at the thought. Oh, it was going to be delightful!

๛

When Jonah reached his exit, he pulled into the first gas station instead of continuing on to Mello Mushroom. He needed to collect his thoughts. Jenn refused to come, and he agreed, but oh, he sure could use her brand of calm at the moment. Jonah's phone rang and he hit the Bluetooth.

"You didn't chicken out did you?" his bride asked and Jonah huffed a nervous chuckle.

"Naw, I pulled into the BP. What's up?"

"All nonchalant, are we? Okay, I'm just doing a little cheerleading before you go in. She called you, remember? She wants to know you. She wants you in her life. You don't have to work for this, ya hear me? Go see her, give her a hug if she wants one, and ya'll just start talking."

"But I'm really not sure what to talk about."

"Ask her about her, what she's been up to. And later, she'll ask about you, and you can tell her how you retired and work me into the story. I will hang by the phone if you have a reunion emergency."

Jonah laughed. "I love you, Jennifer soon-to-be-Miller."

"I love you, too. Now go get 'em!"

Jenn disconnected and Jonah turned the Jeep onto the roadway. He had married Valerie, Elizabeth's mother, right out of the Police Academy, so she knew she had married the Force. Jonah sought the fast track, and worked double and triple shifts to catch the eyes of his superiors, and by the time Elizabeth was born, Jonah had exceeded the detective's requirements and would serve the remainder of his career in homicide. Over the next nine years, God forgive him, he neglected his wife and she strayed. When Jonah discovered the betrayal, he didn't seek counseling (not that Val would have taken any), and he filed for divorce. His wife moved across the country with their ten-year-old daughter and Jonah lived his life as a long-distance dad. He mailed greeting cards and sent money on birthdays, but he had never visited. In fact, he hadn't seen Elizabeth in person since the day she boarded the jet for California fifteen years ago.

Jonah clucked his tongue now pulling into the restaurant parking lot. There were a million reasons Elizabeth would want to connect; Jonah took his last sixty seconds before switching off the car to pray that her reason was a friendly one. *"Please, Father, let me have my daughter back. I don't deserve her, but I will make up for the past. I promise. Amen."*

Here we go.

Jonah exited his Jeep and walked to the doors. Elizabeth's latest text said she had arrived and would see him in the lobby.

"God, help me be the best dad ever," he whispered inside and put on a friendly grin.

ॐॐ

He looks exactly the same!

Elizabeth noticed her father's Jeep and watched him exit the car. His lips were moving and his eyes took in every direction in a glance. *That's probably the cop part,* she guessed and scooted away from the window as he pulled open the glass door to the restaurant. Jonah Miller, police detective, was over six feet, sturdily built, and dressed down in a plaid flannel over a black T-shirt with faded blue jeans and sneakers. Elizabeth didn't know what she expected—maybe dress blues as when she last saw him in uniform, but today? He looked like a dad who might be going hunting later.

He met her eye as if he recognized her as easily as she had him.

"Hey!" he said and Elizabeth liked that his voice sounded the same, too. She'd been ten when they last spoke, but she loved him then. Her heart broke over the first year he was gone, as it sunk in that he wasn't returning. But then, as time passed, she moved him into her memories and grew up with Step-Father-Sean filling the daddy role. Her dad came close and made a few awkward shoulder twitches as if wondering if they should hug. Elizabeth rescued the moment by turning and pointing to a booth.

"Come on over here," she said and wanted to call him dad. Should she? She remembered she was grown and God had her back, and when she took a seat, she gave him a smile. *He'll be nervous, too,* she reminded herself and she put her hand on the table, palm down. Her father covered it with his huge hairy paw—also exactly as she recalled it to be. "Thank you for coming, Dad," she said.

His eyes watered. "Honey, I am so happy you contacted me and I am sorry for letting all this time pass without coming out there to see you. I am so sorry…"

His voice broke and he gave her an embarrassed smile. It was endearing—her larger-than-life bear-sized father overflowing with the sweetest emotions, and she read them all in his eyes. *Those are different,*

60

Elizabeth thought. Her father's gaze had been clear and serious when she knew him. He scolded her quite a lot before the divorce, so Elizabeth didn't recall ever seeing the soft, grandpa-like eyes she saw today. It was time to let him off the hook and she covered his covering hand with her other one.

"It's not all your fault, Dad," she said and another fat tear popped out of his eye. "I've been an adult for a while now. I could've done my part."

"Well, we're here now," he said and wiped his cheeks with his free hand. "Let's make a brand new start. How about that?"

"I agree." Elizabeth freed her hands and smiled. "So, tell me what you've been up to. Are you still catching bad guys in Whitford City?"

Her father paused, lips parted. "I thought you'd go first," he said in a chuckle. "Let's see… I retired last year. Back in January, I proposed to my former partner on the job and she said yes. Her name's Jennifer and I want you to meet her. We both hope you'll come to the wedding."

"Congratulations," Elizabeth said happy to see him so joyful. "When's the wedding? Of course, I'll come!"

"Wonderful," he said and the relief in his face said it all. He had worried about this day for a while. "Jenn and I just built a home on my property in Carrollton and she wants to have the wedding there. It's set for the first Saturday in December, so mark your calendar."

Elizabeth said she would and they gave the server their orders. When they were again alone, her father asked her what she'd been up to and she told him about her divorce and the subsequent move to Alabama. "I chose Montgomery because of a studio space I learned about back home in Claremont. I knew you were in Georgia. I admit that I hoped we could start over." She decided to tell a little more truth. "I guess the biggest news of all is that before my divorce, I was born again. I'm a big Jesus freak. I know you and Mom were never big in it, but I'm going to be irritating I suppose because I don't like pretending." She watched her father's eyes but he was smiling and nodding.

"I got on the Jesus train about seven years ago at a men's retreat," he said with a friendly chuckle. "You won't irritate me one bit. And I am so happy you moved closer. My farm is 138 miles away and I'll hop on the interstate any time you want to visit. You have a standing invitation to our house. I want you to come meet Jenn. She will just love you."

Elizabeth grinned and said she would. Over the next two hours, she and her dad talked about everything they could think of and when their bellies were full and the topics grew thin, they stood for a goodbye hug.

"I love you, honey," he said, holding her like the father she always wanted. "Come see us as soon as you can."

"I will and thank you," she said and did not release the hug until he did. Finally he walked her to her car and hugged her again. When she drove away, he watched without going to his vehicle until she was out of sight, and Elizabeth thanked the Lord in her heart.

13

So we fasted and entreated our God for this,
And He answered our prayer.
Ezra 8:23

"WON'T HOPE BE MISSING YOU?" TONY ASKED THE
doctor who lounged across from him on the leather sofa. He had
arrived without warning, but Tony was not surprised figuring the close
call with John and then his exchange with Sarah grabbed the penitent
vampire's attention.

Mark huffed a laugh. "You don't seriously believe the princess is
up? It's 6AM in Germany. Hope greets the dawn only when there's a
horse to ride. Sundays, she greets the lunch bell."

Tony smiled by reflex unable to imagine the doctor's life—a
powerful mythical creature residing with Hope Brannen, a woman
consumed only with comfort and equines.

"I told you before, her presence gives me comfort," Corescu said
reacting to Tony's thought-stream. Since he had swapped blood with
Paul, he'd swapped it with the doctor by proxy. As a result, Corescu
saw into Tony's mind with ease. "Now, about this depression…"

"I'm fine," Tony said and realized the words were wasted. The
clock chimed 11PM and he had spent the day in worry instead of prayer.
He had even considered calling Sarah to come back over but the doctor
materialized in his room before things got that far.

Thank God he did, Tony thought and Mark laughed again.

"I consider you a friend, Tony, and more than that, a *brother*. Your
flesh cries out to me when you suffer these pains. I'm concerned. Have
you found a resolution?"

"Of sorts," Tony admitted with a shrug. "But God is taking His
time lifting the curse."

Mark *hmmm'd* and looked off thinking and Tony considered how
he'd appeared out of thin air. Tony had witnessed this power the night
the same vampire relaxing on his sofa attacked him, but the question
remained: how does he do it? Tony wouldn't ask, too afraid to learn,
for fear he might grow attached to his supernatural peculiarities.

"That is wise of you," Mark said and sat up. "And I admit, you look well for a man starving to death."

"I'm doing fine," Tony said and tightened his jaw. He didn't want Mark's help; the doctor's solution would boil down to Tony drinking his blood. *"Just a little. Just a tiny bit to get you by,"* he'd say. *No thanks, Doc, twenty-seven, almost twenty-eight days.* He was nearly to forty—the magic number.

"What happens in forty days?" Mark asked, brow raised.

Tony sighed. "I appreciate your concern, but I'm fine. Go home. I'm working it out. It's good." Tony walked to a bookcase and flipped through the titles.

"Your hunger is my hunger and I know you're lying," Mark said getting to his feet. Tony didn't turn, but felt him approach. The doctor stood directly behind, looking down on him. "I sense you are about to do something horrendous to your friends. What if you come to the end of your rope while in the presence of John Jenkins and this woman? What will you do? Will you remember to pray when the lust for blood clogs your reason?"

Mark put a hand to Tony's shoulder and Tony glanced at his fingers until he slipped them away again.

"You are a strong man of God—much stronger than I ever was— but you're still just a man. A man with a devil in his gut that desires to kill everyone you care about. You know what I'm saying is true."

"I'm fine," Tony said and slipped from the closeness the doctor had created. "God will protect John and Sarah. This is on Him."

His guest didn't argue but followed across the room, for now keeping a polite distance. God would protect John and Sarah but sometimes, God's idea of *protection* was different from his own. Sometimes, when he expected God to rescue him, He merely saved him from death. More than once, Tony was forced to endure horrific physical, spiritual, and emotional assaults only to come out *changed* on the other end. Tony didn't want to talk about bloodlust. He attempted a diversion.

"Has Hope been driving you crazy?"

Mark chuckled. "All she wants is a few horses. Or five. Or ten."

Tony laughed with him. "Is she training for the Olympics or something?"

"God, I hope she doesn't get that in her head," he said with a new laugh. "It's been fun for me, I've never had a female companion and every day I learn something new."

"That explains it a little," Tony conceded. "But why so many horses?"

"This is a mystery. As soon as we get one moved in and under training, she finds one she likes better. Then the current one is pushed aside for the new one to take prominence." Mark laughed again, but Tony noted the tenderness in his voice. He adored the beautiful, strong-willed, and opinionated woman Tony used to pine for.

"I will purchase every jumper in Europe if she asks," Mark said and ran his fingers through his thick black hair. "I could go on, but you know why I came. Your *need* calls me. Right now, your aura is reaching for me with fingers of light. Can you see it?"

Tony looked for what the doctor described and the pulses of what reminded him of low-voltage shocks shot from his outline toward the vampire. He pretended it was nothing and looked away. Mark smiled.

"When you hunger, I hunger. In equal measure, and brother, I'm not enjoying the discomfort."

Tony met his gaze. "Wait. If that's true, why don't I reciprocate that? Why don't I feel it when *you're* hungry?"

Corescu was trying to help, but this revelation did not hold water. When Paul was alive, he saw hazy images of what the man was up to, and sometimes, he even saw Big John without the use of his natural eyes. But the doctor? He barely thought of him except when under the bloodlust.

"That is where I come in," Mark replied, his voice soft. "Any instance where you recall the blood you took from my arm, I am feasting on blood on my end of the world. Your spirit visits me when I feed. It is as if *you* pop over to see *me.*"

"That is completely untrue!" Tony replied without conviction as he recalled the last few times he pondered that delicious afternoon in Germany when the doctor made himself into a donor.

Mark laughed, but then became quiet at the expression on Tony's face. "You can bring an end to all of this. *You* control the anxiety enslaving you. Never let yourself become famished. You can drink the blood of animals. It's much better than the alternative."

Tony gave him a blank look, his mind racing with images he would rather not see, all of them involving the drinking of blood.

"I am never hungry," Mark continued kindly. "Thus, I never give the devil a place to attack."

"Drinking blood is an abomination," Tony blurted. "Why has God convicted *me* of this and not you?" Sounding childish in his own ears,

Tony could not help but be frustrated. Corescu drank his fill daily and Tony was not permitted the tiniest drop.

"Is it possible you have convicted *yourself?*"

"I did not misinterpret God's instructions on the drinking of blood. Only devils drink blood, Doctor," Tony said, his tone no longer kind.

"Are you quite finished?"

Tony did not respond.

"Many animals drink blood. Our bodies no longer process solid food. This is a fact. How can we be held accountable for this change in our physiology that we have no control over? Perhaps you need to wrap your mind around the fact that sin is a condition of the heart. If you believe drinking blood is sin, and you do it, you are guilty. If you see it as a necessary process of remaining fed and vital, it is no sin. Understand?"

Tony sighed in frustration. "But we're not animals! Animals are not accountable before God. *We are.* Maybe we are capable of resisting. Maybe we have more responsibility in this arena than you have grasped thus far."

"Your logic is exhausting."

"I'm convinced that if I stick to it, I can feed on spiritual food alone. And I can wait for deliverance. God sent Sarah to help me, I know it."

"But you're starving," Mark whispered and Tony read genuine concern in the doctor's eyes. "How long can you wait?"

"As long as it takes." Tony tore his gaze from the doctor's. "It won't be long. Very soon, God will lift this curse."

"I hope he does." Mark came close to again set one hand to Tony's shoulder. "Look at me." Tony met his eye and turned his body to stand toe-to-toe.

"What?" he said in a sigh as the clock in the foyer chimed midnight. Mark told him to relax and Tony did not object. If the doctor hypnotized him, he could at least have a moment's rest for his frenetic mind. A peaceful warmth enveloped his consciousness as he listened to the doctor speak.

"Maybe if I had resisted more, or trusted God more," Mark said, his voice low and undulating facing Tony in the dark study, "I would not have been an agent of Satan four hundred years. And perhaps you *will* escape decades of painful bloodlust because of Grace."

Tony nodded in slow motion, enjoying his fuzzy head.

"But what's done is done." Mark paused long enough that Tony focused to meet his eye. "I have assurance of my salvation. Do you?"

"Yes. I have never lost my faith," Tony said and because of Mark's hypnosis, felt calmer than he had been in weeks. "If anything, I've grown closer to God than ever. He has surely turned this curse into a blessing."

"*Anathema*," Mark whispered, his eyes searching Tony's deepest parts, seeking the monster of bloodthirst and checking if it would truly be still. "This is the Greek word for a blessing and a curse."

"*Anathema*," Tony repeated in the same low tone. *That's perfect.*

Mark squeezed his shoulders once. "Don't be angry, but I must offer. Will you take my blood? Please. For your own good."

Tony fluttered his eyes and worked to shake off the lethargy he welcomed the past few moments. He gave Corescu a grateful smile. "No, really. Thank you, I am on a roll. Honest."

Mark lowered his chin and pulled Tony closer looking hard into his face. Tony held his breath, waiting to be released from the vampire's will. Would Mark coerce him? Could he resist?

Would I want to?

Recounting the days he had gone without, Tony waited. After a few long moments, he was released and the vampire backed out of reach.

"Okay, my friend," he said. "I will be close by." Then, Corescu nodded once and was gone.

Tony stared into the air where the eyes of the vampire had just been and marveled. Who gave him that ability, God or the devil? Tony lay lengthwise on the sofa to stare at the ceiling.

Lord, is the doctor within Your will when he satisfies his hunger for blood? He is basically living as a vampire. Some sort of Christian monster. Isn't that a contradiction in terms? Lord? Isn't it?

God didn't answer and Tony resisted the urge to call Sarah. It wasn't easy.

14

Though one may be overpowered,
two can defend themselves.
A cord of three strands is not quickly broken.
Ecclesiastes 4:12

"I NEED A DOZEN CASES OF SHITT-AUKY MUSHROOMS, please," the caller said over the speaker and it took Jonah a few seconds to recognize the voice.

"What the heck are you doin', Kranchez? You finally retired?" Jonah said with a laugh and set his shovel against the fence. He'd been clearing stones in the pasture and answered the phone in case it had something to do with Elizabeth. Seems since they reconnected, he thought she might call or text any minute.

"Retire? You nuts? I'm king of the hill here. I'm never giving up my crown. They can knock it off my head before they put me in the casket, but I'm stayin' right here!"

Jonah wiped the sweat from his forehead and gave his friend a new laugh. "All right, your majesty, what's up? Billy okay?" Montgomery Alabama Police Detective Andy Kranchez had a child with Down's which included a malformed palate. Sometimes, a meal sent him to the hospital and Jonah assumed the call might be for some moral support. Andy had no other family and had called before when things got stressful with his son.

"Billy's tip-top. He found a really great assist-home in Huntsville so he moved out. He's loving it. I get a little lonesome for him, but he's thirty. It's time he got to be a man, eh?"

Jonah agreed and waited. His friend had news and Jonah wondered what it might be.

"How's that sexy partner of yours? Ya'll get hitched?" he asked.

"December 1st. You'll get an invite. Now, Andy, I'm pouring sweat in the pasture, what's up?"

"Heh, never could get you to waste time, old man," his friend said. "Remember that Saul White case? The guy who attacked the evangelist?"

Jonah paled. His friend didn't have to say more. The Saul White /

Paul Black Case had been filed by Jonah himself, tucked away until the killer surfaced. Before the trail disappeared, he and Jenn discovered that Black murdered a newspaperman in cold blood. Before they could make an arrest, their person of interest (P.O.I.) revealed (off the record and in euphemism) that Black left the country. Jonah hadn't thought about the case since. He hadn't even questioned the preacher. By the time the person of interest, a man named Agricola, contacted the department upon his return to the States, Jonah had submitted his retirement papers. He had instructed his replacement to release Agricola from all interest and stamp it C-O-L-D.

Kranchez cleared his throat. "Well? We got us a bloodless body."

Jonah snapped awake. The dead journalist had been collecting twenty-year-old unsolved's in which each death resulted in exsanguination—blood loss. "Why are you telling me?"

"Just being a good pal. Speltz asked me to, of course, at the time, I didn't know she'd picked you for a life-mate, hehe. You know I'd be a much better choice for any woman of her caliber," his friend joked.

"What are you talking about?"

"Geez. Speltz asked me to tell her if any more bodies showed up drained of blood. Her phone went to voicemail so I called you. Last night, a homeless boy was brought to the morgue shriveled to a husk. The ME said he didn't have enough blood to withdraw a full syringe."

Jonah looked toward the house. "Did Jenn say why she wanted to know? I mean, she retired, too, you know."

"You better talk to your squeeze. She's a licensed Private Investigator in Alabama, Georgia and Florida. My boss already put her on the OKAY list."

Jonah huffed. Jenn had joked about becoming a P.I. but the conversation never matured. He didn't know what to ask next. His pal continued as if to wrap it up.

"Anyway, the poor kid's being buried in the pauper's lot on Madison. I'll fax the case, Cap approved it. Between you and me, I don't think Cap cares much about a little homeless druggie, but I do. I gotta go, tell Speltz hey."

Jonah assured him he would and disconnected, still looking at the back windows. From his current distance, their new ranch house stood an inch tall and he grabbed his shovel for the trek back up the hill.

What in the world is going on? Jenn goes behind my back to become a P.I. and now someone's draining the blood from the derelicts in Montgomery?

The details of the Saul White / Paul Black case filtered back and he had put it behind him. He'd put homicide behind him.

And I thought Jenn did, too.

As he often did when things grew bothersome, Jonah turned his heart to God and asked questions to the Lord. He found his bride peeling potatoes in the kitchen sink. When she heard him enter, she waved over her shoulder.

"Hungry? I'm cooking us up some homemade mash-taters," she announced in a put-on southern accent. Originally from Maine, she enjoyed poking fun at the Deep South culture when she had the chance. Jonah dove right in.

"Andy just called. Said you filed for a P.I. license?"

"I sure did," Jenn said without looking behind her. "Took the exams online, paid my fees, and got tri-state approval for nosing around." She wiped her hands on a nearby towel and twirled about. "I'm keeping a foot in there. There's room for a handsome new private eye in my company. You interested?"

Jonah's mind still contemplated the news and she tipped her chin.

"What's wrong?" she asked and came close. "You look like you've seen a ghost. It's not this, right?"

Jonah waited for the right words. Dating at fifty-one had been odd. The past decade, he may have taken a woman somewhere two times, so now, having an almost-wife around 24/7, Jonah felt he needed training wheels to figure out what to do. For instance, when your woman makes a big decision on her own… Is that kosher? Jenn smiled when he took too long to reply and she hugged his neck.

"Aww, come on, hug the Jenn," she said and her silly tone brought a grin. When she released, she took his jowls in both palms to mush her lips to his. Still being silly, she made a noise in her throat until they disconnected. "Okay—so why are you so upset?"

Jonah blinked and decided he wasn't. *Move on, Jonah…* "Andy wanted me to tell you that they have a bloodless body in Montgomery. A homeless kid in the projects."

"Oh, geez, dammit," she said and fished her phone from the back pocket of her jeans. She played a voicemail from Kranchez which said what Jonah already heard. Jenn nodded when the message ended and she turned for the stairs. "Follow me, big boy."

Jonah said he would and washed his hands and arms to the elbow. By the time he found her upstairs, she had powered up her Dell and was searching a file.

"Here, look," she said and leaned aside for Jonah to view her monitor. "Whatever it is, it's not isolated. Does this look familiar?"

Jonah adjusted his bifocals and read a few words aloud as he skimmed the documents. "Montgomery, Prattville, Millbrook, Selma..." He skimmed faster as Jenn scrolled his current page. "Elmore, Tallassee." He leaned his palms on the desk and turned to see her profile. "Am I seeing this right? Bloodless bodies in each of these precincts?"

"Yep," Jenn replied and clicked the Montgomery one and typed her new information in the blank areas. "They're all like this one," she said when she clicked open the file Kranchez had attached. "This poor child had two deep punctures in his forearm, the distance apart of teeth mind you—*teeth.*" She sought Jonah's eye to say the word twice. "Why do you look so surprised? You're the one with the Count Corescu theory."

"I was joking," Jonah said, his voice weak. When Saul White / Paul Black "left the country" (they think), Jonah had kidded around that maybe they were dealing with vampires. They had learned that Black's housemate was from Hungary and at the time, Jonah thought it'd be fun to play with his partner's imagination. But now? He wanted nothing to do with that case. He ran through some possible reasons she wanted to know this stuff and he could only guess it was personal interest.

"You want to know why I'm doing this, don't you?" she asked, still entering new information. "I'll show you." Jenn hopped up from her computer chair in such a way that Jonah jumped back to avoid a collision. She jogged to her messy bookshelf and yanked out a pocket folder. Inside, dozens of newspaper clippings had been stashed. She shuffled through with one hand and yanked her choice free only to shove it in Jonah's face. "Read that."

Jonah lifted his chin to read from the bottom of his glasses. "Terri 'B' Joiner, the self-proclaimed 'Hip-Hop King of Georgia', was found deceased in his dressing room by his staff five minutes before his curtain call. A spokesperson for the musician revealed that their client had been 'bitten by a Dracula' and 'all his blood was gone'. Officials are calling the death a homicide. This is a developing story."

"Bitten by a Dracula," Jenn repeated and removed the paper from Jonah's fingers. "Future media updates were useless, but look at what the APD sent me from the M.E."[1] This time, Jonah received a print-out photocopy of their department's medical examiner's report. It showed physical evidence at the scene with a "inconclusive" DNA

---

[1] Medical Examiner

marker. Jonah jerked his eyes to Jenn's. "Yep. I sent it to Billy Austin in Whitford City-IT'S THE SAME BLOOD."

"Wait…" Jonah walked away with the M.E. report in his hand, but his eyes had glazed. "Joiner's killer left blood at that scene on a bullet lodged in the wall. The blood matches ours from the tree where they found the journalist."

"Yep, and you should see Billy." She laughed and tugged the paper from his hand to return to her collection. "Cap re-opened the case."

"You're kidding," Jonah said more as an exhale. Jenn grinned like a loon. She loved this stuff, the mystery, the suspense, the homicide. Jonah didn't want any of it anymore.

"Come here," she said and hugged his middle, laying her cheek flat to his chest. "You don't have to do any police work, babe. This is just my hobby. I'm a big girl—you have your cow-poop and I have Count Corescu."

Jonah kissed her hair and she wriggled loose and headed for the hall. "How about you just give me the highlights," he said and followed her down the stairs.

"It's a deal," she said and returned to the sink. "You might be interested to know that Erkleson put your replacement on our old case. Kid's name is Pension." She turned to flash him an ironic grin. "He's got your preacher friend back in his sights. Get this," she said draining the potatoes, "Every single asset of Paul Black / Saul White has been legally transferred to Anthony Agricola." She lifted her mashing tool and bit her lip when Jonah met her eye for more. "The banking agency that handled the whole shebang is in the Caymans. My internet search brought up a single connective name to this bank and Paul Black. Guess."

Jonah shook his head, his mind racing.

"Dr. Mark Corescu of Whitford City, Georgia."

"You're kidding. How much money are we talking about?" Jonah asked, his throat dry.

"Seven-point-five million dollars."

"Jenn…" Jonah said low. That number couldn't be right.

She nodded waggling her eyebrows. "Nobody gets that much money from a Wanted man unless he's crooked." She faced her pot. "Oh, yeah. Agricola's going down, babe. Pray for him, but he's going down."

Jonah had no words. He leaned against the counter and listened as Jenn shared more about her day and less about Draculas and guilty preachers. Inside, he asked God to make it all pass over them. He didn't want to be involved, that case had been hairy and something evil lurked over the whole thing. Of course, it had nothing to do with vampires, but it was one of those cases where Jonah just couldn't break through. At every great lead, they met a roadblock. And when they solved the case, the P.O.I. and suspect disappeared. Jonah couldn't prove it, but he guessed from Agricola's words as he departed the country that he had killed Paul Black himself.

That would make him crooked, indeed.

Jonah shook his head. He liked the guy. They hadn't met, but the few conversations they had over the phone made Jonah feel a kinship, a Christian brotherly kinship.

And now he's taking payouts from killers. Great.

15

He is before all things,
and in him all things hold together.
Colossians 1:17

"THANK YOU FOR COMING," TONY SAID AND PULLED Sarah across the threshold as she shook his hand. It was Monday afternoon and he could wait no longer to see her. In a bid to be transparent, he added, "For whatever the reasons, I couldn't wait until Wednesday. That's the truth of it."

His guest smiled, her face lighting up the world. "Of course I came on over. I only said Wednesday to give you some room. I didn't want to smother you." Sarah gave a tiny shrug. "I have been accused of being overbearing."

"Impossible," Tony said and turned away to lead her to the familiar study. "What can I get you? Thirsty? Hungry?"

"You have food, vampire man?" she asked and Tony turned to read her expression. Her eyes were joyful and he forced a smile.

"Ah-hah, I see you got awful comfortable about this since last night," he said laughing. "Let's sit," he said and gestured her to the armchair she used the night before.

She chose the long sofa instead and patted the seat cushion. "If you spend ten hours in prayer over something, it becomes *much* less frightening. So, yes, this is how I will deal with it. With humor. Can you handle that?"

"Sure," Tony said and sat near. "I could use some laughter. What did God tell you? Any news on delivering me?"

Sarah shook her head. "Not yet, but I received loads of faith and trust. That's what I prayed for you to receive, too. Around midnight, God asked me to pray for you to have faith."

"Midnight?" Tony asked, remembering the doctor's late night offering.

"Something happen?" she asked and Tony shrugged.

"The vampire I told you about, Doctor Corescu, he visited and around midnight, he offered me his blood." Tony watched Sarah inhale with worry, but he waved his hand. "I resisted. Thank you for praying.

It was no big deal, and you're probably the reason why."

"Wow. I better keep listening. It sounds like God's watching you very closely. Since you left Germany, you haven't consumed any blood?"

"To date, I have not imbibed for twenty-nine days."

"Good. So, *why* would this demonic manifestation have the power to oppress a man of God. I don't ask 'how,' because God decided all things. So I'm studying the *why.*"

"I follow..." Tony said with a nod.

"Vampire characteristics are demonically inspired. Do you agree?"

Tony paused and thought of everything different about him since his transformation. None of the new attributes brought glory to God. "I agree. If anything, my new abilities only serve to make me..."

"Prideful?" Sarah asked watching his eyes. "Bloodlust, immortality, strength, those eyes—" she said and giggled, looking away. "All that stuff could make you exalt yourself."

Tony didn't disagree. "Paul gave himself over to it and became a horrible narcissist."

"Was he always that way, I mean before?"

Tony shook his head after a moment's thought. "Hope knew him better; she thought he was sweet. Kind and gentle. Harmless."

"Uh-huh. How about you? Were you humble before? Before you met the vampire?"

Tony furrowed his brow. "Of course."

Sarah *tsked* and lowered her chin. "That was mighty humble of you."

Tony released an uneasy chuckle. "I suppose I carried a chip on my shoulder. My father was a well-known preacher and the congregation lifted me up on his account. I probably let it get to my head now and then."

"We all do. Look at me? Ten-thousand-seat concert halls have invited me and Ira to preach. We did our share of repenting for pride." She waited for Tony to see and he did. "With this vampire curse, your innate pride will be exponentially multiplied."

"Okay, so I will concentrate on humility and maybe shrug off this oppression?"

"Who knows?" Sarah said and laughed when he frowned. "Come on, lighten up. Being sad and depressed gives power to the devil. Here, tell me something funny. What's the funniest thing that's different about you in this condition?"

The first thing Tony thought of was not a polite topic and God's prophetess saw through his fumbling. She leaned forward and took his hand.

"I want to hear *that* thing. The one you don't want to say. It has something to do with something embarrassing. Go ahead," she teased.

"Sarah," Tony said through a tight smile. He didn't know if he was blushing, but he should have been.

"Tell me, or I'm going home," she said with a smile that Tony took as a true if not well-meaning threat.

"Gee whiz," he said with a grin. "Lots of body functions went away. I don't eat food so there's no waste, understand?"

Sarah nodded. "And?"

Tony faked a groan. "My hair, my beard, my belly fat—none of this has changed. If I shave my beard, it grows back within hours—but only in the shape it was when Paul did this to me. Always this same shape," he said and tugged his neat goatee.

"It's very nice," Sarah said with a wink. "What else? There's something else." Sarah laughed at the end, her eyes twinkling.

Tony smiled back, infected with her mirth. "My eyesight isn't cured—my prescription is the same as before. And I can't sleep. Corescu says I'll sleep once a month. This means I'm awake a lot to worry over everything."

"Fascinating," Sarah said, with expectancy. "And?"

"You are incorrigible," Tony said and touched her cheek. She grasped his hand as he lowered it and kissed his knuckle. He decided he'd say it; it was what she was hinting at anyway. "I don't get aroused anymore. Sexually." He waited for understanding to dawn, but she only made a tight smile to force him to continue. "The only part of me that becomes aroused is my hunger, and it is expressed in these," Tony said and parted his lips. Maybe if he showed her the devil's fangs, she'd stop the game.

Sarah peered where he pointed. Then she leaned back and turned bright red. "Good." She gave a short chortle. "I just wanted to see you smile. It worked, too. For a minute, you were really doing it!"

Tony sighed. "Whew, I'm glad that's over!"

"I wondered about body functions," she said, sounding more scientific than silly. "So, I wonder, can you levitate objects? Can you fly?"

"I don't know and I don't think I should try, do you? If I find out a bunch of great things I can do, it would only tempt me to stay this way, right?"

"Oh, gosh, you're right," Sarah said with a delicate hand to her breastbone. "See how easy it is to get carried away? It's so seductive. I'm glad you have your head on tonight!"

"Stick around," Tony added, flirting. Sarah made him feel normal again, helping him forget he was a *creature*, and possibly a monster, as well. Tonight, for fleeting moments, he felt *normal*.

"Okay, smooth talker, let's stick to what we know. What else is weird that you can do?"

Tony waggled his brow and she giggled, looking all of twenty-one. "There's a kind of telepathy with us—me, Mark and Paul, when he was alive. There are parameters that I'm still hashing out, but sometimes, people's thoughts trickle into my ears."

"Ohhhh," she said drawing in her lower lip. "Mine, too?"

Tony hung his head one dip. "Sometimes, when you're close and thinking about me."

"Oh dear," she said and blushed deep crimson. "I apologize for anything you might have overheard that offended thee!"

"I only heard that you are painfully in love with me and trying to get over it," Tony joked, and this time Sarah paled. He touched her knee. "I'm joking! I never.. I'm just joking. Honest."

"Oh," she laughed and fanned her face with her hand.

Tony jumped in and changed the subject. "The doctor's telepathy is so advanced that he can speak to me from Germany. He uses it like a telephone. I've had to use it and I can call him, too. I've also called Big John."

"Oh, wow—Big John?" Sarah asked puzzled.

Tony explained. "We think it's because Paul drank his blood and I," he swallowed, "drank Paul's. We think the blood is the link."

"So maybe that's why you hear some of my thoughts? Because of Paul's blood in me?" Sarah asked with a grimace. Tony nodded. "Makes sense in a morbid fashion."

"The doctor has been alive four hundred years and his powers are so advanced that I have no idea where they end. He can hear the thoughts of complete strangers. He's the one that located you. He concentrated on your name and found your ethereal signature—that's what he called it—and it gave him your exact location."

"Amazing. I'd like to meet him, this aged creature. I imagine he's fascinating," Sarah said, then added, "Since you said he's safe. I would not have like to have met him before."

"Wise girl," Tony teased and Sarah put her hand to his shoulder. The sensation of her touch triggered a warning in his mind.

This is real. This is real. Vampires are real..."

Tony overheard her rambling and kept it to himself, enjoying the pleasant buzz her touch created in his mind.

"Can you see in the dark?"

"Yes, everything gives off an azure glow. In total darkness, I'm blind, but the tiniest light causes these eyes to illuminate stuff that way."

Sarah drew her hand to her lap and met his eye, smiling. "You can hypnotize people with your gaze, can't you?"

"I don't *try* to, but sometimes I do without even realizing it." Tony recalled John's offering and he cleared the thought.

"Anything else?" Sarah asked.

"There is something. Explain this if you can. The doctor can transport himself from one place to another, instantly."

"You're kidding." Sarah sounded more surprised than before.

"I've never tried it and he's not sharing. He never told Paul how it was done, either."

"Must be because he's so old—," Sarah stopped so short that Tony's eyes widened.

"What's the matter?" he asked, unwilling to end their intimate moment.

"What if he can do that because his flesh is dead," she said and looked at the dark corners of the room. "I'm sorry if that sounds bad."

Tony mimicked her movement. Mark wasn't there, and he didn't sense he was listening. "Do you think he heard you?"

Sarah gave a nervous laugh. "I don't know but I had a thought. He might turn to dust when he's delivered." Her eyes appeared apologetic. "That might be why Paul joined the Lord instead of living on. If he was over a hundred years old, how long can the devil animate flesh? How long before it loses fiber?"

"You lost me," Tony said. "Fiber?"

"The fibers that hold us together. The Bible says everything is made for Him and by Him and it is by His will that we have our cohesion." Sarah clucked and Tony's mind raced over the Scripture she'd chosen. She clapped her hands once. "Put a pin in that one. I'll work on it. Moving on..." Sarah took a deep breath. "Let us postulate, vampires don't exists *to us* because we know the Truth. We're not heathens who live in darkness."

"But, my body...." Tony began.

"Just a second. I theorize that Paul and the Doctor yielded themselves to the *myth*. They discovered what you discovered, yet when they awoke as a new creature, they believed the lie. They believed what the devil wanted them to believe. As far as they knew, they had become full-fledged monsters."

"Go ahead…" Intrigued, Tony leaned forward.

"You woke up and you knew it was a lie."

"And?"

"So, we only have to convince your *flesh* what your spirit already knows. Convince the flesh that it has been reborn. You have to live a holy life. Eat the Word of God. Eat of Him until your body no longer lusts for blood." Sarah smiled and opened her hands. "Yes! This is the answer you have been looking for. God has healed you already. He only is waiting for you to accept that you are healed. It's an exercise in faith."

Tony leaned back to allow Sarah's words to sink in. He had been using the Scripture to feed him, but hadn't thought it through this far.

The Bread of Life. The Bread of Life. Jesus is the Bread of Life.

Sarah was beaming with joy. As far as she was concerned, she had just come up with a cure.

Tony did not return her smile, but instead pulled out his wallet. As she explained her miracle cure, God's prophecy about him, delivered long ago came back to his memory sluggish and hazy. He fished through his wallet, seeking the aged and tattered slip of paper that he had jotted it upon the night the Lord gave it to him. It had been over a year ago, and it appeared to be coming to pass.

"Sarah," Tony began as he flipped through old receipts and business cards. "I had a revelation from the Lord a while back." He smiled as his fingers grasped the tiny slip he'd been seeking. "Before I met the vampires, before anything remotely strange happened to me or my friend Hope, I had a Word from the Lord. I jotted it down here."

Tony pulled the yellowed paper open and Sarah leaned in to read along with him.

"It's funny, but I haven't even *thought* of this prophecy since then. I read it to Hope once and tucked it away. That is so weird."

"What does it say? Come on!" Sarah tapped his shoulder.

"Watch that you are not deceived," Tony began in a serious voice as he deciphered his handwriting. "You have your portion. You have your mantle. Be encouraged and know that your God will protect you. Hold firmly till the end with the confidence you have now. On your journey, keep the word of God in your heart at all times. My Word shall be to you as blood and bread." Tony paused and looked into Sarah's eyes. "My God, did you hear that?"

She was directly beside him and their faces could not have been more than six inches apart. Sarah backed and raised her eyebrows.

"It says, My Word shall be to you as blood and bread. My Word is your shield and your buckler. My Word is living and active, sharper than any double-edged sword and nothing in all creation is hidden from My sight. Trust Me. Follow Me. Remember your First Love."

In an urgent move, Tony stood and looked to the ceiling.

"How did you get this revelation? How did He tell you this?"

Tony's memories of that week were coming back fast and he whirled around to meet his friend's eyes. This time his expression was excited instead of sour.

"It was immediately after I attended you and Ira's Signs and Wonders Conference in Whitford City last year! I went to hear you guys preach and I went down for impartation when it was over!"

Almost shouting with the recollection, Tony stepped close and reached for her hand. She took it and got to her feet, eyes shining.

"You and Ira prayed over me and I had my first visit from the Lord later that day. Also, a man approached me with a prophecy saying a great trial was coming..." Tony sighed, his balloon deflating as he realized the severity of that trial. He caught Sarah's eye. Her face was filled with empathy and he realized that he loved her for it.

"I never in a million years would have guessed that this was what my trial would be." Tony waited for Sarah to agree and he continued. "I hope this doesn't last longer than I can resist," he said. With a sudden lurch, Tony's stomach cramped. "Excuse me!" he barked and trotted from the room. When he reached his upstairs bedroom, he pushed the door closed and dropped to his knees beside the bed. Whispering prayers, Tony waited for the pain to lessen. He pushed away thoughts of Sarah: was she offended? Was she frightened? Would she come up if he called her?

"No! God, help me!" he hissed, and closed his eyes. "Ho! Everyone who thirsts, come to the waters!" Tony had memorized ten verses that applied to thirst and he ran through them in a rush. Looping the first three after going through the bunch once, and the grumbling in his gut abated.

"If anyone thirsts, let him come to Me and drink," he prayed in a soft voice. Downstairs, Sarah opened the refrigerator. John kept the basics in there; she would find food and drink.

"He who believes in Me as the Scripture has said, out of his heart will flow rivers of living water…" Tony mumbled and squeezed his eyes as he waited for the hunger to fade. In the meantime, he found comfort in what Sarah had said regarding the vampire's curse.

"You woke up and you knew it was a lie."

She was right and Tony was thrilled to once again, have new hope.

16

I will stand my watch and set myself on the rampart,
And watch to see what He will say to me,
And what I will answer when I am corrected.
Habakkuk 2:1

PRESSING THE BUTTON FROM THE HOUSE, TONY GRANTED
the policeman entrance through the security gate. He waited on the
front porch as the unmarked cruiser parked at the front steps. He hadn't
thought much about the police since they cut him loose a month ago
and now his mind raced, wondering what they might want to see him
about. As usual, he held his red leather Bible and stroked the cover with
his thumbs as he watched a tall official exit the sedan. He approached
with a frown and behind sunglasses, his brow pointed down. When he
reached the first step Tony switched the Bible to his left to shake hands.

"Good morning," he said and his visitor joined him on the covered
porch. "I'm Tony Agricola. Can I help you?"

The cop swished off his glasses. He didn't smile, but his eyes
weren't as hard as Tony expected based upon his austere countenance.

"Detective Kranchez, I appreciate that, and maybe," he said in a
rush and pointed for a pair of rockers. "Can I have a minute?"

"Of course," Tony said and they sat catty-corner, both leaning
forward to prevent the chairs from moving as they spoke.

"Thanks, this isn't an official visit and it's not an official interview,
'kay?" The cop waited for a reaction and Tony shrugged. "Thanks. It's
like this, I was on the case of that evangelist who got attacked a few
months ago and I know you were attached to the guy who did it, Paul
Black."

Tony nodded, still wondering where he was going. He'd been
released from interest, so…?

"Yeah, well, the folks in Whitford City reopened that case this
week based upon some new evidence they found linking Black to the
murder of a musician in Atlanta."

Tony maintained his expression, but inside, trepidation crept in,
the guy's line slowly leading to the vampires.

"So, the reason I'm here unofficial-like is this. I wonder if you'd come down to the station and leave a blood sample for our guys. If you did that, we could rule you out again."

"Rule me out? I'm not a suspect in either of those cases," Tony said, forcing a calm tone. The cop was fishing and Tony did not enjoy the bait Kranchez dangled.

"*Welllll,* actually, you kinda are," he said drawing out each word. "You got a hefty chunk of equity recently and it's all on the record."

Tony blinked and shook his head. "Everything I received was transferred legally and done by the top lawyers in finance." He shook his head again. "What do you want? My blood? Is that what you said?"

Kranchez shrugged with a *hmmph*. "I'm just trying to save you some trouble. Sooner or later, WC's going to issue a blood warrant so you can get ahead of it by going on the record now. With us."

Tony stood up and the cop followed suit. "No, thank you. I have no reason to do this and I won't."

"I'm just trying to save you some trouble," the man said and reached forward to shake hands.

Tony shook it, but inside he fumed.

Who am I so mad at? The only one to blame is God, right? God must want me to be hassled by the cops again. Geez!

Tony griped to the Lord as the cop handed him a business card and headed back to his Buick. After Kranchez waved over his head, he got in and wound his way off the property.

Tony returned to the rocker and looked at his cell. *I should just call them.* Then he recalled the one he talked about God with had retired. *Is the new guy a believer?* Tony growled again to the Lord and pressed the saved Whitford City contact that would ring at former Detective Miller's desk.

"Pension," a man's voice said and Tony cleared his throat.

"Detective Pension, my name is Tony Agricola. You called me back in June to let me know I was off the hook on the Paul Back case." Tony thought he heard a weird noise, like a phone-button click or a *tsk* and he continued. "Well, a Montgomery detective named Kranchez just came by to tell me ya'll have me back on the radar. Is that right?"

"Kranchez said that?" the man asked, sounding as if he was buying time. "Huh, well."

"Look, Detective, am I being investigated or not?" Tony asked aware he had developed a hard edge to his voice that he never used, before or after becoming a new creature.

"Um, right, Mr. Agricola, we have seen some new developments here," Pension said, still dragging out his words as he worked something on his end. "Can you come see us? I know it's a drive, but it would save us a warrant if you just come on in and let us do a little interview."

Tony covered his face and collected his next words carefully. "I'll call you back." He disconnected and stood, looking at nothing in the sunny yard. Under his breath, he began an argument with the Lord.

"What are You doing? First You turn me into this monster and then You give me a hunger I can hardly control or suffer. You send me a woman I can't romance and a heart for ministry that I can't execute. Now the police are looking into my life again?" Tony stormed into the house, slamming the door with gusto. The glass inset shattered and he didn't turn to see. "I'm not a freakin' superman, Father! I'm NOT Apostle Paul! I can't do it! It's too much!"

Tony stomped to the kitchen and without thinking whipped open the stainless steel fridge. Inside, John had stashed some condiments, cheese and lunch meat, plus a few power shakes.

"I CAN'T DO THIS!" Tony shouted to the ceiling and slammed the door hard. His stomach folded into itself then, bringing him to his knees in a fresh wave of pain. He waited for it to pass, and when it did, his forehead beaded with red-tinged perspiration. Tony allowed his knees to slip long and he lay stomach down to the kitchen floor. He turned his head to the side, his cheek against the cool tile.

"I don't think I can do it," he whispered through weary lips.

"I can do all things through Christ who strengthens me…"

The Scripture popped out from nowhere and Tony closed his eyes and wept.

ᘏᕞ

"Your boy lawyered up," Jonah overheard Andy say on Jenn's cell. They'd just settled down for some TV and ice cream when she answered his call. She put it on speaker and Jonah paused the movie. *"I played my favorite cop trick on him and you shoulda seen his face. Whoo-wee, he's in trouble."*

Kranchez chuckled a moment and Jonah wondered about the details. As much as he wished he could forget he knew anything about the case, his curiosity wouldn't let him stay away.

"You went over as his buddy, eh? Just giving him a heads-up and all that?" Jenn clarified with a knowing smile. "Oh, man, this is good. Anything else?" She shot Jonah a wink.

"Looks like he called Pension over there in your old haunt and asked if he was under investigation." Andy laughed. *"I didn't tell the rookie ahead of time. He probably fell all over himself trying to deliver instructions to Agricola like that all surprised and stuff."*

"Yeah, you're a real pal," Jenn joked. "Way to watch out for the younger Boys in Blue."

"Yeah-yeah-yeah. Anyway, Agricola lawyered up. I'll send you the guy's digits, but it's some huge firm out of Atlanta. Real expensive. I don't see WC getting anywhere near this guy without a smoking gun and a signed confession." Andy chuckled and made his goodbyes.

Jenn set down her phone and looked Jonah's way. "Hiding behind a lawyer."

Jonah didn't want to fight about it, but she was wrong. If a man is aligned with bad guys and he's innocent, his best defense is the most expensive attorney he can afford. *And with seven million dollars, Tony can hire the world...*

Jonah unmuted the show and tucked Jenn under his wing. Maybe she'd let him remain mum. He was in no mood to slander who he felt strongly was God's man.

12

I have become its servant by the commission
God gave me to present to you the word of God
in its fullness—the mystery that has been kept hidden
for ages and generations,
but is now disclosed to the Lord's people.
Colossians 1:26-26

ELIZABETH STARED INTO SPACE, NOT AWARE OF HER DEATH
grip to the steering wheel until her wrists cramped.

"Father, no, no, no," she said inside, her eyes cutting to the way her
new client had exited. "No way is that guy for real." This she said aloud
and cranked the car. Her '00 Camaro roared to life and she babied the
aging sportscar out of the strip mall parking lot. Her appointment had
started on time, Rakha Tep arrived in a gleaming new Jaguar at 7 P.M.
on the nose. But from the moment their eyes met until the man
disappeared out the studio door, Elizabeth's skin crawled.

"But what did I have to fear?" she asked, beginning a conversation
with God. "If You have my back, why was I so scared of that man?"

Elizabeth brought back their introduction. Mr. Tep had been
cordial, shook her hand, spoke the correct pleasantries. He was
handsome in a commanding way, dark eyes, dark skin, immaculate
grooming to his hair, nails, and Elizabeth felt certain his eyebrows had
been tweezed. His suit shimmered as if woven with metallic fibers and
tailored to perfection. When he removed his suit coat, the white dress
shirt underneath had been sheer silk, which caught her attention
because he wore no undershirt and his dark brown nipples showed
through. He was built like an athlete, not bulky, but every piece of him
that touched his clothing was toned.

"So, why was I afraid of him?" she said again, now getting the car
onto the interstate for home. She ran over their conversation. He asked
about the dachshund, she gave him some pamphlets, and he
complimented her work that she had unpacked. Everything he did and
said had been faultless.

Then he asked if I was single...

Oh. At that recollection, Elizabeth's skin prickled anew. For some reason, her body reacted the same way when he posed the question the first time. She had been taken aback and stumbled a bit before saying, no, she was recently divorced. That caused him to launch into a story about his wife who died of cancer.

But I didn't believe him. Why?

Elizabeth narrowed her eyes in concentration. A flash of something else, someone uncorking a bottle—Mr. Tep's hand, brown, elegant, moving as if the man's every cell danced to a silent cello solo.

A bottle?

Elizabeth thought about that—had he brought wine? To greet the new artist? To welcome her to town, to drink in honor of their business arrangement? She couldn't remember this happening, but...

I think he uncorked a bottle and poured... Was it wine?

In the miniscule blink of memory, it had been red, too dark to be rosé; perhaps a merlot mixed with—

"Medicinal..."

The word popped into her mind, and from the lips of Mr. Tep.

Did he drug me? Elizabeth's blood drained from her head and she focused on the road. *"Father-God? Did I drink something?"*

After sixty seconds of asking what and why, Elizabeth allowed herself to calm, remembering no matter what she thought happened, her safety forever sat in God's hands. When she realized the Lord probably sent that thought, she imagined angels dispatched to lay hands on her shoulders. No matter if they did for real or not, but the mental image was enough and she exhaled with relief.

"Okay, okay," she whispered, terrified to think she'd consumed something and not realized it. She checked her body, everything was in order. With her eyes on the dashboard clock and two fingers to her carotid, she checked her pulse. Nothing to report.

Think, Elizabeth. I noticed he was weird from when he first walked in...

Never in her life had she met a person who put her on such high alert. Did God do that? Had that been what the preachers call discernment? In Los Angeles, Aaron shared the stage with a famous man and wife preaching team—the Traceys—and the woman's main teaching had been about discerning evil. Reverend Tracey said the Lord had given her the ability to see into the spirit realm. She had also taught that if a believer desired it, God would teach him or her to discern evil spirits.

I think he was evil...

Elizabeth considered Mr. Tep. Everything about him was attractive, even his voice. He had the most beautiful accent she had ever heard and had commented he should do voiceover work for the entertainment industry. He had laughed and his dark brown eyes sparkled with joy. This, too, Elizabeth noticed.

"He really liked my armadillo," she said low, recalling the way Mr. Tep reacted when she pulled the two-foot long sculpture from his packing.

"He looks ready to wake up!" Mr. Tep had said with glee. "I've been around the world and have never seen the life in a sculpture as you have put in yours!" He stroked the armadillo's head and as Elizabeth handed it over, he ran his strong almost feminine fingers down the animal's back, languid and thoughtful.

Elizabeth's eyes widened.

Oh, Father! I remember!

When the man's hand caressed the sculpture, Elizabeth's body reacted. It was as if the hand on the poly-resin lay on her lower back and when he ran his fingers to the tail, her insides tingled and she had excused herself and left him alone. She had gone to the small bathroom and collected herself. She wasn't wanton; since her divorce—and a year before that even—she hadn't been a sexual person. She did not think about sex. *Period.* But once the client initiated stroking the artwork, the pulsing deep in her sleeping places remained awake.

Elizabeth ended the meeting at the first opportunity. Tep had gone, made a vague announcement of calling her again, and added that he would like to treat her to dinner sometime.

Elizabeth shook her head and asked God to tell her what to do. She did *not* want to see him again and definitely didn't want to believe they'd shared a toast she promptly forgot.

That was my imagination. I mean, if it happened—I'd recall it. I don't have lost time and I'm fine...

Elizabeth huffed, angry at herself for her histrionics.

"Let's keep it in the real world, Father. What happened was that this man spooked me. Please don't make me have to see him again," she prayed under her breath, eyes closed. "Amen."

With every ounce of her courage, she put the subject on the back burner and headed home.

ॐॐ

Rakha steered the Jag west onto Old Selma Road, having left Montgomery city limits and the delicious-smelling church girl behind. He had provoked her to such an extent that he provoked himself and decided a good old fashioned hunt would scratch his itch.

The church girl emanated light and Rakha sensed immense protection around her in the form of energies he could not see with his eyes, natural or supernatural. But his hyperawareness informed him of this wall that could have been angels with swords like in the storybooks or even some of the Unseen perpetrating their deceits by making things difficult for their vampire friend.

. Rakha chuckled. It didn't matter if the wall emanated from the Unseen or the Creator, it was not capable of keeping him away. No matter her invisible hedge, she'd fallen for his host's beauty, she drank his wine, he was inside her now. A two-thousand year old entity had slipped past her lips and even now, with barely any effort, he sensed her. His blood in her system connected their life-threads, and oh, he would weave them together over the next few days. Every ounce of her pain would be his, and pain was what he would search for first. Every living man and woman hid secrets in their innermost souls, and a being as old as Rakha would be able to draw them out at his leisure. By the time Agricola was conquered, she'd be ready to join Rakha, be his servant companion as he moved on to the next adventure in the flesh.

She is so soft...

Rakha grinned at the memory of when the pad of his forefinger brushed the young woman's hand. His nerve endings recorded and extrapolated the data into a full body scan. When he captured her, he'd pet her forever, take her blood and enjoy the softness of her flesh under his palms. Rakha had no memories of sexual intercourse as his original flesh became a vampire while still a virgin, but his brain remembered pleasures of touch, sound, and psychological enjoyments all above and beyond the blood. So he would receive many, many pleasures from steering the church girl from her faith, into debauchery, and he would make her a willing slave to his bloodlust. Did he truly need Agricola if he turned the church girl?

"You will chicken out, we knew it. You have wasted our time..."

"No, tomorrow, I will begin my work with Agricola. I only set up this appointment to plant a seed. You have chosen wisely; I will first subjugate Agricola and then play with my church girl. Have no fear..." Rakha waited to see if the Unseen accepted his promise and it seemed they did.

He hummed a tune and turned onto brittle asphalt which became a red gravel county road lined with pine trees along both sides. The cloudless sky caused the full moon to shine like a million candles in his special vision and he peeked through the brush, slowing the car and extinguishing his headlamps. The hunt, the old way, as if still in the wild, untamed forests of Hungary or the wide-open flats of Turkey, or any number of places his hosts had allowed him to seek and steal human blood.

Then he saw it.

Tail lights flickered and disappeared a hundred yards deep in the trees. These were small and close together, a cart or side-by-side with a rumbling gas motor. Rakha pulled his car to the shoulder and slipped away, heading at first, directly toward where he'd seen the light and then he branched to the side, circling around in the dark, his practiced step making no sound no matter the leaf-strewn forest floor. Then he saw his prey. A man alone, a high-powered rifle slung across his back as he struggled with a deer he'd bagged only minutes earlier. The man wasn't strong, he wasn't fit, and the ninety pound beast was more than he could lift the four feet to the bed of his Polaris.

"Come on, sheez! Dangit!" the man cursed low, struggling and losing what little lift he accomplished before his muscles gave up. The carcass slithered to the ground, its head the last thing to hit the leaves, its glassy eyes like huge marbles. The hunter hung his shoulders for three long seconds and then spun with drama to lean against the open tailgate. He pondered his choices. Knocked catawampus by his bulk against the machine, the hunter's rifle slipped to the side so after a new, stronger curse, he set it into the ATV bed. He fished in a pocket of loose-fitting camouflage coveralls and lifted a cell phone.

Rakha measured the distance between them, approximately twenty feet. He stood against a thick pine and if the man looked directly at him, he'd still only see shadow. Rakha had long learned how to hide in plain sight and he counted heartbeats before he made his attack. Just one. One human heartbeat. He listened out for animals for kicks and heard only the smallest – squirrels and birds – nothing of interest.

"Sheez, Karen, just meet me at the fork, okay?!" the man said in a loud voice and dropped the cell into his pocket.

Rakha chose his moment. In a blur, he rushed the hunter from the front, pushing the man onto his back in the short cargo bed. The man's head rapped the lip hard and he screamed more from that than the attack on his person.

"Come on, man! Sheez! What?" he shouted, the slurred syllables alerting Rakha the man had been drinking. Since he detected no alcohol aromas, he hadn't noticed before now. It didn't matter.

Rakha forced the nails of his right hand into lion-like claws, thick and pointed, but not hooked like a housecat. With them he ripped the man's thick canvas coveralls open at the front snaps and a second heavy swipe ripped his undershirts to the skin. The man yelled for help and Rakha silenced him with a third swipe to the larynx, opening the trachea, but not damaging enough to stop the man's heart. With his lifeblood pumping to his open wound, Rakha surged in, mouth wide and without any need for fangs. The blood sprayed across Rakha's chin and cheeks, dribbling into his shirt as it ran down his skin, and he slurped as much into his stomach as he could.

It took the man four minutes to expire and when his heart skipped once and stopped, Rakha exhaled and propped himself with his palms to the big man's chest to watch his soul exit. The guy didn't see Rakha, but whatever he saw, he went to it and Rakha watched it with his senses, wishing he could see like the Unseen did, into the spirit realm. In between hosts, he saw there—when he did not have a flesh to parade in, he housed in that in-between world of shades of gray. But eyes of flesh, no matter how special, prevented him from seeing into that realm.

Unless I had special permission…

Rakha stared at the dead man a little longer. In another lifetime, his host lived in Palestine. There had been men who saw spirits. Their rabbi taught that the Creator gave them this gift in order to fight the Unseen. Rakha would never get that sort of permission. He worked for the opposite team and he knew it.

The man's phone rang and Rakha climbed off his chest and dropped to the forest floor. With a last glance to the deer, watching everything with its gentle sightlessness, he dissolved into the shadows, backtracking to his vehicle. He drove three miles before meeting another car and he wondered how long until his prey would be discovered. Wherever the fork was to Karen she wouldn't find him there.

But damn…

The hunter's blood worked its magic and Rakha smiled.

Tomorrow, I'll introduce myself to Agricola and I'll show the Unseen what his blood looks like spilled.

18

Do not be overly righteous, nor be overly wise;
Do not be overly wicked, nor be foolish;
It is good that you grasp this.
For he who fears God will escape them all.
Ecclesiastes 7:16,17,18

"MCS?" JONAH ASKED HANDING JENN HER CELL AS SHE scrambled eggs for breakfast. They had chosen this day to drive into town and buy what they needed for the new greenhouse. A long day of shopping at Lowe's and then a fattening late lunch should round out most of the day.

"Montgomery County Sheriff," she replied and stuck the slender device between her ear and shoulder, holding it handsfree to serve up breakfast. "Speltz," she said to the caller in her cop voice and Jonah shook his head smiling. "Uh-huh. Okay. Thanks, you hear?"

Jonah caught it when she allowed it to slip into his possession. He regarded her with raised eyebrows as she pointed to the dinette, carrying two plates.

"You sure you wanna know? I'll play with this by myself. It won't hurt my feelings. It's a hobby for me. I don't mind if you don't do it, too."

"It's the Dracula File?" he asked forcing a light tone.

"Yep," she said and dove into her eggs.

"Well, I've given it some thought and maybe since we worked this one together, let me play, too. I'm not a pansy, I was just lazy. Go ahead. What happened? Another bloodless body?"

"Yep," she said, turning her Maine accent Southern.

"Montgomery County, not town?" he clarified.

"Right. A hunter was drained of blood last night. His wife spoke to him at 8:45 and went to meet him at their spot at 9:45. He never showed and she called the County in for help. They found him around midnight in the bed of his own side-by-side, clothing ripped free at the throat and his upper body slashed to the bone."

Jonah *hmm'ed.* "So no double punctures like on the Hip-Hop King?"

"No punctures, but the M.E. found him down three-quarters of his blood supply. The blood splatter at the murder scene didn't account for it all."

"Does the sheriff think it's a vampire?" he asked as a joke but Jenn answered.

"He's running on a Satanic Cult theory, views this as an isolated homicide, someone took the blood for a ritual. I never mentioned the word vampire, thank you, but I offered to share whatever I had on bloodless bodies."

"And?" Jonah asked, pretty sure what she'd say. Sheriffs had even less patience for that sort of hogwash than the City.

"You know what he said," she replied with a wink. "But I have a copy of this file for my collection." She grinned, happy to show Jonah the bacon in her teeth.

"Sexy," he said and swigged his coffee, thoughtful and wondering if the dead hunter fit in with their... *ahem,* Jenn's newfound pastime. She was still smiling when a minute passed and Jonah grew suspicious. "What else?"

"Andy's the one who clued me in on this new one. He said the dead boy case listed a blue or black newer model Jaguar sited in the area that night. No one had specifics, but it was noted in case it became interesting later."

Jonah waited for the rest. One thing he would need to accustom himself to was jealousy; having another man texting his soon-wife without him in the loop prickled his ire. He bristled and hid it as best he could.

"The County boys didn't have a Jaguar XJ6 near the hunter, but a traffic camera caught a midnight blue one on Old Selma Road in the time frame." She lifted her gaze and winked when Jonah met her eye. "County assured me you can't read the license plate, but I asked for the TC footage anyway."

"You're kidding." Jonah had no doubt that if he was requesting all the stuff his bride had, he'd get nothing.

"The lady in Traffic said she'll share it end of shift."

"Incredible," he said and meant it.

"I know," Jenn replied and finished off her coffee. "Okay, let's get going. I want to play with my Dracula File when we get back."

"Okay, Detective Van Helsing," he said and ate faster.

After unloading the last of the materials and feeding their two Guernseys, Jonah found Jenn clacking away on her computer keyboard. He entered her home office after a cop-knock on the lintel.

"Cracked it yet, boss?" he said and she finished another ten keystrokes before stopping.

"Look," she said and pushed back to reveal her 19" monitor. "I have your notes from the Brannen interview. See what you put on, 'Paul Black-how old?'?"

Jonah adjusted his bifocals and read what he wrote a year ago when they questioned a woman in the Paul Black investigation. He recalled the incidence for many reasons *not* having to do with the young lady's remarkable beauty. For one, Captain Erkleson had approved that he and Jenn fly to Maryland to question the woman. For two, she had been as scared as hell. Her every answer raised his suspicions. The one regarding the age of Paul Black, Hope Brannen had paled, stuttered and then offered he looked like a teenager.

"Our funky blood is found at Nixon's homicide. The same funky blood is found at Joiner's homicide. Paul Black / Saul White shed that funky blood on the evangelist in Whitford City. This is why we suspected Black of everything..."

"I follow," Jonah said trying to read her next thought. "So what does this have to do with Ms. Brannen's evasive behavior regarding the guy's info?"

Jenn shook her head. "Not his info. His *age*. One of my rabbit trails has been trying to find Paul Black's history. His SSN starts in 1980. Before that, there are plenty of Paul Blacks on file across the country, but when we pair Paul Black and Mark Corescu, it narrows to a timeline I can plot and trace." Jenn hit a key and the screen opened an excel spreadsheet.

"You think Paul Black is an imposter? Or you think Paul Black is... what? A vampire?" Jonah was kidding, but Jenn only pointed to her screen.

"Black's first driver's license with this SSN shows up in 1990, and states his date of birth as 1974. Do you think it possible Hope Brannen mistook a thirty-five-year-old man for a teenager?" Jenn blew a puff of air. "Before 1980, there's no paperwork for this guy. So I traced his partner, Dr. Mark Corescu. *His* driver's licenses go back to the 70's. So I dug into his *medical* license, which I can trace to the 1950's." She scrolled a little more and then sought Jonah's eye. "What is the likelihood that Ms. Brannen—and every other woman we spoke to

94

about Dr. Corescu—was talking about a man more than seventy years old?"

Jonah blinked. "When did you look all this stuff up?"

"While you shovel your cow-manure, I dig up my facts. I'm retired, not dead." She returned to the computer and opened a new file. "I have never found a photo of Paul Black other than his driver's license. Here is what I found."

Jonah studied the scanned images. In each license, different states, different dates, different attire, same SSN, and the man looked to be the same age, around eighteen.

"And this page is his partner." Jenn clicked and Jonah looked at five scanned DLs for the physician. As with Black, photographs of Corescu revealed the same man, same age, only the dates, address, and clothing differed.

"You've been calling them partners lately. Is this a theory of them being a couple? I mean, he was dating Brannen. Or am I missing something?" Jonah stared at Corescu's face. His features were striking; but… even his 2D photograph grabbed Jonah's attention and made him uneasy somewhere inside.

"I think partner in crime," Jenn clarified. "I have one more page. Prepare yourself. We're heading into the tinfoil-hat territory." Jenn paused with drama and turned to catch Jonah's eye. "This is the place you might better go to the greenhouse."

Jonah gave her a snarky har-har. "What is it? I'm in, now."

"Okay," she said as a warning and scrolled to the next page of photos.

She rolled several feet away this time so Jonah could move in and lean down to the monitor. Eleven photographs, evenly spaced, arranged in chronological order from newest to oldest, all but three of them in black and white, and the oldest two a silvery, plate-type photo. Jonah stared hard at each. His fingers found the mouse and used the scroller ball to zoom the photos to different sizes. He checked the attire of the subject to the date it claimed. He checked the backdrops for evidence of Photoshopping or fraud. Then he exhaled, stood up and turned to look at the opposite wall.

Jenn had found a dozen photos of a man who did not age. The oldest one showed a physician tending a wounded soldier in an Army hospital. This soldier wore a Rebel uniform and whether it was God or his own inner voice, Jonah did not doubt he was looking at the same man, thirty-five, or thirty-eight tops, from the Whitford City 2018 Driver's License photo.

"Yeah, it's weird stuff," Jenn said, her voice soft as she must have intuited Jonah's mood. "I don't think anything yet. I'll wait for more evidence, but before I looked these up, I was just joking around. Having a bit of fun with the mystery. Now I want to know how these two men aren't aging."

"Okay," Jonah said, still facing away. "I gotta go think on it some."

He didn't know how else to extricate himself from the conversation and he hoped that did it. With a wave over his shoulder, he said I love you and headed back outside. He needed to pray and he needed to stop thinking about movie monsters.

19

See to it that no one takes you captive
through hollow and deceptive philosophy,
which depends on human tradition and
the elemental spiritual forces
of this world rather than on Christ.
Colossians 2:8

ELEVEN LOCAL PASTORS AND EVANGELISTS APPLAUDED as Tony completed his presentation. The United Methodist Church had arranged the meeting in their luxurious conference room and asked Tony to deliver a talk on how to preach the Gospel while making sure your church remains in the black. A friend of his father's had touted Tony's success with Whitford City Presby while he worked there, and so Tony accepted as an experiment; his first such outing to test how the outside world perceived him now. He had a good head for business and didn't mind sharing tricks of the trade that kept his father's church's books in good standing with money left over each quarter.

At the end of the forty-five minute session, Tony found himself amazed that no one seemed to notice he wasn't like them anymore. No one became hypnotized or gave him any odd looks. Inwardly, he questioned why, but he did not get too far when the pastor led them in an exit prayer and everyone stood to leave.

The men and women filed out, each shaking his hand with a blessing or message of encouragement. Tony had made goodbyes with the last attendee when a twelfth man stepped into place for a handshake. This gentleman had not been in the meeting, but wore a smile and put out his hand. Tony shook it.

"Good evening. Do I know you?" he asked and the man's grin went to the side.

"You should," he replied with mystery, but when Tony did not react, he continued. "Mr. Agricola, allow me to introduce myself. I am Rakha and I've been watching you."

"Oh, how about that," Tony said an alert status reaching his brain. The man before him was his height, but unlike Tony, built compact and muscular, with a medium complexion and dark brown hair. His expensive tailored suit shimmered, his coat open to reveal a white silk dress shirt with no tie or undershirt, open three buttons.

Tony noticed all of this as the man looked him over in similar fashion. Tony dropped his gaze to his shirt front, a plain blue Oxford with dark blue jeans and boots. He raised his gaze with a crooked grin but the visitor's eyes were hidden by black-lensed Raybans. The stranger had not spoken again, so Tony picked up the slack.

"Which church are you affiliated with?"

"Hah," he laughed, sounding forced. "I am not affiliated with any church. I am here to meet *you,* Anthony Agricola." The man then backed and gestured for the exit with a large, sweeping of one arm.

Tony's red flag went to full mast.

Am I supposed to be afraid of this guy?

Tony wasn't fearful but couldn't discern why he'd gone on alert. He saw no harm in following the man out, he was headed that way anyway. He nodded and the stranger turned about and led the way.

"You certainly aren't from around here," Tony said with humor as they reached the hall door which led to the side exit in three strides. "Why are you looking for me? I can't imagine why if it's not church related." The stranger replied only after he'd stepped into the night.

"You will have to open your mind," he said and stopped his forward movement once he had them both in the shadows of the ornamental trees that boxed the parking lot. "There are many things in life more interesting than a bunch of whining congregants awaiting the return of the god who abandoned them."

Tony huffed, but had grown uneasy. Now they stood in shadow, the sodium lamps unable to reach so far from the source. Tony saw every detail clearly in his detestable condition, but what of the stranger with the dark sunglasses? What oddball thing would he say next and what exactly did he want? Tony gave him a new prompt.

"Okay, Mr. Rakha, you have officially piqued my interest. What can I do for you?" Awaiting an answer, Tony noticed the man's age. By his appearance, he might be mid-twenties, his skin smooth and blemish free.

"I am *extremely* disappointed that you do not recognize me. I was told you were a great colossus, but how can that be true when you did not even *see me* in that silly gathering just now." Rakha chuckled with derision.

In his mind, Tony looked around the room during the meeting— this man had not been present, he was certain. Then Tony wondered if the man had him confused with someone else. Who told him Tony Agricola was a huge colossus?

"Maybe this will help you figure it out. We share an acquaintance. A priest. Ring any bells?"

Tony thrust his hands into his pants pockets to prevent fidgeting. Who was this priest? The few Catholic clergymen he knew came to mind, but none would be associated with such a strange character. What did he want and why was he so weird?

"Your mind is racing with all the wrong questions," the stranger said, his fingers going to the stem of his Raybans. "Perhaps now," he said with drama and whipped off his sunglasses, "you will ask the right ones."

Tony's jaw dropped. It was a vampire, and worse, when adding a priest to the equation, he realized which vampire he had encountered: Mark Corescu's maker, the original demon from four centuries past. The stranger's face revealed all that he need know; Rakha's eyes held murder and death, hate and avarice, and Tony understood now why his spirit had been on alert.

"Ah-hah! It awakens!" the demon huffed and turned away.

He walked at a casual pace and Tony followed, lining up and prioritizing new queries. Rakha reached a late-model Jaguar and opened the door when it chirped. Still dumbfounded, Tony had not yet sent up a request to God. He couldn't imagine why such an old creature would seek him out—and that stuff he said in the church—*Rakha has been looking for me? Why? This can't be good,* he finally decided watching the vampire fall in behind the wheel.

"Lead me to your house," Rakha said starting his car. "We have much to discuss in private."

Tony's initial response included expletives meaning *no freaking way,* but his spirit piped in; he was *supposed* to entertain the miscreant. He was *supposed* to hear him out.

But why?

No answer returned from God so Tony gave the vampire a half-nod. No one would be at the house, so at least he wouldn't have to worry about John or Sarah's safety.

"Good," the vampire said as if Tony had spoken. "Carry on. And Tony Agricola…you better not disappoint me." He drew in his leg and closed the door with Tony still standing near and looking into the car. It took Tony five seconds to move. He backpedaled a few steps before turning for his truck, finally praying for help and wisdom.

What do I do? Should I call Mark? Am I in danger?

As Tony's mind rambled he closed his truck door. He pulled toward the road and away from the church campus, and a more rational thought came to his aid.

Wait a minute. I'm not helpless. I'm not in danger here. Because of God, I've beaten every vampire who came against me...

Relaxing in increments, Tony picked up speed and led the stranger to his house. In three more blocks they'd be at his gated drive.

I'll find out what he wants, what he knows, and when he's leaving. I shouldn't be afraid. What could he do to me? I mean, really!

Mostly convinced, Tony smiled and prepared his nerve.

20

If anyone comes to you and does not bring this teaching,
do not take them into your house or welcome them.
Anyone who welcomes them shares in their wicked work.
2 John 1:10

TONY STOOD ASIDE FOR THE VAMPIRE TO ENTER,
hoping it was God and not simple curiosity nudging him to bring the
guy in. Tony's mind raced with what everyone knew—you never invite
a vampire into your home. When Rakha entered he stopped in the
center of the marble-floored foyer and spun a circle.

"How extravagantly you live, sir!"

Tony did not respond. Was he supposed to make small talk?
Would he magically know what to say when the time came? Dealing
with stranger-vampires had not been something he anticipated. And as
memory served, Mark Corescu told him his master was dead.

"I'm impressed with your ability to blend into society. And no one
suspects you? You walk in the sun, correct? How curious. So did my
priest."

Tony closed the door, circumvented the man and led him to the
formal living room. Two brocade sofas faced each other there and Tony
waited to see if he would sit. He did and watched Tony's face, probably
wondering why he hadn't yet responded.

"What of the woman? Does she know about you?" Rakha then
added with raised eyebrows, "Do *you* know about you?"

"You don't get to mention the woman," Tony said, filled with
sudden dread when Sarah came to the monster's mind. "What do you
want?" he said using a stern voice he had used with Paul when that
vampire needed correction.

"First, tell me who I am." Rakha crossed his ankles and clasped his
hands atop his thighs. "Surely you should be able to do that."

Tony took a seat in the opposite couch leaning forward. "You're
the vampire that turned Mark Corescu." As Tony spoke the name his
stomach grumbled and forced him to remember taking his blood to
sustain him until he flew home. Across from him, his guest inhaled.

"Ah! I see your thoughts!" Rakha announced as if the ability only just arrived. "Oh, yes, that is my priest, my precious child. But why did he allow this? Nursing on his arm like an infant?"

Tony hadn't answered when he heard in his head, *"Did this simp truly vanquish my powerful favorite son? How? How was this accomplished?"*

Tony sat up. Not only had the monster peeked into his head, but whether he realized it or not, Rakha's lamentations continued to float to his consciousness. Tony was done. "Enough!" he said in a loud voice. "What do you want?"

"I should kill him now! Why don't I fly across the room and crush his skull?"

The vampire's thoughts continued to stream in Tony's head and he realized the demon did not know.

"Is he a danger to me? He is here and my priest is gone. Is my priest alive? And why is this preacher not using the Gift?"

"Have you come to make trouble or make friends," Tony sent to his mind. He would use his power if only to throw off his guest.

Rakha exhaled, a smile touching the edge of his mouth. "I am glad to see you're not completely impotent. Contact my priest. Tell him I am here. He will be delighted."

"No," Tony said as a flat refusal. He relaxed into the couch to appear calm, but inside he asked God for answers and an advantage over the visitor. His guest's eyes flashed, the emotion reading as indignation at Tony's response. He decided to twist the knife if only to maintain the upper hand. "He thinks you're dead. He told me you were burned up by villagers."

"Villagers!" Rakha sneered and stood to pace the room. "No mere man can kill me, you simpleton."

"Well, if you weren't rendered helpless by the townsfolk, why did you let the priest go?" Tony egged the vampire's ire, trusting that whatever words he spoke were given to him by God. Was God even listening? Tony hoped so, although hearing from God had become a thing of the past since his life change.

"Your impudence is noted," Rakha hissed. "I was *delayed,* not dead. A few frightened mortals could never have control over my destiny." His guest continued to pace as if walking off nervous energy and Tony watched every step, hearing in the demon's thoughts that he sought the right moment to attack.

"Why are you here?" Tony asked, his tone neutral. "Answer or be gone. I'm not playing this game any longer."

"I came here to kill you," Rakha said and stopped pacing. He met Tony's eye only a second and shook his head. "Although now that we've met, I don't believe you are what I was told."

Now it was Tony's turn to scoff. He had allowed his spirit to rest, as if his battles were done. But as long as he lived for the Lord, Satan would never cease trying to kill him. "You devils," he muttered. "Is this the newest trick? Resurrect a dried-up vampire to see if perhaps *he* can vanquish the Hero in me?"

"To whom are you speaking? Surely not I." Rakha approached. "Are you so dimwitted that you cannot sense the danger you are in? I could rip your arms off and show them to you before you even knew what happened."

"No, you couldn't." Tony faced the old vampire more fully. "I had to allow you to my home in order to discover your intentions. Now, I want to laugh. You thought you could wander in here and do something that no one else has been able to accomplish? I'll tell you what I tell them all, you're not fighting only me." Tony relaxed his posture and thrust his hands deep into his pockets. He intended to appear helpless, as when he faced off with Mark and then Paul. Each time Tony came against the vampires in the past, God told Tony to drop his defenses so God could battle in his stead.

"You have lost your mind," Rakha said, his fists clenched.

"Not hardly. Have you no concept of the Creator who made you?"

"I know Him well…"

"Then allow me to inform you that the power that created the universe dwells in me, He watches over me, and will never allow you to ruin what He has in store for me. You may as well give up your quest to kill Tony Agricola. I will not die until my Father in heaven wills it."

Rakha laughed. "Are you preaching to me now?"

"No, I am issuing a warning, just as I gave the enemies of God in the past. If you attempt to destroy me, you may be destroyed yourself. God has a plan for me, and what He has showed me so far does not include being vanquished before His timing." The hardness in his voice convinced his guest of his purpose and he thanked God in his heart.

❦

He truly believes his words… Rakha sucked his teeth, holding the man's calm eye. *It's not insanity… No. He knows.*

Angry but not overcome by emotion, Rakha grew still. Agricola had assumed a casual stance, his expression blank. A few more moments of holding his host's gaze and Rakha understood what the Unseen had tried to explain. If he lay a hand on Tony Agricola tonight, he would be defeated by the very same forces that protected the man in the past. The preacher's faith is what defeated his priest and then young Paul Black. Rakha grinned with comprehension.

This is good. It is fine. I will bide my time. I only need to wear him down…

With a dramatic exhale and friendly half-bow, Rakha dropped his domineering stance. "I apologize, forgive me. I am a very old creature and not accustomed to this new age." He gestured for the couches, his shoulders drooped and his eyes averted.

"Speak your piece," Agricola responded, impatient now.

"Please, let us talk. My sources tell me you bested *two* vampires. Will you tell me more about this? I will answer questions for you. You have questions about your new condition and I have been enjoying this Gift for more than two thousand years."

"I have no interest in anything you might say. I know my enemy and you are a liar." His host crossed his arms, his earlier politeness erased. Rakha returned a tight smile, reminding himself to be calm.

"Humor me then. My priest. He is well?"

"If you are who you say you are, you haunted him last year. This is how I learned about the old vampire that turned him."

"Ah, yes," Rakha responded, delaying and deciding what to reveal. He had indeed worked his consciousness into Corescu and his offspring during their chaotic last months, but he had been doing so from the spirit realm and unable to visualize the fleshed dimension. Spirits only see the land of the living if they have *eyes*, as in, possessing a fleshed being. But he would not explain these abstracts to his fledgling *vampyr* host, so he attempted a redirect.

"You would like to know more about me, then?" he asked and the preacher did not say no. Rakha smiled; the more Agricola allowed him to share, the more human sympathy he would arouse. Getting to the preacher through his emotions would be the way to go. "I was born in the year 837 BCE." He paused, satisfied by Agricola's stunned expression. "Born again as *Vampyr* in 800 BCE. I am immortal and expect I shall continue my existence until the end of time. Meeting you has made me young again and I wish to know you better."

"I don't want to know you," the man said without inflection.

"Isn't there anything I can answer for you?" Rakha used every ounce of his mental power to read the youngling's mind, but nothing came forth. He turned to the Unseen.

"He wonders how many vampires roam the earth," they whispered in response and Rakha grinned.

"Now that Paul Black is dead, would you be interested in how many of our kind remain?"

The preacher's brow lifted although he tried to disguise his interest with a scowl. "Why should I care?"

Rakha made a mental count, able to sense them all except the priest. "Counting the two of us and my priest, there are five. Of these, Rakha spawned only the priest," he said with pride, his hands to his sternum. "And only Rakha is able to hop hosts."

"None of this has anything to do with me," Agricola said.

Rakha almost laughed, but he hadn't been thrown out. He maintained his penitent posture and listened to the advice of the Helpers. *"He is curious about the priest..."*

"I will go, but allow me to share about the priest, the one you call Mark Corescu." His host shrugged, but his eyes revealed his great interest. "His congregants called him Father Markus, an oh, how he inflamed my interest. When I laid eyes on him, commanding the spirit realm to protect and bring peace to his parishioners, my heart swelled with desire. He is, so far, my greatest infatuation, and to date, the most difficult to obtain."

He had said the right words for the preacher relaxed his angry posture. Rakha had an idea and he softened the wall preventing Agricola from seeing his thoughts. Then he sent his mind back to the evening he first saw the village priest that would soon become his partner. Their pairing had lasted only a few days, but each hour had been precious. When he sensed Agricola peeking at what he left available, he continued.

"I came upon a small village where a celebration had grown into a bonfire with dancing and music. Oh, the music!" The night returned to his memory in vivid detail and the preacher sat at rapt attention, perhaps as infatuated with the priest as Rakha had been. "I came to see who might make a nice meal and beheld my priest. Ahh! You should have seen him. Strong, comely... You have seen his glorious appearance so you know." His host made a tiny nod. "Father Markus stood before the tiny congregation, blessing them, commanding the very *Creator* to bend to his man-sized will. I determined in my heart that this man would be mine. I had walked alone for many years and it was time I reproduced. And I had found the one I needed."

"Please continue," his host whispered and steepled his hands under his chin.

"From there, I wooed him. I tried many different tactics and it took a long time. See, he knew his enemy and rebuked me often. He was not easy to manipulate."

Inclining his head toward Tony, Rakha indicated his host would cause similar problems for him if it ever came to that. Tony only smiled.

"But I always get what I desire. And he was everything I wanted and more. If only I could have had more time with him, things would have been very different for me."

"That is a very interesting tale," Agricola offered in a soft voice. "But Mark is with God again. When will Satan learn he will never see victory over God? It amazes me that he keeps trying when he knows he has lost."

"He doesn't *know*, Tony. May I call you Tony?" The man shrugged and Rakha continued. "He sees much more victory than your precious Nazarene. I can see your line of reasoning and it leads to those prophecies of the End."

"Yes. In the End, Satan and his angels will be cast into the lake of fire to be tortured forever and ever. Revelation 19."

"The book of Revelation is a *prophecy*. It has not come to pass. Who's to say it is accurate? It is my belief that the devil is writing the End right now. He is ahead in the score count, and look around you. This world bows to him. Every nation, every tongue, he has servants everywhere. And your beloved God has but a handful." Rakha's voice softened. "You are on the losing team."

Agricola sighed and fake-yawned. "Is there anything else?"

Rakha gave him a chuckle. "One more thing. Have you conquered your bloodlust by *feasting* on the word of God? I find this fascinating." He had caught his host off guard and so he added, "Have you not supped on blood since that time with my priest?"

He still did not reply; Rakha had finally hit on a weakness in the preacher's staunch exterior. The young vampire was certain of his God, but not sure of his conviction regarding blood drinking. It was time to turn the screws.

"Can you pray yourself out of this?" Rakha drew his thumbnail across and down his forearm, dragging a ragged gash through his flesh. He leaned forward and held his wound for the man to see. Oh, the anguish in Agricola's face! And there was the other thing all vampires would recognize: lust, and he had it *bad*. The preacher was not cured or miraculously healed. Agricola lusted for blood as surely as all of their kind. In addition, Rakha read in Tony's eyes that he was *starving*.

"Pray, preacher, pray to your unseen God. Pray He will fill you as my blood

106

could," Rakha taunted sending the words to Tony's mind. He did not intend to allow the scoundrel to drink his blood, but he may be able to drive the man to *try*. *"The blood is hot, filling, and alive. You could go several months on one drop of this ancient ambrosia…"*

Agricola's body went on full alert and he could not look away, his eyes riveted to the flow.

"This is everything you have ever wanted, little Tony. Take it, you have earned it. Oh, how hard you have slaved for your God!" Again, Rakha sent his words telepathically because of how it unnerved the struggling vampire. He dipped his finger in the blood and put the finger then to his tongue. "Mmm, Little Tony. Mmm…"

"NO!" His host leapt to his feet and backed to the living room threshold. "Jesus said 'I am the Bread of Life! I am the Living Bread which came down from heaven. If anyone eats of this bread, he will live forever'!" Agricola backed further, now standing in the hall. "It is written, 'The bread that I shall give is My flesh! I give My flesh for the life of the world'!"

Rakha frowned and stood, his wound closed.

This vampire's will is very strong, his devotion much more advanced than that of my priest.

He stepped toward the exit and kept his eye on Tony stepping shakily backward down the hall. He sent the Unseen, *"I see the challenge, my friends. I see what had you so excited. And don't you worry. I can defeat him. I will have to do it correctly and patiently, but his weakness has been revealed…*

"I command you to leave!" the preacher barked from his spot down the dark hallway. "Leave! Now!"

"I will see you again, Tony," Rakha said and reached the front door. Tony's footsteps retreated, scrambling up the stairs. Rakha listened as he entered a room and slammed the door. With a wry shake of the head, he jogged to his car.

"Your favored vampire has deluded himself into a false security. A few old sayings will not supply his fuel for long. He will grow weak and his faith will fade in same measure as his strength." Rakha spoke aloud to his invisible companions always present. "Then I will make him renounce his God. After which, I will kill him, send him to the hell he fears so much."

The Unseen cheered and Rakha worked on his plan. This had been an excellent night.

21

But encourage one another daily,
As long as it is called Today,
So that none of you may be hardened
By sin's deceitfulness.
Hebrews 3:13

WHEN SARAH ARRIVED, TONY HAD HORS D'OEUVRES
and drinks on the ready. He didn't want to be left again without
foodstuffs and since he had always loved to eat, he knew what to stock.

Sarah stepped from the kitchen holding a cup of cocoa and a mini
cheese croissant. "These are delicious," she said saluting her snack. "I
didn't know I was hungry until I smelled these babies."

Tony grinned at her generosity—they were not special, he'd picked
them up at Winn Dixie deli. But she had eaten three; maybe they were
okay. He watched her choose a seat in the study, tickled that she'd worn
blue jeans and sneakers. Before tonight, he'd only seen her in slacks.
The dressed-down Sarah Tracey was even more beautiful.

With a notion he might enjoy a few minutes pretending he wasn't
a creature, Tony asked her about her childhood. For thirty minutes, he
learned how a young Sarah Smithson grew up in Tennessee, the middle
of three daughters, happy, un-traumatic, both parents were in the
ministry, and she loved tiny dogs, Pomeranians being her favorite
breed. Tony gobbled every detail, and the clock alerted them nearly an
hour had passed since she arrived and she set down her empty pastry
plate.

She offered a new smile. "I sure can talk, I know." She widened
her eyes. "Your turn. What's on your mind? There's a definite crease,"
she said and lifted a finger to point to his brow.

Tony grinned and pulled a light chair close to sit near. "You caught
me. I've been putting it off. Something happened last night. I could use
your insight."

"I'm at your service," she said with a sparkle in her huge eyes. Tony
hated to bear bad news, but he asked God to help him do it well.

Tony took a deep breath. "I'll just dive right in. Last night after my
Pastor's meeting, I met another vampire." Sarah stopped chewing, her

brows raised, but she did not interrupt. "He told me his name is Rakha and I learned through conversation that he had come to kill me."

"Heavens!" Sarah offered sitting upright.

Tony admired Sarah for not becoming hysterical since it was all he could do to remain calm. "This creature is the one who turned Dr. Corescu. He has been around for two thousand years," Tony whispered in deference to the statement's incredulity.

Sarah's mind began to trace back time, thinking of past history and what the demon might have witnessed. Tony caught the gist and cleared his throat.

"I didn't let him talk too much," Tony interjected, "because I didn't trust him. I see him as mostly demon so that means he'll spend our time together trying to trick me into screwing up."

"Wow, I agree," she said, still wondering how it went down. "It looks like you did okay. You don't look hurt."

Tony huffed with a wry shake of his head. "There were a few hairy moments when he tried to get me to drink his blood."

"Oh, Tony, I'm so sorry," Sarah said her voice packed with empathy.

"I was tempted. I almost succumbed. I need you to pray for me to overcome this trial. God protects me, but when I faced that monster, my judgment was altered. I don't want him to be able to trick me like that again. And he will be back."

"Yes, I will. I'll start tonight. I care about you..." Sarah stopped herself and said, "I've only known you a few days and God keeps you on my mind every minute. I'm at war for you, trust me."

Tony reached for her hand and she watched as he brought it to his lips to kiss the outside. "Thank you. I don't deserve all that. Thank you so much." She offered a sad smile and when he released her hand, she covered the area he kissed and held it in her lap.

Finally, Sarah sighed with a new smile. "You are certainly the most exciting man I've ever met. I can see that together, we're going to have nonstop adventure."

Tony chuckled and liked that in her mind, they were joined. "I overheard you with John that first time you were here. You said you see demons. What is that like?"

Sarah nodded and dropped her grin. "I was saved in my teens and in college, I attended a Holy Spirit conference where the pastors offered to pray for our future ministries. I went up and they asked what I wanted to do for God. I said I wanted to pray for deliverance." She paused and ran her fingers through her short hair. "My mom and dad were Apostolic and believed in all that, so I watched a lot of deliverances up to this point."

Tony nodded and did not interrupt. Ironically, before he attended Sarah and her husband's worship service a year ago, he spent his life *avoiding* apostolic display. The night the Traceys prayed for the assembly, of which Tony had been part, Tony's life among vampires soon began.

"The prayer team laid hands on my head and I went home. Over the next few days, I began to see demons, and over time, God taught me how to deal with it."

"It sounds frightening," Tony offered although his words may seem silly coming from a vampire. Sarah's reaction did not reveal that; she nodded with empathy.

"If I didn't have the Holy Spirit so close 24/7, it would be. On the flip side, I don't see angels, so that's someone else's job, I guess."

Tony released a small huff and she asked him about it. "I've seen an angel. He came in the form of a sheriff's deputy and saved me from getting pummeled by Paul." Tony's gaze turned to the dark yard.

Sarah beamed a new smile. "Praise the Lord! That's what they're for! 'What are angels if not ministering spirits sent to serve those who will inherit salvation?'" Sarah quoted the Scripture and followed his line of vision to the yard. Tony stiffened and got to his feet. "What is it?"

"It's Rakha. He's in the trees." Tony swiveled to place his back to the window and his body blocked Sarah from view of their peeping Tom. "You head home. He doesn't get the pleasure of meeting you."

"Be careful, okay?"

"I will. Pray for me." Tony walked with her to the foyer and she turned.

"Give me a hug." Without awaiting a response, Sarah pulled Tony close, her arms wrapped tight and standing taller, her lips at Tony's ear. "God bless you and keep you, Tony Agricola," she whispered before releasing.

Tony had only the briefest moment to reciprocate before she broke free and opened the front door. He would have enjoyed the contact a little longer, but he was walking her to her Volvo. When she had belted in, Tony scanned the trees for his nemesis. Rakha remained, for whatever reason obediently awaiting Sarah's departure.

"Call me tomorrow," she said and switched on the car. Tony nodded and by the time her taillights disappeared over the horizon, a stealthy footstep approached from the side yard. Tony turned to face the devil and asked God for help. *Again.*

❧❧

Sarah's mind raced with concern over Tony and that monster's visit. Although certain God held the man in His mighty hand, she worried just the same. When she assigned more thought to her true complaint it came back to this: *Why does that sweet man have to go through all this hell?*

She asked the Lord and heard the same Scripture every time: *God's ways are high above man's ways.* So tonight when she left Tony's house, Sarah drove her antsy self to Barnes & Noble. Strolling row after row of books usually calmed her nerves and gave her pleasure.

The store had very few patrons this late and she checked the time on her cell, 8:15. The first two aisles she perused were New York Times Bestsellers and she gravitated toward the ones with the most striking covers. She lifted a new whodunnit and at the moment she peeled open the book, a siren alerted from the ceiling of the store. It had been some mechanical quirk—a male voice immediately apologized over the PA— but when Sarah returned her focus, she had startled enough for the thick new interior book pages to slice her forefinger.

"Oh, goodness," she said her eyes jumping to both sides for a cloth or tissue. In another moment, she blind-fished into her purse with her other hand, her eyes to the sliced skin. It didn't hurt and even as she grasped a slip of paper in her bag, the wound disappeared. Sarah froze, staring at a miracle.

There it is, Abba—that Tree of Life—it's inside me...

Sarah blinked and slowly daubed the miniscule drop of blood onto her retrieved napkin. She shouldn't be so surprised, but she was, and her mind raced with implications—brand new now that her flesh healed like magic even when away from Tony.

But it was okay. She was okay.

With a wry shake of her head, Sarah left the aisle and headed for the Bible section. She was reading titles and thinking about Scripture and did not notice another shopper scrutinizing her with intent. Sarah finally looked up, the young woman blushed deep red.

"Oh! I'm sorry!" she gushed and stepped close, covering her mouth. Sarah waved away her concern and gave her a smile. It was a young woman, mid-twenties, with an enviable mane of light brown wavy hair and a sweet, heart-shaped face. The young woman put out her hand. "I'm Elizabeth. I recognized you from this," she said and held up a hardbound book, back cover first.

"Hey," Sarah said happy to have Ira's memory returned by surprise. The book had been his last before his death and dealt with soul-ties and forgiveness. "I love that one, truly."

"I saw you and your husband speak in California a few years ago. I'm Elizabeth Hawken; you shared the stage with my then-husband, Aaron."

"Oh! Sure, I remember that," Sarah said nodding. The minister she spoke of had been a smooth one with a face made for the camera. When she realized the young woman called him an ex, she hated to think the reasons why. "So how are you? How did you end up in Alabama?"

"God's providence," she said and tucked Ira's book under her arm to free both hands. "I heard about Pastor Ira's passing and my condolences."

"Thank you," Sarah said with a genuine smile. "Every day with him was a blessing." A pleasant nudge tickled her within and she asked the youngster if she wanted to chat over some coffee.

"I sure would," she said and they made small talk all the way to the café. When both women had a choice beverage, they sat in a 2-seater round high-table and shared a mutual grin. "In the book aisle," Elizabeth said with a waggle of her eyebrows, "did God tell you we should go have coffee?"

Sarah grinned with a laugh. "He did, but I don't usually get called on it!" The young woman's countenance shined and she sipped her coffee, her eyes still in Sarah's.

"Good, because I felt like I should say yes. I wonder why. This is a divine appointment so it means something."

Sarah agreed and they fell into praising the Lord in various testimonies and personal stories, each woman sharing equally. When it seemed only ten minutes had passed, the PA system announced the store was closing. Sarah was about to begin the goodbyes when Elizabeth's cell buzzed and her eyes went to the screen by reflex.

"Rakha Tep," the name read and Sarah's blood ran cold.

Elizabeth picked up the device, scowled, and pushed the off button. She looked up and noted something odd in Sarah's expression. "What's wrong? What happened?" she asked and looked around.

Sarah shook her head. *It can't be. How crazy and coincidental. No way...* Sarah continued to disagree with what she knew in her spirit to be true—the demon that harassed Tony was in contact with Elizabeth

Hawken. But *why?*

"Sarah, what?" Elizabeth whispered, leaning in and putting her fingers to Sarah's arm.

"That name," Sarah began, for spiritual reasons not wanting to say it aloud. "Who is that?"

Elizabeth looked at the dark screen and back, picking up Sarah's seriousness. "A new client. Why?"

Sarah sucked her teeth, buying time and asking God for insight. Finally, she said only, "Tell me about him."

Elizabeth nodded with a grim expression, either from her memory of the man or intuiting Sarah's state of emotion. "He is an awful man who contacted me about my sculpture. Said he learned about me from one of my art professors."

"Why do you say he's awful?" Sarah asked in a near whisper, her spirit assuring her who it was.

Elizabeth took a deep breath and looked at her hands. "I can't put a finger on it, but everything about him makes me uncomfortable. Why? Do you know him?"

Sarah's respirations hyped as she wondered what God wanted her to do. "A friend of mine knows him and… he's not …nice."

The store closing announcement came again and both women slipped off the tall stools to their feet. It was almost nine and Tony could be entertaining the devil right that moment.

Sarah met Elizabeth's eye. "There's a diner next door. Will you come so we can talk some more?" Sarah asked and Elizabeth accepted without reservation. Sarah didn't know what she would say, but she would need to warn the girl to avoid Rakha at all costs.

"How much are You going to want me to tell her about you-know-what?" she asked inside, not willing to say *vampire* to God.

The all-night diner sat catty-corner to the bookstore, so the women walked the distance across the brightly lit lot. It was time Sarah found out how open her new friend was to odd moves of God.

  

Tony leaned against the doorframe watching Rakha approach. The vampire grinned when their eyes met and he climbed the four steps of the wraparound porch to stand a few feet away.

"My precious baby vampire, you are looking well."

Tony sighed for him to see and made a show of pulling the door closed behind him so the two of them remained on the dark porch.

"What do you want?" Tony asked, wishing he had been able to spend many more hours with Sarah and zero with the monster.

"Let's take a stroll," Rakha said with a vague gesture to the yard.

"I'm not in the mood for a stroll. What do you want?" Tony crossed his arms at his chest and assumed his sternest gaze. So far, he felt no fear, but his internal complaint to God had been activated—*why me? Why me? When will this end?*

"Don't be such a *baby*." Rakha reached for Tony who flinched before he caught himself. Rakha laughed. "You're supposed to be this undefeatable foe, this superman, and you're frightened of little old me?"

"I'm not frightened," Tony replied and dropped his arms to step into his unwanted visitor. Rakha stepped back in equal measure, his grin falling. "I'm just not interested in spending any time with you. I don't want you here. I think we're done."

Rakha smiled wider than before as if wanting to reveal his unnatural fangs, elongated even though he was not consuming blood. Tony shuddered at the sight and hated he might appear squeamish.

"Just leave. I can't see you tonight. Be gone." Tony turned for the door.

"I wonder what your friend Sarah would say if she were to meet me tonight."

Tony spun around and faced Rakha, his eyes aflame.

"You have some passion after all!" the vampire teased.

"I will not warn you again, you monster," Tony hissed between tight lips. "Do not speak of her. I will *kill you* if you go anywhere *near* her. Do you understand me?" Tony's face flushed with rage and his heart raced in his chest.

"Tony, Tony. Relax. You're going to give yourself an aneurysm. Look at you. Even with practically no blood in your system, you managed to turn as red as an apple." Rakha was still laughing as he watched Tony pull open the screen door and stomp into the house. "Can I come in?" the vampire called through the closed door.

"No, no more. Go away. You are no longer welcome here and leave me alone!" Tony had lost his temper and had stopped listening out for God's input but how could he allow the demon to haunt dear Sarah? He may have missed something God had wanted him to do, but he continued to argue in his heart.

Maybe I did it my way, but he's leaving. The monster is gone. What's wrong with that?

The vampire had reached his car hidden on the far curb. Tony shook his head. He should have allowed God to lead.

Rakha left with the upper hand. Now he knows how to get me riled up. That gives him power.

Tony kicked himself mentally and switched off the lights in the foyer.

"Geesh, I'm horrible at this!" Tony mumbled his thoughts aloud as he trudged to his study. Maybe he could forget that Rakha had even visited tonight. Maybe at sunrise, he'd be delivered.

Twenty-nine days, so… maybe.

A man could hope.

22

Who will rise up for me against the wicked?
Who will take a stand for me against evildoers?
Psalm 94:16

ELIZABETH AWOKE IN A COLD SWEAT, SITTING BOLT upright even as she returned to consciousness. A movement out of the corner of her eye; she inhaled, for a moment wondering if she was still asleep. But there was nothing to see; her room sat quiet, dark, only a soft white light from the late moon filtered through her slatted blinds. She reached for her phone and awoke the screen. 2 A.M.

What was that? She asked inside. It had been a nightmare, but had no details. She was afraid, but why? She searched her memory and nothing pinged back. She dreamed nearly every night, but nightmares?

I haven't had a nightmare since Aaron asked me for a divorce.

Planned with meticulous care, Aaron had taken her to a busy Italian restaurant, filled her with food and wine, and then brought the conversation around to her shortcomings as a wife.

"When we first married, you were different. You wanted to see me happy and you sought to be my helpmate, the Proverbs 31 wife. These past two years, all you do is complain. You complain when I'm on the road too long and when I'm home, you complain that I don't make enough money. You don't like the way I run the finances, you don't like the way I treat your family, you don't like sleeping with me; nothing I do is right. You've pushed me away so far that I can't come back."

Elizabeth had sat stunned, the rich food threatening to bring on nausea with the sudden stress of his accusations. One by one, as she considered each slander against her marital performance, she found them all baseless or lies. Yes, she wanted to be God's idea of the perfect wife, but she didn't complain to him all the time.

Did I? No, I'm sure I didn't…

Did she disapprove of his bookkeeping? No, he spent a lot of money when on tour, but Elizabeth couldn't remember ever mentioning her misgivings. And she had no issue with how he behaved for her mom and Sean. What did he mean? And what was that about their intimate relationship?

He continued. "This week in Chattanooga I had an epiphany—we're not meant for each other. I married you out of some sort of obligatory emotion, I felt responsible because you fell so crazy for me. I should have been honest with you then and there, but I'm just too nice. I can't keep being nice just so you're happy. I am not happy and God wants me to be happy, too."

Elizabeth couldn't speak. Her entire life, she'd only had one man, one lover, one boyfriend, and she married him. And wasn't he supposed to be a safe choice? A preacher would never hurt you, right? She believed she'd be Mrs. Aaron Hawken forever.

"Elizabeth, say something," he had said when she was quiet too long. "I want a divorce. I hired a lawyer and tonight, I'm going to a hotel. I suggest you get a lawyer because we're selling the house and liquidating everything."

"Aaron," she had whispered, aware that the other patrons prevented her from crying out, "I don't want a divorce…"

Her husband stood up, placed his napkin on his plate, and stepped close to kiss her forehead. "Bye, Liz," he had said. "You'll hear from my lawyer tomorrow."

Then he walked away.

Elizabeth had met him there for their date and so she drove to their house alone. Because the marriage bed only taunted her, she had gone to the guest room and slept on top of the covers, crying until she fell asleep. Somewhere in the night, the demons of hell piled upon her and the nightmares they delivered had her sitting up at 2 A.M. just like tonight.

That's the nightmare, she realized. The night Aaron left is the night she dreamed of being chased, caught, and viciously gang-raped by a faceless trio of men.

But that wasn't the first time I dreamed that!

Elizabeth switched on her bedside lamp and wiped her cheeks, aware that she had started to cry. *The first time I dreamed that was the night of my high school graduation.*

"Oh, God, please erase it!"

Elizabeth covered her face, but the nightmare replayed now that she had called it up. Eighteen-year-old Elizabeth in her cap and gown, walking to the high school gymnasium for commencement. Halfway around the campus, with the building in sight, three men jumped out from nowhere and pushed her to the grass. What was day turned to night and dream-Elizabeth screamed for help, her body now in an enormous cavern. Stalactites reached for the ground in her vision, as lying on her back now, the men ravaged her body. She felt nothing, but the fear was enough to wake her up then as it did tonight.

"Take it away, please," she prayed, this time softly and peeking toward the ceiling.

At eighteen and then at twenty-three, Jesus had removed her fear and the memory enough to go on. She matriculated with her class, no problem. The morning after Aaron dumped her, Sean helped her hire the right attorney to facilitate her divorce. Tonight, wanting to pretend she never met the vile Rakha Tep, she prayed for the Lord to take away the memory of the nightmare and of the imaginary sexual assault that tore more at her peace than her body.

"Rakha and his friends will do this to you…"

Elizabeth's eyes flew open and she covered her mouth. That sentence had not come from her own mind. It came from beyond. Elizabeth reached for her phone, pressed the call icon and stared at the screen. Who could she call? She knew no one.

Call Sarah…

That voice was familiar. That was what she had come to know as God's voice speaking to her spirit.

But I'm too embarrassed…

The famous evangelist had shared her personal cell number and address when she invited Elizabeth to come over the following night. Mrs. Tracey, Sarah, said she wanted Elizabeth to meet her friend Tony who knew more about the horrible Mr. Tep.

Again, her subconscious encouraged her to reach out to her new friend and again, Elizabeth just couldn't imagine it.

I can't tell her about that dream. I just can't. I want her to like me, not think of me as some kind of freak. I'm not a victim!

Elizabeth set her phone to the table, screen-side down. This was the part she could never reveal. This was why she couldn't tell Sarah Tracey or anyone about the dream. Because it was her fault. All of it.

Elizabeth turned off her lamp and lay back. She pulled the covers to her chin and stared at the dark ceiling.

There's no getting around it, it was my fault. I started it.

She'd teased those boys back in 7th grade, called them names, told Jules Kemper he was ugly. Called Allen Hutchens a fart-knocker. If she had simply walked away, they wouldn't have done what they did.

"I deserved it. All of it," Elizabeth said under her breath, and she believed it was true. Even twelve years later, even when two different therapists told her she wasn't to blame, she was. They weren't there, they didn't see how fiercely she taunted those three senior boys.

"I'm sorry," she said to God and to the memory of the boys, crying again. *I ruined my marriage by starting it with deceit...*

She had lied to Aaron about being a virgin. The three seniors ruined her for marriage, but she never told anyone, not her mom, not Sean, not her teachers. The night they dragged her behind the practice field locker room and punished her for being so mouthy...

"There are many more ways to use your body," the evil voice said in her ear. This voice that for sure didn't come from God sounded sort of like those boys, hard, mean, raspy. *"And Rakha has lots of friends who will teach you new ways to please a man. We can't wait to show you these great and wonderful things!"*

"No!" Elizabeth hissed in the dark room, recalling a teaching Aaron had once given about commanding demons. "You hush in the name of Jesus!" she said in the same tone. The horrible voice said no more but the damp chill it brought to the air remained.

Elizabeth reached for her phone with a blind grab and woke the screen. Feeling stronger, she opened the message center. It was not even 3 A.M., she really shouldn't call Mrs. Tracey or anyone else at that hour.

Call Sarah... the gentle voice said again and Elizabeth did the next best thing. With a shaking hand, she texted three words to her new friend: *pray for me.*

Elizabeth then opened her music app and started her favorite gospel album. She closed her eyes and visualized an open field of wildflowers and the sun rising over the horizon. She might forever blame herself for what happened the day she turned twelve, but God would help her go on. She didn't need Aaron or any man. She had a new life in Alabama, a new shot with her father, and a brand new art studio in the trendiest section of town.

"I'm gonna be okay," she told the room. But she wouldn't tell anyone about the nightmare, about Rakha's voice in her head, or about the boys who stole her childhood. "I'm gonna be okay..." And she believed it.

23

"Thus says the Lord, the King of Israel,
And his Redeemer, the Lord of hosts:
'I am the First and I am the Last;
Besides Me there is no God'"
Isaiah 44:6

JONAH COULDN'T HELP HIMSELF. THE IMAGES FROM Jenn's research, the faces of the men that didn't age haunted him and two days later, he still hadn't shaken the eerie feeling that something was going on beyond their perception. Something conspiratorial, and Jonah hated not knowing the truth of a thing. This attribute treated him well during his law enforcement career. He'd grown into a veritable human lie detector by his third year in homicide. This is how he knew Agricola was telling the truth the few times they spoke. But this new evidence revealed the secret the man shielded the police from might be too large to keep to himself now that P.I. Jenn was on the case.

Dr. Mark Corescu and Paul Black, a.k.a. Saul White, hadn't aged. The end. Why? Jonah ran the licenses down on his own when Jenn was on errands, just to make certain someone hadn't screwed with her results for kicks. When he collected the photos himself, he got the same end result. Two males with no wrinkles over fifty years. This is why Friday night at 7pm, Jonah sat at Jenn's PC looking up a certain Reuben Stuckey. Because he was employed by one of their P.O.I.'s—Dr. Mark Corescu—Reuben Stuckey became a P.O.I. as well related to the Saul White / Paul Black investigation. In addition, Stuckey went on the MISSING register. Now that the guy's driver's licenses filtered in one by one, Jonah's heart fell.

Reuben Stuckey, 3344 Sherwood Drive, Atlanta, GA. Race, Black; height, 6'0'; weight, 165lbs; eyes, brown; hair, black; D.O.B., December 25, 1966.

1966. Fifty-four years ago.

Jonah rubbed his eyes. The monitor displayed nine separate D.L.'s assigned to this SSN and name. The dates ranged from 1982 to present and covered eleven states. In every photograph, Mr. Stuckey appeared to be on the young end of eighteen. If he was old enough to shave, Jonah would be surprised. *What the hell is going on?*

Jonah opened all of the pages simultaneously and allowed his eyes to go soft, searching for the common denominator, the missing link, some rational explanation for why three men, all associates, appeared to be the same age in their official documents.

And all the different states…

With a careful count, Jonah jotted down the capital cities the three men had registered a driver's license. Eleven, spanning the continent. *I could scour the database in those states for bloodless corpses…* The enormity of that task caused Jonah to scowl; he wasn't *that* interested.

What about outside the US? Agricola said he had gone to Europe. This thread may be just as ridiculous, but it carried more weight since the other suspect may be hiding overseas. Jonah pulled up his friendliest Scotland Yard associate, sending a message for him to return a call, Priority One.

"Whoa! Stuckey! I forgot about him!" Jenn said in an excited voice, coming up fast behind him to rest both hands to his shoulders. "Look at that! Sheez-Louise, Jonah! Three vampires!"

Jonah craned his face to hers, his expression harder than he liked. He didn't get it softened in time and she withdrew her hands in surrender mode.

"You gotta relax, old man," she said and in a cautious movement, kissed the top of his head. "I was joking."

"I couldn't stop thinking about it." He shook his head and rose from her office chair to grab her in a hug. She fit right into his body and his hug turned into a caress of her back. He sniffed her hair and rolled his face to her cheek. "You sure smell good," he said without thinking and she giggled. "What?"

Jenn stuck one arm out of the hug to hit some keys on the keyboard. "Does it smell like cinnamon?"

Jonah sniffed her hair again and grinned. "It sure does. Is that a new shampoo?"

Jenn laughed again and he released her. She dropped into her chair and reached blindly for his sleeve to hold tight. "I brought you a Cinnabon. It's in the kitchen, but first…"

Jonah looked at the door and she held him tighter. He loved pastries and even with all the stress of the moment, he loved her even more for thinking about bringing him sweets. She tugged his arm and he looked at the screen.

"Okay, P.O.I.'s. Hope Brannen looks normal, but then again, she's only twenty-five." Jenn had pulled up the young woman's driver's licenses for the past few years. "Okay and Anthony Agricola... normal." Jonah was happy on that one and he watched on. "Craig Connie Nixon..." she mumbled and hit some keys. "Normal guy."

"What about the Irish receptionist," Jonah said remembering her mostly for her fun accent. "Fran Booker."

"Francine Booker, yep, yep," Jenn said and the woman's driver's licenses were normal. "How about the redhead, I know you want to see her again," Jenn said joking and she typed in "Opal Jenkins."

Jonah made a *hubba-hubba* and watched the woman's driver's licenses populate. She was the murdered man's cousin and had been a fun one to interview. Jenn elbowed him and he laughed.

"Anyone else?" Jenn asked and then started typing again. She pulled up the evangelist who had been attacked by Black before he left the country. Her D.L.'s were normal. Jenn sighed, happy with herself and she leaned back to look at Jonah upside down. "Wanna eat some Cinnabon?"

Jonah kissed her forehead and she scrambled from the chair.

"Race you downstairs!" she said and she jogged from the room. Jonah followed but his phone chimed with his daughter's assigned tone and he stopped at the threshold.

"I'm hobnobbing with famous people!" the text read and a photograph appeared seconds later. Elizabeth stood in a brightly lit bookstore holding a hardbound book face-out, hugged into a tall, willowy woman Jonah recognized. He spun on his heel to the computer monitor and zoomed the last driver's licenses.

It was her—the evangelist. His worlds had collided and Jonah jogged downstairs to show Jenn.

❧

Sarah invited Tony to her house and he arrived at seven on the dot. She didn't tell him the details, but there was someone she wanted him to meet. In his new condition, Tony caught the stranger's aroma before Sarah opened the door: a floral shampoo or body wash that belied he'd be meeting a woman. Sarah pulled him into the house without delay and wrapped him up in a hug. He returned the embrace, his eyes closed, memorizing her scent and the feel of her lithe body in his arms. His chin came to her collarbone and he wondered why he'd been searching his entire life for a shorter woman. This one was perfect and he didn't pull away until she did.

"Tony, meet Elizabeth Hawken," Sarah said and led him into the living room by his hand.

A bright young brunette stood from the couch and approached. Tony shook her hand and thought of Rakha. The timing was a bit odd, that he'd touch the young woman's hand and suddenly—

His aroma...

It was the vampire's body scent. Tony dismissed it in a millisecond to concentrate on Sarah's friend. The youngster beamed with positive energy and an inner joy pulsated her aura.

"Nice to meet you, Pastor Tony," she said, her accent a bit on the California side.

"Just Tony," he said and grinned at Sarah.

"Come on in. Elizabeth has made an interesting acquaintance and maybe the three of us can decide what God wants to do about it."

Tony's interest piqued anew and he sat in a chair while the women both sat on the short couch. Sarah glanced at the young woman who gave a tiny nod and pulled out her phone.

"Elizabeth is new in town, but a few days ago, she received a text from a man with the name Rakha Tep..."

Tony's blood turned to ice before Sarah could go any further. Elizabeth offered him her cell and Tony took it, his eyes to the screen. It was an email and he scanned it twice; there was no question, it was the vampire. He didn't have to know it with his brain for his spirit yelled it loud and clear.

Tony cleared his throat. "So, Yakol... he is a real person?"

"One of my art professors," Elizabeth said with a cautious eye. "Sarah said I should ask him if he knew Mr. Tep and he said he didn't. I never would have questioned him if I hadn't met Sarah."

Tony nodded in slow motion, his mind racing with questions. Mostly, *why?* What did this woman have that Rakha wanted? Why had he chosen her in particular?

"She met with him Tuesday night," Sarah said, her voice soft and her head at a tilt. Her spirit seemed to be telling her the same thing— that Rakha meant to harm the young woman. Now what should they do about it?

"How did it go? Tell me what he did that gave you this worried expression," Tony asked the youngster. He leaned over his lap and the women also sat forward.

"Yes, well, he didn't look strange, I mean, at first glance. He was my height and well-dressed. He looked wealthy, I did not have any problem believing his story until our eyes met." Elizabeth visibly shuddered and went on. "He had been wearing dark Ray-bans and he sort of whipped them off..." She mimed the move and both Tony and Sarah nodded. "And when our eyes met, something happened inside me. I didn't trust him. I started ending the meeting and he started dragging it out." She shook her head and blew a puff of air. "I almost got him out the door when he started to flirt. It was forced and uncomfortable. When he finally left, I got in my car and locked the doors and just prayed. I felt awful, covered with slime, just..." She looked at Sarah and didn't continue.

Tony ran her story past again and exhaled slow. "We need to figure out how you landed in his radar." Sarah nodded and Elizabeth shook her head once.

"You need to tell me who he is." She touched Sarah's knee and said with a kind smile, "I am blessed to have met you, but you were desperate for me to come tell your friend Tony about this. Why?"

Sarah's lips parted and she turned to Tony. He got to his feet and motioned for the women to remain seated. "If you'll let me jump through a few hoops, I will fill you in as the Lord allows. Deal?"

Elizabeth rolled in her lips and gave a tiny nod.

"Had you seen him before?" he asked and she shook her head. "And you moved here from California?" She nodded. "Did you have an art studio there, too?"

"No, I was married and going to school off and on. When I got divorced, I moved here."

Tony narrowed his eyes, his mind lining up details. "Why here? Family?"

Elizabeth made a more or less gesture. "My dad lives in Georgia and I got a great deal on a studio space here, so it seemed perfect. Close to Dad but not too close." She grinned with muted humor.

"Georgia," Tony said, just mumbling as he thought.

"Yes, Whitford City," Elizabeth said and then corrected, "Carrollton, actually. He retired and is getting remarried in a couple months."

Tony's expression must have changed for Sarah stood and walked to his side. She touched his arm. "What is it?"

"Whitford City," Tony said, his voice croaking. Everything bad in his life for the moment found its origin in that place. He looked to Sarah. She'd been attacked there by Paul, but her face wasn't ashen. He turned to Elizabeth, her Part II even more suspicious. "Your father retired?" he asked, a black trepidation creeping up his spine.

Elizabeth offered a careful nod. "Yeah," she said just as slowly. "He was a police detective."

"Jonah Miller," Tony whispered and the young woman grinned.

"Yeah! You know him? You're from there?" she asked and got to her feet so all three were standing.

Tony inhaled, held it a few seconds and turned away. "Sit tight," he said and left the room. He hadn't been past Sarah's living room in his previous visit, but saw two choices as he hit the hall. One looked to be her personal bedroom so he chose the other, a guest room with an elliptical machine in the corner. The women would wonder what happened, but he needed to think. He needed to pray and God better listen; things were getting dire and the silent treatment was hard to bear. He closed the door and knelt beside the neatly made bed.

"What are You doing? Why involve that innocent little girl in all this hell? And that policeman? You want him in danger, too? These people don't have to suffer, Abba. I'll take it all on myself. Just dump it on me. Please, let me stand in the gap for them all..."

"Tony?" It was Sarah and she stood outside the room, her hand making a single knock.

"Come in," he said, knowing by the sound of their hearts that Elizabeth was with her. They filed in and he changed position to be sitting on the edge of the bed. He gave Sarah a head shake-shrug gesture. "I don't know," he whispered looking in her big eyes. "I don't know what He's doing and I don't want this girl to get hurt." He didn't look at Elizabeth.

Sarah walked close and the young woman remained by the door. "Say those sentences again inside," Sarah said in her softest voice, her gaze as gentle as an angel. She stood right up against him and draped one palm on his near shoulder.

He did as she suggested, his mind emphasizing the word "I" as he imagined she intended. She grinned and his heart swelled with new respect atop his present affection.

"See? It doesn't matter a hill of beans what you want." She peeked at Elizabeth who remained in the door awaiting an invitation. Sarah then whispered low, "God allowed Job's livestock and even his children to die. Job didn't want that, but we learned from Job that God does things his way for a reason." She kissed the top of Tony's head and he grew increasingly peaceful under her gaze.

"I agree," Tony said too low for Elizabeth to overhear. "But I wish He wouldn't send suffering on you guys. It's just not necessary. I can carry it. I want to."

Sarah's face softened and her eyes welled with tears. "You can be certain He knows your heart on this. Your selflessness is noted, I have no doubt. But you forget to consider—everyone's pain is meaningful to God's plan. He needs me to suffer so I can play my role and the same goes for Elizabeth and each person on earth."

Tony exhaled with a slow headshake, not disagreeing but not happy about such Truth.

"But you're right about this; Elizabeth doesn't need to know about *everything*," she said with an eye raise at the last word. "We'll tell her Rakha's a killer and she needs to stay away from him, no matter what."

Tony offered a small nod. His stomach emitted a tiny gurgle and Sarah took a casual step back and dropped the contact. "What about her father?" he asked no longer whispering. "I should at least share something of that connection because it will come up later somehow."

"Dad?" Elizabeth took a step closer but stopped as if being polite. Without missing a beat, Sarah backed to help keep the girl in place.

"I'm from Whitford City," Tony said. "I met your dad last year when he was working a case. I was what he called a Person of Interest and was interviewed a few times about some of the suspects."

"Oh, okay," Elizabeth said as if it was nothing.

"Yeah, well, this week I learned that they reopened it and his replacement might start coming around to question me again."

"But, you're innocent," Sarah added on his behalf and he nodded.

"I'm innocent of what they're investigating. A reporter was murdered last year and I only met him once and went on my way. I don't know anything about his death. The thing that has me in hot water now is that their prime suspect—also dead—left me his entire estate. So your father's replacement and the local cop who stopped by to talk off the record, say I profited from the suspect's death. I'm guilty in their eyes because their suspect was wealthy and generous."

Tony paused. He had glazed over so much of the truth, stretching it as thin as possible to keep the girl unaware of vampires. Her expression remained soft and open, having no trouble believing the tale. He waited for her to speak, but neither of them did. They were both looking at his face. He met Elizabeth's eye and inside counted to five, she didn't blink. Was she breathing? His chin swiveled to Sarah and her gaze had gone soft. *Dammit! They're hypnotized!*

"Sarah! Wake up!" Tony shouted covering his eyes with his palm.

"Oh! Sorry!" she said, her voice high. "Okay, come on, honey, let's get some tea. Tony, take your time." Sarah ushered Elizabeth into the hall and turned to see Tony's face. "Just go on home, eh?" she whispered and blew him a kiss.

He nodded and she disappeared with the youngster to the kitchen. Thirty-three days without sustenance. *My body is going to try to get it anyway. Come on, Abba! Get me out of this! But there I go again. Me me me.* Tony wanted to scream. But instead he clenched his jaw and slipped out the front door.

24

Pray…that we may be delivered from unreasonable and wicked men;
For not all have faith. But the Lord is faithful,
Who will establish you and guard you from the evil one.
2 Thessalonians 3:2-3

"HOW'D YOU LIKE TO PLAY DETECTIVE A FEW HOURS?"
Jenn asked, pulling on blue jeans on her side of the bed. Jonah watched her long enough that she wiggled her behind in extra measure until he chuckled. "Well? Can your mushrooms take the day off?"

Jonah sat up and put his feet to the floor. It was Saturday and there would be no watering or rotation of his crops until Monday. He had been using Saturday to do repairs in the morning and watch baseball after lunch. He rose and trudged to the bathroom, dragging his feet with drama.

"Morning person," he mumbled with humor and made it to the head in time.

"Your favorite suspicious preacher is going to make a statement at the precinct this morning," she called across the room.

Jonah poked out his head. "Agricola? You're kidding."

Jenn grinned, wholly satisfied with herself. "Andy set it up for Pension. Seems his friendly cop routine gave Agricola the willies. He made an appointment for today at eleven to answer whatever questions Pension has for him."

Jonah returned to brush his teeth and spoke through bubbles and paste. "What do they want us there for?" he sputtered. "Erkleson know about it? Us, I mean?"

"Us getting married or us coming?" Jenn asked.

Jonah didn't reply. He finished minimal grooming and joined her in the room to dress. He flipped through the closet choices and when he pulled out a brown suit coat, Jenn whooped and clapped her hands.

"Miller and Speltz! On the case!" she said and turned for the hall to jog downstairs. "I'll put on the coffee!" she belted out and Jonah turned back to the closet. He donned his old regulars, brown slacks, black socks, faded blue long-sleeved shirt, and his dusty leather cop shoes. Maybe wearing the old gear would put his mind in police-mode.

He didn't want Agricola to have trouble, but if he was guilty, he should be held accountable.

The drive to town took an hour and Jonah tucked their Ford F150 into a visitor slot. A few Unis passed without looking at their faces but Jonah recognized them anyway. He didn't want to have any coworker reunions, but expected Jenn would. When they entered the glass front door into the lobby, a dozen citizens ambled about their various concerns and Jonah met none of them in the eye. He headed straight for the back hall and Jenn passed him.

"Kipper!" she barked and waved at a female in blues. Jonah made a polite grin and kept walking while Jenn chatted and then jogged to catch up. She called greetings to several more police officers before they reached the detective den. The first to meet them was the captain heading out.

"Hey, Cap," Jenn said and shook his hand like an old friend. Jonah shook, too, but then moved on. Erkleson and Jenn made small talk and then Jonah heard the captain thank her for coming. "Sure, you can always count on Miller and Speltz. So let me go meet this new guy."

"Take him a lolly, he's green as a pickle."

Jonah snickered at Erkleson's remark and had reached his old desk, now occupied by a thirty-year-old child in an expensive three-piece-suit. The man stood and shook hands, Jonah not liking his limp-fish grip.

"Ammon Pension, Detective Miller, nice to meet you," the youngster said and his eyes flit to Jenn. He put his flaccid paw in her direction and she shook it. "Ammon Pension," he repeated and invited them to sit.

The desk Jenn used to occupy had been moved and now two wooden chairs sat before the detective's desk. Jonah and Jenn took a seat and Ammon did too. The man looked average, normal height, normal weight, his sandy blond hair had been shaved almost off and he sported a bushy mustache and no beard.

"Do you have a partner?" Jenn asked him scanning the room.

"Not so far. Cap-Erk said if I need one later, just say so." Ammon shuffled papers, seeking something in particular.

While Jonah considered what he just called their old boss, he noted the man's ordered mess. Stacks of folders haphazardly jumbled, a maze of paperclips on the chipped wood surface that Jonah used to scribble on, and no fewer than four old Styrofoam coffee cups on the rare empty spots. Maybe he had a system, but the word *chaos* came to mind.

"Here it is. Agricola left the country with Paul Black, eh?" he said not asking but reading Jonah's closing remarks from the case.

"Look close, I said I think he left the country with Black," Jonah said sounding like a grump in his own ears. "We didn't have anything to compel him to stay, so…"

"Yeah, we still don't have any evidence against him, but Cap-Erk felt the receipt of such a bounty warranted a bit more scrutiny. Erk also said you and Speltz could be of some help."

Every time the guy said "Erk," Jonah shot a look to Jenn who would make an invisible snicker. Before he thought of what to say next, their person of interest walked in, looking both directions until a man pointed them toward Pension's desk. The attack victim, evangelist Sarah Tracey had accompanied him and Jonah's mind flashed to the photo his daughter took with her days earlier. The two walked close, and Jonah and Jenn stood up. Ammon stood afterward, looking at the oldsters with a *pshaw*.

"I'm looking for Detective Pension," Agricola said. When Pension stepped forward to shake hands, he finished with, "I'm Anthony Agricola and this is Reverend Sarah Tracey."

"Pension, nice to meet you," the young officer said and pointed to the two chairs Jonah and Jenn had previously occupied. "Please, have a seat. Do you remember Detectives Miller and Speltz?"

Jonah shook Agricola's hand. "We've spoken, never met." Then he sent Tracey a nod and she smiled, actual beams of light seemingly emitting from her face. Jonah looked aside while Jenn shook with them both. She had also only met the woman. Agricola and the reverend settled in and Jonah and Jenn leaned on the nearest desk to be available. The pair looked as innocent as doves to Jonah though he maintained the poker face decades on the Force required.

"Thank you for coming in, Mr. Agricola, Ms. Tracey. Although, we didn't expect you, Ma'am," Pension said, leading, but neither civilian offered an explanation. Jonah thought the pair was peculiar; in his mind, he added it up: Black attacks and threatens to kill Tracey. Some weeks later, Agricola's on a 747 to Europe with the guy running from the cops. How did an innocent lay-pastor end up arm-in-arm with Black's supposed victim? *Supposed? Come on, Jonah,* he admonished himself, *you're not on this case. You're not on the force. Stop working so hard and let Jenn play.* He purposed to stop detecting and listened in.

"Mr. Agricola, I'm sure you want me to hurry, so here are my questions. First, did you leave the country with Paul Black this past September?"

Agricola's lips tightened and he reached into his back pocket to unfold a single sheet of paper. He handed it to Pension and Jenn and Jonah read it over his shoulder. Amid several lines of legal posturing and bravado, the man's attorney had provided a list of things Agricola would not discuss. Leaving the country with Black was one of those. Pension sucked his teeth a long second and set the paper to the messy desktop.

"May I keep this?" Pension asked.

Agricola nodded, leaning comfortably back. He shot a gaze to Jonah, fleeting and maybe accidental, but Jonah's skin prickled. *What was that?* He waited to see if the man would do it again, but he trained his eyes to Pension.

"Okay, let's see," the young detective said low, skimming his interview sheet. "Can't ask about the money. Can't ask about fleeing the jurisdiction..." Pension allowed a pause since he had accused Agricola just then sideways. The man didn't take the bait, but relaxed awaiting a question. Finally, the junior man sighed and looked up. "What can I ask you? Why did you come in?"

Agricola gave Pension a weary gaze and sucked his teeth. "I am innocent and I don't like the cops thinking I'm guilty. I came in to clear the air and let you know I will not be bullied." Agricola leaned over his knees, holding Pension's eye.

Jonah blinked; the young detective had leaned back in response. And did he just go pale?

"Detective Miller did not ask me about my relationship with Paul Black, so I'll give you that. Maybe writing it there in your little case file will give you some peace."

Jonah heard ice in Agricola's tone that he had not heard the few times they spoke on the phone last year. And did his voice sound deeper? Jenn had teased him when they were on the case that Jonah looked at the guy too much like a preacher, an untouchable that God wanted far away from the police. But now? Agricola's cool affect to an extent adjusted Jonah's opinion.

"At the time of the homicide you're investigating, I had accepted the task of spiritual advisor to Dr. Mark Corescu. I met Paul that night and we did not hit it off. He left some time that night as me and Hope Brannen prayed for Mark. Some months later, I saw Paul again and we were more friendly. At that time, I took on the task of becoming his spiritual advisor as well. I moved in with him and we grew close. By the time Sarah was attacked…" Agricola put his hand on the reverend's forearm. "…Paul and I were like brothers. I had no idea he knew Sarah or that he attacked her. I didn't know that until two months ago. In fact, the entire time I lived with Paul, I never saw him do anything illegal."

Agricola turned his eyes to Jonah on his final statement. Jonah knew why—the guy was telling the truth. At least for that one sentence, Agricola had no knowledge of any illegal activity for his roommate.

Pension made a noisy exhale. "I'm sure you feel great sharing all this useless—"

"The reason I'm sharing this," he said, the hard edge returning and he met Pension's eye. Again, the man visibly shrank back and Jonah noticed. "Is to demonstrate, at least to normal folks with common sense and no suspicious leanings, that Paul and I had become brothers in this time. We developed a kinship as deep as any I've had in my lifetime."

Jonah noticed he squeezed the reverend's arm then and removed his hand to his own leg.

"Because of this, Paul's estate was transferred to me by his legal representation."

"Because he died?" Jenn asked, the first time she'd spoken since they began.

Pension snatched Agricola's legaleze from the desk and shot it to Jenn. "Can't ask that."

"No, I'll answer as much as I can," Agricola said, this time looking at Jenn.

Jonah softened his peripheral vision to see if she flinched, but she didn't. Her eyes *did* widen, though, and she parted her lips into a tiny half-grin, which Jonah found just as curious.

"I don't have the cold hard facts about how Paul died, but I know he did. If nothing else, assuming his property legally transferred by his people is enough to convince me he's gone." Agricola ended his explanation and rose to his feet. Reverend Tracey did too, her smile as bright as when they arrived.

"Reverend Tracey, I'm sorry about your husband. I bought his last two books. Great studies. He was a good man," Jonah said without planning to. Everyone present looked his way for different reasons, but the reverend beamed him a new smile.

"Thank you, Detective. Ira was wonderful to me and he loved the Lord so much." She then put her right hand to Agricola's elbow and his eyebrows went up. He looked at her hand and then to her face and grinned. Jonah noted all this and was certain Jenn did, too.

Jonah expected Agricola to turn and leave without another word, but he caught Jonah's eye and tipped his chin.

"Can I have a minute?" he asked and Jonah excused himself, garnering eye-raises from both Jenn and Pension. Agricola walked them to the elevator and left their backs to the others, but turned three-quarters to look up into Jonah's face. "This is uncomfortable and out of my wheelhouse," he said low, pointing a knuckle to their folks at the desk. "But I'm still the same guy. How have you been? How's retirement treating you?"

Jonah took a moment to reply. They hadn't been pals, but the guy had been more preacher-like in their correspondence. Accepting that for a reason, Jonah answered in the same tone, "Fine, it was time. Speltz and I both got out. Getting married in December."

Agricola nodded with just enough emotion that Jonah saw he meant it. But the man wasn't done.

"The other reason I came," he said inching in. "Last night I met your daughter, Elizabeth."

Jonah regretted that his jaw dropped before he closed his mouth and resumed his blank expression. He murmured *mm-hhmm* and Agricola continued.

"She and Sarah are going to be friends now, and you would have heard about this eventually. It's not a secret, but it's probably fair to assume you're hyper-sensitive to anything relating to your daughter."

"That's correct," Jonah said, still low but more eager to hear anything noteworthy about their association. Such as, is Elizabeth likely to become involved in anything to do with this case. As if reading his mind, the man addressed the issue.

"If Pension wants to question me or my associates, or if he gets a warrant to search anything pertaining to me, Elizabeth might be involved because she will be around. Sarah visits me almost every day and the two girls are close already."

Jonah almost grinned when the man compared the reverend to his daughter as another girl, but instead he nodded once. "Understand." Then it flashed across his mind, *is this some sort of threat? That I should dissuade the department from following up?* Jonah narrowed his eyes, still holding the man's intense gaze. *Yeah, they really should just close the case again. There's nothing left to investigate. Paul's gone and he's not coming back.*

"Thank you for all you've done," Agricola said and put out his hand.

Jonah took it, the man's shake a firm and comforting connection involving two pumps. "It's nothing, and I tell ya the truth," he whispered lower than before, "this will blow over. I mean, Black is dead, your lawyers have covered you, Erkleson'll close it today."

"That would be a huge blessing," the man answered and released Jonah's eye to look toward the reverend. Jonah pinched the bridge of his nose. A weird headache had invaded behind his eyes and he turned to rejoin Jenn.

"Whatsa matter?" she asked low, putting her arm around his back and sidling close, wholly disregarding Pension who had turned to his computer monitor.

"Just my stupid head," Jonah mumbled and peeked at the elevators. The pair had exited and he exhaled. "That was weird."

Jenn chuckled. "You're weird." She turned to Pension to close their visit and in another minute, they were passing Erkleson's door.

"Miller," their old boss called and Jonah stepped to the threshold. "Anything we can use from the guy?"

"He's covered, Cap. He became best friends with Black and doesn't know anything about his death," Jonah offered in a monotone. "I say close it and move to something alive."

Erkleson frowned and looked at Jenn. "You agree with that, Speltz?"

Jonah swiveled to see her answer. Her two-second pause told him she did not agree, but she had never spoken against Jonah's opinions to their boss in the past. He watched her face to see if she'd do it now.

"Yeah, he's right. It's going to waste a ton of resources and that baby at Jonah's old desk would have better luck with something he can actually work. You're spoiling him in Cold Cases. He'll never get off the teat."

Erkleson regarded her with a lazy eye and turned to his work as if they had left. Jonah pushed away from his door and walked beside Jenn to the elevator lobby. Once inside and headed down, she elbowed him hard.

"What the hell, Jonah? Did you look into Agricola's beautiful brown eyes and let him hypnotize you into letting him off the hook?"

She waved her right hand in the air in slow motion. *"These are not the droids we're looking for..."* she said in a faraway voice.

"Well? It's the truth. You saw that letter. They're not going to get anything else from the guy. His explanation fits. There's no reason to believe anything fishy is going on." He hadn't been looking at her as he spoke but turned at the last word. Her eyes had grown huge. But, they were on the ground floor and the doors opened. Jenn greeted a few faces coming in and they walked to the exit at a clip, Jenn right beside him looking at his face. As soon as they hit the parking lot, she responded in a forced whisper.

"What the hell?! He grew *so very close* and lovey dovey with Paul Black, a man who hasn't aged in fifty years. There's plenty fishy here!" They had reached the truck, and she was still hiss-arguing. "Do you think they grew closer than he's ever grown to anyone in his life—and I quote—and he never knew the guy was ageless?"

Jonah opened the driver's side door looking over the hood. "I forgot about that," he said and then climbed behind the wheel. Jenn also got in and he started the truck. "But we'd never show Pension that ageless stuff, right?" He watched her face and her ticked-off expression took longer to melt away. "Aren't you investigating the vampire angle for fun?"

She looked out her window. "I guess."

"Yeah, you *know*," he said in a gentle voice he knew she enjoyed. "Let them close it and we'll play vampire detective together, off the record. Whatcha think?" She shrugged, still averted the other direction and he put the truck in gear. "I'll start," he said adding a chipper intonation now, "if Agricola knew he was ageless, then Agricola knew he was a vampire. That's where we're headed, right?"

Jenn looked over. "Right. So if he knew, then maybe he's a vampire, too."

"Aww, wait," Jonah said. "What sort of monsters are we playing at? Vampires don't go out during the day. They don't make heart-eyes at famous evangelist widows, and they certainly don't talk about Jesus to police detectives investigating him as a POI."

"Wel-l-l-l-l," Jenn said with her old humor, joining the game, "he worked some vampire magic on you at the end." She gave Jonah a sideways grin and he only raised his eyebrows. "I didn't hear what ya'll were saying over there, but I could see your face, not his. You looked like a child at a magic show." She assumed a blank stare and a goofy buck-toothed grin. "All you were missing was the drool."

Jonah glanced over and then back to the traffic. "Really?" he said thinking back. "For real, or are you exaggerating?"

"I wish I was," she answered with a snicker. "And Pension nearly wet his pants when Agricola asserted himself. Oh, that was beautiful."

Jonah nodded and said out the side of his mouth, "You were not immune, my pretty."

"What are you talking about? I didn't do anything weird. You two though, hilarious."

"Okay, Ms. Denial," he said with a chuckle and placed his right palm against his cheek to belt out in a high voice, "Oh, Mr. Agricola! You're so handsome! So debonair! You make my heart sing!" When finished, he looked over to catch her eye. She regarded him with confusion.

"I didn't say any of that?"

"Your eyes did," he said and gave her a smug grin. "When you asked him about Black's death and he gave you his full attention. You looked at him like you look at me after two shots of tequila." He chortled and she disagreed with a huff. Then she fell silent, likely thinking back to that moment and wondering if the guy had hypnotized her like she had accused Jonah. In another mile, she reached for the CDs in the glovebox.

"He's a vampire," she said withholding a snicker. "Maybe a special kind, but he's weird. I'm going to keep poking into his business. Keep researching his associates. If he has fangs, I'll find out."

Jonah nodded and had reached the moment to share his newest news. "Remember I showed you Elizabeth's text about meeting Reverend Tracey in the bookstore?" Jenn nodded. "Well, they're best friends now and he wanted me to know, in case the cops get a warrant and she might be at his house."

"Really? That's sort of... I mean, what an ass," Jenn said turned sideways in her seat.

"Naw, it was nice. He wanted to protect her," Jonah said and Jenn softened with a nod. Then he shot her a new grin. "Plus, I didn't think anything of it until today when the same lady arrived arm-in-arm with your vampire."

Jenn grinned. "You're playing!" she said with a huge smile. Then she assumed a more serious expression to add, "Are you okay with that? I mean, did you have an instinct that this was bad news or neutral news?"

Jonah hemmed, allowing his varied opinions to meld into something he could vocalize. "I don't like her being close with Agricola because of his unknown association with the ageless Paul Black." In his peripheral vision, Jenn nodded. "But Reverend Tracey has to be the most gentle and safe person in the world for my daughter to congregate with. I don't know what to think yet." He shot Jenn a new look that included a wink. "I expect my P.I. bride will let me know how the case develops against Count Agricola."

"Count on it," she said enjoying the reuse of his word.

Jonah sighed. "I'd like to be a vampire," he said as if daydreaming. "I'd bite you and make you a vampire, too. Every winter, we'd turn into bats and fly to the Bahamas."

"I'd like that," she said and selected a CD. When she inserted Randy Travis and his greatest hits, Jonah sang along. He had purchased the old country stuff for Jenn back when they were only co-workers, but now, he'd learned the words. It was good.

25

Then Gideon said to God, "Do not be angry with me.
Let me make just one more request.
Allow me one more test with the fleece…"
Judges 6:39a

THE DRIVE HOME FROM WHITFORD CITY HAD BEEN
pleasant. They did not discuss the meeting much beyond saying they
were both glad it was done. Sarah had a strong feeling in her spirit that
they would put the case of interest against Tony to rest for good, and
this gave Tony great peace. Inside, his spirit whispered of its own
accord, *"Day thirty-four, Abba. Almost there…"*

Tony walked Sarah to her door and they stood facing each other.
The sun had set and in Tony's special eyesight, the blue aura
surrounding all things had tinged pink around Sarah's head and neck.
He told her so and she pretended to coif her short hair.

"This day was good," she said, her voice soft. "You ready for
tomorrow?"

"Sure," Tony replied just as quiet, enjoying her full face-to-face
attention. Although not an ordained minister, Tony's lay-pastor
reputation had grown immensely before Paul turned him into a
monster. A local congregation had asked Tony to share a message, and
now that he'd met Sarah, he accepted. They would proceed as she
suggested; Tony would introduce his friends in his stead, launching
their ministry publicly and before the Body of Christ.

"Me, too," she said and Tony overheard a sentiment swirling in
her mind of, *"it will be my first public appearance since Ira passed…"* and he
said nothing. In another moment, her thoughts turned to Tony, how
she wanted to spend more time with him. Tony suppressed a grin.

Now what? If he was mortal, he'd kiss her. Sarah's mind sent a
similar notion, from her perspective, and he pretended he didn't see.

If we kiss, what then? Tony held her eye, thinking about how beautiful
she was, and she clasped both of his hands in hers. *Why does there have to
be a what then? If we kiss, we touch mouths. My mouth works… She's not a sex-
crazed teenager any more than I am…*

138

Tony took one step to be directly under her nose and Sarah lowered to meet his gesture. When their lips brushed, they remained, barely in contact, gentle puffs of air exchanged between them. Then Tony dropped one of her hands and then the other to put both palms to her throat. That done, he allowed the kiss to press in. He'd never kissed Hope, his last girlfriend (albeit how short-lived) before he met the vampires, and before her, he'd kissed three, total. His first real sweetheart had been older—him a high school senior and her a college sophomore. She constituted the only woman he had ever been to bed with. Now, as God's reluctant monster, sex had become a non-issue. But they were kissing...

Sarah moved her hands now to Tony's cheeks, her thumbs stroking his short goatee. Neither had opened the kiss for tongues, but nothing seemed amiss. Tony's lips seemed to melt into hers and he did not want to ever back away. In the end, it was Sarah who broke off the kiss, remaining close, and looking down at him, her eyes huge and watery.

"Good night," she said in a whisper and he moved his hands to her cheeks to pull her close for one more kiss. That done he smiled and backed off the small stoop.

"Good night," he said and waited for her to go indoors. As he walked to his car, the happiness that filled his soul caused his brain to fuzz and he assumed a stupid grin. He made it to his truck when a familiar sensation pricked his subconscious. With his hand to the door handle, he scanned the area 360 degrees.

Where are you? he asked inside and not addressing the vampire. Tony pocketed his keys and stepped away from the truck, facing a deserted playground directly across from Sarah's home. Focusing into the darkness with intent, Tony found he was able to see better as the light of the streetlamps gave way to the light of the moon. Then he saw it, the form of a man in the shadow of a tremendous oak tree on the far perimeter. Tony abandoned the thought of leaving and crossed the quiet road. Night had fallen in full and he traversed the dewy grass, stepping over the low cross-rail barrier, and into the park. Once he cleared the slide and the merry-go-round, he made a beeline for Rakha's silhouette.

"Look at this!" the old vampire said as he drew close. "You aren't nearly as pitiful as I had thought! I was truly hiding. There is hope for you yet. Well done!"

Tony didn't reply, but stopped twenty feet away and crossed his arms at his chest. "What do you want?"

"Oh, what do I want? Let's see…" Rakha thrust his hands deep into his pockets. "I want you on your knees before me, begging for me to save you and shouting curses at the Carpenter." He nodded as if in thought. "Yes, that is what I want."

"Not gonna happen," Tony said in a low voice. "Don't you have anything better to do than tail me around town?"

"Besides run down some supper now and then? No. I spend all my time thinking about *you*. Where have you been today?" As he spoke, Rakha sat on an iron park bench.

"I really don't have time for this," Tony sighed and glanced at the truck.

Rakha thought he was looking at Sarah's house because he added then, "Is there something you need to tell me about that kiss? Is there a flutter where a vampire's flesh sleeps?" He pointed a knuckle in the area of Tony's fly.

"Bye," Tony said and Rakha *tsked* in his cheek.

"Sit with me, Pastor Tony. Right here…" Rakha patted the opposite end of the bench with a sweet smile. "Indulge me. Keep me occupied. Isn't that what your intuition tells you?"

The old monster was right; Tony sensed he was supposed to keep him talking without revealing anything himself. He settled on the opposite edge of the cool bench. "What?" he asked, looking straight ahead and not at the vampire.

"I want to know what makes you tick. I want to know why you sit there with power that defies imagination and do nothing out of the ordinary."

Rakha had turned to watch Tony as he spoke, but he still didn't turn. "I didn't ask for this power, as you call it. It's a curse, and I fully expect it to be lifted any day now."

"Ah, a curse, okay," Rakha said with put-on concern. "How long do you have to wait? Very soon, you'll go insane in the blood thirst and attack everyone around you." He huffed once. "I hope I'm there to see that."

"That won't happen and I will wait as long as it takes," Tony replied. Inside, he ran down helpful Scriptures regarding forty-days. Rakha saw some of it and made a new noise of concern.

"Forty days? Is that how long it lasts?" he asked and nodded as if he'd discovered something amazing. "I will be with you on Day Forty-One and you will take my blood. Do you believe this?"

"I will not," Tony replied and tensed to rise.

"Wait, help me with this. Why do you obey a God you have never seen? I have firsthand experience with the force that compels me, but all you have are rumors and vague visions of ancient peoples."

"That's where you're wrong. I have the Spirit of God living inside me. I'm never alone. I'm safe with Him no matter what I see with my natural eyes."

"You believe very strongly, and that is rare."

Rakha stood and Tony finally turned to see him. Their eyes met and Tony regretted it. In those eyes was a memory of the vampire's blood and how he dangled it before Tony's starving face only days ago.

"Yes, I will feed you when you give up on the Carpenter to do it. I've been doing this for thousands of years and I never fail. In time, you too will bend to my will. I am as patient as you are."

"I will never give up on God," Tony said and rose to his feet. "He keeps His eye on me. He loves me."

"I love you, too," Rakha said in a soft voice. He reached out to take Tony's wrist and he allowed it. "And I would never let you go hungry."

Tony looked down at his captive wrist and turned to face Rakha, placing his other hand on top.

"My faith sets me free from this curse already. I will not give in. I will wait and He will be my food and my drink."

This time, Rakha made no reply, but remained as he was, facing Tony and holding one hand. Tony huffed a sad sound and waited for Rakha to break it off first. Finally, the vampire dropped the contact and returned his hands to his pockets.

"You are irresistible to me. I shall relish ruining you."

"May God's will be done with both of us," Tony offered hoping they were done. *But I'm going to run into him again and again until You deliver me. Hurry, Father. I am getting weaker so You have to be stronger...*

"I love it when you pray," Rakha whispered in an eerie undertone. "Until next time, holy man." Rakha turned to walk away.

Tony made his way to his truck, his forty-day projected end-date circling his mind. He ignored the empty hole in his middle; he was almost there.

۵۰۵

Rakha took the interstate out of Montgomery and traveled west on Old Selma Road, past his previous hunting spot and to the next few small towns, pondering when to overcome the preacher. The woman, Sarah Tracey, carried a blinding aura that all but eclipsed her shape; Rakha did not wish to go near that light, it being much too familiar. The Carpenter emitted such a glow and none of Rakha's kind would approach Him.

I cannot eliminate the woman… he thought and hated to admit that fact. Rakha mumbled aloud to the Unseen, "The preacher will complete his fall according to my will…"

"We're losing confidence in you," an eerie and ethereal voice answered. *"You could have destroyed that man of God already. You know this. The Carpenter is not covering him as before. You should have taken his life already. Your selfish motives will be your downfall…"*

Rakha disagreed. "I will accomplish my mission."

"You should heed our instruction. We have been doing this since time began and you want to do things your way…"

Rakha looked to the black landscape surrounding his luxury sedan as he slowed entering Burkville, Alabama, Population 155. He said low in the quiet car, "I know what I am doing. In the end, I will turn him over to you. You know I am fickle with my playthings. They mean nothing to me after the initial affection wears off."

He heard no reply, and slowed in front of a small community church. A shed at the back of the property revealed a low-wattage bulb burned and Rakha wanted to investigate. He tucked the Jag into the tree line and exited the car. In a low jog, he stayed near the forest that surrounded the structures and reached the shed. Inside, a middle-aged black man leaned over a worktable, repairing what looked to be a small gas-powered motor. After determining no other mortals were about, he made his move.

26

He will be a holy place;
for both Israel and Judah he will be
a stone that causes people to stumble
and a rock that makes them fall.
Isaiah 8:14

"REMEMBER WHEN THE COMPUTER USED TO SAY, 'You've got mail!'?" Jonah sighed. "I miss those days." He scrolled through the list and huffed. "Of course, checking it with my phone set to silent would nix that anyway." He grinned all by himself because sitting across the room at her desk, Jenn's full attention went to the pages of info she'd collected on Tony Agricola's doings. He saw a notification from a Messianic Jewish site he frequented and opened the mail. *"Whitford City's own Pastor Anthony Agricola to speak at Chavurah Yeshua in Montgomery, AL, Sunday, 6 PM…"* A quick read thru and he was ready to do it. Would Jenn go? Probably, if he couched it as a good day for investigation.

"Look at this, hon," she said without turning.

Jonah rose on creaky knees and positioned over her shoulder. She'd pulled up plane manifests and her cursor sat at *Agricola*. Again, he marveled at how easily she procured information with their retired status and he waited for more.

"June 28, Agricola flew one-way from Germany, to Atlanta, where he rented a car to Montgomery." Jenn scrolled and Jonah lifted his chin to adjust his bifocals. "June 26, late afternoon, he purchases two tickets at the counter. One for Agricola and one for White. They used their correct address…"

"Well, why not? We didn't have any evidence on Black. They knew that."

"Hmmph," Jenn mumbled and kept reading. "They land in Hamburg, get a ride to Mausberg where they rent a hotel room in Agricola's name. The concierge said they hired a car. So far, that's all I have. They slept over and drove out together in a car. Something happens so that in less than 24 hours, Agricola purchases a ticket for one and flies home."

Jonah thought of his Scotland Yard buddy who hadn't yet returned his call. Why not let Jenn try? "Check the local paper for bloodless bodies in Mausberg."

Her face whipped to his. "You think? Geez!" She made a note on a slip of paper. "I will. Geez!"

"So we're thinking they went to find Mark Corescu, right? Brannen said he went to Europe and so did Agricola. Search Brannen's travel info."

Jenn punched some keys and sighed. "I'll have to put in a request for it with Powder." She typed a note to her connection and Jonah poked her back.

"While they're at it, have them search Mark Corescu's name for plane tickets," he offered with a shrug. Jenn typed that name in, too. And sat back.

"Well, what now? It'll take a few hours. Powder only helps me when she's on the clock." Jenn looked at her watch. They'd both risen early for a Sunday and it wasn't even 9. Jonah tried out his idea.

"How about a drive to Montgomery? Agricola is preaching tonight at a church I'm affiliated with. You could watch him work and I'd enjoy seeing some of my old friends there."

Jenn jumped on the idea and they decided on a plan that included a huge late lunch and then arriving early. They'd be in Montgomery, so why not try to visit Elizabeth? Jonah called and she was already planning to attend. Excellent.

❧❦

The time had arrived; apparently, God thought Tony was up to standing in the wings while Sarah and Big John brought the Gospel to the public. The size of this experimental introductory venue had been ideal. God controlled who sent invites, but Tony chose Chavurah because it was tiny; with fifteen families, not much bigger than a home church. They had advertised it all week as "Lay-Pastor Anthony Agricola will bring a powerful message!". Before Paul changed his DNA to crave blood, Tony had been booked two and three times a week at various Christian facilities across the tri-state area. Paul attended some of them with him, which is how he ended up meeting Sarah Tracey without Tony's awareness. She had attended a previous service, and by the magic of God's timing, she had been leaving the church the same time Tony went on the stage. But all that changed when Tony heard the congregants' blood pushing through their hearts and whooshing across their systems. He couldn't stand on the bema as God's man when he wanted to take their blood.

Here they were, about to deliver God's truth and Tony would wait behind the curtain. Sarah told him to support them in prayer, but God hadn't been hearing him a while now. Tony hadn't heard from the Creator in a long time and he had begun to suspect this had something to do with Rakha combined with getting close to the magic number. The temptation would be at its apex about now. *Three days until deliverance day!*

For the moment, he and Sarah sat in the rabbi's office. Big John's text read he was minutes away and Sarah had invited Elizabeth, who said she'd be there, too. Tony turned his face to see Sarah sitting beside him on the stiff sofa and she gave him a huge smile.

"This is going to be wonderful. Jesus is so excited to share with these beautiful people," she said with meaning.

Tony nodded as the door opened and the rabbi walked in, followed by Big John and Elizabeth.

"Okay, Tony, let's do it before I lose my nerve."

Tony got up and shook his hand, greeted Elizabeth and turned to the rabbi. "I appreciate this, Simon," he told the man, who gave him a warm clap on the back.

"Sure! Come on, I'm sure they're ready!"

Five-foot-six and round as a ball, Simon led them to the sanctuary. All of them walked to the front, shaking hands here and there, and then they reached the podium and faced the group. Chavurah Yeshua normally met Friday and Saturday nights for Shabbat service, so the Elders had advertised in a local paper. As a result, all of the members attended as well as double that many from the city. Fifty-five folks signed the guestbook and now looked at their rastor (Rabbi-Pastor) for introductions.

"Shalom, everyone and thank you for coming!" he said in a booming voice. He then led the room in a prayer for thanksgiving and said amen. With a quick glance to Tony, he said then, "Let me introduce Anthony Agricola, which many of you know has been sharing the Gospel all over the south and we are so happy he had time for us today!"

Tony waved as the people clapped and he took the bema. He opened with practiced words, anecdotes and a few memorized verses, but he felt none of them. He needed to hand it off because soon, he feared someone would notice he was a monster and not a man. His mind rambled with these thoughts long enough that standing behind him, Sarah cleared her throat to get him back on track. With a chuckle, he introduced everyone on the stage, playing up Sarah's connection to her former international ministry with Ira and Big John's status in his own church in Columbus, Georgia. Once that was done, he stepped back and he and Elizabeth exited the stage to stand behind the curtain and watch out of view. Sarah began with Big John on her right and Tony sighed. Elizabeth stood near and listened with him.

Before the first song ended, the doors at the front of the smallish meeting room opened and in walked the detectives, Miller and Speltz. They wouldn't see Tony and Elizabeth as they were deep in the shadows of the dark backstage area, but he pointed them out to the young woman as her father found a seat.

"I'll go sit with them if that's okay," she whispered and Tony nodded.

He watched her tiptoe from the stage hugging the wall. The detective saw her and waved her over. Tony watched until she was seated and remained back, so he couldn't be seen.

He didn't want to talk to them, to be distracted, to be scrutinized. In fact, at the podium, Sarah launched into her message, and Tony grew claustrophobic and anxious. He narrowed his eyes to concentrate on the sensations and adjust. Sixty seconds later, he only felt worse and Tony turned to explore the backstage with his eyes. He saw plainly into the dark and found boxes and props from any number of productions. Then he found the tiny delineation of an exit door. It's illuminated sign had long ago blown out, but he moved toward it, wondering if it was a working door. When he tested the knob, it turned and the door opened into an alley behind the small church. Taking in a huge gulp of fresh air, Tony stepped into the night, allowed the door to close, and leaned against the cool brick wall.

"I have something you want, Preacher Man," he heard as Rakha materialized at the head of the narrow alley walking toward him. "I think I'll give it to you tonight."

Weary of the vampire and more weary of waiting on deliverance, Tony grunted a greeting. Rakha came within ten feet and leaned against the wall with him, mimicking his posture, both facing the back of the neighboring building.

"I can't imagine what you might have that I would want," he mumbled.

"Oh, you could imagine it if you weren't so hungry," he mused, but Tony did not react. "It occurred to me upon waking that I own something you treasure more than life itself."

His curiosity piqued, if only a little, Tony turned his face. "Okay, what is it?"

"Oh, tit for tat," Rakha said with a chortle. "I want something in return."

"I figured as much. I'm listening."

"Here's the headline: I was there when they hung the Nazarene on the Tree."

Tony's heart swelled in his chest. Could it be true, that this creature watched the crucifixion? Tony sent these questions to God, and like usual, nothing pinged back. In a shaky voice he asked the vampire what he wanted in return.

"Tit for tat," the old vampire cooed. "I will fill you in on every detail, and I have many of those. I will tell you all if you allow me to taste your blood."

Tony huffed in disgust. He shook his head but could not make his lips form the words. He must confess with his mouth to make it official but no words would come out. He continued to shake his head while his mind went over and over the possibilities of hearing a first-hand account of Jesus' last days in the flesh.

"And you can choose how I take it. From your throat, your wrist, your little toe…" Rakha smiled and chuckled. "And I would stay at arm's length. I would not attempt to kill you."

Tony still had not moved as he pondered his options. *Is this devil trying to tempt me? Surely I am not so blind to allow a demon of hell to lead me into sinning against God.* He allowed the stored up breath to escape from his lungs and he shook his head with finality.

"No. Absolutely not," he said with force. He would not bargain with the devil, and any agreement with Rakha would be an agreement with his mortal enemy.

Rakha tensed and it took a moment before he exhaled. "Let's be friends."

Tony shook his head. "You've already stated your intention is to kill me. The only reason you haven't killed me yet is because God will not allow it. You're hanging around, hoping to catch me in a sin that would create a window of opportunity for your attack."

Rakha grinned a little-boy smile and shrugged.

"I'm not going to turn my back on God, so go chase one of your other monsters. I'm not changing my mind."

Rakha offered a fake-thoughtful nod. "Oh, okay, I see."

He was quiet a few long moments, leaning against the brick and breathing steady. Tony said nothing, happy his stomach had not cramped the entire day. Maybe the prayer was working. Maybe getting closer to forty days, he had finally cracked the code.

Then Rakha sighed and stood off the wall to turn and face him, still standing ten yards away. "I underestimated you. You are a power to be reckoned with and I would do well to mind my manners from here on out…" The vampire softened his posture and lowered his eyes.

Tony didn't buy the penitence and looked away. "I'm not a vampire. Go on and play with the real vampires. Very soon, I'll be regular old Tony again. No fun for a devil."

"I find you incredible," Rakha mused with the same humble tone. "I have grossly misjudged you. As a token of good faith, let me give you a sample for free." He licked his lips and leaned back to the wall. "I was not a follower of your Nazarene as I had joined the other team by then." Rakha waited for Tony's reaction.

"Go ahead," Tony mumbled and averted his gaze the opposite direction to disguise his interest.

"I was in my original flesh, a wealthy landowner from Achaia, but I was already on my third natural lifetime. My favorite past time was to ruin those who found joy in the God of Israel. Because of this, I spent much of my time in Jerusalem seeking my prey with excitement and little caution."

Tony *humphed;* the vampire's life had always been about death.

Rakha continued. "The days of the Nazarene were days of terror and chaos for our side. My Helpers were beside themselves with reports regarding the Nazarene's ministry and the signs and wonders that followed His disciples."

Despite his misgivings, Tony wasn't capable of hiding his eagerness to learn.

"Have you considered the spiritual atmosphere before the Jewish Messiah began casting out demons? Before He came, my friends truly ruled. They possessed everyone and anyone; unborn infants, young men and women, children, the livestock, even inanimate objects. Demons had the run of the planet!" Rakha spread his hands with drama.

Tony mused, "I guess they were shocked when a mere Man began casting them out with a word."

"But we saw clearly He was more than a man. At the time, I did not realize His full importance, but my Helpers recognized His deity. I followed the tales of His adventures with great interest."

Tony rolled in his lips, the story leaving him with a mental movie of what the man described.

Rakha stood off the wall and clasped his hands together. "I am leaving for now, but I will call again. We have much to discuss and learn from one another."

"Can I convince you to stop coming around?" Tony asked knowing the answer.

"Impossible. It is for you that I have risen from my sleep. I woke to find *you*. My nemesis. My equal. You are my challenge, my game. And I intend to make great sport of you."

Tony shook his head. "Sounds like you have your mission and I have mine," he said in a morose whisper.

"Yes, only, I will succeed and you will fail."

Tony said nothing, averting his eyes and in another few seconds, he sensed he was again alone. He sent a prayer to God—even if he got no reply—and reentered the church. On stage, Big John had taken over the microphone and his deep voice told the sheep about the Lord's love and mercy. Remaining obscured by the darkness backstage, he peeked at the detectives, Miller and Elizabeth listening with intensity, and Speltz looking at faces, her eyes changing focus every few seconds.

I can't talk to them tonight, Tony said inside and maybe to God. *Five more days, Father. Can I go sit in a cave until then?*

He pulled his gaze to Sarah standing three-quarters away from his position. She felt his eyes on her and she turned to give him a wave. This caused Jonah Miller to look his way, which he noticed in his peripheral vision. Tony backed further into the shadows and then out the alley door.

Once in the cool night air, he shot a text to John and Sarah. *"John, please run Sarah home. I need to go. I'll apologize to the rabbi later, make an excuse. Please. I'm sorry."* Then, in a swift jog, he reached his truck and left the church. Maybe he'd disappointed God by abandoning his first new ministry gig, but what else was new?

27

Kish had a son named Saul, as handsome a young man
as could be found anywhere in Israel, and he was a
head taller than anyone else…
1 Samuel 9:2

WITH A LIVELY STEP, SARAH REACHED TONY'S WRAPAROUND
porch. Big John would be right behind her, saying he needed to call his
wife and he would join her and Tony inside. When she reached the
landing, she stopped with a gasp at the sight of a tall stranger lounging
in one of several cane rockers.

"Goodness!" she said and the man rose to his feet. "I didn't see
you!"

"Pardon me. I was watching for Tony," the man said in a beautiful
round accent before offering a tiny bow. Sarah blushed in his gaze and
waved one hand. Then he added, "I am Mark Corescu."

Sarah exhaled with a small grin of greeting. This man—this four-
hundred-year-old vampire—was 6'4", with a dark complexion and
handsome features, wearing slacks with boots and a black duster across
his strong shoulders. He gave her a friendly smile and gestured for the
chair near his own.

"Have a seat. Tony is about five minutes away."

Sarah looked toward the parking slots, but from her angle, John's
Caddy was out of sight. But why should she not sit and wait with him?
This was Tony's vampire confidante. Convincing herself, she switched
her purse from her shoulder to her hands and sat in the offered rocker.

"I'm Sarah Tracey," she said and did not attempt to shake his hand.
"I am happy to meet you."

"Likewise." He settled into his own chair, eyes going to the
driveway. "Do I hear Mr. Jenkins?" he asked and Sarah nodded with
parted lips.

"Have you met him already?"

"I haven't had the pleasure, but I am aware of him, of course."

Sarah *hmmm'd* not knowing what she should say. Finally, she
decided to go with, "You said he's almost here. Can you *see* him?"

"Yes," Corescu said and leaned over his knees.

"Interesting," Sarah whispered and blushed when she realized her eyes had slowly scanned his body of their own accord. Inside, she asked God to deliver all of them from vampires as soon as possible.

"I appreciate the support you give our Tony. He leans on it heavily, and also upon your counsel," Corescu said his eyes never leaving Sarah's. "It has been thirty-six days since we parted ways in Europe. You are aware of the significance of this fact."

"I am," she answered, worry blossoming for her new friend. They fell silent and she squelched further curiosity regarding the dark stranger.

"Ask," the man said then, his brown eyes kind.

Sarah inhaled, certain he couldn't read her mind. Or could he?

"Some of your thoughts trickle past my consciousness. I interpret them based upon centuries of practice. So, please, ask. If I can answer, I will."

"I guess I was wondering what it's like to move across time and space like this. Is it instantaneous?"

Mark took care with his response, finally answering, "It's instantaneous. It feels a little like being lifted and dropped in the same movement, such as one might experience on a roller coaster."

Sarah uttered a surprised sound and quieted, wondering when John would round the corner or Tony hit the gate. She remembered Tony's friend who lived with the vampire in Europe. "How is Ms. Brannen?"

Corescu smiled, small and to the side. He rolled in his bottom lip, still with the amusement on his face.

"She is well. She has a new horse and has trailered him to a month-long horse camp." Then the man got to his feet. "Tony is turning into the neighborhood." He put a hand out for Sarah but she stood without taking it. When he placed that hand in his pocket to rest, he gave her a tiny huff. "You have nothing to fear from me."

"I know," she replied watching the gate. "But I'm new to this. I hope by the time it normalizes in my brain, Tony will be delivered."

Mark did not respond and they both watched Tony meet the electronic gate and pass through. At the same time, Big John closed his car door with a bang, meaning he'd be coming around the front any moment.

Sarah moved forward to be seen by Tony and John and she couldn't help but feel weird allowing the vampire doctor to stand behind.

But God has me covered... Just because there are mythical creatures suddenly in my world doesn't mean my protector is gone...

Sarah continued to soothe herself with prayer as John came into view watching Tony's truck. What would the big man think of the doctor? Sarah hugged her purse and waited to find out.

꙰꙰

Surreal did not come close to describing what Tony felt when he saw the beautiful and angelic Sarah flanked by the vampire that attacked him a year ago in a misguided show of bravado. He rearranged his expression by the time he exited his truck to jog up to his friends, greeting Sarah with a peck to her cheek. Then he introduced Mark and Big John. The doctor offered a regal nod and stepped aside to allow Tony access to the front door. He invited them all inside and asked Mark to speak in the foyer.

"We'll be right there," he told the others and the doctor remained, a sideways grin in place. He turned to see his face. "What's up?"

"Your spirit called me here. At the assembly tonight," he answered in a low voice, "I sensed you speaking with another, but I could not see who or what it was." Mark put a hand to his shoulder. "You're hiding something and you will now tell me what it is."

Tony took a quiet breath. "Your old master is back in a new body." Tony spoke fast and did not attend the surprise in the doctor's face. "I've told Sarah and John about him and he asks about you often." Mark's eyes flashed with a mixture of emotions and Tony held up his hand to request a chance to finish. "I know he's untrustworthy. I'm only entertaining him for God's sake. I'm not letting him close to my friends."

Corescu sucked his teeth, holding Tony's gaze with a new ferocity. Tony sensed he was choosing his words and when his eye narrowed, he was ready to speak.

"If this creature is back, that would explain the night-visions I've had regarding him. He threatens me in my sleep and I had assumed it was my subconscious. You should not see him again. If he comes back, command him to be gone in Jesus' name. Do you understand? Command him to be gone. You are finished with him."

Tony did not disagree, but he also did not want to consent. How was the doctor to know more than his own spirit?

He did not answer Mark's question the way the doctor wanted and he crossed his arms to say with finality, "I will sit in on your little meeting. I will become familiar with your friends. I have a very strong sense that you might need help in the days to come."

"Come in. I want you to," Tony said and meant it. He motioned for the door and Mark entered and allowed Tony to lead him to the living room where John and Sarah waited.

Once everyone was seated, Mark in a cushioned arm chair, Tony and Sarah on the short sofa, and Big John sitting forward in the recliner, Tony opened with and apology.

"Guys, I'm sorry I abandoned you at the church. It will be a slow process, but I'll stay longer next time."

"You will need to come clean about your mystery visitor in the alley," Mark sent to his mind and Tony pretended not to hear.

Big John cleared his throat, a wary eye on the doctor sideways. "Ms. Sarah introduced me to the detectives. I don't like this, them nosing around again. Do you think they'll drop it?"

"They will," Tony said with confidence. "You won't have to worry about them any longer."

"Did you tell the doctor about Rakha?" Sarah asked then as innocent as a lamb. Tony hadn't mentioned to Mark the old vampire's name. He turned to Corescu who looked back, eyebrows raised.

"Rakha means 'cursed' in Aramaic," he said holding Tony's eye. "Please, share."

Tony inhaled and nodded. "That's what he's calling himself, Rahka Tep. There is something he said that you can help me with," Tony said happy to redirect the attention from him back onto the doctor. "Rakha said there were two other vampires in the world that were not his offspring. When Hope asked you if there were more vampires, you told her no." Tony watched his dark gaze, reading nothing, likely because of his centuries of practice holding his emotions in check.

"There are more? Geez!" John mumbled and stood to pace across the room. Tony looked at his wide back and decided to let him be. He returned to Mark who leaned back and crossed one ankle over his knee.

"I have made no other vampires, so I cannot testify on this topic."

Tony waited. There was more, but Mark had closed off. *"One of them is named Haman. Do you know this name?"* he sent with precision and Corescu blinked once and did not reply.

"Are either of you connected to these other two telepathically?" Sarah asked as sweet as always, looking between them expecting an answer. "Tony said the blood makes this possible. Maybe you share blood somewhere down the line."

Tony remained in Mark's eye and waited to see if he'd give her a courtesy reply. In the space of five seconds, he did finally look aside and give Sarah a kind shake of the head.

"I hear Tony," he said his voice soft. "I do not hear the others."

"Neither do I," Tony said, eyes on Mark's profile.

Across the room, John's irritation hadn't lessened. He could be heard mumbling under his breath, perhaps praying and Sarah got up to check on him. Tony rose and stepped to where Corescu sat and stood close, hovering.

"Are you being dishonest? I think you know something about these vampires," he said in a whisper. Mark got to his feet and as he was taller, he looked down on Tony not enlarging the cozy bubble he'd created.

"I will reveal nothing while you're in contact with that devil. He wants to destroy you, your faith, your ministry..." Mark flicked his chin to John and Sarah across the room. "He wants to kill them, although I doubt he can get close to Ms. Tracey."

"You see it too," Tony said as a statement. If he softened his gaze, much like looking at those secret hidden photo books, her aura shone with blinding glory.

"I do not approve of you obliging this demon further. I am extremely disappointed that you have allowed him access to your life." Mark spoke in a fatherly way, but Tony resisted his chastisement.

"I think you're treating me as if I don't know what's going on," Tony replied, speaking low enough that his friends couldn't overhear. "You have been a vampire longer but I've walked with God longer. I think He's done having me face off with that devil, but who knows? I will answer to Him, not you."

"I'm speaking for God right now," Mark sent to his mind, growing angry in increments. *"Even a fireman can be burned alive if he develops a hole in his suit."*

Tony huffed and in another moment, backed from the doctor's proximity. He cleared his throat and his friends ambled back, speaking words of encouragement to one another.

"Let's pray together and see what God would have us do," he told them and when he turned to grasp the doctor's hand, he was gone.

28

It is the glory of God to conceal a matter;
to search out a matter is the glory of kings.
Proverbs 25:2

"MAUSBERG POLICE ARE LOOKING FOR A YOUNG BLOND tourist to question, re: the murder of three locals. The bodies were found—their examiner estimates—a week after, which puts it in the reasonable timeframe of Paul Black's visit. I sent Black's photo and they're showing it to witnesses."

Jen spoke her piece, eyes to the monitor as Jonah entered the home office. He crossed to stand over her shoulder and watched her scroll her current pages.

"Before you ask, they weren't as giving with the M.E. reports, but they shared the public record. It says two local men died of catastrophic cervical fracture and one of exsanguination." She turned her face to Jonah. "Guess he only needs blood from one."

Jonah sighed and turned for his desk and laptop. He powered it up and in another minute, had his digitized notes from their original case on screen.

"The dead reporter had been investigating bloodless bodies," he said. When he reached the end of the twenty quick-reads, he sighed. "None of those had broken necks."

"Yeah, I saw that, too. I tell ya, my vampire theory is leaning toward *two,* maybe three vampires. The one from Connie Nixon's files is Vampire 1. Twenty cases of exsanguination with no discernable pattern of victim choice. The only similarity is the cause of death." She waited for Jonah to nod. "Vampire 2 is Paul Black. His blood is on Sarah Tracey's clothing, the DNA anomaly in his blood is in the blood found at the Hip-Hop King's murder scene, and also found under the bark at the journalist Connie Nixon homicide scene."

"But Nixon wasn't bloodless," Jonah said low.

"But he was researching Vampire 1. Paul Black, Vampire 2, lived with Dr. Mark Corescu and worked alongside Reuben Stuckey. I think Vampire 1 might be Stuckey or Corescu."

"Then why say three vampires?" he asked without expression.

"Because we have not yet found Corescu or Stuckey. Assuming Black is dead, that means we might have two vampires left, one of which is killing here—the homeless boy and the hunter—that we know of."

Jonah exhaled, his mind seeking a non-vampire solution and coming up blank.

"You'll be happy to know that John Jenkins is normal. After I saw he was part of the ministry team—which is suspicious in itself—I looked into his records. He hasn't had any trouble with the law, works part-time as a bouncer in Atlanta and co-owns a moving company with his wife—the dead reporter's cousin, a.k.a., the red-head you like so much," she said with snark.

"A bouncer in Atlanta?" Jonah said, his memory provoked. He went to his digitized notes from the old case and read to Jenn, "Fran Booker and Glorie Brannen (deceased) were advised by the bar's security staff to call a cab. That staffer's name was John Jenkins."

"You're kidding," Jenn said and craned her face to read his monitor from where she sat. "And Glorie Brannen died in that wreck driving drunk, right?"

"Yes, and we put in our closing report that there had been an APB out on her around the same time for suspected poisoning of her three young children."

"Geez, Jonah, this is messed up! Let me see if Powder got me the travel docs for Hope Brannen and Corescu." Jenn returned to her PC and checked her email and then Messenger. "Heck, I'll check travel on John Jenkins, too. I have his Social right here."

Jonah offered a tiny nod and relaxed back in his chair.

"Okay, Powder says Hope Brannen flew from Georgia to Germany the same day Agricola and Black did. Geez—do you think she was with them? This is sick." Jenn continued to hit keys on her keyboard and Jonah only *humphed*. "I want to question her. Where's her number?" Jenn shuffled her papers and found her collection. Jonah watched her dial, frown, and hang up. "No longer in service. Hmmm. Let's see if she came back."

Jonah made another noise and turned back to his laptop. He had no reply from his Scotland Yard pal, and he huffed. Jenn would have gotten a reply, he mused and skimmed his email with half of his mind on Jenn's theories. Her phone rang and he listened as a familiar voice filled the quiet room.

"Got another one, sugar," Kranchez said and Jonah scowled at the man's endearment. Jenn caught his expression and waved in his direction.

"One what? Bloodless body?"

"Yep. This time outside Lowndesboro. State Troopers found the man's body behind a church when his family reported him missing. No mess this time, just two punctures. The township has no police so Staties handed it to Lowndes County. I sent what I got from their guy."

"Great, thanks, Andy," she said. "Anything else?"

"Yep-p-p," he said stretching out the last letter. *"Your artic blue Jag, LCT15 was spotted by traffic cams that night outside Selma. Good time stamp. Put it in your collection."*

Jenn whooped and disconnected after a quick goodbye. She turned to Jonah. "Vampire 3 drives a Jag and is killing right under our noses. Does Agricola have a Jag? Have we looked up his registrations?"

Jonah rolled his eyes without intention. "Yes, he only has the one truck in his name. He's aging, he's not a vampire."

She grinned. "Just keeping you on your toes, Old Man."

Jenn returned to her monitor and Jonah decided to go tend his mushrooms. Turning manure was much more fun than chasing monsters, which was why he retired in the first place.

29

But God is faithful, who will not allow you to be tempted
Beyond what you are able,
But with the temptation will also make the way of escape,
That you may be able to bear it.
1 Corinthians 10:13

TONY THREW THE TRUCK INTO PARK AND FLED THE
vehicle. Without turning, he begged her forgiveness and asked Sarah to
allow him a few minutes alone. Then he tore away, circling the house
to wind up behind the garage, hidden by shadow.

Lord! What do I do? What do I do? With frantic glances, he took in
the upstairs windows, the pasture behind him, the field on his right, and
the vacant horse barn on his left. He needed to be alone, to shout at the
Lord, to curse and scream and expel the anger he'd been building for
forty days and forty nights. He didn't want Sarah to witness any of it.

Tony turned for the barn, happy his sweet friend so far hadn't
followed. With no effort, he yanked the handle of the gigantic sliding
door and opened the musty space. He had never used the stable which
left it a nest of dust and cobwebs. Still, it was quiet and deserted. When
he pulled the heavy door closed, he sunk to his knees on the dirt floor.

"God! My God! How long will I suffer this torture? How long will
you ignore me?" Tony hiss-whispered, even though far from the house,
afraid Sarah might overhear. "Forty days, Lord. Please!" he begged, his
hands curling into claws where they supported his weight, bent over to
spew hate to the ground.

That morning, Tony watched the most gorgeous sunrise of his life
and that gave way to the bluest sky he'd ever seen. Everything about
the morning exceeded his expectations and Tony had been certain it
was over—he had been delivered. It had been forty days. Forty. One of
God's favorite prophetic numbers. Forty days and nights the rains fell
upon the earth during the time of the flood. Forty—the number of days
Moses spent on Mt. Sanai receiving the ten commandments. Forty
days—the length of time the spies stayed in Canaan. Forty years—the
period the Israelites spent wandering the wilderness because of their

disobedience. Forty days—the length of time Jesus was tempted in the wilderness.

And in 2020, there's me...

Hadn't Tony done his forty days? He had no reason to believe otherwise. If God was fair, Tony reasoned, then as of sunrise, he had survived his tenure as a vampire and the lust for blood had been removed from his flesh. But as the morning headed for noon and he met up with Sarah to preach to a congregation in Selma, the need for blood hit him harder than ever. First he hated himself for it. Then, he blamed the Almighty.

Sarah and John carried the meeting and Tony spent the majority of the time in the truck, hiding, sometimes folded over in misery. For six hours, his partners fed and nurtured the sheep of God while he stayed in the wings, seething and praying for himself.

"But I did my time! What do you want from me? I'm not Apostle Paul...I'm not John. I can't do this anymore!" Tony cupped his face into his hands. Praying to God in his heart, tears sprung from his eyes and he caught them in his palms. *"How long? I'm so...tired, and I'm so hungry..."*

In another moment, he considered the water in his palms, tinged red with blood—*his* blood.

Or Paul's? Or Mark's? Or is it God's?

Tony would not let it go to waste. In an urgent movement, he swiped both palms clean with his tongue, his body feeling like a dried-up husk. Then he heard a step outside the door and as he leapt to his feet, Sarah pulled it open wide.

"Tony, let me help you. Don't isolate yourself from the one person God sent here to help you get through." She gave him her beautiful smile and peeked inside, having opened the door three feet. The lamppost sent light to the floor and she stepped into its place. "What is it? Is it the hunger?"

Tony dusted off his knees with one hand, wiping his face with the other. "I need to be alone a minute. Please wait for me in the house." Sarah was watching him with her big hazel eyes and he looked away, remembering how easily his friends were hypnotized. "Please, Sarah, I need you to leave. *Now.*"

Sarah remained in place, and he saw in her mind that her alarms had gone off. "John texted. He made it home and wants to know if you're okay," she said, her voice gentle and her eyes wide. "I'll leave you alone, but tell me you're okay..." Then her mind whispered, *"I love him so much, Lord. How can I help him? What can I do?"*

Tony met her eye and she took one step toward him. "Don't…"

"You can't hurt me, Tony. Paul saw to that," she said and took another step. "Let me help you. Talk to me. Let's pray together."

"I'm out of prayers," he said almost too low to hear. Then Tony gagged and cried out as his stomach cramped worse than ever. She took another step near and he looked up from his hunker. He didn't meet her eye—his eyes fell to her throat. As soon as he realized this, he jerked his gaze to the wall. "No! You're trying to help, but you're making this much, much worse."

"Why? Because I am potentially a *donor?*" she asked, now only six feet away.

Tony clutched his middle with a new groan of pain.

"Are the prayers not working anymore?"

"To hell with those prayers! I have fasted forty days! Do you know what that means?" Tony's glare flashed with anger. "It means He doesn't intend to rescue me! Forty days! That is a very, *very* long fast!"

Sarah nodded with sympathy and started in her softest voice, "He is still watching over you. You're the apple of His eye. Trust. Believe…"

"And 'hang in there'? Was that your advice?" Tony snapped back. He stepped to an arm's length away. "I'm tired. I haven't rested in weeks. I have not enjoyed *ten minutes* of real sleep since Paul stuck me with this curse…"

Sarah closed the gap between them and folded him into her arms. "I know. And God knows. He wants you to trust. Don't give up."

Without intention, he sent telepathically, *"But I am so tired. I'm so hungry…"*

Sarah inhaled at the sensation of him speaking in her mind, but then relaxed, whispering in his ear, "Rest, dear friend. You'll find rest here with me. Shhhh…"

Tony leaned out enough to look into her face. *"You are so wonderful, the answer to my prayers. How did I ever end up in the arms of the most beautiful woman in the world?"*

Tony's conscience warned him to push her away, but he did not.

"I don't know why you aren't healed yet. I pray for you every day, *all day*. Believe me, I'm on the case," she returned in a whisper. He watched her eyes glaze, staring too long in a vampire's face, he thought with misery; yet, he didn't make her stop.

"Maybe forty days was not what God had planned…" she said in a faraway voice.

Tony released his visual hold and returned to her embrace. He inhaled to take in her aroma: Spikenard anointing oil and tangerine shampoo. It was a wonderful and terrible combination all at once.

"I can smell your soap," he said and nuzzled the skin of her throat. "Go into the house and wait for me there."

He held her close as she debated her next move. His hands dropped from around her back to her sides, then to her narrow waist that ended at full hips. He hadn't allowed himself to study her femininity to this extent, but now, caressing her silk shirt provided immense pleasure and he ran his hands another circuit. She was not going to leave, he saw that she had made up her mind that she should talk him down.

Lord, please send her away now!

"So," she said with light humor above his ear, "you don't like my shampoo?"

Tony sighed and taking two steps backward, he brought her with him as he leaned against the mason brick wall, facing her, his hands sliding to join with hers. "If you had even the slightest inkling of what you're doing to me right now...." Tony waited for his words to sink in. "Will you turn around right now and leave the barn?"

Sarah gave him a new smile, her chin to the side. "Tony, I love you, but you are so melodramatic."

Tony raised his brow, his lips parted and she jumped in to clarify.

"Yes, I've loved you since that night at the party." She gave a little shrug and brought his hands to her mouth to kiss once. "It's a fact and you shouldn't feel obligated or anything—"

"What? Stop—I love you, too, Sarah, since the party. I just can't do anything about it." Tony dropped contact with her and shoved his hands into his pockets. "I can't be a husband to you. I'm not even a man anymore!"

"Shh," she said and reached for his forearms and then when he consented, she took his hands again in hers. "You are a man. This vampire curse will be lifted. You'll see."

Tony held her gaze and his inner mind reminded him to send her out. The monster in his gut begged him to move closer.

Sarah's eyes went to half-mast and she whispered, *"I need to go."* But in a languid manner, she slipped her hands free and unbuttoned her silk blouse three buttons.

"Don't," Tony said, but maybe he didn't. His eyes were trained to her neck and soon picked up the illusion of her blood beneath her perfect skin. He reversed their positions in slow motion, so she was the one against the wall. His eyes fell to her throat. How would it go? What would it be like, biting into her flesh? Even as the thought crossed his mind the odd ache hit his gums. As his teeth elongated in preparation, he hated that his body had become a playground of the devil. Tony's reason was slipping away and the voice telling him to stop grew silent. He leaned forward, Sarah's height putting his face level with her chin.

"Are you scared?" he whispered around his strange new teeth, not wanting an answer. Sarah only inhaled once and gripped his biceps. "I haven't done this before…" His voice had grown husky and did not resemble his own.

"Tony, stop," she said almost too low to hear. "You'll ruin all your hard work."

"God's not paying me any attention," Tony said in his softest voice. "You smell so sweet and your skin is as smooth as silk…"

"Tony… stop…" she said without much force.

Tony set his lips to her throat for a kiss, innocent, between friends.

Sarah inhaled again and this time, whispered, *"In the name of Jesus Christ, Tony… let me go."*

With a yelp as he snapped awake from his self-induced trance, Tony jerked back and stumbled out of reach. Sarah did not meet his eye, but sleepily turned aside and made her way to the light streaming in from the lamppost outside. He watched her escape and sent apologies to her mind that she did not acknowledge.

"Pray for me," he yelped to the empty barn and she peeled away.

With fresh tears of anguish, Tony sunk again to his knees in the dusty aisle. She had seen the monster, the unclean demon no woman of God could ever love. He could not face her again.

I have to leave town… I can escape to… where? Where can I go?

Tony shook his head, his heart breaking. Nowhere. He belonged *nowhere.*

"Tony."

Tony raised bleary eyes to focus on his nemesis. There he was, just as he promised. A deep cry of despair rumbled up his throat as Rakha stepped to a mere four feet away.

"Look at you. I do not think you have the strength to stand." He opened his arms. "What was that display about? You'd never take blood from that sweet woman, would you?"

Tony considered his waiting posture, wanting Tony to make the decision, to accept what Rakha offered. His head pounded, pulsing in time with his labored heartbeat, the acid in his stomach too familiar to separate from the general misery.

Is this it? Is it time to be killed finally by one of these monsters?

Tony had no words and he sat on his heels looking into the vampire's face.

"Come to me, Tony. I have what you need, here, in my veins." Rakha conformed his hands to the top of Tony's head, ruffling the hair with a tender touch. "Little Tony, weak and starving. I will doctor you up. You will feel the power again. You will kick yourself for denying me before…"

Tony closed his eyes under the demon's touch, soothed but at the same time, sure he was about to die. His walls of protection were down, defenseless and godless, it would take no effort at all for the vampire to end his life.

"Why are your fevered thoughts always about death? Are you so very anxious to reach eternity to find that you have been duped? Why rush into that?" Rakha touched Tony's chin to lift his eyes. He grabbed Tony's pained gaze and smiled. *"There's no need for this suffering,"* he sent to Tony's mind, strong but gentle fingers urging Tony to lean against Rakha's thighs as he moved to stand behind him. *"Lean on me…I will take care of you."*

Tony did not resist, but moaned deep in his throat expecting to die.

"Tony Agricola, this is a very sweet moment between us. You have lost your faith and I have gained your trust. How perfectly wonderful." Rakha bit down on the inside of his wrist and his blood welled in the deep gash.

Tony smelled the blood long before he saw it and his eyes jerked up and back toward the source. Rakha lowered his arm to the level of Tony's mouth. He could not refuse. Leaning against Rakha behind him, Tony grasped the vulgar offering and wrapped his mouth around the man's wrist. As the disgusting liquid coursed down his parched throat, Tony cried. But… for the first time in over forty days, he was alive. *Really* alive.

30

There are six things the Lord hates,
seven that are detestable to him:
haughty eyes, a lying tongue,
hands that shed innocent blood...
Proverbs 6: 16-17

JONAH'S RETICENCE TO QUESTION CLERGYMEN HAD NEVER
been as evident as this morning when Jenn awoke with a notion to drive
to Georgia and interview Mr. and Mrs. Jenkins about her Dracula File.
He didn't think she'd ever tell anyone outside the two of them what she
thought was going on, but the more time passed and the more answers
she collected, the more he thought she believed it. This morning, after
a quick phone call to Opal Jenkins, Jenn was ready to go.

"Why did she agree to talk with us, I wonder?" Jonah asked as Jenn
grabbed her keys from the foyer table.

"It's off-off-off the record, that's why," she responded and
reached for the doorknob. "You sure you wanna go? My feelings won't
be hurt (much) if you stay home with your 'shrooms." Jenn had jokingly
shot her mouth to the side to say much, and he smiled.

"No, I'm in. I need to understand it." Jonah followed her out the
door, feeling good about what they had pieced together.

"You're interested in Mrs. Jenkins," Jenn said grinning and she
climbed behind the wheel. "I'm driving."

Jonah chuckled with a nod. He'd admit Mrs. Jenkins was nice to
look at, but he'd rather look at Jenn. Once they were tooling away from
the farm, he told her as much.

"I know," she said and reached across the truck to pat his leg. "I'd
much rather look at you than her enormously strong and handsome
husband."

"Touché," Jonah said with a new nod, agreeing the man resembled
a bronzed Schwarzenegger in his prime. At the church service this past
Sunday, he had enjoyed the message which helped to erase his
disappointment that Agricola did not take the stage. He had hoped to
see the man there, but after the service, when he went up to shake hands
with Tracey and Jenkins, he was informed Tony had gone. Jenn

suggested later that he left because they arrived, but Jonah didn't go that far. He chatted for three seconds with John Jenkins and found him to be friendly and maybe a little anxious because of Jonah's former occupation and connection with their friend. The big guy did not enjoy scrutiny, so why again had he accepted Jenn's interview?

It would take an hour to reach the residence and Mrs. Jenkins arranged it so they'd arrive when her husband was home for lunch. When they rolled into town, they had fifteen minutes to spare. After each downing a quick gas station coffee, they followed the GPS to the address.

"Okay, Detective Miller, my hobby, my lead, eh?" Jenn said low as she rang the doorbell. Jonah chuckled and Mrs. Jenkins opened the door.

"Hey, ya'll," she said in a toned-down Georgia accent. "Come on in. Big is almost here."

Jonah followed Jenn inside and sat where the woman suggested. The man's home was tidy, smallish, but warm and inviting, with modern color palettes he knew Jenn would appreciate. In fact, she designed their current new home herself, every wall, every floor, every fixture. She had asked Jonah's input, but once she got started, he found that she knew exactly what she wanted and he only needed things to work.

"I don't know why he agreed to meet with you," she said and Jonah shot a look to Jenn who didn't acknowledge. "That man, Saul, Paul, whatever the hell you call him, he was awful. John told me to let him do the talking, but let me assure you, that man was a monster." The woman shivered and looked at the front door and back to Jenn, her visage visibly paler. "We didn't file a police report," she said in a whisper, looking to both of them in succession, "and if you repeat any of this, I'll deny it, but…" Jonah and Jenn both leaned in. Opal said in a very small voice, *"Paul Black thought he was a vampire."*

At her last word, the front door opened and her enormous husband entered, hand extended to Jonah. He stood and shook hands, watched the man shake Jenn's hand, too, before settling on the sofa beside his wife. He kissed Opal's cheek and leaned over his knees. Jonah couldn't stop looping the woman's last sentence in his mind. Leave it to Jenn to say her thoughts aloud.

"Mrs. Jenkins, why do you say Black thought he was a vampire?"

"What?! Geez!" the big man said whipping his face to his wife. "That is not true. He was crazy, that's all. Geez, Opal, come on."

Jonah had seen this scene a hundred times in his career and he knew Jenn was watching the woman, too. Opal had spoken what she considered the truth. Now her husband wanted her to lie. Jonah waited to see what Jenn would do—after all, her hobby.

"If you don't mind, and remember this is all off the record," Jenn said and held up a manila folder she'd brought as a prop. "This is a combined career of almost forty years seeking a little closure from our last case. Jonah has a keen interest because of his respect for Mr. Agricola's ministry. I need to know so I can sleep at night."

In a sideways fashion, Jonah read the faces of their hosts. Husband and wife wanted to help but also keep Mr. Jenkins secrets.

Jenn continued, "I'll have to agree, Mr. Black *thought* he was a vampire. Will you share the story you you didn't file a report about?"

Opal looked to her husband, her brows knitted either from being chastised before or from the subject. Mr. Jenkins only gave her a glance and sighed.

"None of this matters, detective," he began and Jenn said he should call them Jenn and Jonah. "None of this matters, ma'am. Paul is dead. He was crazy, tragic, deluded, deceived, and now he's dead." Jenn was about to object but he went on. "Tell them what happened, Ope, but let's keep it in the real world, okay?"

His wife cut her eyes a tiny moment and recovered. This told Jonah that when the cops weren't around, her husband had been plenty histrionic in his explanation of the perp's behavior. Then she gave Jenn a tight smile. "Maybe this isn't a good idea…"

Jonah got to his feet in such a way that John Jenkins did, too. He looked down on the wife and said, "how 'bout you and Jenn talk it over. Me and John'll go catch up on some Jesus stuff. Sound good?"

In his peripheral vision, Jenn's eyes sent huge thanks. John *humphed* an agreement, maybe happy to leave the women to it, and he led Jonah to the kitchen.

"Can I get you a beer?" the big man asked opening a new model stainless steel fridge.

Jonah accepted and they both sat at a small round dinette. "I appreciate you two humoring my Jenn," he said after the first sip. "She told the truth in there; I respect Mr. Agricola and I respect you and Reverend Tracey. I didn't like pestering him back when it was my job. I could see he wasn't involved with anything nefarious."

As Jonah spoke, he watched the man's reactions. As a trained body language expert many years, he read micro movements of self-protection when Jonah said Agricola was innocent. On its own, it didn't mean much, but he'd put it all together at the close of their interview.

"Did you want to talk about this case or Jesus?" Big John asked and Jonah huffed a small chuckle.

"Both, I think," he answered with a humble posture. "I spoke to your wife last year about her cousin, Connie Nixon. That's the end of it. I didn't know until today she had a bad run-in with Black. I'm sorry about that. He was ugly to a lot of people and we probably won't know who all was affected while he lived."

"Well, Tony said he told you everything he knew about Paul," John said and wiped a handkerchief across his bald head. "I was never interviewed about it—I worked for him, but thank God the police never thought I was connected. I don't know if we can be any help closing the details for you."

"Well, I saw Jenn's question sheet," Jonah said with a shrug. "Want to hear a few of them? At least you'll know what she's asking your beautiful wife."

John smiled. "She's a beauty, yes she is," he said and if his skin weren't so dark, Jonah would have seen a blush. "Okay, what you got?"

"Off the top, she'll ask why she thinks Paul is a vampire."

"She said *he thought* he was a vampire," John corrected with force. "It's like this. Paul was spoiled and eccentric—he was very rich, as you know. He liked to wrestle with me, I let him win, and he enjoyed it so much he would pay me to come to Montgomery twice a week for a match. I did this for months and he got addicted to me, I guess."

Jonah listened with nods in the pauses, but much of the man's story was fabrication. Jonah wished he had a video recording of the whole thing, but could only keep watching the clues.

"He was paying me a lot of money, but I had to stop. It was too weird. When I quit, he came here and threatened my wife." His voice broke and he swigged his beer, eyes averted.

This part is one-hundred-percent true, Jonah thought and waited for more.

"Yeah, sorry. So Opal will tell your partner—I mean, Ms. Jenn—that he grabbed her and said some things about drinking her blood or something. I was racing home and missed it, but apparently, Tony came in and begged Paul to take him instead." John shook his head once and daubed his forehead. "She said Tony stabbed himself in the neck and Paul dropped her and grabbed him. She took our son and ran out of there. I met her on the way and by the time I got her safe and returned to the house, Paul and Tony were gone."

Jonah didn't say a word and he hated that Jenn's vampire angle fit into the new information. Plus, he had to face the fact that if Agricola stabbed his neck in that way, he knew the move would cause Black to divert attention. If blood was all it took to get the man off Mrs. Jenkins, and Tony knew it, then he knew Paul drank blood.

Jonah shook his head at his thoughts, unable to put the sentence together, even to himself, that the guy was a vampire.

No, I simply won't admit that. Ever.

"I can see you're as stunned as I was," John said and finished his beer. He offered Jonah a second and he declined looking at the tabletop. "I was happy to hear he died…"

Jonah looked up. "How did you hear about it? From Agricola?"

John nodded with a one-shoulder shrug. "It was for the best."

Jonah's interest piqued at his wording; John had details. He considered pushing the guy on it, but no. If the man knew how Paul died and Jonah asked, he'd toss up his walls and nothing else would be shared. Instead, Jonah nodded as if the topic had closed.

"Jenn will ask her about the knife her cousin asked her to evaluate…" Jonah was interrupted by Jenn calling him from the living room. He and John both rose and walked to the couch. Pinching it with a hanky, Jenn held out an enormous hunting knife with a serrated edge and writhing snakes carved into the handle.

"This is it, and Opal said this is Paul's blood." Jenn waited for Jonah to come close and he noticed the air between the women had grown cozy.

Jonah took possession careful to leave it untouched. It indeed seemed stained with blood at the base and on the carving as well. "Wow," Jonah said and handed it back. "We're off the record, so…"

Jenn waved once with her free hand. "I'll leave it with them. She let me swab the blood. I'll do an anonymous test. For the file." She handed the blade to Mrs. Jenkins who returned it to a leather scabbard.

"Do you want us to turn this over to the police for you?" Jonah asked when the woman's face read disgust at the object.

"No, I don't want to be involved," John answered for her. He moved to his wife and gently removed the scabbard from her hand. He pecked her cheek and walked to the back of the house. Jonah gave Jenn a how much longer look and she exhaled with drama.

"You have been an enormous help and I won't bother ya'll again, I promise," Jenn said and when she went to shake hands, Mrs. Jenkins moved in for a hug.

Her husband returned as they walked to the door and he also made polite goodbyes. Jonah waited until Jenn had pulled the truck onto the main road before he began the reveal. Jenn spoke first.

"I didn't want to belabor it at the house, but Opal said Paul brought that knife the evening before he attacked her. She said he had brought it to play a new game with John, to get John to try to kill him with it."

Jonah swiveled his face. "That man's enormous," he said with awe. "He said Paul liked to wrestle him—which was a lie, although I can't prove it. But wrestle? And now the kid wanted John to attack him?" Jonah *tsked*. "What would make a kid 6-feet, 120lbs think he could best a man 6'6" 330? It's nuts."

"Well, she said he thought he was a vampire. A deep delusion could make him behave that way."

"I guess," Jonah allowed and waited for more.

"I asked how Paul's blood got on it, and she didn't know. She said it was bloody when it arrived, so not in their fight. I sure would like to ask Agricola about that knife. She let me photograph it. If I could see his face when I ask, I'd learn a lot."

Jonah nodded. They both would. But did he want to know Tony was involved? The guy had seemed weird at the station, but also good and just. No matter how bizarre he might have behaved, Jonah liked him. End of story.

For the rest of the trip home, Jenn shared Opal's version of Paul's physical assault on her person and it jibed with what her husband told Jonah. When they were done, they reached a common conclusion, and the sensation reminded him so much of their days on the Force that he mentioned it.

"Deja vu, baby," Jenn said with a laugh. "Must be a glitch in the Matrix."

Jonah agreed and tried to add the pieces up with Tony Agricola in the clear. As a detective, he wouldn't try it, but he was a civilian now. He'd steer his mind off Tony and vampires for as long as he could.

&

Tony leaned his back to the wall where he sat next to Rakha on the vampire's hardwood floor. Morning had come and gone and nightfall crept across the city outside. The past twenty-four hours, since he put his mouth on the monster's arm, Tony had been in this spot, chatting, dozing, and listening to the vampire pontificate on whatever came to his dark mind.

Tony remembered everything: running away to the barn, screaming curses at God, almost latching sharp fangs into the woman he loved, and at the last, accepting the offer of blood from the worst of all miscreants.

But he saved my life…

Beside him, Rakha had fallen silent. The vampire sat in the exact same posture, against the wall, legs kicked out before him, only he wore beige slacks with no shirt and Tony was still dressed.

Thus, from Friday night at midnight to now, Saturday nearing nine, he had listened to the ancient creature's tales of glory. He did not offer any in exchange; how many stories could a man of thirty-three years have in comparison with one born before Christ? Not many. And even fewer that were interesting enough to sit through. But Rakha had talked almost nonstop, one adventure after another. The only lulls in the action of his life were when he forced himself into a type of stasis, a hibernation period he called it, every three hundred years or so. Just to keep him from becoming too bored with it all, he had said. Tony tried to maintain perspective and remember who he was, but he didn't. Instead he *sympathized*.

His phone buzzed with a text. Tony fished it free and dropped it screen-up to the floor between them. *"Where are you? Please call me,"* the text from Sarah read. He had received a couple others and one from John. He closed his eyes, leaving the phone where it lay.

"The family worrying about you, eh?" Rakha asked, smiling.

"They have a right, I suppose." Tony should go home. Rakha hadn't killed him, but saved him. He was well. He could return home and start fresh, the vampire's blood had satisfied him even more than Corescu's and why that was would be a guess.

"It is because I am much, much older than my priest," Rakha said and lifted his hand to grasp Tony's phone. He activated the screen and read through whatever text messages he could see. Tony watched on, not caring. Then, seemingly bored, the vampire set the device to the floor and sighed. He closed his eyes as Tony had done and leaned his head to the wall. "So, go home. You know where to find me and I certainly know where to find you." After a long minute, Rakha laughed to himself.

"What?" Tony crossed his legs and leaned over his lap.

"You make me laugh." Rakha waited for Tony to turn.

"Why's that?"

"You cow to them, the mortals. You're at their beck and call. Not only that, you *serve* them." Rakha laughed again. "You could be *a god* to them. You possess a great power and yet you keep it hidden. This fascinates me."

Tony shrugged, not up for any apologetics. He had not spoken to God or allowed His name to cross his lips since Sarah left the barn. For now, it didn't seem important. He had needed rest and found it. He had needed sustenance, and he had procured it. Whenever he went back, he'd resume his old life, but here? He'd be a vampire.

Rakha snickered. "I like this Tony a lot more."

Tony didn't answer. He shouldn't please a demon, but what else could he do? *I'll ask forgiveness later… for now, I need to reset.*

"Contact my priest," Rakha said in earnest. "Tell him to come."

Tony offered a woeful shake of the head. "He started over. I told him you are here and he thinks we should destroy you. He would never come to you as I have." Tony watched Rakha's face a moment and then resumed with his eyes closed, head back. Then with a playful glance, he sent Corescu a message.

"Doctor, I'm with Rakha. He wants you to come…"

Beside him, Rakha sat up and turned. Tony remained as he was and Mark responded without delay.

"Get away from him. You're being seduced. Leave right now and if you can, destroy him!"

Tony rolled his head to the side and looked at Rakha who rubbed his hands before him, eyes wide.

"Isn't he dramatic! Tell him if he wants me dead, he should come and do it himself."

Tony spoke aloud in the room. "Your old master is seducing no one. He *did* come to kill me but he knows his mission is futile."

"In God's name, Tony, this is not a game. Get out of there!"

"Your priest doesn't trust you. Or maybe he doesn't trust himself," Tony said to Rakha not caring if the doctor rebuked him for his complacency. "I mean, I'm here and I'm doing fine."

Rakha leaned forward and put a hand to Tony's cheek before then running his fingers through his hair. "Yes, you're here and you're doing fine."

Deep in his mind, the doctor shouted a few more worried exclamations and Tony shut him out.

Mark has no idea how far along I've come. I can control it now. And Rakha no longer wants to destroy me—he's having too much fun...

Tony met Rakha's gaze. "I'll go home later. First, I'll rest."

Rakha's mouth curled into a smile filled with a demon's affection. "Wonderful. Close your eyes and I will watch over you."

Tony had no argument and he did not ask God's opinion. Rakha resumed leaning his back to the wall and Tony dozed off.

31

It shall be a statute forever throughout your generations,
in all your dwelling places, that you eat
neither fat nor blood.
Leviticus 3:17

RAKHA STROKED TONY'S HAIR AND THE MAN STIRRED,
having slid down the wall in a heavy sleep. The night and day had cycled
in that time and the young vampyr would likely awaken and stay awake
for a month before such a rest came upon him again. Rakha's victory
had been sweet and more fulfilling than he imagined: bloodlust caused
the man of God to turn his back on everything the Carpenter taught
him. This was more delicious than any simple ending of a life.

Tony woke in stages, considering Rakha beside him and the cottage
in which he sat. He then rolled to his knees to stand. Rakha watched
the man stretch his arms to the ceiling, pop his back in a habit of his
old life and then take a deep breath.

"That sleep was wonderful," the man whispered and allowed his
gaze to fall into Rakha's who remained cross-legged on the floor.

"You ready to fly on home to your people?" he asked and wiggled
his eyebrows. "Because if you would humor an old monster another
hour, I could show you something amazing."

Tony looked at the curtained window and fished for his cell. He
checked the time and returned his gaze. "Okay. Let's see it."

"Excellent!" Rakha got to his feet and ran his fingers through his
hair to straighten the strands. Tony mimicked his movements as Rakha
shrugged on a shirt from the floor. "We'll go in my car. Come." He
tucked his shirt into his pants and Tony did the same.

"Where are we going?"

"Ah! Hence the surprise!" Rakha said with glee and headed to the
car. The clock had struck 9, which meant the fledgling had been with
him forty-eight hours. When his phone buzzed again during Tony's
sleep, Rakha had silenced it and returned it to his pocket. His friends
wouldn't give up and he'd send him home soon. But for now, adventure
awaited.

When he got behind the wheel and Tony fell into the passenger seat, he heard the name Paul in the man's mind. He started the powerful engine and touched Tony's near shoulder. "Tell me about Paul. You think about him a lot." Out the side of his eye, Tony shrugged and clasped his hands in his lap. "If you don't want to talk about him, we won't." Rakha maintained his easygoing tone and it worked. Tony tucked both hands under his thighs and exhaled.

"It was hard dealing with Paul. Living with him. It'll take me some time to break it down, but I cared about him."

"Hmm," Rakha murmured.

"He was mean because of the way he was transformed," Tony added. "He was orphaned, he felt helpless and powerful—a horrible combination."

"Like a lion in a kitten's body," Rakha said his voice soft.

"Exactly." Tony paused and added, "He rescued me when I was starving. I mean, he made me like this against my will, but when I was about to lose it and murder someone on the plane, he came to my aid." Tony shook his head. "All of it is so screwed up, but I don't hate him." His shoulder bounced once. "I just don't."

Rakha made a sound of agreement and considered the preacher. An ocean of emotion roiled in his spirit and the man worked hard to keep it in check. "You *feel* everything so deeply, like a well with no bottom."

Tony only sniffed.

"A desirable quality in a mortal. But in a vampyr? It will make you unhappy."

Tony huffed. "As I have discovered. But what can I do? This is the way I'm wired. I've always been the serious type and I'm passionate about what I consider important."

"I like that about you. You're an enigma. You draw vampires like a moth to a flame."

Tony answered with a sad smile. "I do seem to be the target of every undead creature on the planet. I guess that makes me pretty special."

"Yes, it does. Tell me, has my blood sustained you? It has been two days. Do you hunger?" Tony did not wince at his question, which was an improvement.

Tony's right palm went to his middle and he shook his head.

Rakha smiled with a happy noise and turned his attention to the traffic zipping past as he wound the car downtown. In another few minutes, he reached Martha Street and slowed to a crawl, stopping on the curb behind a yellow work truck. He switched off the car and looked to his passenger.

"Who lives here?" the man asked and Rakha only grinned and exited the car. With a *follow me* gesture over his shoulder, he led the young vampyr to the house.

Rakha climbed the crumbling steps to the green Victorian-style home. The residences on this block were built in the teens and the one they visited had not been renovated as many others had been. Seafoam green paint peeled on the exterior walls and the marble steps and spacious porch floor were cracked and stained. As they stopped at the threshold, Rakha pulled the handle to the tattered storm door and knocked twice.

"What are we doing?" Tony sent to his mind and Rakha said nothing. In another moment, the figure of a man appeared through the opaque circle glass set in the door. After the sound of deadbolts and a chain, it opened inward and a heavyset middle-aged man stepped back for them to enter.

"Mr. Smith!" the man said in an urgent whisper and Rakha led Tony in without meeting the slob's eye. The entryway opened to the living room where a shredded couch faced a cracked-screen CRT television sitting on a broken down book shelf. Behind them, the man re-bolted the door and scurried around Rakha and Tony to stand before them, his hands clasped at his middle. Beside him, Tony's thoughts grew frenetic.

"Why can't I hear from God? I shouldn't have come here. I need to go. I should have gone home hours ago. I can't focus. Where is God?"

Rakha took gentle hold of Tony's bicep. "Harry, meet Tony, my brother."

Harry's beady eyes picked apart Tony's face and body and then returned to Rakha's. "...is he...?" Rakha hushed him and approached. "I knew you'd come today," the man whispered with a glance to Tony over Rakha's left shoulder. "They told me so. I'm so happy to see you. I missed you."

Rakha lifted his right hand to the man's throat. Harry had proven to be a decent medium and the Unseen spoke to him when they needed something accomplished in his dimension. It was because of his communication with these invisible helpers that Rakha revealed himself as a vampire when he arrived to town weeks ago. Without turning, he instructed Tony to draw the blinds.

"Are you about to…" Tony sent to his mind, his telepathic tone hyping. *"Don't do it…"*

Rakha ignored him. Harry bore the aroma of an unbathed hyena, but he was full of blood and he gave it away for free. Something Rakha appreciated.

"Is that guy gonna watch?" Harry asked in a coarse whisper.

Rakha ignored him and spun him around with a finger to one shoulder. Harry turned, familiar with the protocol, and Rakha tugged down the collar of the man's filthy undershirt. On his upper back, three previous visits were healing well. Rakha chose his spot and Harry lowered himself to suit Rakha's height.

"Please don't!" Tony sent to his mind.

Rakha now faced Tony over Harry's shoulder and the young vampire's horrified expression tickled him. He held Tony's eye as he sank his teeth into Harry's pasty skin.

"Please, I can't handle this!"

"Peace, be still," Rakha sent as the volunteered blood flowed to his needs. Such blasphemous use of Scripture pricked the preacher's spirit and he smiled.

"Oh, God," Tony muttered and grabbed his middle, his thoughts again clamoring in Rakha's joyful ears. *"I can't pray! I can't think! God help me! But how can He? I'm filthy. I'm abominable!"*

Rakha pressed his fingers to Harry's punctures and watched Tony fold over and turn his face. His fat donor took over by covering the wound with a cloth from his pocket and Rakha stepped to Tony's position, laying an arm across his back, both of them facing away.

"I will feed you, my son, my precious one. Come with me to my house, take your portion, and go home to your people. You will be fine…" Rakha's silent transmission delivered slowed the man's frantic thoughts and he stood upright. He motioned to the front door and Tony stepped toward it. Harry slumped onto his dirty couch and called for Rakha to stay, but he moved on out, getting Tony to the Jag.

Very soon, they were headed back to his cottage. In the passenger seat, Tony did not speak. In his mind, he continued to send half-hearted and tragic messages to his God and Rakha's heart almost burst with joy over the man's sadness.

"Why did I come here? Why did I stay? Am I insane?"

"Preacher man," he *tsked,* "You certainly enjoy your misery. You hate bloodletting, yet you love blood. You hate the power, but wield it with skill. You curse the darkness, but are only truly alive at night." He checked for Tony's reaction, but his thoughts had quieted and he faced out the window. "What a depressing companion you must have been for Paul Black."

Tony said nothing and Rakha sensed the man rolling up a mental barrier to his listening ears. He decided to add a bit more, Tony's conflict giving Rakha great peace.

"Paul loved you very much, you know. How could he not? I love you myself! Oh, you must have puzzled him to no end. I wish he was here with us. I would have welcomed him. I would have made him feel whole and wanted…"

Tony's immense misery did not break and when they reached his cottage and he parked the car, he turned before opening his door.

"Go home to your friends. Or, come inside. I will comfort you."

"I'm going home," Tony replied defiant, but when he exited the Jag, he headed for the house. "I'm falling apart. I think you should just put me out of my misery."

Rakha caught up with him at the stoop. "You'll be fine. Come in."

Rakha left the door ajar, certain Tony would follow. The man was more confused than ever and was not communicating with his God.

"Just one more time, little Tony," he said in a kind voice as the preacher came near, eyes averted but his hunger returned in force. "Once more and you can scurry home to your friends."

When Tony closed the distance, Rakha opened a vein in his arm as before, not ready—if ever—to allow the man to initiate the move. Tony took the offering, but this time drew more slowly and savored it. Rakha saw this in his countenance and he grinned.

৯৵৶

Miserable in spirit but glorious in his gut, Tony switched his phone off silent and scanned the many messages from Sarah and John. Rakha sat near as before, both of them on the floor against the wall with their legs kicked out long. Watching a man volunteer his blood had been a surprise and now that the image had normalized, Tony pondered the event. Why had he been so appalled? John did the same for Paul, right? Tony had been disgusted by it then, but not mortified as he had been tonight. Then again, he knew why – this time, Tony wanted to taste the man's blood, too.

"Yes, Harry is my John Jenkins," Rakha offered in a soft voice and reached across the space to touch Tony's shoulder. "You can taste him. He'd like it."

177

Tony did not remark. He hadn't mentioned God in a while and he huffed to himself. Why was that? Oh, because he didn't want to be reminded of how he disappointed his Creator, entertaining a demon for a little peace in his stomach.

"Stop trying so hard. Life with me is simple. You make it so complicated with this whine and worry."

"If I could rewind the past year, I'd stick my head in the sand and ignore the lot of you." Tony arose and looked down on Rakha.

"Is it so bad?" Rakha asked without rising. "Go home. I am inside you now, we are connected. Go play preacher and when you are hungry, we'll have our next date." He waggled his eyebrows.

Tony looked at his phone. He needed to call them back. He needed to go home. But... the vampire had a point. Mark drank animal blood.

Heck, he probably has a Harry or two himself over there, Tony thought with a huff. He looked back at Rakha's face, pointed upward, smiling, handsome and sincere. Was the guy a devil? Tony wasn't so sure. He looked at his phone, thought about Sarah, and began lining up apologies.

❧

"Okay, old man, put me on with your woman," Andy said, the fuzzy connection indicating he called from a city car radio instead of his personal cell. Jonah grunted and handed Jenn her phone. It was Sunday night and he'd convinced her to go out for some Italian. She hit the Bluetooth on the steering wheel rather than grab the phone.

"What's up?" she said to the air. "You're on speaker!"

"Damn, woman, take me off speaker if Miller's around," Andy joked but Jonah only sucked his teeth and looked out the window.

"Stop, Andy, you're going to ruin my date," she said and slapped Jonah's shoulder. "What happened?"

"Well, spoil-sports aside, my local love bunnies saw your JagXJ6 tonight downtown. They had time so they followed it to an address on Martha Street and watched two men get out and walk inside. They didn't get a photo, but the description sounds like your Agricola and another man, an Arab gentleman around the same age and height."

"Geez!" Jenn said and slapped the wheel.

Andy chuckled. *"They ran his plates. I'm texting you his DL deets. He looks foreign."*

"You're kidding!" She looked at the traffic behind her and changed lanes. "We're coming to Montgomery!"

Jonah gave her a sidelong glance, but had already conceded in his mind to go where she wilt. Andy had been his friend a long time and the "love bunnies" to which he referred were two patrolies he wined and dined when the mood struck. Tailing a car that wasn't on the official radar was something they'd do on the sly, keeping their radios on and available to peel off at a moment's notice. Tonight, it seems the lack of crime in their sector proved a boon for his lovely bride.

"I'm off the clock, I can meet you at Twirlies," Andy said and Jenn confirmed a time gauging by her mental GPS. When their friend disconnected, she whooped and slapped Jonah's shoulder.

"Hon, get the love bunnies' cell number from Andy and shoot them Agricola's photo for a positive I.D."

Jonah texted Andy's phone and watched the dots for his reply. Jenn loved the chase, and he loved her. It was okay.

32

A wise man's heart discerns both time and judgment,
Because for every matter there is a time and a judgment,
Though the misery of man increases greatly.
For he does not know what will happen;
So who can tell when it will occur?
Ecclesiastes 8:5,6,7

JOHN OPENED THE DOOR AND GAVE SARAH A WARM HUG. "Am I glad to see you!"

"What's going on with Tony? He hasn't responded to my calls or texts since Friday night. Is he all right?" Sarah followed John into the kitchen where he offered her a seat at the table.

"I haven't seen him since Friday. The next day and the next, he didn't text me back. No read receipts, nothing." John poured two glasses of iced tea and pulled out a chair. "Where could he be?"

Sarah pictured her friend as he'd been in the barn, starving, sad, and luring Sarah close without even trying. John read her worry and asked her to explain. She took a deep breath. "Friday night, he ran into the barn as soon as we got here. He wanted to be alone and yell at God." She shook her head. "He reached forty days and in his mind, God was supposed to have delivered him that night."

"Oh," John said, his voice soft. "What else? Your face... He didn't *hurt* you, did he?"

"No. But he was in bad shape when I left. I thought he'd pray himself back to normal like always." She shook her head. "He wouldn't ignore my calls. We've grown close." John's nod said he'd intuited as much. "I think he might be with that demon, Rakha."

John huffed. "Tony's the strongest man of faith I've ever met. There's no way he'd fall for the devil's tricks."

Sarah put her hand over John's huge fingers on the tabletop. "What I saw in the barn was not our Tony. That Tony was at the end of his rope, weary of the battle and furious with God."

John huffed. "Angry or not, Tony won't turn his back on Jesus."

Sarah hushed, her mind racing. How could they find him? "Do you have any way of contacting Doctor Corescu?" she asked and John said no. She thought about Elizabeth, but the demon wouldn't have given out his true address. Then she remembered Tony's silky voice in her head while under his spell. She caught John's eye. "Can you call him with your mind? He said when he was in Germany, he and you spoke that way."

John considered her question. "I've never tried to call him first…"

Sarah remembered Tony's explanation regarding *why* the vampires could communicate telepathically with their victims. She whispered to her friend, "Has Tony ever tasted your blood? He said that makes the link strong."

Big John grunted. "No, but he got some from Paul who took my blood a lot, God forgive me."

"Hey, I don't judge you. Try it now. Try to call him." Sarah watched his face and John bowed his head. *"Tony! Where are you? Answer me!"* he said inside and aloud for Sarah to hear.

"Tell him in the name of Jesus, he must answer. Be adamant." Sarah moved to stand beside John, her hand to his huge bicep.

John paused. "He received me," he said low, eyes closed.

"Command him to answer. Go ahead."

"Tony Agricola! In the name of Jesus Christ, answer me!" John again spoke and sent simultaneously. Then he inhaled when Tony responded, which he translated aloud.

"He's saying, 'Big John, look at you. When did you learn to pick up this line?'" John opened his eyes and gave Sarah an excited look. "He sounds okay. He sounds normal."

"Ask him where he is," Sarah offered, trying to stay calm.

"Sarah's really worried about you. She wants to know where you are." John closed his eyes again.

"He says, 'I'm fine. Tell her I'm fine. I just need a little time away. Tell her not to worry.'"

Sarah swallowed and chose her words. "If he's doing so well, ask him why he hasn't responded to either of us in two days?"

"Why haven't you called us back? Are you with someone there? Are you with Rakha?" John turned to Sarah and mouthed, *he's not alone.*

Sarah's blood turned to ice as a new panic hit her gut. Could Rakha be holding him against his will?

John held up one finger. "He's saying, I am not going to speak to Sarah like this.'" John opened his eyes. "He said he's not in danger and we should trust him." John said then very low, "We trust you, Tony, but we hate the devil and he is going to do whatever he can to separate us. If you don't come home tonight, we'll come looking for you." John looked to Sarah then and she approved of his ultimatum. He waited and said to her in a whisper, "he's with Rakha I think. He's listening to someone else… Wait. He said he'll be home in an hour." John blinked and rubbed his temple with one thick finger. "That gives me a terrible headache."

"Let's pray for him until he gets back."

"Sure, but he sounded fine. Why do you still sound panicked?"

Sarah's eyes widened for effect and she held the big man's gaze. "You're aware that Rakha is the *original* vampire. A two thousand year old monster who works full-time for the devil. What are the chances that Tony was safe with him? If the vampire lets him go, that just means he'll enjoy chasing him later. Tony needs wisdom and discernment because vampires are extremely alluring."

John nodded as if he had knowledge and Sarah didn't prod; saying more wouldn't help their situation.

���

Jonah sipped coffee and listened as Andy and Jenn delved into theories of what Tony Agricola and the mystery Jaguar man were doing together. The love bunnies on patrol positively identified Agricola and the man driving the luxury car. Andy's captain had taken notice of the frequent mention of the Jag around the murders and circumstantial evidence was enough to justify increased scrutiny. At that moment, Jonah thought he heard Andy say "vampire" and he came to attention.

"Wait, what?" he said and both tablemates looked at him as if they forgot he was there. "Did you say vampire?"

"Geez, Jonah, get your ears checked," Andy replied.

Jenn touched his hand on the table surface. "I said Jerry McGuire," she whispered and Jonah wondered what context would cause her to bring up that movie. He didn't want to let on that he'd zoned out, so he only nodded.

"The guy's driver's license can't be legit, right?" Jonah asked. *"John Smith?* Really? And no one pops up out of nowhere like that."

Andy shrugged. "This guy did. Brand new SSN as if he just arrived on the planet six months ago."

With a grumbling shake of the head, Jonah put both palms to the table. "Summary time. Agricola and John Smith were visiting Harold P. Bax, of 112 Martha Street. Harold works for the power company, has

182

for twenty years, and he doesn't have a police record. Not even a parking ticket."

"Harry Bax?" Jenn said with a half-smile and it took Andy a moment to get it. When he did, he laughed louder than necessary and Jonah cleared his throat to jump back into the game.

"Let's sum this up, what do you say?" he asked and they both agreed to let him do his thing. "Mr. Smith drove past a traffic cam at the boy's murder. Three days later a hunter is murdered and Mr. Smith is spotted down the road a ways, but in the time frame. Three days after that, Mr. Smith is caught on camera on the highway that leads to Burkville where the church man was murdered."

"And it's a week later that Mr. Smith and Agricola visit Bax in the middle of the night," Andy summed up.

"And we don't know why they visited, right? Didn't your bunnies hang around and snoop a little?" Jenn asked, jubilant with the investigating.

"They got called away. I asked them to follow up, but so far, nothing." Andy finished his coffee and checked the time on his phone. "You two are fun and all, but I gotta get going. My shift starts in six hours and I haven't been to bed in over twenty-four."

"I told you, Andy, retirement is the answer," Jonah said with half of his normal humor. His friend har-har'd and stood, dropped some bills for the waitress, and in another minute he was gone.

Jenn sighed into her mug. "You said Elizabeth named the guy. Mr. Smith is Rakha Tep. You didn't tell Andy... why?" Jenn had asked her question in a secretive tone and Jonah appreciated her loyalty.

Jonah hemmed, unable to admit to her beloved that his reasons were mostly spiritual. "I'm not sure. I ran the name and nothing came up. I even ran it past Interpol. Tep is well-used, but Rakha?" Jonah shook his head. "In Hebrew it means *cursed.*" He didn't wait for Jenn's reaction. "I think we should keep looking into it ourselves. If this guy has his eye on Elizabeth, I think we should focus our energy on him and let Andy in when we have more facts." He huffed. "If she doesn't have to be involved with official police business, all the better."

Jenn agreed with a nod. "Let's consider asking your friend Agricola about Tep." She watched for a reaction and because it had to do with Elizabeth's safety, Jonah didn't bristle as he usually did. "Good. Tomorrow, I'll see if I can get him or Reverend Tracey on the phone."

Jonah nodded again and asked for more coffee. If they were going to be looking close at Agricola, he hoped they had better luck than last time.

༠⤫ᨆ

Tony entered the side door off the garage, hoping for four extra seconds of peace before his friends lit into him for his escapades. He heard John's and Sarah's hearts, and for the first time he didn't mind that he could. Fighting his nature had been making him miserable. Tonight, he hoped to make it plain that everything was going to be fine. In the hall, Sarah saw him first and jogged close to wrap him into a warm hug.

"Tony!" she said low in his ear and clutching him tight, "Don't ever disappear on me again! I was worried sick!" Sarah then held Tony at arm's length and looked into his eyes. He thought she sought an apology, but he hadn't reached that point.

"Come into the study," he said and led her down the hall, one arm draped around her waist. She allowed it and John entered directly after they did. Tony waited for the right way to say his piece and it did not come easy.

"Are you okay?" Sarah asked, looking him over. "Are these the same clothes you wore on Friday?"

Tony kissed her hand and crossed to sit in his desk chair facing them. "I suppose they are."

"You had us worried. Where've you been?"

Tony diverted his gaze to John's and heard the man thinking, "*He seems different… and what is he smiling about? Can't he see Sarah was worried sick?*"

Tony lifted both palms in surrender and returned to Sarah's eye. "I had to get away, end of story. No drama. No fanfare. I just needed some space."

His words stung Sarah and she inhaled. Her thoughts also trickled past and they were full of worry. *I'm the one he's spending his time with and he's sick of it? Father, is he okay?*

"You should mind your manners. Nobody's crowding you. You wanted us here. Are you still with us, Tony? Or did you hop loyalties?"

Tony leveled his gaze at Big John but maintained his smile, Rakha's words returning to his memory.

"You cow to them. You serve them. But you are a god to them."

Tony exhaled holding the man's eye. *Does he think he can control me? Was he always like this or have I been blind? Have I done anything wrong? All I did was ask for two days by myself. Surely that is no sin.* He tempered his tone to them both.

"I didn't mean to upset you guys. If you haven't noticed, I've been struggling with some major issues that the two of you—*God-willing*—will never understand. I apologize for my absence. Okay?" Tony looked to Sarah with a soft smile. "Can we pretend this never happened? Will you forgive me?"

Sarah nodded that she was satisfied with his apology.

John attempted a smile which came across as a grimace. "Okay, good. I thought you had turned to the dark side."

"Well, I'm not any closer to understanding God's motives." Tony crossed his arms on the desk and propped his chin.

John sighed and got to his feet. "Well, if it's good with ya'll, I'm going home. Opal would be happy to see her husband tonight."

"Thanks for everything," Tony offered without taking his eyes off Sarah. She touched John's arm as he passed.

"John, thank you."

He glanced at Tony and then asked Sarah if he should walk her to her car. She shook her head.

"No, I'll hang here a minute. I'll see you next Sunday, right? We're booked here, in Montgomery that day."

John looked to Tony who agreed. Then with a new sigh he made his goodbyes and was gone.

After a silent moment, Tony said, "Everything's going to be okay. You know that, right?" She nodded and he knew, no matter what she saw with her eyes in the days to come, she believed God would work it out.

And Tony leaned on her faith.

33

In the morning, LORD, you hear my voice;
in the morning I lay my requests before
you and wait expectantly.
Psalm 5:3

JUST AS THE VAMPIRES WARNED, SLEEP DID NOT COME
easy. Tony had slept like the dead at Rakha's and his body absorbed the
rest like a bone-dry sponge in a pool. Now, twenty-four hours later, he
reclined in his own bed and waited to see what might happen. He
peeked at the clock and it wasn't quite 3 A.M.

I'm not a fan of being awake all the time.

With a quick mental calculation, he realized it could be twenty-
five days before the "vampire sleep" returned.

*I'm supposed to stay awake and do what? Think about how hard it's been?
About how God didn't deliver me when I reached the end of my fleece?*

Tony sighed aloud in the quiet room. There had been something
decidedly different about his inner thoughts; he'd been speaking to
himself and not to God. His eyes flit to the ceiling.

You can end this, he told the Lord. Earlier tonight, Jonah Miller's
woman called. Tony had sent it to voicemail, unwilling to be
interrogated. He sent a complaint to God about being hounded *again*
by police and his senses went on alert. Tony put his feet to the floor.
His ears and eyes delivered no answers but a prickle ran up his spine.
Someone was near. He didn't have to guess who it might be once he
ruled out the doctor. Tony paced to the front window and pulled open
the heavy curtain. Rakha was there, toes to the sill, magically balancing
mostly in thin air. Tony lifted the sash.

"What are you doing here?" he asked through the screen.

"I missed you," he said in Tony's mind.

Brow knitted, Tony tugged at the tabs holding the screen in place
until he freed it from the pane. Rakha stepped inside and straightened
his clothing.

"Tada!" he said with playful inflection. "I can teach you to do this.
I have much to teach a willing pupil."

186

Tony wagged a no-no finger, not upset at the creature's visit. Was that because he finally understood his place in the world? Was he to be more the vampire Paul made him than a preacher for God?

"I want you to think about our future together," Rakha said and instead of sitting in a chair, he sat on the edge of the bed.

Tony sat also leaving a good four feet of mattress between them. Just then, Tony's stomach announced itself. Was he to be hungry again simply because he laid eyes on Rakha? He cleared his mind, not ready to admit he might have enjoyed the man's blood too much.

"I like this room, your soft bed," he said and slid an inch closer. "Perhaps I should furnish my house in this manner. I could accustom myself to such luxury."

"Why did you come?" Tony asked, his voice much too low. Again he recalled the ecstasy drinking Rakha's blood aroused and again he forced back the thoughts.

"My helpers are finished watching," he said, his eyes searching Tony's face, rodent-like, in sporadic jerks. The room was unlit, but both of them saw clearly in the dark, the bluish aura delineating everything in varying degrees. "They want me to end my mission and move on."

"They want you to kill me?"

Rakha nodded and scooted another six inches closer.

"But you don't want to?"

"Not yet," Rakha answered and moved the last bit so their thighs touched. He laid one hand on Tony's near leg. "I'm not finished," he said allowing a pleasant silk to his voice. "I have one more task for you and you're not ready."

"What's that?" Tony asked, a tiny cursor in his mind telling him he should send the devil out. Warning Tony, *don't listen to anything he says.* But Tony listened, his tongue swelling as the blood memory would not bed down.

"You want to ask me for my blood, right?" Rakha asked, his tone gentle. Tony shook his head no, and Rakha *tsked.* "See? You're not ready. If you asked me right now, I'd say yes, and my blood would feed you again. Filling you with unimaginable peace."

"True joy comes from the Lord," Tony said very small and then loathed himself as he realized he didn't feel the words as he had a week ago. This time, he spoke words of life and his mind had already bitten the vampire's throat.

"You would enjoy that, eh?" the creature asked then. "It is a very intimate thing, you holding me close, pushing your teeth into my flesh.

The hottest, richest blood on the planet flowing into your mouth and down your throat faster than you can swallow…"

Tony shook his head but his gums ached, the vampire's provocation doing its job. "I want you to go," he whispered.

"You don't want me to go. That is a lie." Rakha leaned back, propped upon his palms. "Why did you let me in?"

"I don't know. It doesn't matter." Tony experienced a new pang of grief at the knowledge of God watching him suffer, yet doing nothing to help.

"Let go. Be what you are. Creatures of the dark need to stay in the dark." He looked about the room. "You sit in the dark; why didn't you turn on the light?"

Tony moved one shoulder. "Who needs lights anymore," he mumbled more to himself.

"Precisely. Why turn on the lights if you can see without them and why speak when you can send your thoughts with less effort?"

Those are good questions… With a new exhale, Tony leaned back on his hands, matching Rakha's posture.

"What do you think of this host? Nice, eh?"

Tony took a new scanning glance of the vampire. Rakha's bizarre and unholy method of assuming a new body upon each resurrection was difficult to swallow. The demon indicated that the mortal gave his flesh to the spirit realm and Rakha had to fight other entities to assume it first. They sometimes indwelt a person in multiples, but Rakha preferred to rule the roost. Tony didn't like it, imagining the poor and deceived men and women who voluntarily sacrificed their lives to demons. It was a tragedy he could not fathom. The vampire awaited a reply and Tony murmured, "You look fine."

"I rather like him. I was born in what is now Cairo, Egypt, and my original flesh lasted over a thousand years." Rakha collapsed backward onto the bed and folded his hands to his middle.

"A thousand years," Tony said low. "You're not immortal."

"My spirit is. The master who turned me ensured that my flesh remained vital a very long time." Rakha pulled Tony's shirt until he fell back beside him on the bed. "This is a nice time. If you weren't such a religious nut, you'd be an entertaining companion…"

Tony issued a weak huff, on his back looking at the ceiling. Rakha's presence and cadenced conversation calmed his frantic thoughts.

"Tony…" Rakha sat up part way and turned at the waist, looking upon him. "Tony…"

Tony looked dreamily into Rakha's face. "What is it?"

"You are not resisting very much." Rakha shifted his body to shove his left arm underneath Tony's upper back. "Don't you want to pray a little? Ask the Carpenter to rescue you from the evil vampire?"

His mind numb and a sense of calm penetrating his entire body, Tony only had one response. "He's not listening to me anymore."

Tony could feel Rakha's movement and then the sound of the vampire biting his own arm. When the monster put the blood to Tony's lips, he accepted, his hands to either side of the wound.

"You're falling in love with Rakha," the demon said in a husky whisper.

Tony made no sense of it, the words too crazy to consider. He slowed his feeding, no longer frenzied, but wistful.

"You are all but conquered. I think your protective shield might be completely disabled..."

"*Try it,*" Tony sent as if from far away. "*If God wants me dead, it'll happen.*"

Rakha released an angry huff and jerked his arm to himself. "Why do you still believe?"

"*Believe in what?*" Tony asked in his mind only, eyes opening with effort and enjoying the blood-induced lethargy. "*How do you ignore that you have a brain? I haven't seen it, but evidence proves it's in there.*"

"You have a brain and you have a Maker," Rakha whispered. "But you misunderstand His role in the lives of the people of this plane." With almost no effort, Rakha pulled Tony's upper body to his face. Without another word, he pressed into Tony's neck and grabbed on with fierce fangs.

Tony exhaled with sleepy surprise and did not resist, his arms limp at his sides. His consciousness floated in a peaceful and shadowy place, the sensation of Rakha's lips to his skin no more interesting than an ant crossing a field. The vampire did not guard his thoughts and Tony listened with macabre interest, disembodied and wishing he could care.

"*So much like my priest, so so so holy... And why did I lose him? I won't make that mistake again. I will make Tony my new priest. This blood is what I need, this is what I want forever. The blood of a brother, a holy brother, will feed me and grow my power...*"

Tony mumbled a few sounds, the sentiment being, "It'll never happen." But the vampire ignored him, drinking and planning, without caring that Tony saw it all in his mind.

"If he can be turned...he could accompany me as I revel in whatever the world has to offer a supernatural earth-bound god. Sure, the Unseen may disagree, but if this one is molded and taught properly...they may allow me to keep him."

In another long minute, Rakha ceased pulling Tony's blood and lowered him to the mattress. Tony folded his arms across his middle. He still wanted to sleep, but the vampire's plans needed to be addressed. Tony tried to say his concerns aloud. "I won't go with you. I want to be delivered..."

"Stop," Rakha responded, his tone harsh. "You want to wed the Tracey woman, I see it in your mind. Listen well—I will be back. I will come here whenever I wish. You have opened your veins to me, your soul is almost mine, and I don't like her. Think twice about adding her to our love affair."

Tony shook his head but did not rise from his defeated position.

"Sleep, little Tony, but dream about me." Rakha rose to his feet and crossed to the window. "Dream about my teeth in your throat and if you behave, you will one day take from me as you will it."

"Don't come back," Tony said, or maybe he only thought it. He allowed sleep to overcome him and he did not dream.

ॐ

On the other side of the world, Mark stood in the shade of an enormous German Oak watching Hope try out a new horse. With no effort, his inner eye watched Tony and the demon he knew as The Other swap blood. It was becoming impossible to *not* intervene as Tony dangerously erred again and again. When Rakha finally exited the man's home, Mark thought to warn him mentally, but Tony was sleeping too hard for him to break in.

I can't even push myself there right now, he said inside as Hope's riding-inspired giggles reached his ears. She needed him. For the first time in weeks, she was home, and her roving ways had him concerned. She returned with the scent of strangers on her skin, male and female, and when Mark asked her what she'd been doing, she never admitted to anything that explained it.

What do I think she is doing? Having romantic trysts? Mark scoffed. He did not think that was the case. But he thought she might be putting herself in danger, living without caution, and always when he was far away and out of sight. Their telepathic link remained strong but she did not "call" him when she was away on her horse adventures. She filled her time with others and only thought about him when she grew bored.

"This is the one!" she said then, pulling the horse to a sudden stop near the fence where Mark waited. "He's ready to move up, too. I'm going to need a new saddle and I think Rhonda will loan me hers until a new one comes in."

Mark nodded and she hopped to the ground with ease, still as fit and beautiful as since the day she arrived.

"What are you thinking about?" she asked and walked closer, the white gelding ambling behind at the end of the reins. "I don't think you were watching me at all." She leaned on the rail facing him. "Is Tony okay? You're worried about him, I think."

Mark forced a smile. When he and Hope first connected, her interest in other people's affairs seemed genuine, but now? She wanted to be Mark's main focus and since that wasn't his nature, she sought stimulation elsewhere. He had to answer so he told her Agricola was fine.

"Is he still a..." She looked left and right and whispered the end. "A vampire?"

Mark licked his lips and tipped his chin, his eye on the animal over her shoulder. "Your horse is enormous. Are you sure he's not too big?"

Hope's lips tightened aware he'd diverted the topic, but she allowed it. She spun away and re-mounted. "I'll show you too big." She used the reins to tug the gelding's face to one side until he moved away and she called to the helpers in the ring. "Set it to three feet!" She flashed her eyes to Mark, the horse sluggishly building into a trot. "Watch this and try to concentrate!"

Mark gave an absent nod. In his mind, though, he looked in on Tony, tapping his subconscious. When he still couldn't rouse the man, Mark sighed and prepared to purchase another Trakehner.[2] He'd keep an eye on Tony and as long as possible, avoid connecting minds with the demon that brought him into the Dark three centuries ago.

---

[2] Breed of European warmblood, excellent for equestrian sports.

34

What is mankind that you are mindful of them,
human beings that you care for them?
You have made them a little lower than the angels
and crowned them with glory and honor.
Psalm 8:4-5

IT DIDN'T CONCERN TONY IF THE DEEP SLEEP HAD BEEN caused by Rakha taking his blood; the rest had been helpful. Sarah called twice before Tony returned to consciousness. Once he'd risen and enjoyed a hot shower, he phoned and invited her over. Minutes before 8 PM, she rang the doorbell.

On the way downstairs, the doctor checked in telepathically, sending a simple *ping*, to which Tony returned an "I'm fine." Happy that Mark left him alone, he pulled open the front door to Sarah's beautiful face.

"From now on, you should just walk in," Tony told her. "I'll get you a key."

Sarah laughed into her hand, demure and with smiling eyes. "I'd probably drive you crazy. I warned you, I've been called overbearing."

"No way," he said and when he had closed the door and turned, she stood close, her posture reminiscent of someone expecting a kiss. Unsure if he read her correctly, Tony lifted on his toes to peck her cheek.

"Thank you," she said with a sideways smile and pointed behind him. The sash to her coat had closed in the door and he hadn't noticed. Tony laughed one short burst an freed her.

"Well, that's embarrassing," he mumbled with a grin and gestured they go to the study.

"No, I mean it—thank you. I liked it," she said and hadn't left the foyer.

"You did?" he asked and returned. "I have another one in here somewhere." Sarah's eyes twinkled. "The other one goes right here," he said with a finger to his mouth.

"Let me see that one," she said and waited while he came close and touched their lips.

The first three seconds he did not press in, but tilted his head ever so slightly to the side and she followed his lead the other direction. Then she moved into him millimeters, and the kiss deepened until she had to lean down to truly engage the contact. When she didn't cut it off, he put his palms to her neck, his gentle hold meant to encourage her to continue. Her hands went to his chest, palms flat to his shirt and in another second, he slipped both arms around her body and their kiss opened fully. He did not count time any longer, enjoying her softness and the tender skill of her technique. When the clock chimed in the hallway, she broke it off, standing close and looking into his face. She'd grown breathless and his special hearing picked up an elevated heart rate. Finally she said, smiling, "That is something we should do again."

"Walk with me in the moonlight," Tony said, still deep in her eyes. "I bet we could do it again there, too."

"Let's go find out," she replied and when he put out his elbow, she took it.

Tony led her into the cool night air. After a few yards, they reached the end of the sidewalk and stepped onto the manicured grass. The air seemed alive with songs of crickets and the warbling of frogs. Beside him, Sarah matched his thoughtful stride, both of them looking upward. Tony's house and land sat eleven miles outside of town leaving the heavens especially clear and black.

Sarah parted her lips and after a long pause, whispered, "Isn't this beautiful? The sky is like ink. I can see a *million* stars."

Tony paused his step and Sarah turned.

"*You* are beautiful," he said with meaning and took both hands in his. "Sarah Tracey, you're the most amazing woman I've ever met. I never want to lose you. And I never want to see you angry at me again."

"Oh, Tony, I wasn't angry at you; I was *worried*. That wasn't you in the barn. You're not a vampire and you're going to beat this thing. I know it."

Tony nodded slowly in her gaze and then turned them back toward the walk. They remained in their own thoughts and he steered them through the iron cow gate into the wide-open pasture. As they strolled, Tony's mind wandered to his most recent liaison with Rakha. How much should he tell Sarah about that? Could he keep it from her? For her own good?

They had reached the end of the fence line and Tony again caused her to turn and look into his face. The night couldn't be more romantic, the air the perfect temperature and the softest breeze flipping wisps of her hair into a halo where the moon shone through. His heart jumped in his chest—it was time. He couldn't stop himself. Tony dropped to one knee in the damp grass, holding her hands and looking up into her eyes.

"Sarah, will you marry me?"

Sarah's eyes widened. "Oh, Tony! Yes!" Sarah dropped to both knees to align their faces and she yanked him into a hug. "I love you so much."

She was crying as she spoke and Tony chuckled against her cheek in the hug. His eyes threatened to tear, but the thought of them being red with blood was enough to cause him to straighten up. He kissed her mouth, once and then longer, and in a few seconds, they had resumed the earlier passion, both of them on their knees in the night air.

When Sarah pulled away inches to catch her breath, she put her hands to Tony's cheeks, her thumbs caressing his short beard. "God showed me in a vision that we'd be married one day, but I thought He meant... you know, after..."

Tony hadn't considered waiting. "Will you marry me now? As I am? I don't want to wait. I need you as much as I love you." He sounded pitiful, but her eyes revealed he'd said the right thing.

"We don't have to wait." Then her breath hitched. "But keep in mind, you're younger than I am. When this curse is over, you might want children and..." she stopped, choking back new tears.

Tony pulled her up with him and covered her lips with gentle fingers. "You are everything I ever wanted in a friend, lover, spouse, and more. It's not up to us if we have children—God decides, right?"

Sarah wiped her eyes and grinned wider than before. "When?"

Tony pretended to look at a watch. "I guess it's too late tonight, but tomorrow looks good."

They both laughed and fell into a new embrace. Tony held her, encompassed her with tenderness and her hands caressed his back, both of them pondering what the future might hold. After a moment, Tony broke the silence.

"I fell in love with you at that party. You will never know how beautiful you looked feeding the Word to those lambs on the floor," Tony whispered in her ear, her lithe body against his own.

"I couldn't keep my eyes off you, did you notice? You took my breath away."

"I thought I spooked you. I was a pretty fresh, you know, *monster* then. But look where we are now." Tony paused with a new thought.

"I can't give you a church wedding while under this curse, but we'll go to the Justice of the Peace and do a proper church wedding later. Is that okay?"

Sarah nodded. "You are wonderful, Tony Agricola."

"You are," he responded with a goofy grin. Somewhere close by, the vampire watched on; Tony sensed him, Rakha's blood sang a song his subconscious listened for. Tony hid his response; he needed to keep Sarah and the vampire apart, and he needed to keep her from knowing that he wanted to see Rakha again and again.

Tony held tight to his future wife and held on to his secret. In his heart, he made excuses to God.

35

And he did evil in the sight of the LORD,
According to all that his father had done.
2 Kings 24:9

GETTING MARRIED BEFORE STRANGERS SEEMED FITTING.
Before heading to the Justice of the Peace, Sarah had packed a bag from
her condo and joined Tony for the trip to the courthouse. On the ride
home, they discussed newlywed logistics, such as moving her in and
where they should honeymoon when the time was right. She admitted
she'd been married to Ira only a few years before he passed and because
of his advanced age and her unfortunate internal conformation, they
had not consummated their marriage.

"In my twenties a doctor described my uterus as 'mis-hung' and
he said I was likely barren," Sarah said during their conversation on
sexual matters. "He also said it could make sex painful." She gave Tony
a small grin. "As it worked out, I haven't slept with a man so I don't
know one way or the other. I wanted you to know."

Tony sensed she wanted him to comment and he only patted her
shoulder, his mind walking two tracks. *I want to see Rakha and take his
blood and I want to be married to Sarah. Why can't I do both? God isn't in any
hurry to lift the curse, so why do I fight so hard to resist?*

Beside him, Sarah still awaited a response and she cleared her
throat.

"I'm sorry," he said and blinked several times. "I've only had one
serious girlfriend." He shot her a wink that he hoped appeared jolly.
"God-willing, you and I can love each other like husband and wife…"
he said and trailed off. He meant the words, but she read his current
mindset—*God's not delivering me.*

With an understanding sigh, Sarah changed the topic to hobbies
and asked him what he liked to do for fun. So much of what he would
answer pertained to "before he was a vampire." What would he enjoy
now? He allowed her to ramble on until they were almost to the house
and she grew quiet. It took him a few seconds to realize her silence was
because of him. He reached the electronic gate of his property and
looked her way.

"Why aren't you talking? Rather I should ask, what are you thinking so hard about?" Her tone was even, but she was irritated.

"Oh," he stammered and to cover his error, said, "I got off in my own head a minute, that's all." She wasn't satisfied and he exhaled. "I keep having to justify every answer with the timing of the question. There's no one in the world I'd rather share words and stories and dreams with, but everything I answer is pre and post curse. I don't know what life will be like as a vampire." He had reached the parking area and he switched off the truck. "I think this is it. I think I'll have to live with it like Dr. Corescu does."

"Anthony Agricola!" Sarah said, her voice stern as she swiveled in her seat to better see him. "This is *not* you! You don't believe that one bit. Stop lying to yourself and rationalizing what you know God is going to deliver!"

The spike of anger did not bring any reciprocal emotion. Instead, Tony turned inside and refused to reply, his beloved revealing why he wanted to keep her out of this part of his new life. She didn't have the demon in her gut torturing her if she didn't give in. And she didn't have God turning His back every time Tony asked him *when?*

"Say it," Sarah said her voice recovering its normal gentleness. "Tell me how God will deliver you of this curse once He has accomplished His will." Tony rolled in his lips so she added more. "When we met, you were fully aware of this fact. You agreed to it and you agreed to allow God to work through you and use this condition in your flesh for whatever He needed."

"I misunderstood all of it," Tony said out the windshield and not looking into her face. "I misinterpreted the Scriptures. I condemned myself, God did not condemn me." He did not want to say more, but Sarah was relentless. He hoped his next sentence would end it. "Do this for me. Pray for me to have the wisdom and knowledge of God, okay?" He turned to finally meet her eye. "Pray He will reveal it to me again, because I don't think He means to deliver me. I waited forty days, I set out that fleece and he rejected it. I'm not doing it again." He shook his head resolute.

Sarah gasped with understanding. "You're giving in?"

Tony shrugged. "No, not the way you think. I'm not going to bite people on the neck, but I might do like Mark." Inside, he didn't think about drinking from animals, but from donors such as John and Rakha... *and Sarah?* He waited to see if his inner mind would attack him for thinking that and it did not. He was truly rearranging his position on all of it. Sarah caught on.

"Oh, I see," she said and opened her side of the truck. "You're not cursed, after all."

Tony also got out of the truck and analyzed her tone. She was angry, but not at him. This godly woman had turned her fury on the devil, accusing him of swaying Tony from the Truth. Whether intuiting or reading the info in her mind, Tony loved her for her selflessness.

He walked around the front of the truck and offered an embrace. Sarah accepted and with his face against her jaw he said in her ear, "Yes, I'm cursed and with you, God will set me free again." He placed a lingering kiss to her throat. "Come upstairs, Mrs. Agricola, and let's see how much a vampire and an angel can do in this condition."

His words brought a giggle and he sensed her anger had passed. She kissed his head and said yes. In another thirty minutes, they found the bed and did the best they could to forget their common tribulations. For an hour at least, they'd just be lovers.

ঔৎৎ৹

Jonah turned in early, but sleep evaded. His mind raced with Jenn's case and he was helpless to stop his mind from doing what it did best.

"Doctor Mark Corescu is a respected member of the aristocracy in Hungary," Jenn said entering the bedroom.

"Say again," he responded opening his eyes.

"I *said,* Doctor Mark Corescu is a certified Count, just like you suggested last year. He owns tons and tons of property across the Balkans and we're not allowed to look into what else he owns. They have protective laws over there; seems the government seizes landowner assets when they reach a certain ratio of wealth to debt."

Jonah sat up in bed. Jenn spoke rapidly, fully awake, and he noted the bedside clock read midnight. He asked her to slow down and she turned to face him, busily removing her shoes and socks.

"Corescu's family line does not hide their ancestry. He does however hide details pertaining to his business in other European countries. I bribed a local barrister to look into the name and he found evidence that the doctor hides assets."

"You bribed a barrister?" Jonah couldn't believe his ears.

"I didn't break international law, detective, honest."

Jonah huffed in wonder. "Okay, what else?"

"Nothing else. I couldn't find him. He's not on anyone's radar in his home country nor surrounding sister states." Jenn disappeared into the attached bath and called from inside, "I phoned Opal and she's never met the doctor. She said her husband hasn't either. But…"

Jonah listened as the toilet flushed and Jenn brushed her teeth. *But…* he thought and wished he'd never met this case. Jenn exited and leapt upon the bed, fresh-faced and wearing one of his giant T-shirts.

"BUT," she shouted and then spoke normally, "I called John Jenkins phone right after—see, I knew he'd be at work—and I asked him if he'd ever met the doctor. Guess what, he said he hadn't. The interesting thing is that he lied."

"Oh?" Jonah lay back down when Jenn reclined. "So you think he's actually met the guy but told his wife he didn't?"

"That's what I'm thinking, based upon voice inflection and word choice. Opal believes her husband never met the guy, but Jenkins bristled, stumbled, and made up a lie when I asked him the same question. Not only does he want to keep this a secret from us, but from his wife, too."

"But he knows him. Knows about him," Jonah said recalling John taking care of Agricola's home when he went to Germany.

Jenn nodded. "Here, I recorded it." Jenn lifted her cell from the night stand and found the app. She hit play and John Jenkins' deep voice emanated from the device.

"When I worked for Paul, his boss had already left the country."

"How did Paul like him? Tony said they were close. Did Paul talk about him a lot?"

(Hemming) *"I g-guess. I don't know. Paul complained a lot about everything. I think he complained about the doctor once or twice."*

"How's that exactly?"

(Hemming) *"Oh, just wishing they were together. I really don't see how I can help you. I never knew the man."*

"And did you say you never met him?"

"I never met him back then and I think when he was around, Paul liked him a lot. Was attached to him."

Jenn looked at Jonah who's brow raised when the man said "back then." With a smug nod, she restarted the playback.

"So you met him recently? Now?"

(Hemming and cleared throat) *"No, that's not what I said. I'm sorry, Detective, I mean, Ms. Speltz, whatever, I don't know anything else. Good luck."* (click)

Jonah nodded, his mind running down their clues so far. *John Jenkins has met the doctor and recently. But why lie?*

"Why not just admit he met him? Is Corescu under investigation? No. Why is Count Corescu in hiding and why does John Jenkins want to keep their meeting a secret?" Jenn waited for Jonah to guess, but he had nothing. Jenn shrugged and switched of the lamp. "It's because Corescu is a vampire and he needs to stay out of the spotlight. He visited for vampire purposes. That's why."

Jonah gave her a nudge with his elbow. "It's hard to sell the vampire angle, but let's piece it together human-style."

"Our direct information starts with Brannen and Agricola going to Corescu's house one night."

"Wait, ma'am, it starts the day before, when Brannen and Agricola are leaving Corescu's house—without going in, they were at the gate, remember? And the doctor was coming out..."

"Yeah, okay, go on," Jenn said, excitement building. Oh, how she loved this part of crime solving.

"The dead reporter came up to their truck and asked if they knew Stuckey. Brannen lied to throw him off and they went on their way."

"Then they go to Corescu's house another night where Agricola meets them both."

"Right. Agricola told us that he was Corescu's spiritual advisor and he didn't like Black to start..."

"Later, he said, they became close, like brothers."

Jonah nodded. "And then he became spiritual advisor to Paul Black."

"Who had killed Nixon by now and maybe the Hip-Hop King of Georgia, and had attacked the reverend. All of which, Agricola professes to know nothing about."

Jonah shrugged in the dark. The man hadn't expressly denied it, but since he didn't offer the info, they could assume he didn't want the police to know he knows.

"We gotta add John Jenkins," Jenn said in a wistful tone. "He said he worked for Black during this time, coaching or wrestling or fitness, some crap."

"Right and that went on a couple of months," Jonah said. If he still wore a uniform, he'd make a timeline board.

Jenn's phone chimed and Jonah covered his eyes as she lit up the screen. It was from her associate Corporal Powder and she read the text aloud. *"Assets of Anthony Agricola include the house on eleven acres, one Chevy*

S10 pickup, and a bookstore in Old Cloverdale." She switched on the lamp. "I never heard anything about a bookstore."

Jonah didn't sit up, but he was wide awake now and curious as she was. "Old Cloverdale. Look it up."

Jenn's fingers flew across the tiny keyboard and she squinted her eyes when they found a Yelp entry.

"Collegiate Bookstore, M-F, 7-7, Sat 12-3, Closed Sunday." She looked at Jonah. "Tomorrow's Saturday. I'm going. Wanna ride to Montgomery? We can see Elizabeth, too."

Jonah nodded, his mind already questioning the staff at the bookstore. He relaxed back and Jenn again turned off the side-table lamp. He fell asleep to the sound of his beloved typing notes to herself for tomorrow.

36

Know that the Lord is God.
It is he who made us, and we are his;
we are his people, the sheep of his pasture.
Psalm 100:3

THEIR LOVEMAKING WOULD BE UNCONVENTIONAL FOR
the time being, but when Sarah awoke the morning after, her heart burst
with happiness as the memory of their intimate evening caused her to
blush a deep red. Tony was not in bed and she didn't expect he would
be. He had warned her that his condition stole his sleep and agreed to
stay until she fell off. Now that it was a sunny new day, she could not
wait to see what the Lord had in mind for them both.

After a quick shower, she headed downstairs, watching for Tony
along the way. Coffee had been brewed, but as for the rooms she
passed, he was nowhere to be seen. Sarah entered the large kitchen and
filled a mug Tony must have set out for her earlier. Remembering that
one of Tony's supernatural oddities was his hearing, she called in a
normal voice, "Good morning, Mr. Agricola! It's a brand new day!"

She heard no reply and sipped her brew and took a seat at the
center island. The stools were tall and she curled her feet in the struts
and leaned over the granite with both elbows, looking at nothing, but
sending up thanks to the Lord in her heart. After a quiet amen, she set
down her cup and strong arms from behind removed her from her stool
with gentle power and in a flash, she was cradled into Tony's arms.

"Oh!" she exhaled with surprise and then kissed his cheek as he
held her like a child and with no obvious effort.

"Good morning, Mrs. Agricola," he said low in her ear.

Sarah did not struggle in his careful support and instead used both
hands to cup his face and kiss his mouth. Tony responded and for a
long moment, they resumed a special kiss they had developed in bed
the night before. When he pulled away, his eyes shined with humor and
exhilaration.

"See, you can still feel enough!" she joked and he agreed, carefully
lowering her feet to the ground. Sarah loved his happy face and his joy

gave her hope after their rough start the night before. "I guess you're feeling better?"

"I feel better than better. I feel *perfect.*" Tony took a deep breath and exhaled with drama. "This is a beautiful morning!" Tony made his pronouncement looking at Sarah and not out the sunny picture window. "After you fell asleep, I went before the Lord. I repented for waffling and I think He was listening. For the first time in weeks, I feel hopeful. I think He's preparing for us a breakthrough. What do you think?"

Sarah nodded and said with caution, "But don't put a time limit on Him this go-round. He has something to accomplish. If we turn our prayers to asking what that is, maybe your concern over *when* will fade into your subconscious. Let's focus on doing His will and let the curse fall off in His timing."

"Okay, I agree. I'm in." Tony's eyes shone with joy, appearing fully rejuvenated.

Sarah thanked the Lord and grabbed Tony into a new hug. "I just fell in love with you all over again!"

Tony smiled out of genuine pleasure. "I'm sorry about the way I acted last night. There's no excuse for that. Vampire crap or not, I should never bring you any sort of grief. You are a human angel, Sarah, and I want to be like you, to love the Lord the way you do. To care about His work selflessly."

"You do, honey, you do all that," she said but he shook his head.

"I think maybe my selfishness is why I haven't been delivered. You said it just now—the past forty days, I focused on Tony. Me, me, me. When will God deliver me. When will He help me. I had no idea I'd become so important in my own eyes. But I see, now, and I want you to pray that I will continue to seek after God's will and not my own."

Sarah wiped happy tears. "Of course, I will. I will never stop praying for you and what God has for you to do in this life." She hugged him one more time and from the island top, her cell phone vibrated with a call. When she lifted it, they both read Elizabeth's name.

"Sarah, he was here. Last night, Rakha Tep came to my house." Elizabeth did not sound hysterical, but she was tense.

"Oh, honey! Tell us what happened. Tony's here, too," she said.

"First, I'm horrible—congratulations on your marriage. I just…" The youngster grew quiet and Sarah waited. They had alerted Elizabeth and John of their courthouse wedding and didn't expect them to do anything except wait for the big one later. But the demon at Elizabeth's?

It was all Sarah could do to not fly over to her house without waiting for more.

"Did he hurt you?" Tony asked listening from the side.

"No, he didn't come inside, but he was there, on my curb in his car. I called the police. He left before they got here. I've been having nightmares, too. I'm afraid I somehow let him in. I… I…"

"Hush now, nothing he does is your fault, do you hear me?" Sarah said in a gentle tone. "I'm coming over there. Sit tight."

"No, really," she said meaning it. "Dad's coming by. He heard about me calling the police and got worried." She chuckled a sad sound. "I didn't realize how it worked with retired cops. Now he's concerned about Mr. Tep, too."

Sarah looked at Tony who had grown serious.

"Elizabeth, will you talk to Tony a minute?" Sarah asked and she handed off the phone. She didn't know what Tony would say, but his concern about the retired detective was written all over his face.

"Hey, I'm glad you're okay," Tony said and held Sarah's eye as he continued. "Will you keep Sarah in the loop concerning whatever your dad thinks about Rakha? I'd be interested to know what the police think. And if they have any evidence against him."

"I will, and I feel so much better just talking to you guys. Thank you for being there."

"Elizabeth," Sarah said back on the phone, "you should have called us last night. Never think you can't call us, any time, day or night."

"Okay, I knew you were just married so I tried to handle it myself."

"You are a doll, but please, always call me. I'm never too busy to help. Tony, either."

Sarah watched Tony's eyes and the youngster said her goodbyes and was gone.

"I don't want her to know about the vampire stuff," he said to Sarah who agreed. "Detective Miller wants to drop it, he has a spiritual nudge to keep his nose out, but his fiancée drives him to investigate. It was the same way when they were investigating Paul. Every time they got close, God kept them back. I had the feeling God was protecting them. I hope He keeps them clear of Rakha. He's so much more dangerous than Paul ever was."

Sarah considered his point and decided her prayers for the next hour should be about Elizabeth.

ॐ

"Why the hell is this guy stalking my daughter?" Jonah did not expect or even want an answer, but Jenn had one ready.

"Because she's friends with Agricola's woman. I tell you, hon, this has to do with your preacher friend. Something's off with him. I think he's connected. But we're almost there. We'll figure it out."

Jonah didn't need to say it, but he did anyway. "Please don't mention Dracula—"

"I won't," Jenn said and shot him a 'cross-my-heart' gesture.

"Andy's keeping surveillance up for a few days. He convinced his captain she was a priority witness."

"That Andy, he's a good guy. How long have you been friends?"

Jonah hid his unfounded jealousy. "Met him back in my academy days at a joint-agency workshop."

"Well, he's like us, laid-back. When he retires, we need to find him a little wife and move him near us."

Jonah peeked her way but she watched out the windshield. "Sounds like a plan."

They had reached his daughter's house and he slowed beside a city car with a man behind the wheel. Jonah flash his driver's license but the guy was already nodding.

"It's all good, Andy gave me your deets."

Jonah thank him. "Any sign of the creep?"

The guy said no and Jonah pulled into her driveway. Elizabeth opened the front door and watched them park.

"Hey, Dad," she said with a cautious smile. "Jenn."

Jonah came close and engulfed her into a hug. Jenn hugged her, too, and she invited them into her cozy living room. Once she sat them on her two-seater sofa and offered them something to drink, she sat across on a ottoman and told them everything about her stalker.

"Why would he do that? I mean," she paused and waited for Jonah's eye. "I mean, I wasn't scared-scared, but I was spooked. Tony and Sarah told me he was dangerous. Who is he? Do the police know what he wants from me?"

Jonah shook his head. "There's nothing on him anywhere. It's like he appeared out of thin air. They located his residence by tracking his vehicle registration, but all of the information he used to purchase and lease is clean." Jonah sighed. "It doesn't link him to anything nefarious. The guy is clean." He looked to Jenn who touched his knee with a kind nod.

"Why do you think Reverend Tracey said he was dangerous? Do they know him?" Jenn asked, of which Jonah was glad.

"Huh," Elizabeth said as if considering the possibility. "I didn't get the idea they know him very well, but Tony knows something about the guy. He wasn't specific, but he told me to stay away from him."

"That's weird," Jenn said and this time Jonah spoke over her last word.

"How do you feel about Agricola? Tony? Is he a good guy?" Jonah asked.

"Yeah," Elizabeth said and met Jenn's eyes, too, before sighing. "He's sort of moody. Eccentric. But he loves God and really loves Reverend Sarah." Then she met Jonah's gaze with a new thought. "He wants me to tell him what the police think about Mr. Tep. Is it okay for me to tell him what we talked about just now? I don't want to break any police confidences."

"I appreciate that, honey, but Jenn and I only know unofficial stuff these days. As for telling Agricola, just use your best judgment. If you think he's okay, then he probably is."

"Then what's worrying you? Is it because of the guy who died? The guy he used to live with?" she asked. Jenn answered in Jonah's stead.

"Your dad likes the guy, has from the start. I've been suspicious of him. So to cover your bases, follow your gut. It will always steer you right." Elizabeth said she would and Jenn got to her feet. "I'm heading over to the Collegiate Bookstore in Old Cloverdale. I can leave you and your dad to visit a while…"

Elizabeth stood. "Oh, let's all go. I have a couple of books to swap out and two on hold to pick up."

Jonah's jaw dropped. Elizabeth was familiar with Agricola's store? "Honey, Tony Agricola owns that bookstore. Did you know that?"

Elizabeth's brow lifted, her mouth an O. "No way, I go there every week. I never asked and they never mentioned it. What a coincidence."

"What a coincidence," he repeated. The overlapping of every single detail of this case unsettling Jonah to the core.

They decided to go together in the Explorer. Once they were loaded, Jenn and Elizabeth made small talk about books and Jonah pondered what God might be doing.

"Why does my daughter need to be involved? This stuff is too close, Lord. It's too close. Keep her safe. I mean it…"

Jonah knew God was listening, but he didn't feel any better by the time they reached the small establishment.

The bookstore was well-lit and eleven patrons milled about, Jonah counting them at a glance as if still a policeman. Jenn found the cashier was also the manager and began asking about Agricola right away.

"Sure, Tony's great. A good boss. He lets me run the place. Never doubts my decisions. Why?" Rachel sounded sincere and truthful, so Jenn tried a new tact.

"The store had two owners. Did you meet his partner, Paul Black, or maybe you knew him by Saul White?"

This time, the young woman paused, and did she blanch? She allowed a customer to distract her and Jenn and Jonah waited for her to finish. She turned back, still pale.

"Who, now? Mr. White?" she asked, delaying. Jenn nodded. "Sure, I met him once. The day I was hired, he was here."

"Tell me about it," Jenn said and Jonah did the cop-thing, stepped closer and lowered his eye. They could not compel an answer and hoped she didn't think too hard about it.

Rachel shook her head. "He was weird, that's all. He acted weird." She sought the right words. "He laughed for no reason and Tony had to sort of, well, control him."

"Huh, that's weird," Jenn said leading.

"Yeah, and their friend was here, a wonderful guy named John. He's been by here since to check on me. He's very nice."

"John Jenkins," Jonah said and gave the girl a smile when she darted her eyes his way.

"It would help if you could tell us anything specific about Mr. White's behavior. We're connecting him to some other things, so anything you have might be helpful." Jenn spoke her piece flawlessly and Jonah followed her lead with a serious nod.

"I guess the weirdest thing was Tony told him to wait outside while he and John spoke in the office." She pointed to a stairwell at the back of the store leading to a door in the wall. "It turns out they were praying in there and Mr. White thought it would be hilarious to send me up there to interrupt."

The young woman gulped and Jonah peeked at Jenn. She noticed it, too.

"And that's about it," she said.

"Why are you afraid of Mr. White? Last question, I promise," Jonah asked, stepping on Jenn's toes, but she only nodded.

"Oh. I don't know. His eyes, maybe? He was like a mean kid who pulls wings off butterflies. I can't put it any better than that." She shrugged.

Jonah looked to Jenn who sighed. There was more in there, but the girl had locked the rest down. Jonah watched her thank her just as Elizabeth hit the register with a stack of books.

"Hey!" Rachel said with recognition. "How are you?"

"I'm good, thanks!" Elizabeth answered and Jonah stepped back to make room. "I just need these here."

Rachel rang up the first two and held the third longer to read the back. "*Ancient Beings, Demons, and Fallen Angels?* Whoa, this should be interesting!" she said. "Are you writing a book?"

"Oh, no, personal interest," Elizabeth said and lowered her voice. "I think there's a spiritual attack against me and I'm going to get ahead of it!"

Jonah watched on, in wonder at his daughter's knowledge of spiritual warfare.

"Oh! Geez!" Rachel said and her hand went to her mouth. "The last time you were here, a very creepy man asked about you." Her eyes flit to Jonah. "He asked about Tony, too!"

"What did he say?" Jenn asked for them all.

"Well," the young woman said and her eyes narrowed. "I can't remember. But I remember him asking for Tony's information and for your name."

"You didn't give it, did you?" Elizabeth asked.

"No, but…" She thought back. "I don't know. It's fuzzy. But still, I just remembered when you mentioned spiritual attacks. He was evil. I just know it."

Jenn showed her the print-out of the man's driver's license photo.

"That's him. He was nasty. I'm very happy he doesn't come in here."

Jonah and Jenn thanked her and moved off.

"We have to speak to Agricola," he said low to Jenn. "Let's see if Elizabeth can get us an audience." Jenn nodded and in another five minutes, the three headed for the truck. Once seated, Jonah swiveled to see his daughter in the back.

"Hon, we need to talk to Tony. Since we're in town, do you think we could run to his house?"

"He got married yesterday," she said as if to herself, scrolling her contacts. "But Sarah said I should call any time, no matter what. Let's see..."

Elizabeth pressed send and Jonah didn't start the car to keep it quiet.

"Elizabeth! What a pleasant surprise! Did you have a nice visit with your father?" The reverend's happy voice rang out through the earpiece.

"We did, but we have more news on Rakha Tep. Turns out he was looking for me and for Tony at the same time. Here, at Tony's bookstore. Dad wanted me to ask if the three of us can come by the house to compare notes."

Jonah looked to Jenn, both of them proud of how she worded her query. Reverend Tracey told them to come on over and she disconnected.

"Head out Taylor Road toward Mitylene. I'll tell you where to turn," Elizabeth said and relaxed in the back.

Jonah started the ignition and pondered what they'd ask the man and he also pondered if Jenn would give him the benefit of the doubt or call him a vampire to his face. Jonah smiled to himself and hoped he was joking.

��

Tony and Sarah had been sweeping cobwebs in the stable when Elizabeth's call came through. Within fifteen minutes, he heard the whine of the electronic gate and told Sarah they were here. She shook the dust from her hair and went to the barn door to wave them over. Tony set his broom aside and prepared himself. He had no problem talking to her father off the record, but if they got too specific, he'd have to recuse himself. He cued Sarah on what not to discuss and she agreed. No talk of vampires.

The cop's SUV rolled to a stop in the lot and the three got out. Tony remained in the shadow of the barn and watched them approach. Jonah walking with pride, probably reflecting the joy of being with two women he adored. Jenn walked ahead of them and reached Sarah first, putting out her hand.

"You're a dear to let us come on such short notice," the woman said and Sarah pulled her into a Southern hug. Tony wasn't surprised and he watched Jenn mimic the move.

"Oh, we are thankful God had you near when this was discovered. Isn't He marvelous! Setting everything up so neatly!"

Jenn's eyes reached Tony and he gave her a curt nod. Before the vampire curse, he probably would have shook her hand or maybe even half-hugged like a proper man of God, but now? He didn't like anyone close except Sarah and she knew how to protect herself if the demon seeped out of his pores.

Jonah hugged Sarah when he reached her and then he headed toward Tony who grinned and put up his palms.

"That's close enough, Offisuh," he said with humor and the big guy chortled.

"Thanks for letting us stop by. That Tep character asked about you and my daughter a month ago. She checked the date —the 24th of July." Jonah shook his head. "Who is this guy and what does he want?"

Tony also gave one long shake of the head and added a befuddled sigh. "I didn't know he was interested in Elizabeth, but he approached me, oh, I'd say… about a week after that. I'd been giving a presentation at a church and he introduced himself at the end. It was bizarre. I have no idea where he came from."

Tony watched the retired cop nod, the whole while picking apart every word and gesture, deciding if Tony was lying. Because of this, Tony told the truth as much as he could. Such as who the demon is— *I don't really know that.* And why he wants Elizabeth? *God help us; I have no idea.* Then Tony's mind said, *I could ask him…* and he erased the thought as her cop father continued to jabber.

"…are watching his house. If he sneezes, they'll know it."

Tony's ears perked. "That's fantastic, but how long will they do that? Isn't it expensive?" He still wanted to visit the old guy as he worked out his angst; a house surrounded by cops wasn't something Tony wanted part of.

"Only through the weekend, and then they'll just check on patrol…" Tony commiserated with a frown as Jonah slammed him with a pointed question he hadn't expected. First he checked the position of the women behind them, all three involved in their own conversation. He then asked Tony in a lowered voice, "You could help me with this. Between you and me…" He shot one more glance toward his woman. "Why did you go to Martha Street with the guy if you don't know him?"

Tony drew one hand down his face buying time, aware the guy read his every gesture. What could he say? Nothing without incriminating himself, but if he refused to answer, Miller would assume the worst.

As if he could; none of them would ever guess what's really going on. Tony turned in such a way that Jonah followed. Once they reached the back of the longish barn aisle, he faced him with a sigh.

"All of this is off the record and if I'm ever asked officially, I just made it up for kicks." Tony lowered his chin still holding his eye. "I'm going to tell you as close to the truth as I can. Ready?"

The retired lawman nodded at rapt attention. Tony liked him, had liked him last year. He was a good guy, a great cop, and he sought after the Lord's will even when it went against his employer's commands.

"Earlier this month I had a mental breakdown, right here, in this barn." Tony pointed to the general area it happened, which only helped the guy believe. "I had a fight with Sarah and she left. That man, Rakha, was watching and he came in here when she was gone. He caught me at my lowest point and offered to give me some peace." Tony paced his story, now wondering what to translate the bloodthirst into. He had a notion. "Off the record, remember?" he reiterated and the cop gave him a blink. "Years ago before I knew God the way I do now, I had an addiction."

He hemmed, partly on purpose, but partly because the lie he had decided to go with was pretty huge. Jonah gave him a sincere "continue" nod.

"I'm straight, but," he said and read in the man's eyes he was trying to guess ahead. "I used to be addicted to…" Tony lowered his voice and moved close to Jonah's ear, *"male prostitutes,"* he whispered with a slight movement toward his fly. Then he resumed the lowered voice. "The night I broke down, I had given up. I was in pieces over everything that happened over the past few months. I can't tell you all of it for legal reasons, but I've been devastated since Paul died." He caught a question in Jonah's eye and he jumped in front of it. "No, we weren't lovers, but I grew close to him, like a brother. Like I said, I'm straight." He peeked at the women far away and back to Jonah, mixing lies and truth. "I've never slept with men, but in my twenties, I had a problem, like, with what I said before. Just receiving… you know."

"I got ya," Jonah said low. "So, Rakha Tep brought you something of that? When you were at your lowest?" he offered with deep compassion.

Tony nodded. "I was mad at God, mad at Sarah for being so kind and godly. This guy, whoever he is, he knew me and knew what I needed. I voluntarily left with him." Tony tried to appear self-mortified as he admitted, *"I stayed with him three nights."*

"Geez," Jonah breathed, his eyes still soft.

"The third night, I went with him to Martha Street. In that house is a man who is into the same thing." Tony shook his head as if in shame, but he was happy at how well he'd disguised the truth with an unexpected lie. He held his palms up in his own defense and said, "I didn't let that man touch me. Just seeing him sort of broke my fugue. I told Rakha I wanted to go home and I did."

Jonah nodded a few times, eyes averted in thought. Tony guessed he was deciding whether or not to believe him. The story was too embarrassing to be fake so Tony held his face and waited.

"Does the reverend know?" he asked, but only in the sense that he didn't want to spill any beans.

"I haven't told her yet. But I will. If you can keep this to yourself. I mean, tell Ms. Speltz, sure, but not Elizabeth or Sarah. Please."

"I won't say anything." Jonah sighed and thrust his hands in his pockets. "So this guy stalked you and took advantage of you when your guard was down. Why is he interested in my daughter? She only just met you and Reverend Tracey."

Tony shook his head, sincerely wondering what Rakha had in mind. The demon hadn't mentioned the girl to him at all. *And I need to warn him about his police detail. They're watching him. He needs to know...*

Jonah had run out of questions and he made an excuse for the two of them to see what the ladies discussed. Tony followed and let Sarah lead the topics. The two ex-cops wished them a good evening and then invited them to see them wed in Georgia in December. Tony made all the correct responses, but he also sensed his hunger returning and his gut wanted a date with Rakha.

37

Truly I tell you, whatever you bind on earth
will be bound in heaven, and whatever
you loose on earth will be loosed in heaven.
Matthew 18:18

TEN DAYS AFTER SAYING, "I DO," SARAH HAD COMPLETELY
moved in. Putting her townhouse on the market would wait; for now,
she sensed more than ever how important it was to be close to Tony
during his transition.

God, I hope that's the correct word, she thought and headed from the
bedroom to the laundry room downstairs. In the past several days, Tony
seemed happy, normal, not at all a vampire thirsting for blood. It was
as if the episode in the barn cleansed him of the terrible cramping his
suffering caused. Sarah was eternally grateful, but so far had no peace
in her spirit regarding when he would shed the curse.

Sarah pulled clean towels from the dryer, mentally checking the
time. Tony and John had run an errand having to do with the tractor
and that had been hours ago. When she texted him at 5, he replied they
were nearly done. Now it was close to 9 PM, and she had no word on
when they'd return. Sarah carried the towels to the staircase and her
phone chimed in her pocket.

"Sorry! Leaving now. See you in an hour."

Sarah returned a heart emoji and started up the stairs, her mind
returning to Tony's hunger. Had he finally found the answer? Was the
Scripture helping that much? It wasn't hard to believe, she'd seen plenty
of miracles in her life. Only, something in her spirit caused her to keep
thinking it over and she sighed.

"Okay, Lord, please help me understand what You want me to know..."

Sarah pondered the Lord's reply as she put the laundry in its
proper place. Five minutes later, she headed back down the stairs. The
moment her foot touched the landing, the hairs on the back of her neck
stood on end. She was not alone.

Sarah searched the dark corners and flipped each light switch she
passed on her way to the great room. When she met the threshold, a
lamp inside beside the couch illuminated the space.

"Did I frighten you?"

Sarah did not know the creature's face, but it was him, Rakha, Tony's nemesis. With adrenaline flowing to her limbs, Sarah resisted the urge to flee. Instead, she forced her mind to praise the Lord in her heart, reciting a Psalm she used to bring herself comfort. Then as she registered the surprise in the monster's face, she slowly turned her back and walked to the main staircase.

"Ma'am?" the thing said, and Sarah enjoyed the waver she discerned.

He wasn't accustomed to being dismissed and she would be out of sight by now. With a stern command and in Jesus' name, she told the demon to depart. When she reached the top stair she looked backward. Rakha had trailed behind her and stopped in the front entry, looking upward to her position. She pointed to the double doors behind him.

"You are no longer welcome here, Rakha. I live here now and my God will not permit you entry."

"I'm here. I got in," he said, but his voice did not carry its earlier confidence.

"I don't care how you got in. Right now, in Jesus' name, I will only say one more time—depart."

"Or what?" the demon asked, still speaking low and unsure.

"Or I will bind you up so bad you won't be able to move for a week." Sarah held her passive expression and waited to see what the vampire would do. In her heart, worship flowed to the Father and her initial fear response evaporated.

"You will *bind me up*? I have come to see your husband. He asked me to come. He wants me—"

"Rakha!" Sarah interrupted and took a deep breath. "You have nothing to say to me or my husband. We're not interested in you. By the name of Jesus, I bind you and compel you to be gone!"

Sarah's words worked on the vampire's haughty smirk, causing it to fade to a scowl. He looked as if he wanted to move toward her, but couldn't. The creature dropped his eyes to his feet and made a noise in his chest. Then, with his horrid mouth gaping, his sharp fangs erupted like a B-movie Dracula. Rakha howled, spun a 180, and ran out the front door.

"Thank God!" Sarah shouted aloud and sank to sit on the top stair. She needed to go down and close the front door, but first, she'd catch her breath. *"Thank you, thank you, thank you,"* she repeated and in her mind, she laughed at the vampire's boasts. He was in for a big surprise.

❧❧

An incredible weakness traveled across Rakha's frame and he half-crawled the final few feet to his car.

I knew better! She has the light! I knew better! Rakha shouted to himself. He never anticipated becoming paralyzed. Even as he steered the car away from the property, an all-consuming numbness poured into his bloodstream.

"What is happening? You must tell me!" Rakha beseeched the Unseen to explain, afraid he might not make it home before he lost the ability to move.

They answered laughing in a dozen voices. *"If you would only follow our instruction, you pitiful creature! You have met the Carpenter face-to-face. Did you not recognize Him? Oh, you should have listened to us. You may not recover. You may not make it to the safety of your dark room. We might be watching you melt in the sun very soon!"*

Rakha gasped and barreled home. Before his foot hit the stoop, the weakness hit him in full and he fell across the threshold. Kicking the door closed with a numb foot, he lay flat and face down on the floor, unable to move. Was his curtain drawn? He had made it a practice to keep it drawn at all times, but what if? Rakha didn't know and he couldn't turn his face to see. In his mind, the Unseen taunted him with glee.

"He might have broken you for good. Look at you…kicked to the dust by a woman. You should thank us for getting you home. If we hadn't dragged you into the house, you would still be sitting in your car waiting for the sun. So, so sad…we had such hopes for you."

Rakha did not respond or argue. As the Unseen berated him helpless on the floor, he began work on Plan C. It was all a learning exercise. Now he knew what the enemy was capable of. This was good. And surely the invisible bondage would not last forever. He would wait; he was a patient creature and he'd wait as long as it took.

❧❧

Tony waved goodbye as Big John headed away from the house. He hadn't intended to spend such a long time at the tractor shop, but one thing led to another and the boring part of owning a large property came into being. John hadn't asked him anything about his "condition," and Tony liked that. Since the wedding, Sarah hadn't mentioned much either and he liked that, too. Somehow, with the passage of time, he didn't worry over it nonstop as he had in the past.

Of course, Rakha's blood might be doing that…

Tony cleared his throat as if someone might overhear such a thought. In eight days, he had secretly visited the ancient vampire three times, twice at Rakha's cottage as Sarah slept, and once in his study when she left for a meeting at the church.

It's simply not a big deal and I blew the whole thing out of proportion before.

In fact, Tony grew increasingly embarrassed at how he treated the vampire upon their first meeting.

And all that stuff about wanting to kill me…

Tony shook his head. He didn't have all the answers yet, but one thing was certain—swapping blood with Rakha was keeping his loved ones safe from his teeth. There could be nothing wrong with that.

Tony wasn't hungry now and it had been twenty-four hours since he'd seen the old guy. With his hand to his middle in an absent manner, he headed for the den where he heard the television. Sarah turned to see him as he entered and gave him an enormous smile.

"There he is!" she said and hopped up to wrap him up in a hug. "This place sure is lonely when you're not here!" Tony nommed her neck with a crazy noise until she laughed and pulled away. "You look happy. Tractor-repair is your joy!"

"Hah, no," he said and led her back to the loveseat where they both sat facing the television. Sarah hit mute on the remote and they sighed in unison.

"What did you do today, milady?" Tony asked intertwining his fingers in hers between them.

"I studied the Bible. I cooked some pasta. I went for a walk. I did the laundry, and in Jesus' name, I bound up the demons in the vampire Rakha."

Tony's brow knitted and he turned his face. "What was that last one?"

Sarah nodded with a sly grin. "Rakha came in like he owned the place. I told him he wasn't welcome and that we didn't want to see him anymore."

"You're serious?" Tony's expression must had read something weird because Sarah laughed as if he made a joked.

"He was shocked! He barely got out the door. I don't even know if he made it home. Walking all stiff," Sarah said moving her arms as if she had no joints. "His muscles seizing right before my eyes. It was amazing to see!"

Tony's mind raced with too many questions and some of them he could never ask Sarah. "Sarah...I am so sorry..." Tony started but didn't know what else to say.

"It's not your fault, honey, and don't expect him to come back. If you'd seen the surprise in his face...." Sarah said and looking Tony's way, her grin faltered. "What's wrong?"

"Nothing, that's just amazing," he said and looked aside. *Is he gone for good? Should I check on him?* Tony cleared his mind, afraid that she might see his uncertainty. Of course it was good Rakha was prevented from hurting her—*wait. Why did he come? He came at a time she would surely be awake.* Tony rolled in his lips, not willing to go to that corner, that the vampire had intended to harm his wife.

Beside him, Sarah had continued to another topic, explaining a Bible passage she'd been pondering a while, having nothing to do with vampires or demons. And Tony pondered Rakha and if he was okay.

☙❧

A week had passed since he and Jenn visited Agricola at his opulent newly-inherited mansion. Jonah had confided in Jenn the man's story regarding how he knew Tep and how he ended up going to Martha Street. Jenn didn't believe him ("That story just doesn't hold water!"), but Jonah had seen the man's eyes—he'd been *mortified* at his admission. Jonah had a food addiction as a younger man and used that to commiserate. But he'd known plenty of addicts, including sex addicts, on the job and in the perp walk, so he certainly did feel for the guy. For the moment, he sat alone in the living room, lights out, TV on mute, thinking.

Elizabeth hadn't seen any sign that Tep had been around since that one time, no one at the department had seen him leave his house and of course, by now, they had removed the surveillance. Bookstore girl hadn't seen him either, of which she was thankful, she told Jenn who had checked back. Jonah found the most frustrating thing being he lived so far away from Montgomery. He wanted to be there if his daughter needed help, but 138 miles took time to drive. It was all he could do not to go down there daily. But he didn't. He tended his farm and Jenn tended her Dracula file.

Jonah *humphed* with a wry smile. That's where she was right now, upstairs on her computer, researching tidbits from whatever she could find on the public database. Andy would look things up for her if she asked, but Jenn had raised his suspicions by being too gung-ho about a case they had to put back to bed.

"JONAH!"

Jonah sat up with a grunt, unaware he'd dozed off. It took a moment, but Jenn shouted again, adding, "LOOK AT THIS!"

Shifting his weight with care he rolled to his feet. He'd turn fifty-one in another month and hadn't been treating his old bones right since retirement.

Heck, I slacked off gym-time five years ago...

Jenn called a third time and he bellowed he was on his way up. In the home office, Jenn glowed with excitement, whipping her face to his when he entered. It happened in a flash, but Jonah took in her bright eyes, messy mane of thick brown hair and that smile, bookended by deep dimples.

"What?"

"Nothing, you look happy," he said and stood behind her to place his palms to her shoulders.

"You called it. Look. This is unbelievable!" She gestured with a knuckle where to begin and Jonah adjusted his angle to suit his bifocals. There it was—Jenn had landed upon the question he hadn't wanted to ask when it occurred to him to research bloodless corpses in every state the three "vampires" registered. Jonah made an "ohh" noise and began to read.

Jenn had typed three columns:

2020-2010	Georgia	1125
2010-2000	Tennessee	1255
2000-1991	Maryland	3121
1991-1985	New York State	2000

And on, and on, to eleven states with varying third-column numbers. Jonah caught her eye. "Okay, go ahead. What is this exactly?"

"I'm glad you asked!" she chirped with a new twinkle in her eye. "These are the dates from the doctor's driver's licenses. The other guys line up so close that I didn't specify if they were off a year or so. The states, obviously, are where they registered and thus, the number is statewide cases of exsanguination where the medical examiner listed blood loss as the cause of death. It looks like a lot, I know, so this..." Jenn clicked to the next document, this one an excel sheet with more of the same. "These are exsanguination cases across the nation. Turns out thirty of fifty contiguous states have about the same number of cases."

Jonah pursed his lips. "So, why are you so happy?"

"Ah-hah!" she said with humor. "Because I took a page from the deceased." With the flick of a single key, a third doc opened, this one with fewer numbers and columns.

Alabama 15

Tennessee 34

Maryland 99...

Jenn nodded as he read on. "Connie Nixon died, we think, because he got too close to *the ageless three*." She shot Jonah a new grin. "I dropped the vampire label. Now I call them The Ageless Three, or TAT for short."

"Like that," he said and she tipped her chin for a kiss. He acquiesced and she continued.

"Nixon narrowed his search to cases of exsanguination that were unsolved. I didn't specify that the first few hours and that's why there are so many. Then it occurred to me that Nixon had cold cases so I went back through. Here, look..." She clicked one case previously hyperlinked. "They found this guy's body in the Tuskegee National Forest months after his death. Bloodless with two puncture wounds in his neck. In the movies, the vampires hide their puncture wounds or decapitate the victims. Why doesn't this guy disguise the method of withdrawing blood?"

"Is that what the report reads? There was suction on those punctures?" Jonah asked to clarify.

"Exactly. This one," she said with a new click. "Atlanta, Georgia, five years ago. A man, Asian, 6'5", former basketball pro indicted for murder, out on bail. Dead with puncture marks, suction at the edges."

"Murder?" he asked.

"Curious. The vampire killed a murderer." Jenn offered a smug grin. "So I took a shot. Tuskegee man? A murderer. He was found beside a hidden pond. Inside the pond, fifteen women of varying death-dates, the cops traced back to the bloodless guy. TAT killed another murderer."

"Huh," Jonah said his wheels turning. "Go on."

"The Hip-Hop King left bloodless with punctures in the exact same place as Tuskegee Forest guy, and he was under suspicion of homicide and domestic violence."

"Wait. Your sum-up?"

"I'm 50% through looking up the additional extra-case info but 100% of my bloodless unsolveds have evidence against them. Our driver, Reuben Stuckey—" Jen shuffled the docs back two pages on her computer. "Nixon probably died for the one dealing with Clara Stuckey, by records, his mother. Cops say she murdered several johns and the M.E. report says she'd had multiple non-surgical abortions, at-home coat-hanger types. She was a killer, killed by our TAT."

Jonah shook his head in wonder. "Your vampire's a vigilante."

"My TAT's a vigilante."

"So… what now?" Jonah wasn't asking. Jenn grinned and returned to her monitor. The case just wouldn't die. *Dammit.*

38

Woe to the world because of the things
that cause people to stumble!
Such things must come, but woe to the person
through whom they come!
Matthew 18:7

IT DIDN'T MATTER HOW MUCH OF THE PREACHER'S BLOOD
he drank, nor how willingly he handed it over—Rakha could only read
the man's thoughts when he was in sight. This shortcoming threatened
his chances of success now that he'd allowed the woman to shout her
curses.

"You will do it tonight, then?"

It was the Unseen. Rakha felt their anticipation as they scrambled
about in their own dimension. They were done with the game. They
saw a defeated man in Tony Agricola, a man at the end of his rope, and
they smelled his imminent destruction. But Rakha did not answer. He
crossed his arms behind his head and closed his eyes, aching from the
binding spell, but finally able to move. For three days he had been
unable to twitch the smallest muscle, but the ropes slipped away one by
one, until he could roll over and sit up. Now he had grown hungry and
he longed for Agricola's powerful blood.

This is why I need to keep him, convert him to my will and keep him about…

"You will fail. You will fail," the Unseen chanted barging into his
private thoughts. *"You can't beat him so you cook up this alternative. The
woman frightened you, how pitiful you have become in your old age!"*

Rakha did not take the bait and the Unseen repeated the same
sentiments in various contortions. Finally, they threatened to leave him
for good and Rakha offered a calm response.

"I have never let you down. You should have more confidence in
your servant." Rakha paused and heard no reply. "Are you going to
trust me? I have something in mind much better than we initially
planned. Can't you see my preaching vampyr is succumbing to our
wiles? Humiliation galore! And we'll bring down his entire ministry
along the way. Don't you think this would please your master more than
a single soul brought to ruin?"

The invisible minions argued amongst themselves and Rakha pondered his boast. How many souls do they bring into the Carpenter's kingdom during the average week? The number meant nothing to him, but meant the world to the Unseen's princes.

"If this comes to pass and they all fall, we will be very impressed…"

Rakha grinned with victory and turned his mind again to Tony Agricola. He could not reach him, but he asked the Unseen to nudge the guy over. Tell him how much his old friend across town wished he'd come by. Rakha's stomach growled and he looked up at the door. He'd unlock the deadbolt and appear helpless and so pitiful…

Tony will feel so sorry for me. His emotions run so-o-o-o-o deep.

Rakha laughed aloud in the quiet room and waited.

❧

Tony slipped out from under the heavy comforter and made his way soundlessly to the door. As had become their habit, he went to bed with Sarah and snuggled until she fell asleep. He still had two weeks before his vampire sleep returned so again he snuck out of the room without rousing his wife.

And it's been three days since she bound Rakha up. How is he faring? He hasn't been back or even slunk by to call me from the yard. Guilt assaulted Tony as usual when he fell sorry for the monster, but… *shouldn't I care? I mean, he is a living being…*

Tony padded down the staircase to his study. He faced the desk, his thoughts scattered and racing. He had enjoyed three great days recuperating under the tutelage of his Spirit-filled bride, but a worry for the future gnawed at him, too. Tony's hand went to his Bible on the desk and he flipped open a random page. The first Scripture that popped out was from Jeremiah. *"I know the plans I have for you…"* it began and Tony closed the book to look aside.

Those plans have put me in a very bad way.

Tony narrowed his eyes, again wondering what he could have done to turn God against him.

"But He didn't. He loves you. You need to trust that He is doing something wonderful with all this!"

Sarah's words; they helped in real-time when she inspired him and ministered to his pain and suffering. But tonight, he wanted what Rakha offered. The ecstasy the vampire delivered had no equivalent at night when God seemed asleep.

Shouldn't I check on Rakha? Determine his status? Confirm he's no longer a threat to my loved ones?

Tony turned for the dark hallway leading to the front door. Such thoughts were definitely outside the will of God and his bride, but didn't they make sense? If Rakha was his mortal enemy as Sarah attested, shouldn't he know where they stand? As he used to do before the curse came upon him, Tony quieted his mind to hear from God. Nothing happened for several seconds and he closed his eyes. The only sentence he heard besides the Scripture he read minutes ago about God's plans was, *"I'm done listening to nothing..."*

He turned his eyes to the dark ceiling and crossed his arms at his chest. *"If You want to tell me something, do it! I'm not a normal man anymore; don't I deserve more than normal grace?"* Crickets. Tony sighed and walked for the foyer. *"I'm going to check on Rakha. Thanks for the input, Lord."*

He paused to listen for Sarah upstairs and didn't think twice as his supernatural hearing picked up her rhythmic breathing from across the large house.

I am becoming so accustomed to this that I wield it without even thinking. Eventually, I'll turn into a full blown monster. Is that the big plan? Destroy Anthony Agricola?

Tony winced at his vehement heart-speech but still walked to his truck. Once again, he was stepping outside God's will.

But, hey, I'm finally getting good at something besides complaining! he snarked inside and climbed into the S10. *Maybe I'm testing God because I want to die. Maybe I'm tired of His game.*

Tony didn't believe it, he didn't want to die and he wasn't that tired. But he was extremely curious now about the centuries-old vampire down the road. An innocent query presented sideways to Elizabeth two days ago revealed that the police no longer watched his house or hers. To the police, he had gone silent and since they had nothing on him but circumstantial evidence, they wasted no more department resources on surveilling his movements.

So, I can go see him...

Tony headed toward his neighborhood, his stomach rejoicing at the promise of the creature's donations.

When Tony's truck turned onto Rakha's road, he scanned the curbs for city-issued cars, either undercover or marked. He made it all the way to Rakha's driveway when a patrol car turned onto the street ahead of him. Tony pretended to be moseying on by and he didn't meet the policeman's eye when they crossed. Frustrated, Tony tightened his lips and circled the neighborhood. He thought about making another cut in, but the police car had stopped to enter a different house only three doors down from Rakha.

Tony exhaled and drove another large circle, taking in the side neighborhoods as well in order to swing near the vampire's house in another five minutes. The cop car remained and had been joined with several others.

"Come on!" he hissed and considered his options. The police presence for the other family could take hours to settle and he had already stalked the area for twenty minutes. Sooner or later, he'd be noticed. With a dissatisfied groan, Tony gave up and headed back. He'd go back to Sarah and try to make sense of what he had become.

What sort of man have I turned in to? Why do I do what I don't want to do and I don't do what I want to? He smiled then, realizing he'd just quoted Apostle Paul, another disciple who simply tried to do his best when his checkered past constantly dragged him down.

𝔖𝔍

I have been crucified with Christ and I no longer live,
but Christ lives in me. The life I now live in the body, I live by faith in
the Son of God, who loved me and gave himself for me.
Galatians 2:20

IT WOULDN'T BE FAIR TO AWAKEN SARAH AT 2 AM AND
expect her to be at full charge so Tony waited. From the time he raced
home from Rakha's to 6 AM, when his wife arose to tend to her
morning duties, he prepared his confession. He started a pot of coffee
in just the way she liked and put a roll of croissants into the oven
slathered with butter. By the time he'd set placemats and jam before the
island stools, she was heard descending the stairs. Sarah rounded the
pillar and inhaled deeply with a huge smile.

"This is a prophetic moment, Mr. Agricola," Sarah said with a
wink. "I prophesy here and now that I'm going to eat all of those and
not even feel guilty!" She came close for a hug and when she pulled
away, she noticed his expression. "What's wrong?"

"You said that you and I are yoked together, for better and for
worse, against all of the dark powers of this world, looking forward to
the road ahead with apprehension, but even more joy and gratitude for
what God has done to bring us this far…"

"That is exactly what I said," she laughed and hugged him again.
"Perfect recall must be another vampire superpower. Well done!"

Tony huffed a tiny laugh, but felt a separation of their spirits caused
by his deception. Now that she stood close, her fresh, clean scent, her
shining countenance, Tony felt more unholy than ever, as if her
goodness made him detestable. Nothing was black and white and he
was forever finding excuses for the most heinous of decisions,
rationalizing his shortcomings before the Lord and in his own heart.

"Tony, what is it?" she asked softly and leaned out again.

It's happening. The vampire's curse is changing me, body, soul, mind and heart.
And Tony knew why: the blood. The more he consumed of the
demon's blood, the more he lost himself in the lie. *But what do I say to
Sarah? How do I say the most horrible truths to this beautiful woman of God?*

"Tell me." Sarah grasped his biceps and looked him square in the face. "What has you so upset?"

"I've been lying to you," he said with his eyes cast aside.

"Okay, about what?" Her voice remained soft and full of love.

"I've been lying and I'm afraid." Tony met her eye but his chin still tilted down. "I am afraid for my very soul."

Sarah held him at arm's length and made a small hum in her throat. She licked her lips and said, "God wants you to remember that you are hidden in Christ. You're losing your perspective. You are a son of our mighty God and He will not allow you to perish in this vampire form. You believe that, right?"

When Tony didn't reply, she gave him a warm smile.

"Tell me what has been happening behind those eyes of yours. Don't be afraid. I won't let anything happen to you…"

Tony tried to read what she meant, then admonished himself; Sarah had no agenda, she hid nothing. *And I believe her. If anyone can kick Satan to hell, she can.*

"Sarah," he said in an anguished whisper. "I fell off the path. I've been seeing Rakha. I invited him to come, I let him fully in and I went to see him last night…"

"Okay, I hear you. Go on…"

"I needed him. I was so tired and so hungry. And I was convinced God wasn't listening, that He had tuned me out, rejected me for my sin and disobedience…"

True to her word, Sarah did not judge or condemn him for his admission. Encouraged by her empathy, he continued.

"My first night with Rakha, I slept more peacefully than I can ever remember, and awoke feeling like I could conquer the world. I couldn't imagine how that was a bad thing, to need rest and find it."

"And he didn't hurt you?"

"No, all he did was talk. He told me about his past incarnations and his victories. For twenty hours, we sat on the floor like stoned hippies, just talking. By the time you reached me, I'd decided he wasn't so bad, that I had misinterpreted everything." Tony swallowed. "I was *enjoying* his company. I didn't want to leave. What does that say about me? How long will God strive with me in this state?"

With a slow shake of the head, Sarah cupped his cheek with her warm palm. "Forever. You were deceived. It is the oldest trick in the book and it is not unforgivable. We can set things right again, this very night."

"But there's more…" he said and she waited to hear what he'd say. "I wanted his blood last night. You went to sleep, and like a demon myself, I snuck out and went to his house. The only thing that saved me was that there were police watching it. My shame is complete in that I wanted to warn him. If he had a phone…" Tony wiped his mouth and did not go on.

"God did that, see? He prevented you from going in so we could do this right here. He has had this planned from the beginning. Now the police are onto Rakha and he'll have to leave town. We are about to close out the entire misadventure and start a new one. Do you feel it?"

Tony wanted to, but his stomach rumbled even now. "If God doesn't lift this curse, I'll fail again. I can't conquer my flesh. I see now that I never will."

"That is a lie," Sarah said allowing a stern tone. "You think you caused mayhem and destruction to God's plan, but you haven't. You've only hurt yourself. Think about it. Rakha has convinced you that you're like him, like the doctor. Do I have that right?"

Tony frowned. "I am. I want blood. I stopped wanting to quit. I started wanting John's blood…" He looked aside. "I've fantasized about yours, too. My mind wanders with unclean thoughts and as much as I hate the devil, I can feel my flesh calling to his minion *even now.*" Tony lowered his voice and glanced out the window.

"There's no reason to fear. You've been through *so much;* why would you stop now? Why would you let the devil have you when we're so close to the end?" She kissed his cheek and led him to a barstool. "Tony, my love, we will break the strongholds that keep you from accepting your thorn. Then we can move into God's purposes. He has a great adventure in store for us both and this vampire curse is a big part of it."

"How do we go on? I am still *hungry…*" Tony whispered, miserable for complaining.

"First off, we go before the Lord. God will help us. His love is great toward us and the faithfulness of the Lord endures forever."

"Yes, pray. He'll help me if you ask…"

Sarah chuckled. "You'll hear from him now. Let's pray."

Tony closed his eyes and she stood beside him, both facing the granite island. First they prayed silently, but before long, Sarah prayed deliverance and healing with powerful words Tony never would have thought of. For an hour, they used God's word against the devil and when Sarah said amen, Tony's gut had been sated.

40

Listen to my prayer, O God, do not ignore my plea;
hear me and answer me.
My thoughts trouble me and I am distraught
because of what my enemy is saying,
because of the threats of the wicked.
Psalm 55:1-3

THE TEMPTATION TO CHECK HIS DAUGHTER'S STATUS
became too much to bear and Jonah had grabbed his keys and asked
Jenn if she wanted to ride to Montgomery again. Now they were
splitting off, intending to meet up later to compare notes over dinner
on the east side. Jonah pulled the SUV to the door of the precinct and
Kranchez strolled out in civvies—jeans and a distressed black The Who
T-shirt.

"You sure you don't mind, Andy? I know I'm driving you crazy
with my new hobby." Jenn had her door open and one foot to the curb
as their friend reached the truck. She waited to see his response before
piling all the way out.

"Heck, I don't mind. When I spouted off at you the other day, I
was puttin' on a show for Cap. Come on. I got 'em lined up for you,
starting with that Real Estate agent."

Jenn turned to Jonah and leaned in for a kiss.

"I'll pick you up here at six, okay?" he told her and she nodded.
But Andy shoved her door closed, took her elbow to maneuver to the
sidewalk and then leaned into the truck through her open window.

"We're gonna be on the east side. I'll bring her to Red Robin at
seven. That's where you're meetin', right?"

Jonah's eye flit to Jenn who nodded and he said okay. When
Kranchez backed away, Jonah waved his fingers to Jenn and pulled off.

Keep your hands to yourself, he said inside and then had to chuckle.
There was zero chance Jenn would cheat or even think of such a thing.
They may have only been romantically hooked a short time but being
partners on the beat made them closer than lovers in a real sense of the
word. Jenn knew what she wanted and could never be manipulated or

228

tempted away from her man. Just couldn't happen. So Jonah wondered about her plan for the day instead.

Jenn's search of the bloodless dead who had been murderers brought nothing. She had never found a shred of evidence linking any of them to any of her TATs. Today, since they were headed into Andy's town, she asked if he'd take her to meet the agent who sold Black and Agricola the house. Andy said over the phone that Veronica Law, of Realty East, said Saul White was "terrifying," and that she felt he was "about to kill her every second." Jenn found this fascinating and simply *had* to ask the woman more. Kranchez also offered to take her by a few of the churches Agricola preached in last year, including the one where Reverend Tracey was attacked. All in all, Jenn was in for a fun afternoon of playing detective.

Jonah on the other hand hoped to tool over to Elizabeth's for a quiet visit. Now that they'd been reacquainted, maybe they could have the deep father-daughter talks they needed to move forward. When he reached his daughter's house, her expression said she was overjoyed to see him and Jonah thanked God in his heart.

Two hours later, Elizabeth pulled away and Jonah watched until her taillights disappeared around the turn. Their visit had been easy, no stress, no strangeness, just a father and his kid talking about life. He also determined that his daughter had a great disposition and tremendous faith which made her daily life more enjoyable. When they mentioned the latest uncomfortable events with Rakha Tep, he could see she had moved on, not afraid or fearful he'd return. She cut their ending short because of a meeting with a client—not Tep, thank God—and now Jonah needed to plan his trip to meet Jenn in town.

He set off to Vaughn Road and glanced at the dash clock and then to his GPS. He was early. Not willing to sit on his hands a half-hour, Jonah saw the exit for Taylor Road and swung in, heading for the address he'd recorded for their unofficial Person of Interest, Rakha Tep. The sun had just started to set and with a sentimental smile at the beauty of the painted sky, he thanked God one more time for the time he had with his daughter.

Driving a full-size Ford Explorer was no way to hide or even blend in, but with practiced ease, Jonah snuck up on Tep's abode and parked several houses down. He saw no police cruisers on the place and a close look found no undercovers, either. It was as Andy said—they pulled off for live cases and Tep went on the back burner.

Jonah sighed. He didn't want to catch the guy; he wanted Tep to leave his daughter alone, that's all. To kill time and feed his curiosity, he trained his eye to the guy's door and sunk low so only his eyes peered through the slots in the steering wheel.

It was only ten minutes later that Jonah saw movement. The sun had set and the front door opened. The man described as Rakha Tep stepped onto the stoop, his head scanned both ways, and then his face stopped, pointed in Jonah's direction. Jonah remained low, hidden in the dark cab, peeking out. The dim lighting of the shadowy front porch kept him from seeing any detail, but Tep appeared to be staring at Jonah's truck. Jonah waited, inside counting the seconds. The man remained, frozen in place, face aligned with Jonah's mostly-hidden one.

What is he doing?

Then the guy moved his hand.

What's he doing now?

Jonah did not rise from his hunker but his puzzlement grew. The lighting could be tricking his eyes, but it looked like Tep was giving him the *come-here* gesture. Jonah watched and the guy did it again, plainly drawing Jonah to him with one graceful hand.

Well, what do I do? Drive away? Drive over and talk? I could tell him to stay away from my family…

Again, Tep's hand fluttered. When Jonah didn't move, the man swiveled to reach inside the house and a porch light illuminated the area. Now Jonah could see clearly and Tep pointed at Jonah with one hand and the other waved him over.

Dammit, I should just go. I mean, I'll tell him to stay away. I'm not gonna make trouble, but he should know not to contact Elizabeth ever again…

Decided, Jonah huffed and sat up to start the ignition. He put the truck in gear and rolled slowly past three yards until he reached the two-foot cinderblock boundary of the man's tiny house. Tep crossed his arms and watched as Jonah parked and got out. He adjusted his suit coat and pulled out his cell. Jenn didn't pick up so he left text.

"Be a tiny bit late. I swung by Tep's. If I don't check back in five minutes, send the police, JK."

When Jonah dropped the phone in his pocket, Tep uncrossed his arms and opened his house door, still facing his approaching guest.

"What can I do for you, Officer?" the man asked when Jonah was twenty feet away, his accent clean but evident.

Jonah shook his head with a small wave. Jenn played with fire allowing folks to think she was on the job, but Jonah had always been more by-the-book. "Just Jonah. I'm retired. I guess since you noticed me, I'll just tell you why I'm here."

Tep took a step backward, his arm gesturing into the house. "Won't you come in?"

Jonah did not want to go into the dark space and he stopped moving and stood square. "I prefer to speak out here. I know who you are, Mr. Tep—"

"You are Ms. Hawken's father?" he asked his chin to the side.

Jonah wished for more light. The porch bulb rested behind the man's head, bathing his face in shadow. His voice was gravelly and it brought dread to Jonah's bones. His reaction wasn't logical so Jonah took a step forward to prove to them both he was not unduly afraid.

"Look, Mr. Tep, I don't want to sound rude, but I will if I need to be. Do not contact my daughter. She does not want to have anything else to do with you." Jonah took a breath and expected the man to interject, but he listened on, his head still to the side and his eyes too deep in shadow to read. "MPD is watching you, too. We don't know what you're up to, but we know enough to keep an eye on you. So what do you say?"

"Well, I'm *flabbergasted* at this news," the man said in a sugary voice. He again indicated inside the dark front room. "Ms. Hawken and I are dating. Did she not tell you?" Jonah sharpened his gaze and the man added with false surprise, "Oh, she didn't. Maybe she's keeping secrets, Women do that, right?"

Jonah took another step and stopped, his ire up. Every fiber in his being assured him Elizabeth would never date this guy.

Why would he say it? Why lie about something so easy to disprove?

Jonah said in a low voice, "Stay the hell away from her, you hear? I won't tell you again."

Rakha turned to go in the house, not closing the door. He said from a few feet inside, "Tell her yourself. She's in my bed as we speak."

What? In a surge of anger Jonah closed the distance to the stoop and poked in his head, both palms to the lintels. "Elizabeth? You here?"

A very faint noise emanated from within, muffled but feminine, and Jonah clambered inside, pushing past Tep. His eyes searched the first room as his ears listened for his daughter. "Elizabeth! Where are you?" he barked taking another three steps to a long hallway with closed doors on both sides.

"Why are you so upset? She's right down there, third door on the right. She came on her own. I did nothing wrong..."

Behind him, Tep spoke and followed matching Jonah's pace. When Jonah's jogged for the suggested door, Tep also increased his speed, so that when Jonah turned the knob, the man stood inches behind. Jonah opened the door with flourish and felt for a light switch. The muffled cry for help came from inside and when he found a toggle, he flipped it, causing a dim floor lamp to light across the room.

"Elizabeth?!" he said again with more urgency than before. The room held no furniture, just the lamp and a throw pillow against the wall. The sound reoccurred and Jonah jumped for the only closed door, a closet he guessed, and he yanked the knob. It didn't budge. Jonah's hand dipped into his pocket for his cell and in the same instant, his arms were cemented to his sides, wrapped up by steel bonds.

Jonah bellowed his rage and the arms increased their pressure, squeezing his chest cavity until he could no longer expand his lungs. In a harsh whisper, he cursed his attacker and demanded to be released.

"Your daughter prays a lot," Tep said in Jonah's ear, his voice scratchy and evil. "It turns me on so much and when I grab her like this, she prays even harder."

Jonah wanted to shout, rage, threaten, anything, but he couldn't breathe. The last ounce of air in his body had been absorbed and his head grew fuzzy as he found it impossible to draw oxygen.

"Are you one to pray, sir?" Tep asked even softer, his putrid breath moistening Jonah's neck.

Tep jerked the contact in such a way that Jonah's knees buckled to the pressure and he slumped to the hardwood floor. Tep came down with him and once to the floor, he used his body weight to force Jonah to lay out flat. Jonah resisted and in another second, a rib cracked, the sound like dry tinder in a fire. Jonah could only squeeze his eyes at the new discomfort; he was passing out. As if from far away, the sad sounds of a woman crying into a cloth filtered through the closed door only two feet away.

"Wait," Tep said, the arms disappearing and switching to hands to Jonah's shoulders from behind. "Don't pass out yet. I have two things to show you." The man's tone had turned giddy and he maneuvered to keep one hand to Jonah's shoulder and still reach the closet door.

Jonah took a huge breath and his fractured rib stabbed inside with an explosion of new pain. The needed oxygen corrected some of his vision and he looked into the closet as it opened, his heart bursting for his daughter's safety. Then he met the eyes of a stranger, a teenager, a girl of maybe fifteen with black hair cropped short and thick eye makeup. She'd been gagged and as Jonah watched, Tep dropped contact with him to put both hands to the girl's thin neck.

"Watch, Jonah," Tep said and with the smallest movement, his fingers crushed her larynx and she thrashed in panic, choking and afraid for her life. Jonah's body sent adrenaline to his every muscle, but he still could not move enough to help. He was able to roll onto one side, his face craned to the poor victim, and he opened his mouth to call for help. He couldn't fill his lungs, one of them already collapsed and the other not filling properly.

The child's eyes met Jonah's and he would never forget that moment for the rest of his life as her light dimmed, his struggle to help worthless. Then he remembered his God.

"FATHER! STOP HIM! Look at what he's doing to this baby! Take me instead, Father! Save her! Let me stand in the gap! Please! FATHER!" he shouted in his mind and heart.

Tep's attention swiveled, his eyes wide and his lips parted. He released the girl and she tumbled to the floor of the closet like a ragdoll.

"Ah! You're praying," Tep said and turned to roughly roll Jonah onto his back.

Jonah continued to pray, the pain of his cracked ribbed flashing neon in his consciousness. He closed his eyes and begged God again to save the girl and take him instead. Tep slapped his cheek hard.

"Look, Jonah!" he rasped, his voice more gravel than ever and altered as if he held something in his mouth.

Jonah squeaked open his eyes and gasped, causing a new jab.

Jenn's vampire!

Tep's lips had parted and his mouth opened several inches revealing two sharp fangs, curving and snake-like. The hands possessed unimaginable strength as he jerked Jonah's body upward to press his gory mouth to Jonah's throat. Despite pain strong enough to cause him to pass out, Jonah fought back. He did not make any headway before the man plunged his teeth into his throat. Jonah was helpless, which he knew the moment the penetration occurred.

I'm going to die!

Jonah softened his focus, closed his eyes, and concentrated on saying goodbye. He'd practiced this, wondering what he'd say to God when his time came. He never really expected it to happen, at least not for many years, but it seemed to have arrived.

"Father, thank you for this life. I thank you for Jenn and my daughter. And thank you for letting me know her before time to go. You are worthy to be praised and I look forward to seeing you soon..."

Tep was sucking his blood. Part of Jonah noticed, but mostly, he pretended he wasn't there. He imagined he was in a huge field of wildflowers, the sky was blue, and he walked it smiling and seeking the Lord. Very soon he'd see Jesus walking toward him, ready to take him into His arms and bring him Home. The last thing he heard before he relinquished his will was Rakha Tep's voice, very low and as guttural as before.

"I love it when you pray..."

Jonah blinked out.

❧

Rakha hadn't been paying attention and the police had his house surrounded.

"Montgomery Police Department! Rakha Tep, open the door or we'll bust it in!"

Rakha withdrew his fangs from the retired detective's flesh. As he stood he allowed the man's body to remain on the floor and he crossed to look out the window. This room faced the backyard and shadowy figures peppered the border, Rakha seeing them in detail. The police shouted their warning again, this time adding a canine to the threat. Rakha rolled in his lips. He didn't like dogs and they didn't like him. He looked at the girl and then Jonah Miller, both of them still lived. He needed to snap their necks.

CRASH!

No more time. The front door had been breached and less than a second later, the back door, too. Rakha had to go. With fierce concentration developed over centuries, he pictured a place to translate his flesh to and went.

Poof.

Rakha opened his eyes in Elizabeth Hawken's rented studio. It was closed, dark and locked, which he had hoped it would be. He'd chosen this spot because of his urgency. Now that he had time, he'd plan the next move.

"Pitiful! Pitiful!" the Unseen chanted, having lost all confidence that Rakha would ever complete even the smallest part of his task.

Rakha ignored them and set his mind on Church Girl. Her father behaved irrationally when he thought his daughter needed help. This

234

could work for Agricola, too. Rakha couldn't get close to Sarah Tracey, but Church Girl? He'd grab her and Agricola would come running. Agricola would also crumble at the thought of harm coming to an innocent. Plus, Tony would be hungry.

Rakha smiled and told the Unseen to bug off.

"I have work to do." And he got to it.

41

As for me, I call to God, and the LORD saves me.
Evening, morning and noon I cry out in distress,
and he hears my voice. He rescues me unharmed.
Psalm 55:16-18

ELIZABETH HAWKEN LIVED IN A QUIET NEIGHBORHOOD off, off, *off* the main drag in what the locals called Old Cloverdale. Rakha had tailed her there four times and only once did she become aware of him and grow anxious. The previous visits were pure curiosity, and maybe a little reconnaissance; after all, he really did want to turn the girl away from her God. It was only after the situation with Tony grew more complicated did he consider either leaving her be or taking her life outright. Now that her father had come to her rescue, Rakha felt it best to use the girl as a weapon and end the game once and for all.

For the moment, he leaned against the back wall of her cottage, hidden by shadow. He hadn't been inside, so the closest he could come when magically translating his flesh across space was her yard. Rakha scanned the entire area in a glance. The neighborhood sat quiet. With a sudden fond memory, Rakha touched his middle. The retired detective's blood had exploded with flavor when he fell into prayer. Be it adrenaline or spiritual specialness, the blood tasted better when his victims prayed.

Church Girl's blood would be delicious, he thought. *But I'm too full to eat again. Dammit. I wish I could save her for later, but...* Rakha sighed. It had to be now. He'd find another church girl another time.

Elizabeth was home, her car sat in its position and one low light shone in a back room. Without a sound, Rakha reached the back door and tested the knob.

Locked.

He wasn't surprised. Rakha ran down his plan once more and worked the deadbolt. He'd always been a proficient locksmith.

જ઼ઌ

236

"Elizabeth, honey, your dad's hurt. Can you get over to General? He's in surgery, but when they're done, he'll be in ICU, third floor."

"Dad! Oh, no! What happened?!" Elizabeth spoke as she grabbed her purse and headed for the front door. On the phone, Dad's fiancée explained he'd been found beaten and near death in Rakha Tep's house. Elizabeth had reached her car and fell behind the wheel when Jenn told her about the teenager found in a closet, her windpipe crushed. She was also alive, but in critical condition. "Oh no! Jesus help them!" she said aloud and backed out of her driveway, her eye catching movement in her front window—a smallish man, bald, with piercing eyes. *Rakha Tep!*

"Jenn! Rakha Tep is in my house! I'm driving away but I know I saw him! He must have been coming to get me!"

"I'll call the police. Watch the road and get here safely," Jenn said and Elizabeth said okay and hit Sarah's icon on her phone. When her friend picked up, she launched into the whole thing.

"Rakha tried to kill my dad. He's at General and I'm headed there now. And Rakha's at my house! I told the police."

"Oh, honey! Did he attack you?" Sarah asked.

"No, I got out just in time. Jesus helped me get away! Oh, Sarah! Please pray for my dad to recover. He's in surgery."

"Tony!" Sarah called to the side and then continued. "Elizabeth, what are his injuries? Did they say?"

"Jenn talks in police-speech, but she said they think he has a fractured rib, a collapsed lung, and he lost a lot of blood. He's stable. And there was a teenager there. She's in critical condition. Please pray for her, too!"

"I will honey, drive safe and we're on our way."

Elizabeth found peace in that promise and she disconnected. It was a ten-minute drive to the hospital and she prayed for her dad and the little girl, all the way there.

আ✑৯

Tony stepped from the shower and set about drying off with one of the new bath sheets Sarah preferred. Before she came along, Tony had little use for proper towels, dishes, anything. He'd lived as bachelor for so long—*and then a bachelor vampire,* he thought with misery—that he had always gotten by with whatever he had on hand. Now their home had new everything, towels, washcloths, dishes; everything used daily had been upgraded. And he liked it, having her tend to the more mundane household things that brought her joy.

The shower had done the trick. An hour ago, John arrived for the trio to plan the next month's ministry dates. The plan had been monthly powwows where the two eaters would have pizza and cola, while they chose which invitations to accept and schedule. John came in, took a seat, and when he passed by and went out of view, Tony's face flushed hot. Sarah noticed and had asked him if he was okay. Tony only had to think a tiny moment before realizing his hunger had been triggered. When John's body heat crossed his, every memory of bloodletting returned to his mind at once and Tony ran upstairs for a cold shower and some prayer.

Well, it worked, he mused and began to dress. As he buttoned his long-sleeved shirt, he heard Sarah saying goodbye as if on the phone.

"You're kidding," John said and then, *"Is he okay?"*

"She thinks so," Sarah returned and called for Tony in a shout.

Tony headed for the stairs and replied he was coming. He found them both in the kitchen, pizza boxes arrived but untouched.

"Who's hurt?" He pecked Sarah's cheek and she told him all that Elizabeth said on the phone. Tony's empathy surged at the thought of the policeman in Rakha's deadly grip. It had to be the grace of God the man survived. And Elizabeth's escape? Definitely God's doing. Sarah and John were saying all of this and Tony nodded, in his mind trying to guess what the demon would do next. Then his instincts grew sharp edges and he met Sarah's eye.

"He's here," he whispered and put out his hand, palm down. "Shh, let me listen." Tony concentrated on the sounds of the house and heard nothing. After a moment, Sarah said almost too low to hear, "He can't come in here. Call the police. If he's outside, they'll get him. He can't get in this house."

Tony rolled in his lips and lowered his gaze.

John said the words Sarah must have been only thinking: "You let him in again?"

"Not expressly, but I sense he has a loophole with me." He looked back at Sarah. "You and I own the house in spirit, but until we go to the courthouse, my name's on the deed. Rakha will use that to come in." Tony heard a noise upstairs and thought about his bedroom, the place he entertained the devil the most. "My room."

Sarah frowned, unhappy at Tony's logic, that the demon could use man's law to circumvent her binding in Jesus' name, but she didn't argue. She asked if they should leave. Tony considered the door.

"If you go outside, he could grab you."

"If we stay in here, he could grab us," John said.

"Let's call the police," Sarah repeated and palmed her phone.

Tony nodded and the noise recurred upstairs. "He's in my room." Tony stepped out of the kitchen and looked at the upper landing. "John, stay with Sarah."

"Be careful," Sarah said and punched the emergency number.

Tony gained on his room in a blur and flung open the door. The room sat empty but the window was open. Tony walked in to close it when he sensed Rakha materializing behind him. He whirled around, but the much-older vampire closed cruel hands about his throat before he could react.

"We must end the dance, preacher man," he said in a low voice already squeezing and not allowing Tony to speak. Tony fought against his touch. Punching led to kicking and no matter how he contorted his body, the hands of iron did not budge. How would Rakha kill him?

"Decapitation," Rakha whispered. "And I hate to do it."

The vampire shot his eyes to the door and it slammed shut. Tony heard the lock click.

"When you pass out, I will remove your head. The Unseen will be glad. Their princes will rejoice..." Rakha did not meet Tony's eye but only squeezed, waiting for Tony to faint. "I'm not happy for it. I had wanted to play a bit longer. Get you to truly follow me and not just be addicted to my blood..."

Tony couldn't concentrate. What was the demon saying? He mentioned blood, what else was it? Tony wanted to understand, but the sensation of leaving his body approached with cat feet. In a moment, he'd be gone, floating in that dream-space where one sometimes died and never came back.

Tony didn't pray.

His eyes still open, he stared at Rakha's profile. The vampire refused to look over. He said more things, spoke more about how he wished he didn't have to kill Tony, but he wouldn't meet his eye.

And still, Tony did not think about praying.

Rakha looked over. "Why aren't you praying?" he asked maybe hearing Tony's last thoughts. "Have you lost your faith?"

No, that's ridiculous...

Tony concentrated on God. Why didn't he pray? He had no answer, except, he didn't feel it. God hadn't heard a single word he'd said in a year, and certainly not since Paul made him a vampire.

I'm about to be erased; why don't I pray?

Tony only had a moment left. His vision blurred and his thoughts grew fragmented. Old scenes from high school scampered past, his first job, his last car before buying the truck, stupid stuff paraded by his mind as his vision faded.

"Father? Please keep Sarah safe..." Finally, he asked God the only thing on his mind.

Then, he was free.

Rakha's grip disappeared and Tony went to his knees. He crawled to the door. Taking several ragged breaths, he turned bleary eyes to where he'd been nearly choked to death and squinted at the sight of Doctor Corescu and Rakha in hand-to-hand combat.

"Get your people to the yard," Mark said his voice jumping as Rakha wrestled in his grip. The demon was strong, but for the moment, not stronger than his offspring. Then he sent privately, blocking out the oldest among them, *"The police have arrived and are surrounding the house. I will hold him here and by the time the police come upstairs, I can be gone."*

Hacking and pounding his own chest, Tony nodded and used the wall to gain his feet. He had almost been killed because of a lack of faith. This fact swirled in his mind and he backed out, amazed at the fury in Rakha's face as Mark held him about the chest with strong arms. The doctor was several inches taller and outweighed him by fifty pounds. Maybe that would be enough.

Tony wanted to ask God to help Mark. He made it into the hallway, an inner voice telling him God wouldn't listen, but another voice told him to try. After all, he'd just been rescued directly after his prayer for Sarah's safety.

"Please, Abba, help Mark. And please help me get Sarah and John to safety," he whispered through a bruised throat, although because of the curse, he felt no pain. He took the stairs two at a time and heard the police banging on the front door. Sarah and John reached the foyer at the same time and he whispered just before the door opened, "Dr. Corescu's up there holding him. Let's get outside."

The double doors came open, kicked by the police, and after a split-second of confusion, they escorted Tony, John, and Sarah to the safety of the perimeter. Tony broke away to find the one in charge and recognized Kranchez. In as few words as possible, he described Rakha's location in the house and then joined his friends at the ambulance where medics checked them for injuries.

"It's all yours," he sent the doctor but heard no reply.

In his heart, he heard a small voice that he remembered well. *"You have done well; you are My son and I love you. You will find rest."*

Tony sighed and turned away when fresh tears of joy welled in his eyes. One peek at his fingers and the water was tinged red. But he'd heard from God. Everything was going to be okay.

ॐ

Jennifer Speltz was a stranger, but she loved Jonah Miller and witnessing such unabashed devotion warmed Elizabeth's heart. For the moment, she and her father's fiancée stood in the hallway facing his door allowing privacy as the nurses checked his bandages. When she arrived, her dad was coming out of surgery and only stayed an hour in ICU. When they rolled him to a private room, she learned that the police department had arranged it, making certain he'd have VIP service all the way even though he was not local (nor active duty) law enforcement.

"You will never know how much that man loves you," Jenn said then and being an inch taller, dropped her arm across Elizabeth's shoulders. "The day you sent that text, he blossomed into a brand new being."

Elizabeth's face grew warm at the sentiment. She could see he was happy they have reunited, but to hear it from someone else meant it shone to all with eyes. Finally, Elizabeth swallowed and offered a bit of truth herself.

"Well, he talks about you nonstop," she said, watching his door with Jenn right beside her. "You should know that as far as he's concerned, you're an angel sent from heaven to make sure he lives a happy life."

After a small noise and a nod, Jenn inhaled, sniffled and shook her head. "I shoulda been there," she said low. "It's my fault. I'll never forgive myself."

Elizabeth turned to see her face and Jenn's arm fell away. "Don't say that. No way. It's not your fault."

With a sad new shake of the head, she disagreed. "I watched his back five years. Day in, day out, sometimes seven days a week, sometimes ten, twelve, fourteen hours a day." Jenn swallowed and wouldn't allow Elizabeth to interrupt. "We faced madmen, domestic battery dangers, even wild animals, for Pete's sake and I never let anything happen to him. Ever." Her voice lowered to a hiss as she berated herself further.

Elizabeth put her hand to Jenn's forearm. "It's not your fault. You didn't make Rakha attack Dad. Stop that," she admonished in her gentlest voice.

"You don't understand," Jenn said, not meeting Elizabeth's eye. "We would have been together today if I hadn't been chasing this stupid cold case, my stupid hobby. This hobby almost got him killed."

"You can't blame yourself," Elizabeth reiterated and inside a small voice told her the same thing. *And neither can you, Elizabeth…*

"Honey, I appreciate you trying to comfort me, but today I left my partner to go play detective. Add to that…" She wiped her nose with the back of her hand and looked to the ceiling. "I did it so Andy would be happy. *Dammit!*"

She'd whispered her curse to the side and Elizabeth squeezed her arm. "But it's still not your fault." And inside she heard, *…nor is what happened to you, your fault…*

"Your dad would never have left me like that. If Polly Policewoman smiled, flirted and said she'd do his hobby with her, your dad would've told her to buzz off. I was having too much fun chasing pretend monsters, soaking up Andy's attention—" She swiveled her face to Elizabeth's. "—that I don't need. Your dad is the most wonderful and attentive man in the world. I just lost sight, lost focus, I just wanted to figure out this case."

"Look, Dad knows you love him, and he told me about his friend Andy. He said he's a good guy. He's not worried about you doing P.I. work together." Elizabeth held her gaze to transmit her sincerity. In their visit, her father didn't reveal case details, but made a few lighthearted jokes about his friend's sad and fruitless chase of his woman."

"I let him down." Jenn sounded done and Elizabeth took her arm.

"Dad went to Rakha's house on his own. He confronted the man on his own. Rakha attacked Dad on his own. It had nothing to do with you." Elizabeth watched to make sure she didn't offend. "And one more thing, because Dad went there, he saved that little girl's life. Will you take credit for that?" she asked with a cautious grin. "Do you see what I'm saying?"

Elizabeth sensed a surge of love and compassion, not only outward toward Jenn, but inside, as if God wanted her to be at peace about the boys that raped her. The voices of her therapists saying it wasn't her fault never did the job, but now? The still, small voice of the Holy Spirit saying the same thing rang 100% true. For the first time since that horrible event, Elizabeth began to see she had no control over what those boys decided to do. She mocked them, but they made the decision to take her behind the lockers.

Peace flooded Elizabeth's mind and the memory of the attack on little Elizabeth, for the first time, didn't cause dread and fear. Right now, standing in the hospital hallway with her father's fiancée, she was joyful. *Everything happens for a reason*, and she needed to share that with Jenn Speltz.

"You made a decision to go different ways today, but beyond that, everything else was not up to you."

Jenn exhaled not yet agreeing.

Elizabeth added more with kind eyes. "God did this. All of it. I know you're not big on God-talk, but facts are facts. That girl would be dead if Dad hadn't gone to Rakha's house."

Jenn's posture softened and she lowered her chin. "I guess. I mean, I can't argue with the fact that he saved that poor little girl..."

Elizabeth nodded and the door to her father's room opened with a quiet swish. The nurses exited with a wave and she and Jenn filtered back in, flanking his bed. It was beautiful seeing her father so in love and Elizabeth's heart swelled with a new gladness. The past few hours had been harrowing, but every step of the way, she could see God's hand on it all. As her dad comforted them saying he was going to be fine, she praised Jesus in her heart.

42

Do not repay anyone evil for evil.
Be careful to do what is right in the eyes of everyone.
If it is possible, as far as it depends on you,
live at peace with everyone.
Romans 12:17-18

ALLOWING HIS FORWARD COMPLIMENT TO SWEEP THE FIRST floor, Andy Kranchez passed the homeowners who were being rushed to waiting medical staff. He offered Agricola a perfunctory nod and pointed to two senior officers, instructing them to accompany him into the house. With succinct directions regarding where to look, he took his two and headed up the stairway to the third door on the left. Agricola had spouted, "be careful. He's not armed, but he's insane. He will attack with teeth and claws."

Whatever.

Kranchez and his men reached the room and called the standard warning. Tep made no reply and he heard no noise. A second barking of the command to surrender and he and Bailey, each standing to either side of the doorframe, heard the sound of a struggle, furniture scrubbing the floor, a decided "oomph!" and then silence. At the mouthed count of three, Bailey kicked in the door and all three policemen jumped past the threshold, fanning out and taking instant cover. Molding his body to the near wall, safety off and ready to defend, Kranchez's his eyes grew wide at what he saw.

A man's silhouette faced him, tall, strong, with dark hair and flashing eyes reflecting the light from the hallway. This man had fixed his mouth to the smaller man's throat, yet his eyes angled to Kranchez as if he'd been awaiting a certain moment to act. With a shout, Andy called for Bailey's torch and the forward space was flooded with halogen light.

The tall man was gone. *Dissolved.*

Weirder... had he seen fangs dripping blood?

Or is Speltz's bloodless bodies investigation finally screwing with my head?
Kranchez didn't have time to wonder, for the very millisecond
Tep's bonds were removed, he lunged for the flashlight bearer in a blur
of movement. Andy's torch then bathed Tep and Bailey with light in
time to see his friend's neck snapped and his limp body falling to the
floor.

"Don't move! I'll shoot!" Andy shouted while in his peripheral
vision, Pouncey flanked the man while avoiding crossfire. There would
be no conversation. With his hands free of Bailey's corpse, Tep turned
for Pouncey and lunged, but received every .9mm projectile the junior
man had loaded into the magazine. Not down with eleven bullets in his
torso, Kranchez emptied his service weapon as well. Tep went down,
but to his hands and knees, lifting a face to Kranchez that would haunt
him forever.

Jenn's Dracula file! Good god!
White skin, black orbs for eyes, and a red mouth full of razor-sharp
teeth. It could have been a Halloween mask if he wasn't standing four
feet away and absorbing every detail in the weak light.

The smallish attacker moved his left hand, dragging at across the
hardwood floor as if to crawl toward Bailey's body. Having reloaded,
Pouncey emptied a second magazine and the man called Rakha Tep lay
still.

"Sarge," Pouncey rasped barely audible, "what the hell?"
Tossing the rulebook, Kranchez followed a nudge deep inside and
fired one more bullet into Tep's forehead. The single report clapped
through the room, causing new shouts from his fellow officers lining
the hallway ready for the word to enter. On Andy's behalf, Pouncey
took control of the scene and called instructions, his voice breaking
with emotion and adrenaline. Kevlar-girded officers filed in, bustled
into the small space and searched the room as Kranchez rolled Tep
away from their fallen friend. He then tipped him onto his front,
positioning the man's lifeless hands behind his back. Pouncey dropped
to one knee and met his eye. Holding a gaze both men shared,
amazement, anger and confusion, his partner handcuffed the dead man
without a word. The image of those fangs in the one who vanished and
the those in the one on the floor caused him to doublecheck everything.

Kranchez stuck to protocol the remainder of the scene,
performing his duties with expertise. One peek and Tep's face revealed
it was normal—no crazy teeth, dead eyes at half-mast as normal as any
man's. Kranchez marveled at the hallucination. He'd ask Pouncey about

it. Not now, but later, when appropriate. Or maybe he wouldn't. Maybe if he waited long enough, he could pretend he hadn't seen anything. Jonah and Jenn would never know and he definitely wasn't putting anything about a second man nor a fanged perp in the report.

43

He said, "Praise be to the Lord,
who rescued you from the hand
of the Egyptians and of Pharaoh,
and who rescued the people
from the hand of the Egyptians."
Exodus 18:10

THE MOST DRAMATIC PART OF THEIR CURRENT TRIAL
seemed to be behind them, but once Big John and Sarah passed
inspection by the medics, Tony asked John to return to Opal. He was
happy to oblige, none of them ready to discuss an air about their giant
friend that he was done with them and vampires in general.

"He'll be okay," Sarah said in Tony's ear as John spoke to
Kranchez and fell into his Cadillac. Tony nodded and sighed. They
needed to get to the hospital and check on Jonah. Kranchez walked
toward them and didn't meet Tony's eye, instead, he focused on his
cheek and took their statements.

"John came over so the three of us could plan our ministry
calendar and Tony heard Tep's voice upstairs." Sarah allowed the cop
to jot notes before continuing. "Then Tony went up to investigate and
made sure it was him. Then he came down and we met your men at the
door."

Kranchez looked to Tony's forehead. "That's how it happened?"
"Yes."

"And there was no one else with you?" Kranchez asked with less
volume. "A tall man with dark hair..." he began, looked left and right
and then met Tony's eye. "No one else was up there with Tep?"

"No, just me, Sarah and John were here." Tony wondered how
much the guy saw. He was spooked.

"Okay, thank you. I have your number. Take the wife somewhere
else tonight, deal?" Kranchez spoke while walking away. He tucked his
notepad into his pocket, interview over.

Tony walked Sarah to the truck and they prepared their hearts for
the next hour. Jonah Miller was stable, last they heard, but he'd been
bitten by a vampire—he would know that now. How much would he

tell his fiancée and daughter? Plus, Rakha was dead—when his life blinked out, Tony felt it in his middle. That meant Mark did, too. Would Rakha be back? *Could* he come back?

All the way to the hospital, he nor Sarah wanted to speculate, so they prayed instead.

Elizabeth's father slept in a private room and Tony was glad for that. This also meant he wasn't in ICU, another good sign. The door to his room had no window, so Tony and Sarah both paused before entering, preparing themselves for whatever God did next. Neither expected Dr. Corescu to tap Tony's shoulder.

"Mark," Tony said, surprised, and he turned. The doctor had come prepared, dressed in a lab coat with a name badge for Whitford City Memorial, his old job. Tony shot him a small grin. "Is Dr. Corescu here to see his patient?" he asked and the three of them stepped away from Jonah Miller's door.

"Ma'am," he said with the utmost respect to Sarah before resuming his conversation with Tony. "Your life, more correctly, *your blood*—" he said the word in a whisper leaning in and then stood back again, "calls me. It is incessant. Now that your detective friend has seen the truth of it, I am interested in how exposed I am. How exposed we are." He gave Sarah an apologetic nod. *"Secrecy is key…"* the doctor sent silently and Tony agreed wholeheartedly.

"I'm glad you're here," Tony said low, truly happy to see him. Mark smiled, too, and Tony caught Sarah's eye. "Honey, Detective Miller only knows Mark as an elusive physician connected to Paul Black. During their investigation, as far as they thought, he was MIA. He and his partner be surprised to see him. Let's play it by ear to see how they react."

Sarah nodded and said to them both, "He hasn't broken any laws as far as they know, too, so they'll just have to deal with being surprised. That's the way I see it."

She was bang-on and after a grateful nod, Tony looked at the doctor. "I'll introduce you. It might help Jonah normalize everything if we act as blasé as possible."

"Assuming he hasn't mentioned vampires to his women," Mark added telepathically and Tony exhaled.

"Sarah!"

Elizabeth Hawken exited the room at that moment and leapt into Sarah's embrace. Mark remained back and Tony waited to catch Elizabeth's eye, sure he would read something if her father had been telling her he'd been attacked by a monster. But Elizabeth turned after ending the hug and gave Tony her normal nod, keeping her distance as he had set up their relationship from the start. With a satisfied smile, he pivoted to introduce Mark.

"Elizabeth, before we go in, let me introduce Mark Corescu. He's a good friend of mine."

Elizabeth stepped closer and put out her hand to the doctor who shook it and returned his hands to his pockets. "You seem familiar," she said and then moved back to her father's room door. "Ya'll come on in. Dad's awake."

Tony wondered at her words and they filed in, Mark in the rear. He strode to the edge of the bed, hoping to meet Jonah's eye before he looked at the doctor.

"Thank God you're okay," he said and took Jonah's near hand for a gentle shake. "What happened? They said Rakha attacked you? What did he do?" Playing innocent, Tony made his voice incredulous. The retired cop had been traumatized, that was plain. What would he say now that Tony had asked him point-blank in front of everyone?

Jonah looked to his left and Jennifer Speltz moved closer, her right hand stroking his sweaty curls. Then he looked to Sarah and gave her a nod. Finally, he looked over Tony's shoulder. "That's...that's..." he whispered and reached for Jenn's hand. She took a closer look of the stranger among them.

"You're Dr. Mark Corescu!" Jennifer Speltz said then, moving around the bed toward Tony, which was also toward Mark behind him. "Where the hell have you been all this time?"

Before he could answer, she looked back to Jonah and her words prickled Tony's spirit.

"There he is, just like they said. He can't be more than forty years old!" She turned her face to Mark again. "I've seen driver's licenses of yours going back decades; what the devil is going on?!"

"Jenn!" Jonah said, his voice cutting the air despite his weakness.

Tony had no words, but in his peripheral vision, Mark stepped closer. At their eye-meet, her brow furrowed with multiple emotions.

"Pleased to meet you," the doctor said and Tony watched Jenn's face soften. "I have been in Germany for several months; forgive me for not coming forward earlier."

Tony made an invisible smirk. Mark was hypnotizing the woman and she abruptly ceased the probing questions.

Mark added, "I heard of your trouble today and am here to offer my support, to you and to my good friend, Anthony."

"That's nice," Jenn said in a new monotone. She swiveled robotically and resumed her place at Jonah's side.

Tony moved inches aside to block Mark from the woman's view. She'd been investigating them pretty hard if she pulled driver's licenses. He didn't want to guess how much she learned to this point so Tony gestured to Jonah's bandages. "What did he do? Choke you?"

"Yeah, Dad," Elizabeth said, standing to the left on the opposite side of the bed, "What's this?" she asked, her fingers going to her own neck to reflect the gauze wrapping on Jonah's.

"Oh, honey," he said and his eyes went to both of his women before skipping past Mark and hitting Tony's. "He strangled me a little and stabbed my neck. The doc says I'm going to be okay." Miller's eyes held Tony's. "Honey, Jenn, I have a huge favor," Miller said to the room without looking away. "I need a moment alone with Tony and Dr. Corescu."

"Sure, honey," his fiancée said still in a faraway voice.

"We'll be right outside," Elizabeth said and Sarah took her hand to walk out with them. Speltz passed Mark without even a glance.

"Can she see you?" Tony asked him silently.

"Hmm," Mark responded with unusual levity, *"somehow, she's forgotten I was here."*

Mark ended with a mental chuckle, both of them awaiting the retired detective's next words. The women closed the door and the doctor remained over Tony's shoulder. Tony sent Jonah a new grin but he shook his head.

"I guess he's one, too, then?" Miller said, his voice barely carrying. Tony and Mark remained quiet and the man continued. "Tep, what was he? Some sort of bad vampire and you two are the good ones?"

Tony allowed silence to fill the room several moments and finally said in a soft tone, "You know we won't answer questions like that, right?" Miller's eye narrowed and Tony tried again. "You're safe. Your family is safe. Tep is dead. When you leave the hospital, you can put this behind you."

Miller shook his head. "There's no such thing as vampires," he whispered lower than before, his eye flitting to the exit as if thinking of his women.

"There sure isn't," Tony replied. "Tep was insane. Paul Black was insane. Dr. Corescu and I are not. You have discerned correctly—we're the good guys."

Miller parted his lips to speak, exhaled, and then closed his mouth. He looked to Mark who remained near the door and then back to Tony. "Listen to me," he said his voice quiet but stern. "Stay away from me. Stay away from Elizabeth. Do you understand?" He looked at Mark. "You, too."

Tony offered a slow nod. "I'll ask Sarah to visit away from the house. Elizabeth will not see either of us unless it is in passing. Deal?"

Miller nodded very slowly. "I can't believe Jenn was right. Wait…" Miller struggled to sit up and when Tony moved in to help, he shrank back. "I got it. Not so close." Miller arranged his thoughts. "Since we're keeping secrets together," he said with weak snark, "who killed the journalist, Connie Nixon?"

"Paul," Tony answered without hesitation, hoping to cement a measure of trust.

"Ah, I thought so. And who killed Paul Black?"

Tony shook his head half-way and hemmed. "We think he died because it was time. He died praying, so we think he went to Jesus."

Miller's jaw softened and he relaxed a tiny measure into the pillow. "Reuben Stuckey?"

"Didn't kill anyone, but he's dead, too, by Paul's hand." Tony took a step back and Mark did, too.

"Wait—," Miller rasped and Tony stopped his movement. "And there's no vampires. Tep was crazy. Like Black."

"Right," Tony said and behind him, Mark resumed to the door.

Miller then made a noise of disgust and averted his gaze to the window on the opposite side of the room. The moon was full and easily viewed through the fat slatted blinds. "I saw those freakin' DLs, too," he said looking away. "Give me a rational explanation for that, dammit. Jenn won't let that go."

Tony rolled in his lips thinking and Mark offered nothing from behind him. Jonah still faced the other way and he sighed with a growl.

"Great. Just great." He faced front and lay back onto his pillow. "Okay. I'll tell Jenn and Elizabeth that Tep was crazy. I say the DLs were staged for, I don't know, hell—insurance purposes. Fraud. But don't, I'm deadly serious," he said, lowering his voice with a new edge, "do not go near my people. Do you understand?"

"I promise," Tony said and Mark opened the door to the hallway. Light spilled in and the women chattered and exclaimed their way back into the room.

Tony and Mark made their excuses and left them to talk. He walked with the doctor toward the stairwell and once in the quiet space, he leaned against the cinderblock wall with an audible sigh.

"I guess that's the best we can ask for," he said to the doctor who seemed deep in thought.

"Elizabeth Hawken has consumed The Other's blood," Mark said and Tony gawked.

"No…" he stuttered, his mind racing back to why he thought of Rakha more than usual when she was around. But, that didn't have to mean…

The doctor held his ground. "Pretending it's not true isn't your style," he offered, his head to the side. "It will be some time before she becomes aware of the regeneration in her flesh. Let some time pass. Let them return to their lives. Then, you can be prepared when the time comes to tell her."

"Or maybe with Rakha dead, she's back to normal," Tony said but realized his error mid-sentence. He added, "Maybe we'll all be delivered before I have to say anything. I don't want that girl to not have to deal with this." Tony shook his head.

Mark laid a comforting hand to his shoulder. "I will come if you need me."

Tony nodded and his mind went to Big John. Mark nodded as if following his thoughts.

"He wants to get away from you, from us. I read this in his thoughts."

Tony shrugged. "It's God. He moves us around when and where He wants. God will move John to pastor a church. He'll be okay."

"That leaves tonight's adventure. Are we exposed? The policeman, Kranchez, he saw me."

Tony shook his head. "I saw his eyes; he talked himself out of it. And with Miller no longer investigating, he'll let it fade. Trust me."

Mark nodded. "How are you? How is the hunger?"

Tony touched his belly and considered the question. He felt sublime, not the least bit hungry.

"Good, maybe with Rakha dead, you can keep the demon of bloodlust at bay."

"I think so. I feel lighter. Hopeful," Tony said and then tipped his chin. "Speaking of, are you going back to Hope tonight?"

"Ms. Brannen is not at home," Mark said and met Tony's eye. "I will return to an empty house."

"Give us a week; Sarah and I will come. She'd love to honeymoon in Germany." Tony watched the vampire's eyes brighten. He lived the past century with an adoring Paul Black. Not too surprisingly, he craved companionship.

"You would be welcomed."

Tony shook his hand. "Look for us on Sunday after next."

Mark nodded, and before another moment, dissolved from view.

Tony returned to the main hall and leaned against the wall to wait for Sarah to finish her visit. With his eyes on Jonah Miller's hospital room door, he sent praises to God. In return, the Holy Spirit fell upon him and Tony knew—beyond the shadow of a doubt—that very soon, in God's timing, he would be delivered and made a brand new man.

He would be patient.

It was good.

Anathema, The Corescu Chronicles Book Four, arrives June 20, 2020. Please signup for Ellen's newsletter to be alerted of all new releases and freebies. Link: https://dl.bookfunnel.com/z0c7dpe1am
Or at the CONTACT link at www.ellencmaze.com
Or by clicking "Follow" on Amazon.

ANATHEMA, Greek for "a blessing" and "a curse," is what Mark and Tony must deal with as a new (old) vampire nemesis creeps in from the distant past to complicate their lives. Mark finds comfort and companionship with Jonah Miller's daughter, Elizabeth, and Tony faces severe punishment for breaking his oath to God. You won't want to miss this!

Available for Kindle PreOrder NOW & launches 6/20/2020

The last installment of The Corescu Chronicles is entitled, NOVUS, which means in Latin, "new beginning." Readers will see the resolution of all familiar characters and a brand-new journey ahead for the new ones brought into the Dark life of vampirism…

Available for Kindle PreOrder NOW & launches 7/20/2020

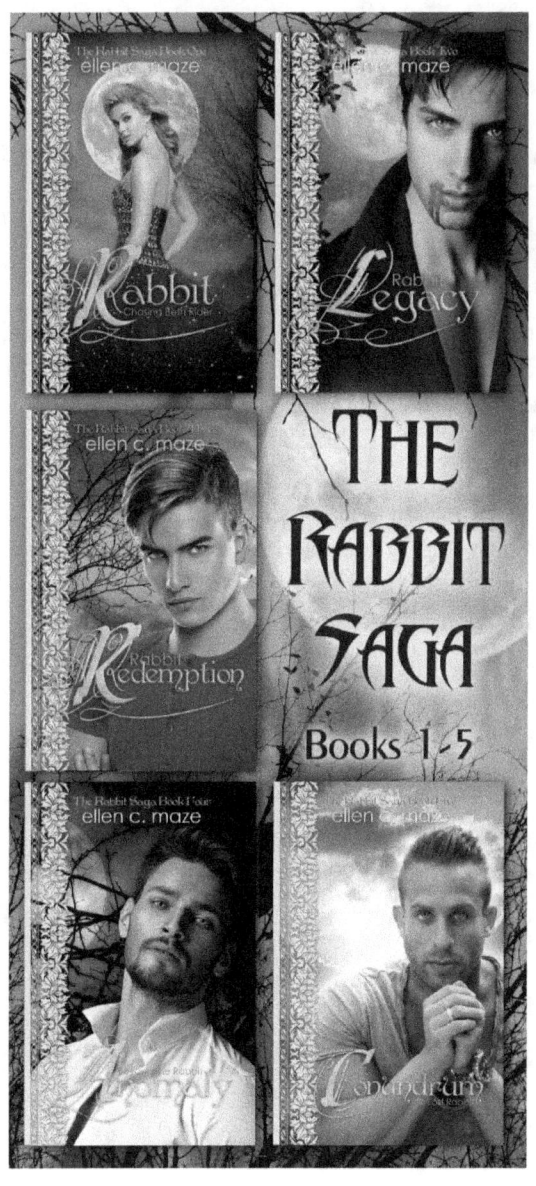

ellen c. maze

The Judging and *Rabbit: Chasing Beth Rider* Connection

In Ellen C. Maze's *Rabbit: Chasing Beth Rider,* a bestselling novelist finds herself on the run from a bloodthirsty race of beings whose leaders despise the affect her novel, *The Judging,* has on their people. Here is what readers are saying about *Rabbit's* fascinating and unique look at the vampire mythos:

Praise for *Rabbit: Chasing Beth Rider*

"Maze's storytelling is fast and fun, overflowing with ideas and spiritual insight."
~ Eric Wilson, author of *Fireproof,* and *Valley of Bones*
(The Jerusalem Undead Trilogy)

"What a great book! It kept me on the edge of my seat, waiting for what was going to happen next. With all the strange powers at work in this world, this book reveals the greatest Power of all."
~ Rabbi John Giddens, *www.ChavurahShalom.org*

"I absolutely love it when an author can take a myth or legend and weave them neatly and efficiently into a brilliant and original tale. This book is definitely not simplistic in nature. Ms. Maze gives us a fast-paced plot with many twists and turns, not just in the action, but also for the mind. *Rabbit: Chasing Beth Rider* will grab your attention from the first page and will not let go until the end, and maybe not even then. Enjoy the chase!"
~ Stephanie Nordkap, *Bestsellersworld.com*

Maze takes us on a vampire journey with a one-of-a-kind twist! Rabbit is a fast-paced, action-packed, exciting vampire thriller. As an avid reader of vampire fiction, this gem unexpectedly has become one of my very favorites.
~ Marcia Freespirit, CEO, *JimSam Inc. Publishing*

"Riveting and eye-opening…a powerful testament to the often overlooked spiritual strength within us all."
~ *Apex reviews*

256

[i] Isaiah 44:6